Dirty Like Zane

TITLES BY JAINE DIAMOND

CONTEMPORARY ROMANCE

Dirty Like Me (*Dirty #1*)
Dirty Like Brody (*Dirty #2*)
2 *Dirty Wedding Nights* (*Dirty #2.5*)
Dirty Like Seth (*Dirty #3*)
Dirty Like Dylan (*Dirty #4*)
Dirty Like Jude (*Dirty #5*)
Dirty Like Zane (*Dirty #6*)
Hot Mess (*Players #1*)
Filthy Beautiful (*Players #2*)
Sweet Temptation (*Players #3*)
Lovely Madness (*Players #4*)
Flames and Flowers (*Players Novella*)
Handsome Devil (*Vancity Villains #1*)
Rebel Heir (*Vancity Villains #2*)
Wicked Angel (*Vancity Villains #3*)
Irresistible Rogue (*Vancity Villains #4*)
Charming Deception (*Bayshore Billionaires #1*)

EROTIC ROMANCE

DEEP (*DEEP #1*)
DEEPER (*DEEP #2*)

Dirty Like Zane

JAINE DIAMOND

Dirty Like Zane
by Jaine Diamond

This book is a work of fiction. Names, characters, places and incidents
are the product of the author's imagination or are used fictitiously.
Any resemblance to actual events, locales, organizations or persons is coincidental.

First Edition December 2018

ISBN 978-1-989273-81-4

Cover and interior design by Jaine Diamond / DreamWarp Publishing Ltd.

Published by DreamWarp Publishing Ltd.
www.jainediamond.com

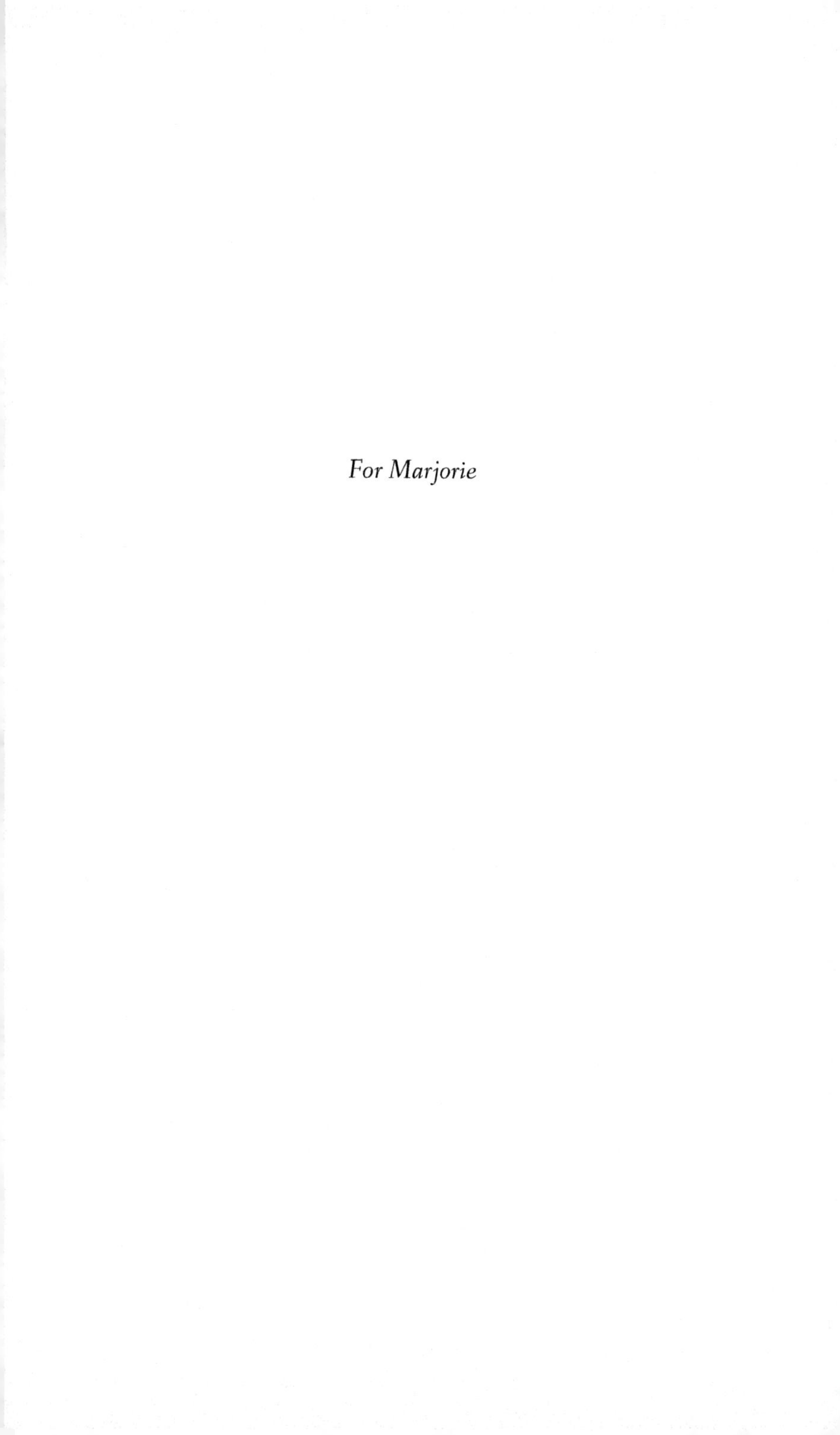

For Marjorie

AUTHOR'S NOTE

The characters featured in this book were introduced in the earlier Dirty series books. I recommend that before reading *Dirty Like Zane* you be sure to read 2 *Dirty Wedding Nights*, which contains prequel stories to this book.

This is the final book in the Dirty series—but the stories of the characters within continue on in the Players series, which is a spinoff that takes place in the Dirty universe, and beyond!

It's been an *incredible* experience bringing the Dirty family to life! THANK YOU so much for coming along on this romantic rock 'n' roll journey with me.

With love from the beautiful west coast of Canada
(the home of Dirty!)
Jaine

CHAPTER ONE

Maggie

ALL YOU HAVE *to do is avoid him.*

That's what I'd been telling myself in preparation for this day. This tour.

Just keep it platonic.

Keep it professional.

And when all else fails... Avoid.

I took a sweeping glance across the parking lot; the members of Dirty were meeting up behind their former rehearsal space, which was now Jesse's wife Katie's art studio. There was room for a few of the tour buses to pull into the lot, but the sporting goods store across the alley had a larger lot where the rest of the buses had filed in.

It was a commercial-industrial neighborhood and not much else was stirring; it was ungodly-early for a January morning, the sun just starting to lighten the sky, and I could see my breath as I looked around.

I glimpsed a few of the band members. Jude's security team. A few of our road crew milling about, those who hadn't already headed south yesterday with the trucks. Our tour manager, Alec, counting heads, his assistant passing out coffees.

Not one sign of Zane.

All clear.

I raised my mochaccino to Alec; he waved back, and I turned to head across the lot.

"Hey, Maggie." Zane's bodyguard loomed in front of me, and I almost pissed myself. For a giant man, Shady was incredibly light on his feet. He eased back, seeming to realize he'd almost literally scared the piss out of me. "Uh… good morning?"

"Hey, Shady," I mumbled, dashing past him.

I waved a hasty hello to my bus driver, who was talking on her phone, and beelined for my bus. I'd already glimpsed it across the alley, parked behind Katie's studio. While the rest of the buses were silver-and-black, mine had a purple swirl down the side.

I turned to cut between two of the massive buses.

And there was Zane.

I stopped so suddenly, I almost spilled coffee all over myself. It slopped out the sippy hole in the lid and burned my hand.

Fuck.

I licked the coffee off my skin and glanced up.

Zane hadn't seen me. His left side was turned toward me.

I wasn't even sure what he was doing.

He was just standing there, alone, in the shadows between the buses, staring at the ground and kinda muttering to himself… like he did when he was nervous before going onstage, or when he was working on a song in his head.

Then his hand raised to his mouth, trailing smoke. He was smoking a joint—because, you know, that was a normal thing to do at the ass-crack of dawn.

If you were Zane Traynor.

He wore biker boots and fitted jeans with the knees ripped out, a white Henley shirt with pushed-up sleeves and one of his trademark black leather vests. He had maybe a week's growth on his jaw and his blond hair had been freshly buzzed on the side into a swatch of velvet, the long part on top falling forward.

Gorgeous.

Dangerous.

Dirty's lead singer.

My legal husband.

Technically, he was also one of my employers. And the one man I'd have to avoid as much as humanly possible on this tour, without making it totally obvious.

Because no one was supposed to know about *us*.

About the fact that we'd secretly gotten married in Las Vegas almost two years ago.

Or the fact that he made my heart race and the backs of my knees sweat... and occasionally made me spread my legs for him and scream like I'd never screamed for any man before.

To all the world except for the very few people who knew the truth about us, I was simply Maggie Omura, Dirty's assistant manager, and he was Zane Traynor, Dirty's lead singer, and we were nothing more to each other than co-workers and, on a good day, friends.

We definitely weren't a married couple who weren't really a couple but who occasionally fucked, fought, and generally had a totally fucked-up relationship.

I just stared at him, afraid to move and not breathing at all. My heart was beating too hard and several parts of my body were starting to sweat, right on cue.

Zane tipped his head back and ran a ring-laden hand through his hair, smoothing it back from his face as he looked up at the sky. He took another drag from his joint... and I slowly backed up.

I got the fuck out of there before he caught me staring at him.

I pretty much ran for my bus, and when I got there, I frowned to see Jesse's guitar tech, Jimmy, stepping out. Jimmy was definitely one of the good ones; he'd carried my bags for me, whisked them away before I was even out of the taxi—but still. He was a dude.

I gave him a look and pointed at the pretty pink sign I'd posted on the window of the front door yesterday, when I'd personally decorated the bus. It said, in giant silver glitter letters: NO DUDES.

Jimmy smiled sheepishly. "Your bags are inside, Maggs."

I gave him a curt, "Thank you," then disappeared up the steps inside. I set my coffee down on one of the tables in the lounge, glanced around and called out, "Hellooo?" But clearly none of the other girls were here yet.

There was a loud, staticky *blip* that almost made me jump out of my skin—apparently, I was that tense—and a voice spoke over the walkie that lay on the table.

"Hey, Maggie. You there?"

I picked up the walkie and replied cheerily, "Hey, Alec!"

"You seen or heard from Zane or Dylan yet this morning?"

"Nope!"

Half-true.

I'd definitely seen Seth, Elle and Jesse in the lot. I hadn't seen Dylan, but our drummer was pretty much always late, so no panic there just yet.

And Zane, well... Alec would find him soon enough.

"Oh, here's Dylan," he said. "Hopefully Zane checks in soon."

"Uh-huh. You know, we can always roll out without him. If he misses the Seattle show, Jesse can cover his vocal parts, right?"

"Uh... okay?" Alec chuckled. "Just let him know I'm looking for him if you see him?"

"Will do!"

I tossed the walkie on a couch with my leather jacket and headed down the back hall, where the bunks were. I supposed Alec didn't share my little theory that we didn't really need our lead singer, but this was his first Dirty tour. Maybe his opinion would change; Zane had that effect on people.

Either way, no way was I holding Zane's hand—or anything else—through this tour. If he couldn't "check in" with Alec, not my problem.

After stashing my pretty makeup bags full of toiletries and cosmetics in the washroom, I started unpacking and putting away some of my clothes in my designated closet/locker. Then I made up my bunk with the bedding I'd brought; soft sheets, velvety-soft blanket and a multitude of cushy pillows. There was no window by my bunk, but there was air and temperature control, some recessed lighting and a little cubby where I could store a few things.

Comfy enough.

This would be my home for the next four months while we toured North America, before we headed overseas to continue Dirty's *Hell & Back* world tour. We rarely traveled by bus on other continents but here at home we had so many tour dates, especially in the U.S., that it made the most sense, both economically and comfort-wise, to travel by bus.

These days, every member of Dirty had their own luxury bus—except for Elle and Seth, since they were a couple. Our road crew traveled on other buses with a bunch of bunks in them. Once we rolled into a city, the band and management would stay in a hotel, but for the most part everyone preferred traveling this way—for each of us to have our own space, with our own stuff, set up the way we liked it; a home-away-from-home that rolled right along wherever we went.

For my part, I was already in love with my bus.

The Lady Bus.

It was the bus for the female crew, and there really weren't many of us.

There was me.

There was my assistant, Talia, whom I'd begged to come on the tour at the very last minute. Since my boss, Brody Mason—Dirty's manager—had a new baby and wasn't coming on this tour full-time, he'd offered me both a promotion and an assistant. I was pretty sure he did it out of guilt when he saw how stressed I was leading up to the tour, but he really didn't need to feel guilty. My stress had little to do with my workload.

I'd turned down the promotion, as usual, but jumped at the chance to take on an assistant, and Talia was my first choice. I was actually afraid she might say no since she was in school, but as it turned out, the opportunity to go on tour with Dirty—one of the biggest touring rock bands in the world—was too much to pass up.

Lucky for me.

I adored Talia. She reminded me of a younger, blonde—and very possibly hotter—version of me. She had a work ethic to rival my own and, in my opinion, the fact that she was a babe with impeccable fashion sense was just a point in her favor.

It had always irked me when certain men in this business—and there were a lot of them—took one glance at me and assumed I didn't belong here, or worse, that I was just some fangirl. If you asked me, women could be pretty, sexy, fashionable—or anything else they damned well wanted to be—and kick ass.

I'd spent the last eight years of my life proving that was true. In high heels and a manicure.

Talia and I would be joined on the Lady Bus by Elle's assistant, Joanie. I liked Joanie, too. No bullshit, great work ethic, and she'd been working closely with Elle for years. She knew the lay of the land.

Bonus: I'd never seen Joanie or Talia so much as bat an eyelash in Zane's direction. When Zane Traynor walked by, women tended to get starry-eyed, stupid, and slutty.

Myself included, unfortunately.

But not these women.

And then there was Sophie, our newish merch girl; girlfriend of our longtime merch guy, Pete. On the last Dirty tour, Sophie had proven herself an asset; tons of fun, zero drama. She had an easy, hearty laugh, and though I was pretty sure she was devoted to Pete in every way, she tended to laugh heartily at pretty much everything that came out of Zane's mouth.

Nobody's perfect, right?

Pete was riding on one of the crew buses, and while Sophie really could've stayed on there with her man, I'd definitely upsold her on the perks of riding on the Lady Bus.

Perks that included pretty decor, cleanliness and a fresh, unoffensive scent.

So, along with our female driver, Bobbi, we had five ladies traveling on a luxury six-bunk bus—just enough for me to convince Brody that we needed our own bus.

Thank God.

No way was I ending up on a crew bus crowded with farting, snoring men. Been there before, repeatedly, and paid my dues in full.

And no fucking way was I ending up on a rock star's bus.

Elle and Seth had Flynn and Bane, their bodyguards, on their bus. Jesse and Katie had Jude, our head of security and Jesse's best friend and bodyguard on their bus. Dylan had his girlfriend and our tour photographer, Amber, with him, as well as his bodyguard, Con.

And Matt, the bassist we'd hired on for this tour, had his own people.

Which left Zane, who had nobody on his bus with him except his bodyguard, Shady. Our ADHD-afflicted lead singer was the one rock star on this tour who probably needed some kind of assistant-slash-life-manager-slash-therapist on his bus. For a biker, Shady was a lovely man, but I'd literally had to teach him how to open an email so he could access the tour schedule; no way he was gonna assist Zane with anything other than watching his back and maybe rolling him a joint.

I was organized as hell, and while I certainly *could've* helped Zane sort out his clusterfuck of a life, *fuck that*.

Brody knew nothing about my fucked-up secret marriage to Zane, but he did know, possibly better than anyone, what a lunatic Zane Traynor could be. And he respected me, deeply. I really didn't *think* he'd suggest that I bus with Zane, but there was no way in hell I was willing to risk that conversation.

The Lady Bus was my insurance policy and my sanctuary.

My dude-free safe haven, as indicated by the NO DUDES sign.

There was also a large pink neon sign in the shape of the female symbol that I'd hung on the wall of the lounge (overkill much?), and an overabundance of fresh flowers to welcome the other ladies onboard.

Whatever.

I surveyed my work and I was pleased. The Lady Bus was warm and welcoming, cozy and comfortable. For the next four months, it would feel like home. We'd have girl talk and peace and quiet, a dude-free zone where we could escape all the madness of touring...

I sighed with satisfaction and turned toward the door.

And Zane was there.

I froze. My entire body immediately broke out in goosebumps, and not because he'd startled me.

My nipples actually hardened.

He stood at the top of the steps, all six-foot-whatever of his tall, built, Viking body filling the entrance to the lounge.

I crossed my arms over my chest as his ice-blue eyes wandered over me, and a hot-cold flush skittered through my body; I was starting to sweat again.

He'd let himself right onto my bus. Did he not see my sparkly sign?

Yeah. He saw it.

"I thought you were Talia," I said stupidly, as if to explain my staring.

"Nope," he said.

Then he just stood there.

And I just stared.

Shit. Where the hell were my ladies?

Through the front window, I could see Bobbi over with some of the other drivers, chatting, drinking coffee. But the rest of the girls?

Fucking late, that's where they were.

I glanced at my watch.

When I looked up again, Zane had cocked his evil-gorgeous pierced eyebrow at me. He definitely hadn't missed that I was wearing the watch he'd given me for my last birthday—when he was in hardcore trying-to-win-her-over mode.

With Zane, there were exactly three modes—where I was concerned.

Trying-to-win-her-over mode.

Trying-to-fuck-her mode.

And pissed-off-at-her-and-fucking-other-women mode.

All equally devastating for different reasons.

I would've given the watch right back, but since it was the only ridiculously lavish gift he'd ever tried to give me—other than the engagement ring he'd tossed my way the morning after we got spontaneously, stupidly married—and it was actually practical, I kept it. It was Cartier, definitely worth more than my car, and perfect for me; silver with a touch of pink gold on the face and a subtle ring of diamonds.

But mainly, it would be useful on tour.

Or so I'd told myself.

"*Fuck*," I muttered, starting to panic as he took a step deeper into the lounge—and every hair on my body stood on end. "Everyone's late."

"I'm not."

"Yeah, but you're not supposed to be here. See the sign? *NO DUDES*." I gave him the fakest smile in the history of smiles. "That means *ever*, and that means *you*."

Zane appeared totally unfazed by my sign or my attitude. "We're not even on the road yet, Maggs. Come on, I wanna see your bus." Then he shouldered past me with his broad man-shoulders.

"For fuck's sake. We're leaving soon."

"Got twenty minutes."

"Alec's looking for you."

"Just saw him."

I huffed a sigh and stood in the middle of the lounge with my arms crossed, waiting for this to be over as he poked around. Then he disappeared down the back hall.

When he reemerged, he looked around, his gaze lingering on the flowers and the strings of twinkly lights I'd hung, the fluffy pink pillows and the neon lady symbol on the wall. "So, no dudes, huh?"

"Yup."

"Why?"

"Because," I told him as icily as I could, "dudes ruin things."

His eyelids dropped a little, and his gaze drifted south of my waist. I was wearing jeans and a little sleeveless top, both were tight, and now I was wishing I'd worn a much longer, baggier shirt. Or maybe a garbage bag. "What things?"

"For one, you're smelling up my Lady Bus with your man smell."

His eyes met mine again and the corner of his gorgeous mouth twitched.

And my knees wobbled a little.

It was true; I could totally smell him. He smelled like pot, a bit. But then there was that heady, sexy scent of his that had always driven me fucking crazy. Or driven my sex parts crazy. I was pretty sure the mere smell of this man had made me spontaneously ovulate a time or two. And by now, I knew exactly what it was; this spiced-chai bodywash he used combined with the leather vests he pretty much lived in... and *him*. Yup. Zane just smelled *that* good.

Totally unfair.

When Zane Traynor walked into a room—or in this case, my tour bus—he came armed with an array of weapons: his bad-boy blond hair, his ice-chip blue eyes, his devilish smile, his smoky voice, his rock-hard body... and that pussy-wetting smell of his... to name a few.

You know, like any natural predator.

While I felt like some poor, soft snail caught without its shell, utterly defenseless as he sauntered over to me, his eyes locked on mine.

"You can smell me?" he asked, in that lazy, suggestive way of his when he got close. "Over all that potpourri shit?"

"Potpourri?" I glared at him. "What is this, 1983 at your grandma's house? It's incense, it's Fresh Rain scent and you're ruining it."

He stared at me, his tongue swiping slowly over his bottom lip, and my eyes tracked the movement. I couldn't stop staring at his mouth.

Maybe because I knew exactly how that tongue and those soft lips felt... all over me.

He nodded toward the back hall. "You got a bunk back there?"

I tightened my arms over my chest, even as my stomach dropped.

Fuck. Me.

I was so woefully ill-equipped to handle this shit.

I needed to avoid this man like I needed my next breath. Because whenever he got near me, he hacked my feeble defenses right down to the quick. And when he got my defenses down, he got me alone.

And when we were alone, like this... he could do *anything*. Because no one was here to see it, and I'd be unable to stop it.

He could get in my face.

Mess with my head.

Put his hands on me.

And once he did that...

"Well," I said cooly, "I don't sleep hanging from my feet like *The Lost Boys*, so yeah, I've got a bunk."

Attitude.

Denial.

Avoidance.

These were about the only defenses I'd ever had when it came to Zane, and as time wore on, they'd only grown less effective.

Avoidance; total avoidance was the only defense I really had left.

If I couldn't avoid him, I was screwed.

Literally and often.

"Which one?"

I just glared at him. *So* not his business.

"Lemme guess. The one with the pink velvet blanket and the military corners. And the five hundred pillows."

"It's not velvet," I said, my tone frigid.

"Felt like velvet."

Fucking great. He'd fingered my bed. It probably smelled of him now, too.

"It's pretty small," he observed. "You know... you ride on my bus with me, you get a whole bedroom with a giant bed."

"Mm-hmm. Which I get to share with you."

"That's just one of the perks, Maggs." He said that slowly, his blue-eyed gaze drifting over my face and lingering on my lips. "No one else on my bus but Shady. It's gonna get pretty quiet."

I said nothing.

"A guy might get lonely..."

"I'm sure you'll find someone to keep you company," I told him, deadpan.

I was sure. Women would be lining up to warm Zane Traynor's bed on this tour, just like they did every other day of his life.

"Should really be my wife," he said, his tone sharpening.

"If you had one."

He stared at me.

I glared right back.

"You ever want to come check it out, door's open."

"I'm sure it is."

He didn't respond to that. He didn't get mad or defensive or argue. He didn't crank up the trying-to-fuck-her charm.

"So let's just be clear about this," he said, in his low, dead-sexy voice. "I'm offering to share my bus with you. And you're turning me down."

I looked away. "I'm not turning you down, Zane. I have my own bus."

And we already talked about this... ad nauseam.

He didn't say anything.

But he was so close to me now, there was nowhere for me to look to avoid his chiseled, gorgeous face, but *down*... at his chiseled, gorgeous body. The Henley shirt, closeup, was thin, stretched over his sculpted muscles. The leather vest was narrow and open; I could see his left nipple and the piercing in it poking against the almost see-through white fabric. The shirt was haphazardly tucked into his jeans in one spot, the rest slopping out, but it definitely did nothing to cover the insane bulge in the front of his jeans.

Was he already hard? I couldn't exactly tell. Zane had a huge dick, and while he usually wore loose-fit jeans, these ones were pretty snug.

I didn't want to stare.

I really didn't.

But there was nowhere else to look. He was *everywhere.*

Then his hand, suddenly, was on my face. Just lightly cupping my cheek, his warmth radiating into me.

I jerked back, startled, and butted up against the partition between the lounge and the driver's seat. He'd cornered me—and as usual, I didn't even notice it was happening.

The fact was, anytime Zane had gotten me alone he'd been able to corner me.

And fuck me.

At least, since we'd been married.

There were really only two reasons we hadn't been fucking *daily* since our wedding night.

One, he let me off the hook a lot. Stayed away when I asked him to. Respected my boundaries, for the most part.

And two, I'd managed to avoid him a hell of a lot. I'd worked my ass off to keep a physical distance between us, most of the time. Because I knew anytime he got me alone... it was only a matter of time.

A few tense moments. A few hungry glances. A few heated words...

And it was all over.

He'd corner me.

I'd somehow let him.

And his giant dick would be in me.

Before I knew it I'd be halfway to my next screaming, scorching, mind-fucking orgasm.

I allowed myself to look up into his waiting eyes... and a wave of longing rocked through me.

I bit down on my tongue.

He stroked his thumb over my cheek, lightly, and over the corner of my mouth, tugging on my lip. I felt the urgent thud of my pulse between my legs, and I sucked back a breath. Then I held it, tight, like it was my life. Like if I let it go, I'd die.

"We're gonna get through this," he told me, in a low, rough, almost-whisper. "Together, Maggie."

Then his lips met mine.

Warm.

Soft.

He gave me the most feather-soft, barely-touching kiss... and the floor dropped out from under me. The world turned upside-down and my throat constricted.

My heart pounded right to a stop.

I didn't move.

I couldn't.

I knew I was a masochist when it came to Zane; that had already been established. I was a strong woman, but I was weak when it came to him.

I was just trying not to be a total moron and fuck him on day one of this tour.

We cannot fuck around on this tour, I'd told him, the last time we were alone together. Two months ago.

And again only three days ago, over the phone.

Yeah, Maggie, he'd said. *We sure as fuck can.*

Which meant we were at a stalemate.

Again.

Always.

His hand dropped away, his lips left mine and he brushed past me, leaving me with a whiff of his sexy man-scent. Then he dropped down the steps and off the bus, and he was gone.

I exhaled hard... then inhaled, deep. My lungs ached from not breathing for so long.

At least my heart had started beating again; pounding. I could've sworn it'd really stopped for a minute there.

And my pussy *ached.*

Truly, one of the worst problems with being madly, insanely, stupidly in lust with a man whom I firmly, deeply, to-the-marrow-of-my-bones believed I could never be with was that it made it difficult to be with anyone else. Impossible, actually. Which meant that I hadn't been. With anyone.

Anyone but *him*, since we were married.

Almost two years ago.

And it was slowly killing me.

I, Maggie Omura, was suffering a slow, slow death by desire.

Unsated desire.

Or at least, rarely-sated desire.

It dawned on me, too slowly, that the blinds were open on the lounge windows... and panic hit me like a lightning bolt to the spine. *Shit. SHIT.* Did anyone see that shit?

Jesus, what the fuck were we doing?

I walked straight to the back, to the bunks, and rolled into mine. And then it really sank in.

Oh dear God.

How the hell was I gonna get through this?

Hiding from Zane the entire tour... Was that really my plan?

I stared at the ceiling, which was actually the underside of Talia's bunk, and sighed, because yeah. That was my plan.

My ridiculous, futile plan.

I heard someone come onboard and I didn't even poke my head out to see who it was. I just lay here, breathing slowly in and out, my head still reeling from that kiss.

"Good morning! Why's Zane on our bus?" Talia appeared. "I thought it was no dudes allowed."

"It is," I said, sitting up. "It most definitely is. He's got the memo on that now. Feel free to kick his ass out if you catch him sniffing around."

"Okay," she said, though she sounded uncertain. Probably didn't love the idea of having to tell our lead singer to take a hike, but she'd learn; sometimes telling Zane Traynor to fuck off was the only sensible move a girl could make.

"Where've you been? We leave in like fifteen."

"I was here half an hour ago." She looked stricken, worried she was in trouble. "I was just talking to the crew..."

"Oh." I slid out of my bunk and stood up. "Sorry. I didn't sleep much last night..." I muttered a lame apology and headed out to the lounge. Talia followed. "Can you find Joanie and Sophie, and get them in here? We should have a quick meeting before we roll out."

"Of course. I just saw Joanie pop into Elle's bus, and Sophie was with Pete. I'll get them." She dashed out the door.

So... my ladies weren't late.

Well, good.

I forced myself, again, to breathe. Why was it so damn hard just to breathe?

It was like Zane did something to the oxygen, made the environment inhospitable to female life.

I sipped my mochaccino and tried to regroup. To start this day over again. Just pretend Zane's little invasion into my sanctuary had never happened.

But it did.

He'd touched me.

He'd kissed me.

On day fucking one—no, moment one—of the tour

And now my whole system was out of balance.

I lit more incense to burn away the lingering smell of him. A little meeting with my lady crew to start this tour off right was what I needed—so I could go over the rules of the Lady Bus with them.

Rule number one: *No dudes.*

That meant any dudes, for any reason.

Boyfriends.

Hookups.

Pushy lead singers.

Unless this bus caught on fire and we needed someone to ax us the hell out... from this moment on, absolutely no dudes were setting foot on this bus.

Only problem with that plan was I couldn't exactly hide in here forever. And I'd still have to deal with Zane *out there.*

I'd have to see him, talk to him, work with him.

Every. Day.

And the truth was I *wanted* to see him.

I hugged myself as I looked around the bus, at this pretty little cocoon I'd created to insulate myself from the world outside. From him.

And I knew; the purpose of the Lady Bus wasn't to keep Zane away from me.

It was to keep me away from him.

CHAPTER TWO

Zane

I HEADED OFFSTAGE at the end of the Seattle-Tacoma show irritated as fuck.

The first night of the tour, and already too many fuck-ups to count.

Everyone was quick to pat me on the back, nod their approval, tell me *Great show*. No one said a fucking word about how my mic cut out in the middle of "Dirty Like Me," or the fact that I'd accidentally clubbed Seth in the face during "Blackout" and probably gave him a fat lip.

Or any of the other minor fuck-ups that had happened throughout the night.

Or how motherfucking tense I was.

I'd swiped Jesse's mic to finish "Dirty Like Me," and I was pretty sure no one even noticed me hitting Seth other than me and Seth. It was the kind of inconsequential shit that the crowd never really cared about in the grand scheme of things, but it bothered me.

A fuck of a lot.

When I was onstage, I *hated* fuck-ups.

I wrapped Seth in my arms when he came offstage and kissed him on the side of the head. "You alright, man? How's your lip...?"

He smiled at me a little painfully, and his bottom lip was definitely swollen. "No worries."

"What happened?" Elle pulled Seth close as I released him, and he laid a hand on her belly.

"Ah, I kissed Zane's mic during 'Blackout.'"

"Oh, baby..." Elle fussed over him, examining his lip and gently kissing it. Even though she wasn't taking the stage on this tour, Elle still looked the part; platinum-blonde hair, kickass boots and a sexy little dress hugging her pregnant curves as she pressed her swollen tits against her man.

And fucking right, I was jealous of that shit.

Not jealous of Seth or Elle in particular. Just jealous they could do that shit anytime they wanted, right out in the open—and they did.

All the fucking time.

Just like Jesse and Katie.

And Dylan and Amber.

And Brody and Jessa.

"Can we get some ice for Seth's lip?" I muttered as Jude came over. His woman, Roni, was somewhere backstage, and any second now they'd be all up in each other's shit, too.

These days, I was fucking surrounded by horny, happy couples.

I got the fuck out of there before one more person could pat me on the back and tell me *Great show, Zane.*

It wasn't a great show.

Not for me.

I hit the shower in my dressing room. Then Brody, who'd flown down for the show, came by to talk to me, feel me out. He had his concerned manager face on, and he definitely felt the tension radiating off me a mile away.

"You've gotta relax into it, yeah?" he told me. "This is the first show of like a hundred and forty. Don't be so fucking hard on yourself. You hear that sound?"

That sound was the thunderous stomping, yelling and singing of the crowd as they gradually left the building. Happy fans.

"I'm good, Bro," I told him, mostly so he'd stop talking, and he fucking frowned. In his motorcycle jacket, tattoos and button-up shirt, he looked like he was ready to kick my ass if necessary—or worse, negotiate me into a better mood.

So I moved on before he could.

I joined the rest of Dirty and our opening band, Steel Trap, meeting some fans Jude had allowed backstage. They all had Dirty stickers on their shirts, a few of them scribbled with Dylan's initials, which meant he'd invited them back himself. Must've met them outside before the show or something.

I did the rounds, signed some shit, posed for photos and tried not to look like a grumpy asshole. Usually the fans let that shit slide after a show, figured you were burnt out from rocking your ass off.

Shady stuck close to me the whole time. I'd already given him his instructions for this tour: *Keep the fangirls off me.*

Oh, and *Keep the weed coming.*

That was pretty much the extent of it.

This was Shady's first Dirty tour, so for all he knew I gave my bodyguard those same instructions on every tour.

But this tour was different.

It was the first tour I didn't actually want the fangirls all over me.

It was the first tour since I was—secretly—married to Maggie. And last thing I needed was anything making things worse between the two of us than they already were. She wasn't in the room right this minute, but she often was. And either way, I knew she'd be watching me. Even when she pretended she wasn't.

I knew she was still pissed at me. And I understood why—in a way.

I knew she was pissed about Dallas.

I knew she didn't trust me not to screw my way through this entire world tour.

I finished up with the fans, fast, and told Shady to get me out of there. While Alec and Jude organized cars for us, I rolled up a fat joint outside and smoked up with Dylan and Jesse. Went a little way to making me feel better. Or at least feel distracted as we fucked around, waiting for the girls to get their shit together.

Apparently neither of my band brothers seemed to think the show was as bad as I did. But they weren't the ones who'd fucked up the show.

Then their women, Katie and Amber, came giggling outside from wherever the fuck they'd been, smelling of booze, and we rolled out.

No fucking sign of Maggie.

Whatever.

I'd already made it known, to Jude, that Maggie's presence was required tonight, which meant he'd make sure someone dragged her along.

Not even Maggie could get away with buzzkilling everyone by bailing on the first-night-of-the-tour party.

I got into a limo with Shady and some of my band, and by the time we arrived at the bar, the rest of Dirty, Steel Trap and a shit-ton of other people were already there. Even Seth was there.

None of the guys in my band were single anymore, but at least they still partied with me. Jesse and Katie were pretty much night owls, always good to go out. Dylan was usually down, often with Amber in tow. It was Seth who usually stayed in, since Elle, in her pregnant state, was usually in bed long before midnight. But tonight, he'd come out.

First night of the tour, no one had any excuse to stay in... except Elle.

By the time Jude got security organized and I'd smoked up again outside the bar with Katie and Roni, Maggie had arrived with Alec and Talia.

We all made our way into the bar, working our way through the crowd to a section near the dance floor where most of our group was hanging out and a bunch of our security guys were making a nice solid perimeter. I was one of the last to arrive, and when I did, there was an empty seat waiting for me, right next to Seth and across the table from Maggie—with a big bottle of Perrier, a glass of cranberry juice and a smaller glass filled with lime wedges.

No one but Maggie would order this shit for me.

As I sat down, I looked hard at her. She was so fucking pretty. Her dark hair was smoothed straight down around her face. She was wearing a little makeup, but she didn't need it. Maggie had flawless honey-toned skin and striking features, the kind that stopped a guy in his tracks. Round cheekbones and sweet little chin, full, sculpted lips and those pretty gray eyes. Filipino, English, German.

All beautiful.

The kind of girl who just got more beautiful the more you looked at her. I'd looked a lot, and Maggie was fucking gorgeous to me. She looked hot as fuck tonight in her sexy little black dress and lime-green suede jacket. And I knew she could feel me staring at her.

I poured some Perrier into my cranberry juice and sat back. Everyone else had beer, and they were firing more drink orders at the waitresses who were circling our tables. Except Seth, who had a takeout coffee.

He raised his cup to me and I nodded.

Seth was always drinking coffee. I wasn't much of a coffee guy myself, and I didn't much like Coke or other pop. Reminded me too much of drinking it with about ten fingers of booze, like I could still taste the remnants of it and smell the whiskey fumes. Definite no-go. So whenever I was in a bar, I stuck with water. Mineral water, sparkling water, fruit-flavored water, I'd tried it all. Any way possible to change up what was otherwise a pretty fucking boring drink. I liked cranberry juice, of all things. Half-water, half-cranberry juice, wedge of lime.

I would've drank it more often if all these assholes didn't call me an old man whenever I did. *Granddad cocktail*; that's what they called my drink of choice.

I took a sip and stared at Maggie until she finally looked at me. I smirked. She rolled her eyes and looked away, and kept ignoring me.

But fuck it. That wasn't gonna last.

I did not believe for one second that Maggie Omura didn't want me. That she didn't want *us*.

That there wasn't some part of her that wanted to be my wife.

Even though she'd avoided me backstage at the show tonight. Even if she ignored me all fucking night. She could ignore me all she wanted. At least, she could try.

Reality was, I was a hard man to ignore.

Especially for Maggie Omura.

I could still feel what went down this morning on her tour bus, when I'd kissed her... how she'd reacted to my touch. The way she'd stopped breathing, stopped moving, and every nerve in my body started firing in response to her desire for me... It was so fucking pungent in the air between us. I could practically smell it. *See* it. Her repressed lust was like a splash of vivid color in my brain. And her taste on my lips? I could practically taste her lust for me right fucking now, just looking at her. And I was not gonna forget any of it.

Because it told me exactly what I needed to know.

This wasn't over.

No way was anything finished between us. No matter how long she denied me, no matter how long she avoided me, no matter how long she lasted before she finally broke and let me fuck her.

This was far from over.

Which meant I was gonna do every-fucking-thing in my power to make this happen.

Me and Maggie.

I was gonna break down her wall of stubborn, for good.

Brick by fucking brick.

Of all the things that Maggie might've underestimated about me over the years, she'd most definitely underestimated my patience.

Two fucking years.

It'd been almost two years since we'd been married, and I'd waited this long. Twenty-one months, to be exact. And I'd waited six years before that, before I'd even gotten my first taste of her.

I was thirty years old. Maggie was twenty-six. We were fucking young.

We had time to work this shit out.

This tour was a year-and-a-half long. At least, that's what was planned out so far. There was always potential for it to go longer. Really, we could tour as long as we wanted to.

Neither of us were going anywhere.

So I sipped my drink, signed some shit for a few fans Jude tolerated getting close, and I talked with my boys. I watched people dance, and I listened to the music.

Despite the fact that I didn't drink, I still loved bars. As long as the music was good. As long as it was loud and the sound system had it right. Didn't even care what kind of music it was.

Rock. Electronic. Fucking jazz.

Didn't matter.

Just give me some loud music and a good vibe.

No idea who'd chosen this place, but it was cool. The DJ was spinning a steady stream of at-least-two-decades-ago, all the filthiest hits from the 2Pac, Biggie and Snoop Dogg catalogue, and at the moment it was Eminem, "Shake That." The crowd of hipster college kids was fucking loving it, and the girls were shaking that all over the dance floor.

Including Katie and Amber, who already looked drunk. Nice to see Dylan's little hippie girl relax; Katie had really seemed to take her under her wing. Amber was wearing sparkly leggings with her little blouse, and I couldn't remember seeing her in heels before.

As for Maggie... she was still firmly planted in her seat and ignoring me.

I elbowed Seth. "How many shots you think it'll take to get Maggie on that dance floor?"

He chuckled and glanced at Maggie. "Thirty?"

I watched her, deep in conversation with Talia. By the looks of it, it was an overly-serious conversation for half-past midnight at a bar. Really, I figured I'd be doing Talia a service if I got Maggie drunk tonight. The girl was barely legal to drink and no doubt would rather be on that dance floor than talking business.

As it was, Talia kept glancing over at Katie and Amber longingly. They were shaking it up in clear view of our table, maybe putting on a little show for their men... which seemed to be entertaining Dylan and irritating Jesse.

Jesse got jealous anytime any guy looked at his wife, and when a girl looked like Katie did—all curvy and petite, with her thick, dark hair and creamy skin, and that sweet smile on her face—and shook her ass like that, guys were definitely looking.

I wouldn't mind seeing Maggie dance like that. Maggie was sexy as fuck when she danced. She just didn't often loosen up enough to do it.

At least not when I was around.

Or when she was too sober.

I looked for our waitresses; they were buzzing around Dylan and Matt, and the Steel Trap guys at the next table. Bunch of boozers. The wait staff had stopped showing love to our end of the table the second they sniffed out that Seth and I weren't drinking.

Seriously, who did an alcoholic rock star have to finger around here to get a drink?

"How you doing?" Seth asked me, eyeing me with a look I didn't love. Maybe he thought I was jonesing for a drink of my own?

Or scoping out the waitresses for other reasons?

"Good. Surprised you made it out tonight. You know, fat lip and all. Figured Elle would be kissing your wounds all night."

He just laughed, like a guy who knew I was jealous.

And sure, maybe I'd threatened to fire him if he didn't come out with us. But I did that a lot—even though it pissed Elle off; I told her it was just a joke, but she still wasn't too fucking impressed.

Truth was, unless we caught Seth with a needle in his arm, fat fucking chance we'd fire him again for any reason. As it was, we were all trying to make up for past wrongs, for lost time. Just wanted to resolidify that bond we'd had with him so long ago.

"You know," I told him, "you keep holing up, fucking your pregnant woman all the time, you're gonna drill a dent in that kid's head."

I'd told him the same thing before, several times, and just like before, he raised his eyebrows at me and kinda smirked at my apparent lack of understanding where pregnancy was concerned.

I just liked to bust the guy's balls.

Wasn't really fair he was so in love and his woman was about to squeeze out his kid. But then again, Seth probably deserved it more than anyone did, after all the shit he'd been through.

"How's she doing?" I asked him.

"Sexy as fuck," he said. "Pregnant women are sexy as fuck." He said that with a smile he couldn't even suppress, and I had to grin. Then I shook my head.

Fucking figured.

Normally, I'd be down for details on that. Right now, I really didn't want to hear about all the sick, sexy shit Seth and Elle were doing together.

He got talking with Jesse anyway, and I managed to wave over one of the waitresses, finally.

A couple minutes later, Maggie and Talia had two shots sitting in front of them—each.

Talia smiled at me. "Thanks, Zane."

I gave her a nod. Talia had dark brown eyes and blonde hair, and I wasn't sure what her story was but she was cute as shit; I'd put money on someone scooping her up long before the end of this tour. Day one, and the dudes were already circling. Jimmy, Jesse's guitar tech, for one, who'd been drooling all over her backstage. And Lex, one of Jude's security guys, who kept staring at her like a creeper from the shadows.

I'd be happy to watch them fight it out, actually. Would be pretty fucking entertaining, even if Jimmy didn't stand a chance.

Talia lifted her first shot and looked at Maggie... who was glaring at me. At least I had her attention now. And I could read that look on her face like a book.

What the fuck do you think you're doing?

I cocked an eyebrow at her. *Loosen up, Maggs,* I told her with my eyes as I sipped my granddad cocktail. *Have a shot.*

She glared at me some more, but finally lifted her first shot and clinked her glass with Talia's. They threw back. It went down decently smooth for a whiskey shot; it was a Double Jack—Jack Daniels and Yukon Jack, which was strong as shit but kinda sweet. You wanted to do a whiskey shot with a chick, this one was a pretty safe bet.

The next one wasn't so smooth.

It was a Kick in the Balls—Jack Daniels, Yukon Jack and tequila.

As soon as it went down her throat and Maggie fucking shuddered, she glared at me again.

Totally worth it. The shots did their job, taking the edge off. Maggie's shoulders softened a bit and her mannerisms got more fluid, her body language infinitesimally looser as she chatted with Talia.

She even shed her jacket.

For the next round, I asked the now-attentive waitress to bring whatever was the dirtiest, sexiest shit they had. She made some suggestions—while bent over, her tits in my face. Was her shirt yanked that low the first time she came over? I passed on the Red Headed Sluts; she had red hair, and this wasn't my first rodeo.

But a round of Slippery Nipples sounded good to me.

They definitely went down a little smoother than the whiskey. This time, when Maggie glared at me, there was a little flicker of relief in her eyes.

Thank you for not being a douche, that look said.

I winked.

Next up was a round of Blow Jobs.

They came in tall, curved shooter glasses with a wad of whipped cream on top. "Proper way to do them," the waitress informed us, "is to stick the shot in-between the guy's thighs—" she pointed at my lap, "—and the girl picks it up with her mouth and shoots it back without using her hands."

Fine by me. I was already seated, so we were good to go. Seth, however, flatly refused to participate.

Pussy.

So it was me and fucking Lex, who mysteriously materialized out of the shadows to pull up a chair on my other side. We stuck the shooters between our thighs as I beckoned Maggie and Talia over. They came around the table—or Jesse and Dylan pretty much propelled them—as the waitress cleared out of the way, obviously disappointed she wasn't offered a lap.

By the time Maggie was on her knees in front of me, a small crowd had formed. Amber had come off the dance floor, and because there was definitely some sort of god who occasionally looked out for me, she'd brought her camera with her. People were yelling and clapping as she aimed the giant lens at us and started taking photos.

Yeah. There was definitely a god.

And he or she wanted me to get Maggie drunk.

Maggie's gray eyes peered up at me, a combo of irritated, embarrassed, and inebriated. I was pretty sure she'd only been nursing one beer since we'd arrived, but those three shooters were sinking in. And sure, she was annoyed as shit I was making her play this game in front of everyone.

I just sipped my granddad cocktail and smirked at her. She really didn't have to be on her knees in front of *me*. She could've chosen Lex's lap.

I know, babe, I told her with my smirk. *No way you wanted Talia sucking that Blow Job out of my lap.*

Lex had put his shooter close to his knees, being a gentleman about it. He even held Talia's hair back for her as she leaned in, picked up the shooter with her mouth and tossed it back. Everyone cheered, Amber took photos, and as Talia plucked the shot glass from her mouth, she smiled halfway at Lex.

He flashed her his pearly whites and those badass silver canines of his.

Myself, I'd been a dick about it and put the shot glass up near my crotch. Maggie's nose bumped my dick when she picked it up. She shot it back to more cheers, then slammed the empty glass on the table.

"You can't get me drunk," she informed me, wiping whipped cream off her mouth.

Challenge accepted.

"And even if you do, it won't matter. You. Won't. Win."

"Win what?" I stared at her, and I wasn't even gonna lie to myself and pretend that when she gazed up at me like she was doing now, kneeling in front of me with that soft, boozy look on her face, I didn't want to dive right into it. Smash my mouth down on hers and melt the fuck into her... the taste of her mouth, her tongue coated in booze. Make out with her right on this table and drink everything the bar could pour, get loaded with Maggie and fuck her brains out and fall the fuck apart.

And pay for all of it later. Whatever it cost me and my sobriety.

Maybe just for a moment, looking down at her face, I didn't care what it would cost.

The desire was strong.

The urge.

The motherfucking temptation.

The desire to fuck Maggie so hard she'd feel it for a week, right here and now, was stronger than the desire to drink. This girl was temptation and everything I'd ever wanted late in the night, fucking tossing and turning and aching in my bed.

Never wanted a girl like I wanted this girl on her knees in front of me.

Add some booze to the mix and that soft look in her eyes... that fucking itch starting to quiver at the back of my brain as the blood pumped to my cock... and this was all starting to seem like a bad idea. Getting Maggie drunk was a bad, bad idea.

But I really wasn't a man to quit what I'd started.

Not where Maggie was concerned.

She put her hands on the arms of my chair and pushed herself up, wobbling a little, and my muscles tensed. I had to fight every instinct I had not to reach out and grab her, haul her into my lap and kiss the shit out of her.

I let my eyes wander from her face to her tits, then all the way down to her crotch in her short black dress. I could *almost* see her panties. I could see the curves of her thighs and her soft bare skin through the holes in the diamond pattern of her tights.

She never did answer me, but her gray eyes narrowed as I palmed my swollen dick and adjusted it in my jeans. I didn't even care who else saw me do it.

So they'd know I'd just sprung massive, throbbing wood for Maggie. How could I not, with her looking like that and sucking shots out of my lap?

No one would exactly be shocked.

She wasn't shocked. Her eyes widened when she noticed my obvious hard-on, but not with shock.

Then she turned her back to me.

She looked good from this angle, too... Jesus *fuck*, that dress was short. I could *just* glimpse the start of the curve of her sweet little ass cheeks... Until she seemed to feel my stare and wiggled her dress down to cover up.

"Hey." Seth gave my shoulder a little shove. "You probably wanna reel it in, before she slips in it."

"Huh?"

"Your tongue," he said, and I tried to focus on his eyes. "You're drooling all over the floor."

I just stared at him. Seth knew about my marriage to Maggie—as in he knew I'd married her in Vegas, though he didn't know much more—so in his way, he was probably looking out for me. And maybe I was being a royal douche staring at her ass like that, like I wanted to be all up in it.

I knew Maggie didn't want me giving our shit away, but what the fuck was I supposed to do when she was right in my face looking sexy as hell?

Seth's mouth twitched in a tiny, pitying smile. *Great.* Now Seth felt sorry for me. "Heads-up," he said, and nodded at the waitress, who was hovering, waiting on our next order.

I blinked at her, at her rack, which was bursting out of her shirt. What did she do, stuff half a roll of toilet paper down there since we walked in? I tried to remember how to speak about normal shit, hyper-fucking-aware that I was sitting in the middle of some random bar with a hard-on, and Maggie's pussy three feet from my face, and I couldn't touch her.

How the fuck did this become my life?

I was a rock star, last time I checked.

I had women, literally and on a daily basis, throwing pussy at me like fucking confetti... Offering me booze, drugs, gifts... Asking me to marry them. Offering me their bodies, their hearts, their fucking bank accounts and their wombs... And I couldn't get Maggie Omura to look me in the eye in public and smile.

I glanced at our table. Katie was shouting something at me. The other girls wanted in on the next round of shooters, so fuck it. I ordered up a shit-ton of Legspreaders, then some Orgasms, then some Screaming Orgasms. Then something called a Passed Out Naked on the Bathroom Floor, which the guys decided they needed a few rounds of themselves.

Then our merch girl, Sophie, arrived. Sophie was fucking cool, with sleeve tattoos and a retro pinup girl hairdo. She was kinda chubby, in a sexy way, with big tits and a big laugh, and the guys fucking loved her. When she started helping the cocktail waitresses pour Upside-Down Margaritas down the guys' throats, things really got sloppy.

Somewhere between the Legspreaders and the first round of Orgasms, Maggie hit the dance floor with Katie.

I watched her dance, my eyes fucking glued to her as she tore it up to "California Love." They seemed to be having fun. Laughing and spinning each other around and bumping their asses together. Maggie in her little black dress and sexy tights and high-heeled boots. And her tight, round ass cheeks almost showing... but not quite.

It was good to see her loosen the fuck up like that. Even as uneasy as I felt sitting here in this bar right now, surrounded by booze and chicks and everyone drinking... and my dick fucking splitting in half watching her dance... it felt good to see her like that.

Sometime after that, she disappeared.

She'd just downed her second Screaming Orgasm when she grabbed Talia's arm and said to her, "Get me out of here before I do something stupid." She said it right in front of me and on *stupid*, she slapped her hand on the table and gave me a look that was half-angry and half-victorious.

How long are you gonna play this game? that look said.

As long as it takes, beautiful.

I watched her lace her fingers through Talia's, like the girl was some sort of security blanket. Then they left the bar with Lex on their tail.

I left right afterwards.

I knew Lex would get them back to the hotel safe.

I also knew Maggie probably didn't want me to follow her.

And since she was drunk, I didn't.

CHAPTER THREE

Maggie

I HAD A HEADACHE.

It was mild, fortunately, and nothing a few Tylenol couldn't fix. So I pounded those back and tried to do some work. I couldn't sleep anyway, and I'd rallied myself out of the hotel a little early, skipping breakfast.

After all the shooters last night, I miraculously didn't feel sick, but I didn't feel very hungry either.

With a little luck, I'd tire myself out and I could take a little nap on the road, then grab a late breakfast when my appetite came back.

It was raining and the Lady Bus was quiet on the way to Portland, everyone tucked away, playing on their phones or listening to music in their headphones. Resting up.

I made a few calls, worked quietly on my laptop at one of the tables in the lounge.

Then, inevitably, I went over last night in my head... trying to figure out what the hell had gone wrong. At the show... and afterward.

And why it felt like Zane had won some small, fucked-up victory because he'd gotten me drunk.

From a business standpoint, the night had gone perfectly. The show was sold out, we sold a shit-ton of merchandise, we got plenty of local media support, and many, many happy fans left the concert with autographed stuff and smiles on their faces.

It was the first show Steel Trap had ever opened for Dirty, and they were a great fit. We'd all miss the Penny Pushers on this tour, for sure; we'd toured with them so often. But Steel Trap was joining us for almost every show on the North American leg of this tour and if last night was any indication, it was gonna rock.

Brody had flown down for the show, and he seemed really happy with everything.

Security was tight and Jude seemed pleased with his crew, which consisted of several regulars and some new guys he'd brought on for the tour. His new girlfriend, Roni, had also flown down; she'd be traveling with us for the first few shows, and Jude looked pretty damn happy holding her hand backstage.

Clearly, the band was happy, too.

Dylan was adorably thrilled that his girlfriend, Amber, was on the road with us. I'd never seen Dylan Cope so lost over a girl; not even close. The way he looked at her, the way he listened when she spoke, the way he was always fetching her a drink or pulling her onto his lap. For her part, Amber was already working her ass off as our tour photographer. And seeing her take photos of Dylan in his kilt at last night's show, watching him sit her down at sound check and try to teach her how to play? Nauseatingly cute.

Elle definitely wasn't happy that she wasn't playing bass on this tour, but she did have that pregnant glow about her. And when she watched her man onstage, reunited with Dirty, I could see how proud she was. Seth fit right back in with the band, almost as if he'd never left, but even better; there was a fresh sense of excitement, respect, and appreciation between all the band members. The members of Dirty were as glad to have Seth Brothers back as rhythm guitarist, backup vocalist and songwriter as he was to be back.

Plus, Seth sizzled onstage. With his short beard and aviator sunglasses, he was all soulful artist wrapped up in mystery wrapped up in sexy man, and the fangirls fucking loved him.

As for Jesse, I'd never seen him happier or in better form than when his wife, Katie, was backstage, dancing and singing along to every song. Which was saying something; with his leather pants, wavy dark hair and dazzling grin, Jesse was always in great form. He kissed Katie every time he went onstage, every time he came off, every time he switched guitars, every time he had any excuse to do it. Marriage suited him. Katie suited him. And every one of us would reap the benefits of his good mood on this tour. When the sun shone on Jesse Mayes, you just had to smile.

And all of us were definitely happy with our newest member, Matty Brohmer.

Matt was a maniac on the bass and he brought something fresh, exciting, and enjoyably unpredictable to the stage and to Dirty's performance. He was filling in for Elle on this tour, and I'd be the first to say we made the right choice with him. He'd rehearsed his ass off and knew all the songs inside-out. Plus, he was a nice guy. Matt was an old friend of Dirty's, had played with Zane on-and-off in his supergroup side project band, Wet Blanket, and really, we were lucky to have him.

And then there was Zane.

Zane Traynor was, to put it mildly, an integral part of Dirty. And there was no denying that I cared about what happened to every member of this band on the road. Every show, from the moment they all stepped onstage until they stepped back off, I cared. I cared if they were having an off night, if things weren't going well, if something didn't go as planned. I cared how it affected them, and how that would end up affecting us all.

We were a team and a family, and I cared.

But it had been so long since we'd been on tour—since before Zane and I were married—that I'd kind of forgotten, until they were onstage last night, how *much* I would care.

How much it would bother me when I saw Zane out there, struggling, and something wasn't right.

My gut was in knots for the entire show.

I'd never felt that way before at a Dirty show. Well... other than at the very last show of the last tour, the night after Zane and I were married. Although, to be fair, I'd missed half of that show, since I was drunk; apparently, I didn't take the whole discovery that we were actually, legally married, and Zane presenting me with a massive diamond ring, all too well.

At last night's show, I was fully-present and sober and I was watching everything from backstage. I saw and heard it when Zane's mic cut out during "Dirty Like Me."

Really, it wasn't that big a deal. I'd seen pretty much every type of screw-up there was, and not just at Dirty shows. I'd seen band members crash into each other, fall off the stage, forget the words to their own songs.

Shit happened.

Even to practiced, polished, professional musicians.

But I knew the mic thing would upset Zane. Despite whatever chaos the man wreaked in his personal life, when it came to his voice and his onstage performance, Zane was a consummate professional.

And he was a perfectionist.

He did not like shit going wrong.

I knew it would bother him even more when, in the very next song, he smashed Seth in the face with his mic. The both of them went right on with the song like nothing happened, because that's what professionals did.

But when Zane screwed up, it stayed with him. And I knew he'd blame himself for the whole thing.

After the show, I didn't approach him. I gave him space and time to cool off. I knew I should probably check on him. As management, it was pretty much my duty. I knew Brody had talked to him, but I should've made sure he was alright.

The truth was, putting aside all our marriage bullshit... I felt for him. The show was fantastic, overall, and everyone else was happy—but Zane just wasn't himself. Brody and I both saw it. We both heard it.

I *felt* it.

Zane was often a little tense before a show, right before he went onstage, and we all knew that.

But once he took the stage, he owned it. He owned the room.

I'd rarely seen a frontman do what Zane could do—which was saying a hell of a lot. Over the years I'd seen a lot of incredible bands play live. A lot of musicians who made magic onstage.

Zane *was* the magic.

Usually.

Last night... not so much. At least, not as much as usual.

And at the bar after the show... he was definitely on-edge. About the show, probably, and about me. I knew he was frustrated with me, and he was trying to push my buttons.

Nothing new.

Zane had always treated *us* like some giant game; like chasing me was some sort of blood sport he'd just keep playing, no matter what it cost him, until he won.

And maybe he could afford to just keep chasing me, indefinitely.

When we weren't on tour.

But being in the spotlight all the time, under the media microscope? That was different than being at home, cutting an album and just generally living life.

I'd realized that last night.

And now I was worried about him. Worried that his performance would suffer on this tour. That *he* would suffer.

Because of me.

Because of this fucked-up shit between us.

I really should've talked to him after the show, figured out if his tension onstage was in any way my fault.

But I didn't.

Instead I'd let him push my buttons at the bar.

Feed me shots.

Make me suck a shooter out of his lap in front of everyone—because he knew I wouldn't say no. That I'd be afraid of making an even bigger scene if I refused.

That I already felt bad about avoiding him at the show. He knew that, right?

Yeah, probably. And he'd only use it against me. See it as an opening to try to fuck me.

He'd definitely gotten the hard-on from hell right there in the bar, and didn't even try to cover it up.

Obviously, I knew there was a danger in letting things go any farther. That if he kept watching me dance with that look on his face... If I had one more of those ridiculously delicious shooters... There was gonna be a disaster.

A naked, sweaty, orgasmic disaster.

He'd try to get me alone and he'd try to get his dick in me, and he'd succeed.

I played a tough game, but the truth was I was so damn ready and willing to give in, it was pathetic.

Which was why I had to walk away.

Thank God he didn't follow. But even though Zane didn't get me into bed last night, it felt like he'd had the upper hand. Like he was in control.

And I couldn't afford to let Zane have control.

No more letting him buy me shooters, then.

No more sitting anywhere near him in a bar.

No more ordering his favorite drink for him.

No more acting like I was his wife, when I wasn't.

When we were about a half-hour from Portland, Zane texted me.

Zane: I'm glad you're on the tour

I hesitated to respond. I considered not responding at all.

I was still kinda mad about last night.

And I was scared.

I was sad, frustrated, irritated, and every emotion in-between.

I was tired, and this tour was barely twenty-four hours old.

But... it was a nice thing for him to say. And it didn't come with a heated come-on.

Me: I'm always on the tour.

He responded immediately.

Zane: you should ride on my bus

For Christ's sake. He wasn't gonna let this go, was he?

No. Of course he wasn't.

This was Zane.

As soon as he had me on the line... let the chase commence.

Me: I have my own bus.

Zane: we could be fucking right now

And there it was.

Not a question. Not an invitation. Just a statement of plain fact.

Because if I was riding on Zane's bus right now, we would most definitely be fucking, and apparently he knew it as well as I did.

Zane: you telling me whatever you're doing on your lady bus is better than that?

I didn't respond to that.

Zane: I like having you around

I didn't even know what to say to that. I really needed to stop looking at his texts.

But every time my phone pinged, I looked.

Zane: you make everything better

Zane: sunshine

Zane: cloudy day

Zane: something about the month of May?

Oh, sweet Jesus. He was serenading me with "My Girl" over text.

Me: Don't get cheesy.

Zane: Motown, baby

Zane: it's a classic

I didn't respond.

Zane: I'll Go is about you

I stared at his text as the words sank in. Slowly.

"I'll Go" was an epic love song on the new album, written by Zane and Seth. Entirely acoustic, with Jesse and Seth on guitar and searing, haunting vocals from Zane. It was some of his best vocal work on the album, for sure.

There was a line in it about gray eyes. I assumed it was about Elle, that Seth had written it for her. Though I didn't ask.

Maybe I just wanted to believe that was true.

Zane: come see me when we get to Portland

Shit.

I tucked my phone away.

Zane was constantly texting and calling me—at home. Flirting, coming on to me, reminding me how awesome it would be if I just spread my legs for him.

And yes, there were times when I did spread my legs for him.

But at home it was easier to just avoid him most of the time. It wasn't like he lived right next door. Here, I'd have to be around him all the time and I knew he was going to put the pressure on, flirt with me.

But worse, he was going to be sweet with me to try to win me over.

And when Zane was sweet with me... it totally fucked with me.

It made me imagine what it could be like if I let him love me. It made me want his love.

It made me want to love him back.

It crossed the wires in my head, lighting a fire in me that would just keep burning, hotter and hotter until I found some way to douse it out.

Usually, I threw a bucket of cold water on it when I reminded myself what a manwhore he was.

I'd tell myself whatever I needed to, to convince myself to keep away from him.

But in the meagre hours since we'd rolled out of Vancouver on this tour, I was already considering many more interesting ways I could douse that fire.

Or stoke it.

Everything just seemed so different away from home. Maybe it was like the Vegas thing; like whatever we did here, on the road, somehow didn't count or something?

Or maybe that was just an excuse.

It counted. I knew it did.

Because what Zane and I did in Vegas changed *everything*.

There was no taking it back. No pretending it didn't happen.

Even if we got a divorce today, Zane would never let me forget what I'd done, and he'd probably never stop digging to find out if it meant more to me than I'd told him it did.

In the days and weeks that followed our wedding, when it sank in for Zane how mad I was that the whole thing was real, he'd accused me of being full of shit. I'd told him that even if the marriage was legal, it still wasn't *real* because I didn't know what I was agreeing to when I said those vows.

When he refused to agree to an annulment or a divorce, and I was the angriest I'd ever been with him, I'd told him that none of it mattered anyway.

The marriage didn't matter.

But it did matter, and we both knew it.

No matter how much we fought about it, no matter how much we disagreed, no matter how much I told him I wanted a divorce and he denied me, no matter how many times he slept with other women... it mattered.

All of it mattered, because we were friends. We were coworkers. Our lives were intertwined in our shared passion for Dirty.

And we cared about each other.

We were still married, even though we weren't living like a married couple. And the truth was we were still married because we both still wanted to be.

Because neither of us was willing to let it go.

Which meant that whatever we did on this tour would matter. A lot.

If I let myself cross the line with Zane, I'd just be giving him another glimpse of the truth. Sex revealed my attraction to him, but more than that, it let him closer to my heart and all my fucked-up feelings for him.

It made me vulnerable to him, which should've made me hell-bent on staying the fuck away from him...

He wrote a song for me.

I grabbed my phone and opened my music app. I pulled up "I'll Go," put my earbuds in and listened, really listened, closer than I ever had before.

It was a song of longing and devotion. Of wanting someone who was far away, out of reach... yet so close you could taste it. Someone who was standing right next to you, but you couldn't have.

I'll go where you are
gray eyes, so far

with you (come with me)

I'll go there (with you)

wherever you are

And hearing Zane sing those words, knowing they were about me... I got a giant lump in my throat as the familiar, dangerous longing flared to life in my chest.

Desire.

Fear.

More fear.

I knew I was afraid to let myself fall for him...

I knew I was afraid he'd already fallen for me.

I knew I wanted him... and that wanting was just never going to stop.

The only thing I didn't know was what the hell I was going to do about it.

CHAPTER FOUR

Zane

AFTER THE PORTLAND SHOW, I headed straight out to my bus alone and told Shady not to let anyone in. Fuck meeting fans and fuck everyone else.

I was not in the fucking mood.

I dropped onto one of the couches in the lounge, dug out my weed and rolled a fat joint. Then I sat back and let the green start to do its thing...

I just needed to smoke, and think things over a bit.

Like why the fuck was I so bent out of shape over another night of inconsequential fuck-ups?

Second show of the tour and I was definitely not feeling it. I'd lost count of the number of small fuck-ups tonight. I'd tripped and almost fallen on my face, for one. And I'd run into Matty countless times, almost knocking him down twice. Would've liked to blame that on the new guy, but wasn't his fault.

I was all motherfucking tense and out-of-body, not even fully conscious of where the hell I was. My body was on that stage, but my mind was somewhere the fuck else.

Total lack of commitment.

Worst of all, I'd fucked up the words to "Road Back Home," a song we'd been playing live for a fucking decade, and I did not do that shit.

Tonight, I'd done it.

Started singing the wrong fucking verse, in a song I knew by heart, upside-down and inside-out, in my sleep and fucking stoned. Stoned or not, when was the last time I'd fucked up the words to a Dirty song onstage?

I couldn't remember it. Maybe back when I was drinking... eight years ago?

Tonight, I'd done it in front of an entire arena filled with fans.

And Maggie.

Yeah. *Fuck.*

I took a long, deep toke. That was what was up my ass, right?

Fucking *Maggie.*

I'd performed in front of her for almost eight years.

I'd been famous as Dirty's frontman for longer than that.

But I'd never been on tour with her while we were in this fucked-up relationship before. We'd never had this bullshit push-and-pull, kick-and-claw tension between us, this messed-up secret marriage shit that was screwing with my head.

Straight up, I'd never worried what Maggie would think of my performance before. Sure, I'd probably always wanted to impress her. But this... this was different.

It was like I was performing just for her, singing every song to her... and waiting for her to pass judgment on me.

Waiting for some kind of thumbs-up from her that was probably never gonna come.

She didn't say one word to me, either before or after the show. She didn't talk to me all day. I'd barely even seen her in the last two days; she'd been avoiding me ever since she ran out of that bar where I was feeding her shots the other night.

I'd seen her in the shadows backstage, but she wouldn't even meet my eyes.

Christ.

All those fuck-ups… They'd just compounded in my head with the pressure of knowing she was watching.

A few minor fuck-ups were pretty normal, typical at the first few shows of a new tour.

And yet the entire show tonight was sitting all wrong with me.

Again.

Even the weed wasn't helping as much as it should.

I shouldn't have needed the weed anyway, but fuck it, what else did I have? It wasn't like Maggie's pussy was waiting for me, warm and ready when I came offstage.

And touching another woman was out of the question.

I didn't need any other woman.

But I needed this tour.

I needed the music and I needed the shows.

For some addicts, touring knocked them right off the wagon. Every time. It was the constant partying, the free access to all the shit that came along with the partying.

Booze. Drugs. Sex.

For me it was the opposite. It was the band, the music, the touring that kept me sane and sober.

But I needed it to go a certain way.

When it came to my talent, some people called me a perfectionist. So be it. The bar I set for myself and those around me was incredibly fucking high; I knew that. And yes, that high bar was probably half the reason I was an addict in the first place. Got me drinking, then drinking to excess, because reaching for that high bar all the fucking time? It was exhausting and damn near debilitating.

The constant striving.

The almost crippling fear of failure.

But once I got sober, I still reached for that high bar. I reached *higher*.

And good thing.

Those high expectations I set for myself, for my voice, for my performance… they kept me sharp. They kept me engaged and wanting more, always pushing to be better.

They kept me at the top.

And they kept me from ever thinking about giving up.

I could never give up on anything once I'd decided I wanted it. Just wasn't in me.

Even if the pursuit of it destroyed me.

That's why I would never give up on Maggie.

She'd have to sue me for divorce and marry someone else, and I'd probably still be pawing at her door, trying to win her over.

Yeah. That was the truth.

I wanted to be Maggie Omura's husband like I wanted to be Dirty's lead singer.

I *had* to be.

What the fuck else would I do if I didn't have Dirty? If they ever voted me off the fucking island? I'd be lost without them.

I could sing with another band, but it wouldn't be music.

I could fuck a lot of other women.

It wouldn't be love.

Someone was knocking on the door. I had no idea how much time had passed, if someone was waiting to take me back to the hotel, if the guys were heading out to a bar, whatever. I just ignored it and kept smoking.

Then the door popped open and Shady stuck his head in. "Maggie's outside," he told me in a low voice. "Said she needs to talk to you."

I sat up and brushed the weed aside. "Let her in." I took a final hit from the joint, then crushed the rest in an ashtray.

Shady stepped back and Maggie poked her head in the door. "Need to go over a few things for tomorrow," she said. No expression on her face. No warmth. No *How the fuck are you?*

I nodded and she came up the steps, shutting the door behind herself. She lingered there, barely inside the lounge, one foot practically out the door.

She glanced at the weed on the table but she didn't say anything about it.

She used to say a lot about it.

These days, she chose her battles with me carefully.

She wore tight jeans and a long, loose sweater that hid her petite curves. Gray, to match her eyes. Her dark hair was smoothed down straight around her face, as usual. She looked a little tired... But those fucking *lips*. I only realized she was talking because her lips were moving.

Kinda got lost looking at her mouth...

"... three phone interviews in the morning," she was saying. "The first is at eight—"

"Eight?" Christ, I was barely out of bed at eight. What about the gym? And breakfast?

And maybe a morning lay?

"East coast," she said. "Brody wants you to do it." She watched as I got to my feet and moved toward her. "Talia will be over at five-to to get you set up..." Her eyes widened as I got close, as I reached past her and flipped the lock on the door. "You'll probably want to set an alarm..."

I drew the curtain behind her, closing off the front steps and the driver's seat, blocking the front windows so we were totally alone in the lounge. The blinds on the windows down the sides of the bus were already shut.

Then I went back over to the couch and sat down.

Maggie just stood there with her arms crossed, watching me.

"That all?" I said.

"For now."

"How was the show tonight?"

She stared at me for a moment, searching my face, like it was a trick question. "That screw-up on 'Road Back Home'?" she said. "It wasn't as bad as you think. You handled it really well."

"Come sit down." I nodded at the couch beside me, lounging back.

She cocked her head as if to say, *Seriously?*

"Do I have to play the employer card? You know, I am yours." I rarely played the employer card with her, but hey, I wasn't above it.

Definitely wasn't above letting my "employee" get down on her knees and suck me off with her gorgeous mouth, if that's what she wanted to do.

"What do you want, Zane?"

"I want you to come sit down."

She took her sweet time about it, but finally she came over and sat on the couch, tense as fuck.

"How was the show?" I asked her again.

"Overall, it was good. I mean... it was awesome." But she didn't unclench when she said it. Her arms were still locked over her chest.

"So, this how it's gonna be?"

She stared at me, totally fucking guarded. "What?"

"You gonna play it cold the whole way through? Avoid me? Talk to me about not one thing but business? Tell me the show was awesome like some yes-woman with a stick up your butt?"

Yeah. Pretty much. I could read that plan all over her face and her *Fuck right off, Zane* body language.

"There's nothing to talk about but business," she said.

"And nothing to do but talk, huh?"

I put my arm up on the back of the couch. I could just reach her, and brushed her silky hair back off her shoulder. Couldn't help it. I had a chance to touch Maggie, fucking right, I was touching her.

In response, she twitched with irritation. Actually, she looked about as frustrated as I felt. Probably needed a good, hard fuck.

I knew I did.

And I was just the guy to give it to her. She knew that by now, right?

She bristled as I drifted my fingers over her shoulder again... and yeah, she knew. Maggie could put up one hell of a fight, but she knew. And fuck if it wasn't the sweetest thing I'd ever tasted—that moment when she started to soften, to give into what she wanted...

Always loved getting her there.

And no mistake, I was getting her there.

It was one thing to avoid me when we weren't on tour. When we were living in separate houses. We'd even been living in separate cities, though I'd remedied that when I'd moved back up to Vancouver last fall.

She'd still managed to avoid me, mostly.

Fine.

I'd let that shit slide, *for almost two fucking years*, knowing we'd eventually get *here*. New album done. World tour, on the road, me and Maggie—unavoidable.

And once and for all, she'd have to face our shit.

Because no way were Maggie and I on a world tour together for the next year-and-a-half, traveling and working together every single day, and not fucking the living shit out of each other all along the way.

No. Fucking. Way.

Not even possible. It was scientifically, chemically impossible. Like even if we never got around to fucking consciously, we'd wake up one morning with her pussy riding my dick.

Because Maggie's pussy and my dick?

Magnetized.

Get them too close—like on the same couch with no one else around... and they were gonna collide.

Only a matter of time.

We both knew it.

I shifted closer to her, and her gray eyes went wide.

Fucking *loved* that look.

"You remember that night... when Jessa went into labor?" I trailed my finger down her shoulder, over her soft, sexless sweater. "Her water broke and Amber called my phone looking for you. You had to take off to help... and we never got to finish what we started..."

She remembered.

It was the last time we'd gotten anywhere close to having sex. Two months ago.

"You were naked beneath me," I reminded her. "And my tongue was about an inch from making you scream."

"I wasn't naked," she said stubbornly.

"Yeah... you still had those skimpy little panties on..." My gaze trailed down her body. "If I didn't get that call from Jessa's number, and you didn't make me answer it... imagine what would've happened next."

"Thank God she called."

"I would've been all over you with my mouth," I informed her, licking my lip for emphasis. I was rewarded when her eyes tracked the movement. "Could be, right now..." I drifted my fingers down to her hip and lifted the edge of her sweater. "You let me at that soft skin..." I snaked my fingers under the sweater and touched her bare waist... and she let me.

Her eyes flared, but she didn't pull away.

My dick swelled.

"You ever have sex on a rock star's tour bus?" I ran my finger up the bare curve of her waist and back down again, watching her eyes. And the answer to that question had better be a giant fucking no.

But she didn't answer. She just gave me a *when-hell-freezes-over* glare.

"You think I'm gonna be in here, fucking groupies after every show." It wasn't a question. I knew that was exactly what she thought. "Ever occur to you that the easiest way to keep my dick away from other women is to entertain it yourself?"

"Entertaining your dick is not in my contract, Zane."

"Kinda what you signed on for, though," I challenged, "when you said those vows at our wedding."

Her eyes flashed with anger. "Yeah, but I didn't know those vows were *real*. I thought the wedding was fake."

Right. So she was still sticking to that story.

And I still wasn't sure if I believed her.

Did it really matter anyway?

Any way you looked at it, we were still married.

"Just say the word, Maggie." I dropped my hand to my swollen dick, adjusting myself a little. My jeans were getting way too tight. "You want this all to yourself? You can have it."

Her eyes drifted down to my lap... And when they met mine again, they had that look in them that always did me the fuck in.

Lust.

Maggie, getting hot, made my brain shut off and my cock take over. I squeezed myself, just trying to ease some of the pressure. Felt better and worse at the same time.

She swallowed. "What word?"

"*Mine,*" I said. "All you have to say is *That cock is mine, Zane.* And it's all yours." I leaned in close, until my lips brushed the soft curve of her ear. "You want this mouth...?" I drifted the tip of my tongue over her earlobe, even as she stiffened. "It's yours, Maggie." I sucked the soft skin into my mouth—and she gave up a little gasp.

My cock jerked under my hand.

Motherfucking *yes.*

Maggie's wall was going down.

Fast.

Now.

And I wasn't gonna miss my window...

I slid my hand up under her sweater and cupped her breast. Silky bra, no padding. I could feel her nipple, hard against my palm. I squeezed her as I sucked on her earlobe.

Then her mouth fell open, those full, sexy lips of hers parting as her breath caught—and it was all the opening I needed. I pressed my mouth to hers and pushed her back on the couch, giving her a quick but thorough taste of my tongue.

In seconds, I had her laid out beneath me, panting softly, wanting more.

Then I pulled my mouth away.

"Maggie..." I tugged up her sweater, uncovering her tits as I pinched and rolled her nipple through the silk of her bra. "You want this...?"

She didn't answer me with words. But as she looked up at me, her eyes darkening... I knew what she wanted.

She wanted it all.

I yanked her bra down and swiped my tongue over her perfect nipple. A dark, dusky pink, it was hard, delicate. She sucked in a breath and her body arched with desire beneath me.

"Zane... *shit*..."

I sucked her other nipple into my mouth, licked and teased until both nipples were flushed dark, taut.

"*Fuck*... you're so pretty, Maggie..." My voice was tight, rough. I tongued my way quickly down her body; I knew I had to move fast, before she changed her mind. Before her brain caught up to what her body was letting me do.

My fingers pretty much vibrated as they obliterated the obstacles of the button and zipper on her jeans. My heart was already pounding, pumping blood to my dick double-time as she buried her hands in my hair. I shimmied the tight jeans down her hips, taking her silky panties with them... baring that perfect little triangle of dark hair and the sweet dusky-pink softness below.

Maggie's pussy.

My fucking kryptonite.

This girl... everything about this woman was my kryptonite.

I kissed her silk-soft hair, swiped my tongue in the little crease between her thigh and her pussy. She wriggled and gasped, clawing her fingers in my hair, gripping me.

"You want my tongue, sweetheart...?"

She made her aggravated little Maggie sound, that soft growl in the back of her throat that made my dick spasm. She bucked beneath me, wanting my mouth—but I held back, taking my time, totally fucking relishing her desire.

"Zane. *Come on*," she panted, as I teased her with my tongue... never quite hitting the sweet spot.

Or anywhere close to it.

"What, you want my tongue? You can have it, babe." I looked up into her gray eyes. "You can own it. Like I own this." I swiped my tongue over her clit.

She bucked again and gasped, fucking *shuddered*, her body

begging me to do it again—but I didn't. All kinds of chemicals were flooding my body, endorphins and pheromones and all that happy shit... Even as Maggie looked more and more pissed-off.

"Worked for this, Maggie," I muttered as I kissed her soft skin. "Fucking *months* I've been trying to get this, get my mouth on what's mine, and I'm gonna enjoy it..." I swiped my tongue, slowly, right alongside her clit and watched her squirm.

Fuck, yeah.

"Why... *Why* do you have to make everything so damn difficult?" she hissed. Yeah, she was mad; furious that she was giving in.

That she wanted this so bad.

"Me?" I yanked off her boots and stripped off her jeans and panties. "I'd park myself permanently in your pussy if you'd let me." I spread her thighs and wrapped them around my head as I nuzzled in between her legs.

"No..." She wriggled and moaned as I kissed the tops of her thighs. "You make everything a battle. You always get what you want, the way you want. You always have to *win*."

"Win? I don't want to fucking win. I want you to win, with my tongue between your legs." Then I buried my face between her thighs and took her whole pussy in my mouth, making her whimper and kind of angry-sigh.

God, yeah...

That sweetish, musky taste of her...

Maggie.

Her thighs tightened around my head, and as I licked her in a slow, teasing rhythm, she breathed hard and fast, fisting my hair, holding me where she wanted me.

As if I was going any-fucking-where.

"I know about Brandi," she gasped out.

I looked up into her eyes again, but I didn't stop eating her out.

"I know about that girl," she said, watching me from under her dark eyelashes. "That Australian girl at Summer's party."

I sucked on her clit until her eyes rolled closed.

"I fucking hate Dallas," she whispered, her voice gritty with that hatred.

I didn't stop. I lapped her with my tongue and smoothed my thumb over her pink flesh, teasing her open. I kissed her, sucked on her with my lips and teased her with my tongue. Fucking worshipped her.

I'd never worshipped any woman's pussy like I worshipped Maggie's.

Definitely never worshipped Dallas' like this.

I knew Maggie hated Dallas. And not just because she was jealous; she seriously hated the woman.

I learned that one the hard way.

"You think I want any of those girls...? They're not here, Maggie," I told her as I kissed her clit, my voice rough with lust. "No one here but you. No pussy here but yours." I licked her in long, slow strokes, from her opening to her clit, and swirled my tongue around, making her whimper and cry out. "Whose gorgeous pussy is this in my mouth...?"

She growled again, like she was truly fucking pissed at herself for enjoying this as much as she did. Like she was pissed at us both.

Because she was fucking *loving* it.

I sucked her into my mouth again, flicked her clit with my tongue until her hips lifted off the couch. I was pretty bent on making her scream, even though she kept biting her lip, trying not to. She ground herself against me, hard, fucking bruising my lips, and I just kept at her. She jerked her hips, totally unselfconscious, hungry for more as her hands clawed my hair and pulled me against her.

"Yeah..." I muttered against her skin. "Never get enough of this sweet pussy..."

I worked my way down, spreading her open with my thumbs, and thrust my tongue into her. Couldn't stop myself, even though I knew I'd have to fuck her when I did. When I felt Maggie's insides... so slick and smooth. So tight, and so wet for me...

I buried my face in her, dug my tongue in deep and rubbed my nose against her clit. She cried out, her entire body bucking. I wanted her to fucking beg for my fingers, for my cock, so I fluttered my tongue around inside. So she felt how deep I was.

How much deeper I could go, if she let me at her with my dick.

But then she yanked herself away.

"Wha—?" I panted, stunned.

Fuck, no.

She shoved at me, hard, and I fell back a bit. Then she got up on her knees—and tore off her sweater.

Great sign.

I let her push me back against the couch and she was on me quick, kneeling over me, climbing the cushions to get her pussy in my face. *Fuck, yeah...* I gripped her tight ass with both hands and squeezed, pulling her to me. I sealed my mouth over her clit and sucked as she fucked my face.

"*Yeah...*" she gasped, desperate. "Get me off, Zane..." She still sounded pissed, but a shiver of arousal rolled through my body.

Those words, in Maggie's breathy, husky, horny voice...

I couldn't hold back.

I dropped one hand to my dick and rubbed hard, scraping the heel of my hand against the length of my hard shaft.

So fucking good... and painful at the same time.

My other hand, on her ass, dug deeper, my fingers delving into her slippery pussy. She was dripping for me and I smeared her juices around, rubbing her opening, starting to finger-fuck her.

She rode me in small, fierce jerking motions as my mouth just tried to keep up. I sucked and slurped at her and fucking moaned—until her clit pulsed against my tongue, her pussy squeezed my fingers and the waves of pleasure snapped through her body.

My dick spasmed under my hand. I probably could've come right now if I wanted to... but I was too fucking mesmerized by what Maggie was doing.

Her hips jerked a bunch of times and her head rolled around. She cried out again and again, her voice getting breathier, ragged. She was holding back, and I knew she was trying like hell not to scream. She pounded her fist into the couch cushion… trying so hard not to lose it.

Motherfucking yes…

All I wanted to do was get Maggie off. Every day. Every fucking way.

Just make her come, again and again and again…

Dripping all over my face.

Tearing at my skin.

Screaming the fucking walls down.

But she was already pulling away.

She fell back and looked at me, still breathing hard.

I wasn't breathing so normal myself. I swiped my hand over my mouth. Her gaze trailed down my body and landed on my dick, hard as a metal pipe in my jeans—and my hand absently squeezing it.

Her eyes flicked back up to mine.

Then she was on me again, tearing my jeans open and grabbing my cock with her small hands—and I fucking melted with relief. Was half-sure she was about to run away, just take off and leave me like this, fucking dying of a raging hard-on. But her hands were strong and warm and soft, and they were all over me.

She pulled on me like she wanted to rip my dick right off.

I just lay back on the couch and took whatever she wanted to do to me. Maggie, turned-on, was a force of fucking nature. A tiny, ferocious hurricane.

She jerked me off, fast and angry, her body slithering against mine like what she really wanted to do was fuck the living shit out of me… her firm, perfect tits half-out of her bra, jiggling in my face… as she panted like a horny madwoman.

As I got close I grabbed her, wrapped my hand around the back of her neck and pulled her to me. I wanted to kiss her, but she turned her face so I couldn't. So I settled for pressing my forehead to hers instead.

She kept stroking me, slowing a bit as she twisted one hand around the head of my cock, tugging at the base of my shaft with the other… and her gray eyes suddenly met mine.

And I blew like a fucking volcano.

Earthquake, the world splitting open… hot lava everywhere.

I smashed my face to hers and somehow I got her mouth. My lips pressed to hers, so fucking soft… I panted against her skin as the spasms tore through me… totally wrecking me. In seconds, I was fucking shattered.

Orgasms with Maggie always left me in pieces.

Her pussy. Her mouth. Her hand.

Didn't matter.

It was all her. *She* wrecked me.

And Maggie knew how to milk it…

She kept stroking me, kept squeezing the hell out of me until she'd wrung out every last drop, every last shiver.

Then she let go.

I fucking collapsed.

She sat there on her knees, kind of panting and staring down at me, one leg tossed over mine. Her gray eyes were shining as she blinked at me.

She'd felt that one.

She'd felt… something.

But she said nothing as she reached for my shirt and used it to wipe my come off her hand. Then she got up and pulled her clothes back on.

Fuck.

She was still mad.

Madder, probably.

And as usual, nothing I could say would make it better. If history was any indication, would probably just make it worse.

I just lay here, fucking destroyed. I was sticky, covered in come. Couldn't even feel my feet, much less find a coherent thought in my brain.

"Maggie…"

"See?" she said, slipping on her boots. "You always get what you want." She didn't look happy about it as she smoothed her hair. She looked neat and composed like she always did, but her lips were dark and swollen.

"If that was true," I said, stuffing my dick away, "you'd be staying."

Her face softened a bit, but she didn't say anything.

She didn't stay.

I watched her walk out as my heart pounded, my entire body still thudding from her touch.

CHAPTER FIVE

Maggie

I WINCED a little in the morning sunlight as Talia and I walked through the lot, headed for the Lady Bus. I was hungover again, and this time I couldn't even blame Zane.

After getting off on his face last night, I'd taken a cab back to the hotel and found Katie and Amber drinking in the bar and decided it was a great idea to do shots again. Just a few, but that was more than enough.

As it turned out, Baileys and self-disgust didn't go down all that well together.

The crew was still packing out from last night's show, and the band was starting to arrive; I saw Elle and Seth talking over by their bus, Seth with a coffee in hand. We'd hit the road in about an hour, but the trucks and crew would roll out later, heading straight to San Francisco, while the rest of us took our time.

I said a quick hello to a few people and checked in with Alec, steering completely clear of Zane's bus, where I saw Shady having a smoke outside.

When I was almost at my bus, I checked my phone.

There was a text from Zane, sent about twenty minutes ago.

Zane: come to my bus

Just four words. And I knew what they meant.

I stopped in my tracks and stared at my phone.

If this was about work, he would've said more. Given some indication what he wanted to see me about.

This wasn't about work.

This was an invitation for sex.

Which meant I was probably gonna end up on his dick in about five minutes.

Shit.

I'd already shoved my pussy in his mouth on day three of the tour. Here we were, day four, and I was twitching with need.

Despite how many times I'd already told myself to get over it, to forget it, to let myself off the hook for one stupid screwup that didn't have to happen again... my body just seemed to laugh at me.

And get hornier.

According to my body, last night was just a tease. A fucking appetizer.

And now it wanted the main course.

Zane, for his part, would be more than willing to serve it up.

No surprise there.

I glanced around. Everyone was preoccupied, and no one was even looking at me. It's not like anyone would *know*.

Other than me and Zane.

I texted him back.

Me: Right now?

Zane: now

I glanced around again. I wasn't even sure why Zane was already on his bus, or why he was even awake at this hour. Usually he was one of the last people to drag his ass out of bed, holding up the caravan.

"You coming?" Talia had paused at the door of our bus and looked back to find me standing here.

"Yeah. Soon."

Talia headed onto the bus, and I dropped down into a crouch and just stared blankly at my phone.

What the hell was I doing?

now

I just kept staring at his text. Those three tiny, demanding letters.

You're thinking about it.

You're really thinking about it.

And that was my mom's voice in my head, popping in to call me on it.

She'd been doing that more and more lately. I hated to admit she'd gone kinda silent on me last year. People told me that would happen. That as time went on, I'd eventually stop having conversations with her and even forget the sound of her voice.

But when things really fell to shit between me and Zane, she still spoke up.

And I spoke back.

Yes. Yes, I am thinking about it.

Of course I'm thinking about it.

This did not make me crazy, having imaginary conversations with my deceased mom in my head. However, thinking about fucking Zane right now probably did.

I knew the man was a hazard to my mental health.

And I knew I was flirting with fire even thinking about him in any nonprofessional way. But the ship had left the port on that about eight years ago, when we'd first met, and never came back.

I knew I'd only made things worse for myself every time I'd touched myself while imagining it was him. And when I'd told myself *No Screwing The Talent*, then went ahead and broke my number one Rule.

Repeatedly.

And yet, somehow, here I was—actually considering taking the massive risk of having sex with Zane while we were on the road together.

A *lot* of sex.

I'd spent the wee hours this morning awake in bed, thinking it over in vivid detail. Thinking about how I just might be able to do it —and get away with it.

Because sex was *rampant* on tour, right?

Everyone was fucking.

It was always this way.

Too many people in close quarters working long hours together, partying together. People who were married or in relationships back home suddenly found themselves crossing lines, cheating, breaking up with longtime partners. Others brought their spouses with them or flew them out to meet up as often as possible, so they could keep the fire burning at home. And those who were single? All bets were off.

There were hookups in hotels, in bars, on the tour buses, backstage. If you could find a place to slam a couple of bodies together, sex was on the menu.

Everyone.

Everywhere.

Was. Fucking.

It was like a rule on the road or something. Sex was just part of the deal. *What happens on tour... stays on tour.*

For the most part.

Except that I'd never been the sort of girl to go full-slut on tour, screwing my way from city to city.

I preferred to keep things professional.

And I knew if I slept with Zane on this tour, it wasn't staying on the tour.

It was staying with *us*.

Zane was never gonna let either of us forget it if I fucked my way around the globe with him.

And yet...

When I was pretty sure no one was looking, I turned and made my way over to his bus. I walked right past Shady without a glance in his direction. I knew he saw me, but he didn't stop me or say a thing.

Which made me wonder what Zane had told him about me.

The door was unlocked.

After I got on the bus, I locked it behind me. I knew no one would open it without knocking first; even Zane's driver wouldn't unlock it without knocking.

No one was in the lounge. It was quiet in the bus, and it smelled like Zane. And like pot. One of Jesse's acoustic guitars lay on one of the couches with a hat that belonged to Seth.

Looked like the guys had a late-night jam session after I fucked Zane's face.

I shivered and tried not to think about that. But it did make me pause and take a breath.

Everyone was busy outside. We weren't leaving for another hour, and some of the band wasn't even here yet. My inner slut really couldn't have asked for a better opportunity to say *Fuck you* to my inhibitions and go nuts.

I was just so afraid, though, of the consequences of that. So afraid, I almost turned around and got right off the bus.

It wasn't just that Zane would hold it over me if we fucked.

It was that I was afraid every time I let him touch me, it would only make me want him more. It would make me want to abandon every inhibition I'd ever had with him.

It would make me want to fall for him.

And I could never let that happen.

Every time I had sex with Zane, it took me weeks to get right again. To get my head right. To drag my heart out of the daydream that he and I could really be together.

That we could be in love.

Forever.

That it could really work between us.

But then something always happened to remind me why it couldn't. Usually in the form of him getting stoned and moody and generally being an asshole. Or, you know, some other chick he was fucking showing up.

Or chicks who wanted to fuck him showing up, swarming like a tide of locusts.

The chicks just kept showing up. He was Zane Fucking Traynor, which meant that they always would.

But so did the daydream...

I found Zane in the bedroom in back, sitting on the bed in his jeans and not one other thing. No shirt. Bare feet. Those beautiful feet of his; long, strong, graceful. He was playing with the phone in his hand, his head tipped down, blond hair in his face.

"Hi."

His head snapped up. Clearly, I'd startled him. "Maggie."

I wrapped my arms around my waist. "Yeah."

He stared at me for a moment, blinking, like he was kind of in shock. "You came." Then he swiped his hair back with one hand and tossed his phone aside with the other.

He was up and closing the gap between us in a heartbeat. He slipped his hand around the back of my neck, under my hair, his heat bearing down on me.

I didn't say a word.

Neither did he.

I didn't know what to say or what to do. I couldn't even look at his face.

I was still struggling with the fact that I was here.

Last night, it had pissed me off how quickly I abandoned my resolve in pursuit of his touch. How quickly I let him get me on my back. It made me livid-mad, but the anger had only fueled the desire, the need to make it happen and happen fast. I was mad at him. I was madder at myself.

I wanted him to get me off so I could get the fuck out of there and berate myself for being so damn weak.

And just maybe... I just wanted it to happen. Maybe I knew it would happen when I got on his bus, and I didn't care.

Maybe I wanted to distract him from whatever was bothering him. Make him feel better.

Maybe I wanted him to make me feel better.

Maybe all I really wanted was to feel my body rock with orgasm as I clung to him. To experience that moment of ecstasy in his arms... The pleasure of it tearing me open and giving me permission, for just those few sweet, terrifying seconds, to love him.

Holy shit...

Was I ever fucked-up.

When I finally looked up into his eyes, his pupils were wide; black smothering all that icy blue. He leaned in and kissed me, fast, like he had to seize the opportunity before I went up in smoke.

I gave in. Immediately.

I kissed him back.

My arms went around him... his hot body, the muscled V of his back. I pulled him to me and he smashed against me, flattening me against the wall.

He kissed his way down my body, fast, tearing off my clothes as he went. My jacket. My T-shirt. My jeans; by the time he got those off, he was on his knees and I was wiggling out of my panties myself.

He buried his face between my legs and started feasting on me, like he did last night—except this time he didn't hold back. He wasn't trying to tease me.

I moaned and grabbed his hair in fistfuls.

Jesus Christ, his tongue...

"Oh God... *please...*" I heard myself gasp. Because I wanted this.

I. Wanted. This.

He knew I did, as much as I fought it. Obviously, he knew.

I'd given in so easily last night, literally climbing on his face. I was giving in again right now. Giving it up.

So. Fast.

I pushed him back, stopping him, and he looked up at me. My heart slammed in my chest.

We stared at each other, both of us breathing these insane,

ragged breaths, like we were halfway to death. Like we'd die if we didn't get to fuck each other.

Maybe that was it.

Maybe I *needed* to fuck him. Fuck him out of my system or something?

Fuck this insatiable, never-ending need away?

"Get on the bed," I whispered.

He got back on the bed and I undid his jeans. I yanked as he lifted his hips so I could pull them down his muscular legs and off. He wasn't wearing underwear.

He was naked, laid out in front of me, just staring at me. A sculpted, golden god, all taut muscles and washboard abs and long, strong thighs... and that *dick* of his... and I definitely wanted to fuck him.

That's what you did with a man like Zane, right?

Anyone could see he was *built* for fucking.

Designed to get a girl off.

"Condom," I gushed, breathless.

That seemed to snap him out of his daze. He got one from a drawer and returned, working it on as I climbed on top of him. I pushed him back on the bed, and as I straddled him, he looked up at me in awe.

Fuck... That *look.*

I'd seen that look on his face before.

Other times when we'd fucked, definitely.

When I'd done something nice for him, or said something nice about him.

When I'd married him.

I put my hand to his throat and held him down.

God, don't give me that look...

I grabbed his hard cock and lined it up where I needed it, and drove down on top of him... hellbent on wiping that look off his face. I couldn't take him all the way until I'd worked my hips up and down a few times. His mouth dropped open. Then he was fully in, my weight and all my strength bearing down on him.

I rode him, frantically, and he closed his eyes.

When he opened them again, he seemed to notice I was still wearing my bra. He tore it off as I went to town on him, fucking him so hard he could barely seem to process it.

It was like he was in shock or something.

Fuck-struck.

That's what he'd call it. I'd heard the guys throw that stupid term around so many times, but I'd never actually experienced it with a man until I saw it on *him*. That look on Zane's face when I took the reins and fucked him, hard.

Shock. Awe. Pleasure. Maybe a little pain... All smeared across his gorgeous face.

For all I knew, I looked like that too.

Then he seemed to recover. He snapped out of it.

He fucked me as hard as I fucked him, his hips pumping into me from beneath. He grabbed me; my hips, my breasts, my face, trying to pull me down to him. A few times, he succeeded.

And when he did, he kissed me.

We kissed like we were dueling.

We fucked like we were in it to win.

We came together grunting and panting and sweating.

It was passionate. Hungry. Aching with the desperation of starvation, of longing and wanting and going without for so damn long.

Months. It had been months since we'd done this.

And it was kind of angry.

I was still angry that I was giving in, that I felt so out of control. That I was so fucking scared.

We were only four days into the tour, and I knew this was dangerous.

Dangerous... for so many reasons.

It only really hit me once we were already fucking that I was in his room.

Zane's bedroom.

I'd never been in Zane's room—in his home, in a hotel, or otherwise. Not since the night we were married.

We'd done it in the back of a limo.

We'd done it in my cabin at Jesse and Katie's wedding.

We'd done it at my place, on my couch.

We'd never done it in his bed.

Now, I was surrounded by his things, all his shit everywhere that he'd half-unpacked and didn't bother to put away. By the smell of him, all over the sheets.

By *him*.

I was in Zane's space, and everything about it was making me uncomfortable. And it was turning me on.

There was just something about the sight of his jeans tossed on the bed... his socks on the floor... his leather vest slung over the built-in desk in the corner. The scent of his spiced bodywash in the air.

The look of him, laid out beneath me... gazing up at me.

Jesus.

He looked fuck-struck again.

He palmed my breasts. Kept lifting his hips to meet my thrusts. He dug his feet into the bed and pounded up into me, faster, harder... then slowing right down...

"Yeah, Maggie," he murmured as he watched me, as he read my body in that way he did. As he *felt* my orgasm build.

And he knew just what I needed to get there.

Each slow stroke, each firm thrust, was designed to hit me how I needed it... until my orgasm hit like rolling thunder. I started to shake and fall apart.

I rode him with the pleasure gripping my body, the shocks and shivers running up and down my spine. I gasped and screamed without even trying to hold back, because I was pretty sure no one could hear me but him.

While I came, he pulled me down to him. He gripped my hair at the nape of my neck, holding me tight, his other arm locked around my waist as the pleasure lashed through me.

"Feel that..." he whispered, just before his hips snapped up and he came, straining against me. He groaned, his cock jerking inside me. Then he pressed his lips to mine.

We squirmed against each other, panting, as the aftershocks rippled through us both.

When we eventually went limp and Zane's arms loosened around me, I pushed away. I got up while he eased off the condom.

I started to get dressed.

"Stay," he said.

But I knew I couldn't stay. I knew I shouldn't have been here at all.

I knew I'd just set something in motion that I couldn't take back. I wasn't sure I wanted to take it back.

I wasn't sure about anything.

Which was why I had to go.

I peered at him and told him, "I shouldn't be here."

Because I knew I couldn't be with him.

I couldn't be with him… but maybe we could fuck?

NO.

Fucking *no*.

Stupid.

Terrible fucking idea.

The worst.

"Like hell," he growled. "You're my wife."

"I'm not."

"You're gonna be," he said.

He was still on the bed, his chest rising and falling as he caught his breath. Just lying there staring at me, totally unconcerned with his nakedness or the fact that we'd just fucked, or the fact that all of this was just going to end up hurting us both.

"One day, Maggie, you're gonna be."

I left without another word. Because there was nothing else I could say that wouldn't be cruel.

Because I knew he was wrong.

CHAPTER SIX

Zane

NEXT TIME I saw Maggie we'd stopped for a late lunch at a diner in the middle of pretty much nowhere, sometime in the afternoon. Jude knew some guy, who knew some guy who ran the restaurant. It was pretty empty when we walked in, just a lone trucker up at the counter and an old couple in a booth.

Between the members of Dirty, Steel Trap, management, various spouses and security, there were nearly thirty of us who piled into the place. They actually flipped the *Closed* sign for us, because the dude working alone in the kitchen was barely gonna be able to handle us.

And maybe we scared the other customers away or something? By the time we started ordering our food, they were gone.

Dylan, who'd had an honest job flipping burgers in high school, went back into the kitchen to help the cook out, and a couple of the Steel Trap guys went with him.

When the lone waitress, who was probably in her fifties but looked about eighty, started bringing out the food, Maggie and Talia got up to help her and so did Katie. Which meant Jesse got up to help, which meant I had to join in, because no way was I letting Jesse Mayes come off as some kind of hero.

We were all packed into the booths while we ate, and Maggie sat about as far away from me as possible, down at the other end of the place. She hadn't spoken to me or even glanced my way since she ran the fuck out of my bus mere minutes after I made her come—again—but we had all day to get down to San Francisco. We also had tonight off. Which meant plenty of time for me to chip away at her fucking wall and get her back in my bed.

I'd lock her in my bus if I had to. Buy her every shooter from here to Los Angeles if that's what it took to get her to look my way again with those soft gray eyes.

Inevitably, I'd get her naked again. Get her to see that resistance was fucking futile.

Because I was never gonna give up on her.

Patience; I had it.

I was never gonna give up on what I wanted.

And what I wanted was my wife.

I looked over at her now, down the row of booths—and some-fucking-how, Xander, Steel Trap's pussy hound of a drummer, had ended up wedged in right next to her.

Fuck me.

I'd already noticed him sniffing her out backstage. Xander was an old friend of Dylan's, and we'd always been cool with each other, but the dude was a rotten, filthy fucker when it came to women. I could see the way he was looking at Maggie, and it was making my food go down all wrong.

It was housemade chili, it was good, but at the moment it was kinda stuck in my throat in a hot glob.

I cleared my throat, sipped my water and tried to pretend I was interested in whatever Elle was saying next to me. I waited for my chili to cool down a bit, and I watched Xander sling his arm around the back of Maggie's seat while he talked to her. Dude was sitting totally sideways, all wrapped up in her.

Then I watched him reach right for her tits.

Classic douchebag move.

He was going in for her necklace—so he could touch her, *almost* touch her tits and see how she reacted.

The necklace was pretty; the delicate silver chain with the clear pink stone that her mom had given her. It stood out against her smooth, warm-honey skin. She was wearing a V-neck sweater, and the stone sat flat against her chest, right between her breasts.

Maggie's gray eyes went wide as she suddenly clocked what Xander was doing; she saw it coming a lot slower than I did.

He scooped up the stone.

A spoonful of chili hit him right on the side of the face. Temple shot. Saucy beans and meat running down his cheek.

"THE FUCK?"

Xander turned to look down the line of booths as pretty much everyone turned to look in my direction.

"Sorry," I called over. "Did I get you?"

"Yeah, you fucking got me." Xander grabbed the nearest grab-bable food—half-eaten burger off Dylan's plate—and whipped it at me. "Fucker."

I ducked.

And a food fight broke out.

"Come on," Dylan protested, "I was gonna eat that..." But his voice was lost in the ensuing chaos.

Food filled the air and shit got out of hand quick. Chicks screamed and dove under the tables or fled to the corners of the room as condiments, full dishes and drinks flew.

Then it ended about as fast as it started—me with fucking mustard all over my leather vest and ketchup in my eye.

Jesse got the worst of it. Seafood sauce dumped on his head, all over his face, and dripping down his shirt.

I might've had something to do with that.

"You're all a bunch of assholes," he said, wiping seafood sauce off his face. But he was grinning when he said it.

"*Shit*, brother." I laughed so fucking hard I snorted ketchup; it was up my nose, too. "You are gonna fucking *stink*. Good luck getting laid tonight."

"Zane!" Katie called from wherever she was hiding across the room. "Don't ruin my man!"

Everyone was laughing and shoving at each other and wiping food off their clothes when Jude broke up the party and started kicking asses out. When Xander walked past me, I gave him a shove that he was smart enough not to return.

Dirty was my fucking band, Maggie was part of Dirty, and he was out of line. He'd been thinking with his dick, and I'd called him on it.

The chili was a warning shot, and he knew it.

"You're a dick," he muttered, and I smiled.

At the door, Jude made all the musicians cough up whatever cash they had in their pockets as I paid the bill with my credit card. Then I handed Jude's wad of cash to the waitress.

Her eyes bugged out at the sight of her tip.

"Sorry about the mess," I said.

Maggie leaned in. "Zane would be happy to sign something," she offered pleasantly, "for your kids or whoever. He's very famous." She fake-smiled at me, pleased with herself.

The waitress, who clearly didn't care who I was, scanned my mustard-smeared vest and face. "Well, my grandson likes the metal. Maybe he's a fan."

Maggie handed me a Sharpie and a Dirty T-shirt she'd pulled out of her ass, because Maggie was always prepared like that. It was a shirt for the *Hell & Back* tour, with some of Katie's art on it. And it was already signed by everyone else in the band.

I signed it, and Maggie handed it over to the woman.

"If your grandson's not a fan," Maggie advised her, "trust me, sell it on eBay." She glanced at me, gave me a pleased-as-fuck-with-herself smile—a genuine smile—and walked away.

The waitress glanced at the shirt, then at me.

"I like her," she informed me.

"So do I."

I was second-last to head for the door. When I glanced back, Amber was lingering, stacking up dirty plates. "They think because they're famous and rich, they can do whatever they want," I heard her tell the waitress, and I stopped. "Can I help you clean up?"

The waitress looked Amber over as she cleared a table. "What's your name, hon?"

"Amber."

"And what do you do, Amber?"

"I'm a photographer."

"Then take a photo, and go enjoy your tour." She nodded at the camera slung on a strap around Amber's neck. "We're the only diner for miles and we're open twenty-four hours, and this county is ripe with bikers. I've seen my share of food fights. Least this one didn't end in gunfire."

Amber's eyes went wide. "Oh. Okay..." She lifted her camera and took a couple of photos of the chaos, the waitress cleaning up, then headed for the door. "Thank you."

I held it open for her and we walked outside together.

"You don't wanna be famous or rich," I informed her, "you're in the wrong place, with the wrong people, sweetheart."

"You can be famous and you can be rich," Amber said, wiping a smear of what looked like cheesecake off her cheek, "but you can be nice about it."

"You don't think tipping her more than she makes in a month in this dump is nice?"

"Hmm," she said.

I tapped a joint out of the little cigarette case I carried in my pocket and Amber lifted her camera, pointing it at my face. I lit up, tossing a panty-peeling glance down her lens as she took my photo.

When she lowered the camera she kinda shook her head at me, then headed over to her bus, where Dylan was waiting to sling his arm around her.

Then I noticed Maggie.

She was over by her bus with Talia, and she was giving me a look I couldn't read. Too far away, and she had sunglasses on... but she was definitely looking at me. Watching that exchange with Amber.

Wondering if I could be trusted with Dylan's new girl, maybe. Trusted not to be an asshole... or worse.

Didn't blame her for scoping me out when I was talking to any chick... but really didn't know how I was ever gonna convince her I was trustworthy.

I might be an asshole, but I was never gonna make a play for Amber or anyone else.

Maggie disappeared onto her bus, before I could make a move in her direction.

Shady was standing by, waiting for me, and we had a smoke while Jude's friend, some biker dude, rolled in with a couple of other dudes on Harleys. Jude introduced us; they were affiliated somehow with Jude's motorcycle club, the West Coast Kings. I didn't ask how. Learned long ago, you don't ask questions like that.

Jude's guy was letting him take his bike for a rip, and as the bikers headed into the diner, Jude got on the Harley and Roni got on behind him.

I'd never been into motorcycles myself, but Jude Grayson made that shit look good. Big and dark and powerful, kinda like the machine itself. And with Roni at his back, all sleek black hair and curves in her leather jacket and tight jeans... I watched as she wrapped herself around her man. Then they rolled out of the lot and tore up the highway.

Jesse and Katie stayed back with their bus to wait for Jude and Roni, while the rest of us rolled out. And as I watched the Harley disappear into the distance, I felt that thing again... that fucking jealousy I always felt around my friends who had the shit I wanted.

I texted Maggie on the road to San Francisco. It was a long drive and I wished she would've just rode on my damn bus. It wasn't like everyone would instantaneously think we were fucking—or married—just because she rode on my bus for a stretch. We could've been talking about business or whatever.

I pointed that out to her in my texts.

She didn't text back.

Then I tossed my phone and lay back on my bed. I smoked some more green and I thought about Jude, rolling out on that Harley with Roni at his back, looking like they belonged together. I'd never seen him like that with a woman.

So right together.

Seeing them like that made me wish I'd never fucked Roni, once upon a time. Wasn't all that proud of it, given Jude's reaction when he'd found us in bed.

But that was long ago and I'd been drinking then. Just one of about a million things I'd done when I was wasted that I'd live to later regret.

Fact was, I regretted a lot of shit I'd done, even when I was sober.

But not Maggie. I'd never regret one moment with her.

Even all the mistakes, the stupid fights, the long stretches of fucked-up silence. Because every moment of our relationship had gotten us where we were. And even if I'd been confused about it in the past, I knew she had feelings for me now. That much was obvious.

Feelings she was trying like hell to avoid. Which was why she avoided me.

Or tried to.

But fuck that. I was just gonna have to make her face her feelings. Make her face *me*. Make her look me right in the eye while I fucked her, again and again, and then I was probably gonna do something stupid, like dare her to tell me she didn't love me.

She wouldn't dare.

At least, I didn't think so.

I knew she was scared, and I knew why she was scared. She'd told me often enough.

The stakes for her were real.

Her job; that was the worst of it. She was afraid of losing the job she loved.

And then there was the fact that she thought—somewhat justifiably—that I was an unrepentant, irredeemable manslut.

Maybe I was, in the past.

But people could change.

Grow. Mature. Motherfucking evolve.

I had my flaws and I had a lot of them, but I'd come a long way since Maggie and I met.

True, I was still an addict. I'd always be an addict. An addict who didn't drink.

An addict who smoked pot but probably shouldn't.

An addict who was probably borderline addicted to pussy. Difference was, these days, there was only one pussy I craved.

I was just gonna have to prove to her that she was wrong about me.

I didn't need any other woman.

I didn't want any other woman.

No matter what Maggie Omura might think, I was not gonna touch another woman on this tour.

That night, after we rolled into San Fran, Dirty met up for a late dinner in the hotel restaurant. Dylan's idea. Just the band and spouses, Maggie and Jude and some security.

Ashley Player, lead singer of the Penny Pushers and Dylan's best bro, who usually toured with us, was down in L.A. and had come up to meet us. He was trailing a couple of random bimbos when he arrived, but that was nothing new.

Bimbos or not, Ash was always welcome at Dirty's table.

I loved this guy. And I was glad that whatever shit had gone down between him and Dylan over Amber, it didn't seem to fuck with their friendship. At least, not seriously. Maybe Ash wasn't coming around as much as he used to, but he was still around.

I was one of the first people to give him a hug when he joined our table at the back of the restaurant.

It was a good night. Everyone was happy. Most everyone was drunk, but Maggie was sipping water and avoiding my eyes. She was sitting across the table from me, a couple of seats over, making forced-polite conversation with one of Ash's girls.

Every time I caught her looking at me, I eye-fucked her steady.

After dinner, as soon as things started getting rowdy, she slipped away.

I was standing up on the bar in my socked feet, with Ash, who was drunk off his ass, belting out a duet of "Stop Draggin' My Heart Around." It was playing quietly over the restaurant's sound system while the bartenders tried to convince us to climb down. *You're not supposed to be up there.*

Huh? Says fucking who?

I took off my boots. So maybe we broke a few glasses; send me the fucking bill. What was I gonna do, let Ash sing all by himself when he jumped up here and started singing Stevie Nicks' parts? Nope. Not what a brother does. I got right the fuck up here and covered Tom Petty.

By the time we hit the chorus, arms slung around each other, our whole group was on their way out the door but everyone had stopped. Matty and Katie started singing backup, Roni and one of Ash's girls were dancing and we had most of the room singing along. Girls were starting to scream as they realized who the fuck we were. Dylan and Jesse were pissing themselves laughing, Amber was taking photos to commemorate the moment... and Maggie fucking *escaped* when she thought no one was looking.

But I saw her do it.

I jumped down from the bar and got my boots on, leaving Jude and Dylan to haul Ash down. He was still singing as everyone spilled out into the lobby and started rolling out, looking for someplace serious to drink.

I grabbed an elevator and caught up to Maggie at her hotel room door.

She was just about to swipe the key card over the lock when I came up behind her. She looked up, startled, but she softened quick. Her shoulders dropped as she glanced past me at Shady.

She let me inside without a word, if only to avoid Shady overhearing anything. But once I had her inside... I could already feel the wall coming down.

I didn't even have to touch her. I barely opened my mouth.

"Maggie—"

"Zane," she said. "We shouldn't do this." But there was no conviction in her voice.

"Says who?"

"Me."

"Why? Because you're afraid of someone finding out? Shady's not gonna say anything."

She pinched the bridge of her nose, the way she did when I was driving her insane. "Is this how it's gonna be? The whole way through the tour? You flirt, you get me drunk, you wear down my defenses until I give in? Cat and mouse bullshit, over and over again?"

I pretended to consider that carefully, as if I didn't already know. "Yup. Sounds about right."

She sighed.

"You got a problem with that?"

"I just think we should stop."

"I think you should take off your clothes. It's just a difference of opinion, Maggs. We can work it out." I slid off my vest and peeled off my shirt, dropping both on the floor as I wandered deeper into her room. "See? I'm willing to negotiate."

I turned to face her.

Her gray-eyed gaze moved down my body as I undid my belt, drinking me in. And she definitely looked like she was dying of thirst.

Yeah; for whatever reason, Maggie didn't have much fight in her tonight.

Fine with me.

Fighting with Maggie could be hot-as-fuck foreplay. But I didn't need to fight with her to get it up.

"Come here."

I undid my jeans, and after the world's tiniest hesitation, she came. I slid my hands into her hair, tilting her face up to me. "What do you want, Maggie?"

She shook her head slowly, but she didn't answer me.

"I want your mouth on my cock," I volunteered.

Her eyelids lowered. "Don't talk," she said, swallowing. "If we're gonna do this... maybe, just don't talk."

Then she got down on her knees in front of me and peeled my jeans open. And half of me couldn't believe this was happening. The other half wanted to ram my dick right down her throat and leave it there a while.

I wasn't wearing any underwear to get in her way, so she had my hard cock in her hands in seconds; good start.

"Yeah... *shit*, babe... that feels so good. Fuck. Does dirty talk count...?" Because there was all sorts of dirty shit I wanted to say to her right now.

"Don't," she said softly. Then she took the head of my cock in her mouth and my brain went kinda blank.

I groaned and grunted as she sucked me off, her little tongue and those gorgeous lips all over me... as I pushed my cock into the back of her throat, as far as I could jam it in without making her squirm and start to gag. I was pretty big, she was pretty small, and she couldn't take all that much of me, but what she took... Maggie had a talented mouth.

And what she couldn't suck... her soft hands took care of the rest.

Before I knew it, I'd lost all sense of time. It could've been an hour. It could've been thirty fucking seconds that Maggie's mouth was blowing my mind. But I had to pull out as a shudder racked my body.

Too fucking *close*.

"Wait," I said, panting. I pulled her to her feet, then shimmied up her little dress, wrapped her around me and pressed her against the wall.

She wrapped her legs high around my hips as I fumbled to get a condom out of my jeans pocket and onto my dick. Then I yanked her panties aside, my cock lined up with her slippery pussy.

She wrapped her arms around my neck as I drove into her, slow.

I did her up against the wall with her body wrapped around mine. I loved how she had to cling to me, had to hold on so tight. I ground into her hard, going slow because I had to, pausing every time I needed to yank myself right back from the edge.

The urge to piston my hips and fucking explode into her was building fast, the pressure inescapable...

"Fuck, Maggie," I told her as I fucked her, "you better fucking come, because I'm about to go off..."

I was slamming her into the wall, grinding like hell into her clit as I sucked on her neck. She was breathing in choked gasps, her nails digging into the backs of my shoulders, her thighs squeezing my waist.

"Don't..." she gasped. "Don't you dare give me a hickey..."

"*Shit*... give it up, Maggs," I demanded.

Her eyes met mine. She was biting her lip and bearing down on my dick so fucking tight...

"Yeah," I urged her, "give it to me..."

Then I started to blow, even though I didn't want to just yet. I wasn't even sure if she was with me... But then there she was, giving it right up—her back arching, her tits pressing into me, fucking screaming as the orgasm took her down.

I pounded into her, sloppily, trying to make every last thrust count even as my legs quivered... fuck her through her orgasm so she felt every last twitch.

And I knew she felt it—all of it.

Maggie was a screamer. I fucking loved that about her. That she was so damn prim and proper most of the time... yet I could get her to this place where she completely lost her mind. This tiny, horny beast in my arms, screaming and shaking and sweating for me.

Fuck. Yes.

When we'd both finished, I slumped against her, pinning her against the wall. I looked at her face. Her mouth was still open as she tried to catch her breath.

She gazed up at me. She didn't say anything. And this time, she didn't even look angry.

Thing was... she definitely didn't look happy, either.

CHAPTER SEVEN

Maggie

I WOKE up in my San Francisco hotel room with sunlight streaming over my face.

And Zane in my bed.

I knew that was true even before I opened my eyes.

In the aftermath of my first couple of hangovers on this tour, I'd been avoiding alcohol. I'd had zero to drink last night. Meaning I was one-hundred-percent sober when I had sex with Zane up against my hotel room wall, and afterward, when he followed me into the shower and we did it up against that wall, too.

And when he followed me into bed, spooned me, put his hand between my legs and massaged me until I came again, then fell asleep. Still spooning me.

And I let him.

I let him do it all.

Which meant that while I was completely sober, I was clearly losing my mind.

I was definitely questioning my sanity mere seconds after I'd woken up, as I felt his arm snaking around me, his hot, hard body pressing up against mine, his hand seeking out my happy zone again—and I let him.

Again.

He'd spent the night.

It was the first time since our wedding night that we'd spent the whole night together. That we'd slept together.

That we'd fucking *cuddled.*

We were naked together under the sheet as his fingers slid over my clit, moving around and around, drawing lazy little circles as he gradually increased the pressure and my body woke up to the pleasure...

Kinda made it increasingly difficult to think about anything else clearly.

All I knew was that we were taking bigger and bigger risks here. And not just the risk of getting caught.

We were risking *everything.*

Everything that mattered to me.

At the moment, with Zane's hand between my legs and his teeth biting gently into my neck, I just couldn't find a shit to give about it.

I shifted my hips, slowly riding his hand as he kissed my neck, grinding my ass against him. Against his cock, which was standing at attention, long and hard and nestled between my butt cheeks.

You wanted to let a guy know, without words, that you were down to fuck... that was pretty much it.

He groaned in his smoky, rough morning voice, gripped my hip and rolled me over onto my back. Then he was on me in one smooth motion, his toned body poised over mine as I hitched my legs up around his hips.

His eyes met mine. The sun was hitting the side of his chiseled face, setting his blond hair aglow. It hit his eyes; a clear ice-blue, whitish flecks in the irises... the velvety black of his pupils, the golden tips of his dark lashes.

He pushed into me and I closed my eyes.

Slow. He filled me slow. He moved against me slow, and he started kissing my face. He kissed me everywhere he could reach... My throat, my shoulders, my chest.

I started kissing him, too. His shoulders, his neck... his chest. I flicked his pierced nipple with my tongue, sucked it into my mouth, making him groan. I kissed my way up his throat until our lips suddenly met and we melted together.

We slithered against one another, our bodies undulating in a reciprocal rhythm, our hearts beating together, our breathing becoming one panting, shuddering rhythm as our mouths fused.

This wasn't fucking.

Nope; we were no longer fucking.

This time, we were making love.

We clutched at each other, every muscle in both of our bodies locked up tight. As the delicious friction built between my legs, the pleasure radiated through me, my entire body aching for the release of this sweet, sweet pressure. I bore down on him, riding his dick and rubbing myself against him as hard as I could.

He broke our kiss, gasping.

"Fuck, Maggie... Come on my cock."

"Yeah..." I breathed.

"Give it to me," he ordered, kissing my face. "I want to watch you come..."

He pounded into me, rolling his hips, digging for fucking gold—until he made me come. The orgasm tore through my body; a hot, fucking delicious burst... then it washed through me in waves and sparks. I was pretty sure I made a bunch of ridiculous, greedy, ecstatic sounds.

But it was like my brain and my body were in two different worlds. My brain, briefly disconnected from reality, projected somewhere into outer space... while my body writhed and screamed in Zane's arms.

"*Fuck*," he groaned. "I can't get enough of that. Can't get enough of you like this... so fucking tight. You're fucking strangling me, sweetheart..."

He kept groaning, muttering dirty shit all the way through my orgasm. And it felt so fucking good.

Amazing, otherworldly good.

The way it always felt with Zane.

His words.

His voice...

His kisses on my face.

Then he started to come, pressing me down with the force of his hips slamming into me over and again until he completely lost it, went rigid, and let go. I felt him blow, deep inside me.

Then slowly he relaxed against me, breathing hard. He gave a few more random, lazy thrusts as he moaned against my neck. He was murmuring more filthy shit about how beautiful I was, how tight and hot my pussy was...

Then he said the dirtiest thing of all.

I heard him say it, but I wished I didn't. I didn't want to acknowledge it, and I definitely didn't want to believe he felt that way about me.

I love you.

I heard the whisper of his smoky voice. Felt his breath on my ear. His lips softly brushing my neck.

And I knew I had to get out of here.

I had to stop this.

I pushed him off. He grabbed at himself, narrowly saving the condom from slipping off.

Fuck. *FUCK.*

I didn't even notice him putting the condom on or give it a split second of thought. I was sleepy, barely awake when he rolled me over and started fucking me, but that was no excuse.

It definitely wasn't the first time I'd let Zane fuck me without making sure he had a condom on. It wasn't the first time I'd left that particularly important detail up to him.

What the motherfuck was wrong with me?

Fucking *seriously.*

This was such a mistake.

I wasn't even on the pill. Hadn't been for years. I got all kinds of weird side effects when I was on birth control; it just didn't work for me. Yeast infections and cysts and all kinds of shit the doctors could never quite explain, but I knew it was the hormones in the pill.

Every time I was on it, same problems. When I was off it, no such problems at all.

Which meant that as a presumably fertile twenty-six-year-old woman who wasn't on birth control, I was particularly vulnerable to pregnancy.

Not to mention the fact that every time I fucked Zane I was potentially getting into bed with every skank he'd ever screwed.

And there'd been a *lot* of skanks.

What the hell did I want to do, end up just like my mom? With some surprise pregnancy, mother to the child of some womanizing rock star who'd never even wanted to be a daddy in the first place—and turned out to be a horrible one?

And with some fucking venereal disease to boot?

Just *fuck*.

Zane had rid himself of the condom and was staring at me. He must've been reading all the shit I was thinking on my face, because his eyebrows furled and he started shaking his head.

"Whatever the fuck you're thinking in that overactive brain of yours," he said, "just stop. Right the fuck now, just stop, Maggie."

"Fuck this." I flew out of bed and started pulling on clothes. I tripped on his stupid boots, banging the hell out of my knee on the coffee table. "FUCK."

"I told you," he said, "just stop." He was sitting back on the bed, leaning against the headboard like it was his fucking throne or something, all king-of-cool and naked and gorgeous, and all I wanted to do was get the fuck out of this room.

Before I ended up on his damn dick again.

Fully dressed, I yanked on my high-heeled boots.

"You can't run away from me forever," he informed me.

"Can't I?"

"What's the point of that? You know we're just gonna end up talking about it anyway."

And here we go.

I ignored him, checking myself out in the mirror. I ran my hands through my hair; I'd straightened it yesterday, so it was nice and smooth. I still had yesterday's makeup on, too; I rarely slept in my makeup.

Just another sign that my life was falling apart.

I licked my finger and quickly cleaned away the little smudges of raccoon eyes from under my lower lashes. Otherwise, I looked okay.

Good enough, anyway.

Zane sighed. "We need to talk about this, Maggs."

"Talk about what?"

"Our relationship. Our fucking marriage."

Right.

I should've known. I should've known he'd turn this into an argument.

He couldn't just fuck me and leave well enough alone.

We had eighteen months, at bloody minimum, to get through, and he couldn't just keep his mouth shut for a mere few hours?

"This isn't a relationship, Zane," I said, hunting for my purse. "This is two people using each other."

"Using...? What the fuck are you talking about?"

"Using. Each other. Fucking. You get me off, I get you off." That was all it could ever be, anyway. "Let's not complicate it with other bullshit."

"What bullshit?" He got out of bed slowly, and started getting dressed while I finally located my purse. "The fact that we care about each other? Because I think the ship has fucking sailed on that one."

I looked him dead in the eye. "I care about you. I care about a lot of people." I started digging through my purse for my phone. "This isn't special, Zane."

"Like fuck it's not."

"It's not to me."

It wasn't. It couldn't be. I was still trying like hell to convince myself that it couldn't be.

Zane was a sex god and that was that. I wasn't immune to it, and neither was my pussy.

I never had been.

But I wasn't gonna make the mistake of letting it become something more.

Something so fucked-up, it would destroy my life.

Not even Zane Traynor's godlike dick was worth that.

"Meaning what?" he growled. I'd found my phone and glanced up at him; he stared back at me, anger sharpening his features. "You're gonna go do *this* with whatever other guys you care about, too?"

I started checking messages on my phone. "If I want to." I sent a text to Katie.

Me: Breakfast?

I tucked my phone away and found my hotel key card. Then I looked at him calmly. "It's not as if you've been faithful to me."

He hadn't. He definitely hadn't.

Not that I'd ever actually expected him to.

And yet I'd been faithful to him. The entire time we'd been married.

Because I was a fucking masochist like that.

His jaw hardened, his nostrils flaring as he sucked in a breath. "Faithful to what?" he said. "A marriage you want no part of?"

"Right. Because when it suits you we're married and I should play the doting wife. And when it suits you we're not married and you can fuck whoever you want. Sounds like the marriage of my dreams." Now I was just getting pissed off. Why did he always have to do this? "I'm not holding you to it," I informed him. "I never asked you or expected you to stay married to me. I've asked you for a divorce, many times."

"So? I thought we were past all that bullshit. I thought maybe you were actually gonna give this a fucking chance."

"*So*, it's your fault we're still married!" Yep. I lost it. Started yelling, which was something I'd promised myself, after the last round of bullshit with Dallas, I wasn't gonna do anymore. I was not gonna lose my cool with him and yet here I was, screaming at him.

"And it's your fault you can't stay faithful to the marriage! *What the fuck* do you want from me?"

Then I turned and walked out before he could answer.

After yelling at Zane and storming out, then berating myself for all of it—for fucking him, for making love to him, for yelling at him and storming out—I avoided him for the rest of the day.

And the next day.

Even at the show.

After the show, I went along with everyone to some bar, but I stayed the hell away from our lead singer. I definitely wasn't drinking any of his sexually suggestive shooters tonight. I didn't even stay long.

The next day, I communicated with him only through text message, and only about business.

After the buses rolled out of San Francisco and I still hadn't spoken to him, he sent me a single text.

Zane: please take down your wall

I didn't respond.

Once we arrived in L.A., it got a little easier to avoid him.

Besides the two shows Dirty was playing while we were in town, Zane was also playing a show with his side project band, Wet Blanket, which meant he was extra busy.

He had a ton of interviews to do during the day, as usual, a few appearances to do with Dirty, rehearsals with Wet Blanket, and he was pretty much busy around the clock. As was I.

Our second day in L.A., the band drove out to Death Valley anyway, to meet up with a film crew and shoot the video for "Somewhere," a gorgeous ballad written by Seth which would be the second single off the *To Hell & Back* album. It was a long day; they were gone before dawn and got back after midnight.

I didn't go to the shoot. Talia did.

Fortunately, we were getting into a pretty decent groove—Talia and I. A groove whereby I had her dealing with Zane on my behalf. Dealing with any texts, emails, phone calls or in-person business involving Zane in any way.

I spent most of my time in my hotel room, on my laptop and my phone. Or at the gym, doing yoga. Nothing like a whole lot of downward dog to keep a girl feeling strong. I was not gonna let anything—even my fucked-up relationship with Zane—mess with my health.

My physical health, at least, was in great shape.

My mental health was a whole other disaster.

The day of the first of our two L.A. shows, I avoided sound check and the venue until showtime. Once I was backstage, I made myself busy talking to whoever else was around so I could avoid having to talk to Zane.

And it wasn't fun. It was far from fun.

Avoiding him, and spending so much mental energy avoiding him, completely sucked. It was exhausting and torturous.

After the show, both bands went barhopping, and I went with them—because I was trying to make an effort. Not let my bullshit with Zane turn me into a hermit. But I skipped the limos and took a taxi with Talia. We ended up at Dylan's nightclub, where I danced the night away with the girls. The dance floor was a pretty safe bet; Zane didn't like to dance.

He definitely liked watching me dance, though.

He also seemed to like several fangirls who were circling around, flirting with him and Matt.

The girls were everywhere. When I really cared to pay attention... they were everywhere Dirty went.

As always.

Begging Jesse to take selfies with them.

Trying to get Dylan's attention while Amber was busy talking to someone else.

Following the Steel Trap guys around.

Xander had two chicks all over him. They were sitting on him, and one of them had her hand happily planted on his crotch.

When I left the club, I saw Ash outside making out with some dude up against the wall in the alley. No sign of the chick he'd walked in with about an hour ago.

I had to stare for a sec, because really, Ash was super fucking hot —all angsty, badass rock star in his tight black jeans and sleeveless shirt and mussed-up black hair. And sucking face with some hot blond guy?

Holy shit.

I would've found it sexy if I didn't feel so sorry for him.

Ash had been a hot mess ever since whatever number Dylan and Amber had done on him. I loved Dylan, I liked Amber already, but I liked Ash too, and honestly, I felt horrible for him. It was pretty clear he'd had his heart broken and was on some booze-and-sex spree, and I didn't even know all the details.

Wasn't sure I wanted to know.

Too fucking depressing.

The whole idea of having to be around someone you cared about, maybe were in love with, while they were happily in love with someone else...

Painful.

Depressing.

Not the kind of shit I'd wish on my worst enemy.

I was in enough pain of my own. But at least Zane wasn't in love with someone else.

Back in my hotel room, alone, I kept looking at his text.

And I kept wondering if he'd come back to the hotel or not. If he was alone.

Zane: please take down your wall

He hadn't sent me another personal text since that one. He hadn't followed me back to my hotel room or tried to get me alone tonight. He hadn't tried to get me drunk.

He really hadn't tried to get near me at all.

He'd definitely stared at me every chance he got, though. With a penetrating, accusing, expectant stare.

A *when-are-you-gonna-get-over-your-bullshit-and-talk-to-me* stare.

By now, I knew that stare well.

I knew he wasn't happy that I wasn't talking to him. I knew he was mad at me and probably hurt.

I was mad at him, too.

And I'd been hurting for years.

I'd watched him drink himself stupid.

I'd watched him hurt himself.

I'd watched him with other women. And not just since we were married.

I'd known the man for almost eight years, worked with him pretty intimately, built a pretty amazing friendship... and I had watched him hook up with literally hundreds of women who weren't me.

When it came to Zane, I had wounds and I had scars.

Fresh wounds. Old wounds.

Ancient scars.

Some that were fading and some that may never fully heal.

Some that had burst back open, over and again.

I didn't want to punish him for it.

I'd never wanted to punish him.

Zane was who he was. I never even wanted him to change. Not at his core.

It was the bullshit destructive behavior, the kind that hurt him, that hurt everyone who cared about him, that hurt *me*, that needed to go.

I'd never asked him to change, but now he was married to me, and he kept telling me he wanted to be married to me, and yet he still couldn't see all the ways he was hurting me.

All the ways he was still hurting himself.

Zane: please take down your wall

I kept checking my phone and staring at his last text, long into the night. I started to reply, a few times, then deleted whatever angry bullshit I'd written.

Eventually I let down my wall, just a bit, and wrote back.

Me: Please don't ever drink again. Please don't smoke pot anymore. Please don't sleep with other women. Please just stop.

His response came in moments later.

Zane: please be my wife

Early the next morning, I lay in bed and tried to formulate some kind of plan. I was always armed with a plan; it was my thing. One of my greatest strengths.

But with Zane, every plan just crumbled to dust.

Usually because whatever plan I had was abandoned the moment he got me alone and got his hands on me.

I wanted to be stronger. I'd always thought I was strong.

But with Zane, I was all over the fucking place.

Maybe we could keep having sex.

Maybe we couldn't.

I really couldn't stand the thought of never touching him again.

I wanted him like I wanted my next drink of water. I could put it off for a while, but eventually, if I didn't have it, I'd wither up and I'd die.

So much for being strong.

I was nothing but weak. Weak and confused and in pain, wanting someone who would only keep hurting me. I did want him, I would always want him, and wanting him would always cause me pain.

I knew this.

I'd been in a constant state of pain for so long now, I'd learned to somehow live with it. To stuff it down. To endure.

Now that I was around Zane all the time on tour, I was also in a constant state of tension and fear, and it was wearing at my nerves. My emotions were frayed, my convictions were shot, my strength was failing.

I no longer had any idea what to do.

I had no plan, and no idea what to do about it.

I just didn't know how to live this way. I felt utterly lost, out-of-control, and terrified that I'd never figure out what to do about it.

Eight years. It had been almost eight years and I still didn't know what to do about my feelings for Zane.

Worst of all... I was terrified that maybe I was losing him, that I was losing my friend and I was going to lose my job, and that was the only ending there was ever going to be to our story.

And by fighting it, all I was doing was delaying the terrible inevitable.

And by trying to tell me he loved me, he was only speeding it up.

It was a simple matter of time, of *when*, not why or how or if. We were fighting over moments between us that, fast or slow, were never going to change a thing.

Any way you looked at it, we were falling apart.

I'd come to this depressing conclusion right around the time a note was delivered to my room on hotel stationery.

Scrawled on the envelope in a familiar hand, it said:

Maggie,

I wrote this to you in February last year, just after Jesse's wedding.

Then things seemed okay between us, and I didn't give it to you.

Then things got worse.

Then things got even worse, and I never gave it to you.

But every word is still true.

Obviously, I knew who it was from.

I set the envelope down on a table, and I went about getting ready for my day. Once I was showered and dressed, my makeup on, my room tidied up and my day organized, I picked up the envelope and looked at it again.

I stared at it for a long time, mildly shaking with adrenaline and dread, hope and fear.

Then I sat down on the bed and I opened it.

I took a breath, and I read every word, slowly.

Maggie May.

That night we spent in Vegas rocked my world.

What happened the next morning... blew it wide open.

What happened in the weeks that followed almost killed me.

Pretty sure it almost killed you too.

You wanna look me in the eye and tell me you don't love me? Go ahead.

I'm waiting.

But sweetheart, I'm guessing that isn't happening anytime soon.

I know I've fucked up.

You're probably thinking if I could take it all back, I would.

You'd be wrong.

Maybe you're waiting for me to apologize, but babe, I'm never gonna do that.

I'm never gonna apologize for loving you.

Zane.

CHAPTER EIGHT

Zane

AFTER I SENT her that note, Maggie avoided me like I was the motherfucking plague incarnate.

Like if she got anywhere near me she'd be struck dead.

I actually saw her turn and hightail it the fuck out of the room or the hallway or wherever we ran into each other, several times. And it was pissing me off.

Worse, I missed her.

Almost made me regret sending her the damn note.

But fuck it.

I meant every word I said. She didn't believe me, or it scared the shit out of her or whatever, that was her deal. At least I was honest. At least I was willing to talk to her. Even if talking meant fighting.

Fighting was better than nothing.

The cold-shoulder bullshit had gone on all fucking day when I finally snapped.

It happened in the hotel elevator.

I'd just come back from a band dinner and got into the elevator with Shady; Dirty had a show tonight and I had to grab some things. Maggie got in on the next floor. She didn't come to dinner, said she had work to do; at least that's what Talia told me.

When the elevator door opened and she was standing outside the hotel spa in a robe and slippers, she saw me and her face totally fell. She stepped into the elevator and made fake-cheerful small talk with Shady—since she had to mind her professional appearance and all that shit—while my jaw ticked and I stood stone-silent between them.

When the door opened on our floor, Maggie was the first one off the elevator. I followed. I muttered something to Shady about waiting for me and caught up to her. Then I grabbed her by the arm and pulled her the rest of the way down the hall—to my room.

As soon as we were inside, I lit into her.

"The fuck are you gonna do? Just ignore me for the rest of the fucking tour?"

"No," she said. "I'm not ignoring you—"

"Save it. You want a divorce? I'll give you a divorce, if that's what you really want."

Yeah. I was annoyed enough, frustrated enough to say that to her.

Even if I didn't mean it.

Maggie looked stunned.

"Unless that's not what you really want," I pressed.

She blinked at me, her mouth open, but she didn't speak.

I got close, cupping her head in my hands. "Is that what you want, Maggie?" I softened my voice and got right in her face. "You want a divorce?"

She shook her head long before the words finally found their way out of her mouth. "No." Her voice was small and fragile. "I don't want a divorce."

Fuck, but I was relieved to hear those words. It wasn't like she was agreeing to be my wife. But at least I knew she didn't really want to let this go. She didn't really want an end to our marriage, as fucked-up as it was.

She didn't really want to lose *me*.

And Christ, it turned me on.

"I want in you," I told her. "Now."

Her gray eyes widened. "Now?"

"Right now."

Her jaw kinda dropped, but she didn't say another word. When she didn't protest, I fumbled around, opening my jeans and reaching up inside her robe to yank her panties down. I *needed* inside her, because when I was inside her it was the only time she got real with me, ever. It was the only time she let me actually get close. Let me see and hear and taste and feel how she wanted me...

I got her panties down around her ankles, hiked one leg up over my hip, and sank into her.

And *fuck*.

Maggie's heat. So silky soft. Wet. Slippery and tight.

Fucking *bare*.

So intense...

"Zane... we can't do this," she protested, even as she clung to me and moved her hips to meet my thrusts. "You have to put on a condom."

"I know." I sucked on her neck as she clutched at my back, pulling me close. "I know, babe. I'm gonna pull out. Just... for a minute..."

"Oh, God..."

"Mmmm..."

Jesus Christ... so fucking good. We were both melting, fucking struggling to keep standing as we came together, right up against the door.

"I'm not on the pill," she said. "You have to get a condom."

I met her eyes, but I didn't stop fucking her. My hips and my dick were on autopilot. She'd told me that before, that she wasn't on the pill. But right now, my brain couldn't process it.

Then someone knocked on the door.

Maggie froze.

"Shit..." I breathed.

She shoved me away, wiggling her way off my dick, and scrambled to cover herself with the robe.

I put my dick away, awkwardly, and that shit hurt. My jeans were still open; no fucking way was I trying to zip them up right now.

I could practically feel Maggie cringe behind me as I yanked open the door.

It was Shady.

"Uh, sorry," he said, his gaze flicking from me to her. He looked genuinely fucking shocked that he'd just interrupted me feeding Maggie my dick. "Sorry. Uh… you didn't answer your phone, and it's time to go…"

"Thank you, Shady," Maggie said in her all-business tone. "He'll be right out."

I shut the door. I knew I had a show to do. I had to get going, but Maggie wasn't exactly dressed and ready to go, and fuck if I wanted to leave her like this.

"How could you?" she hissed, smacking me on the shoulder.

"How could I what?"

"Open the fucking door, Zane! It could've been anyone. You didn't even look through the peephole. Or give me a chance to hide. Or do up your fucking pants." She growled in a way that normally would've turned me on, but right now, just pissed me off. "And you didn't even put on a condom!"

I swiped my hand through my hair, fucking aggravated. My dick was aching, my balls were throbbing, and she was pissed at me again? "Hide? What are we, fucking teenagers? Why the fuck do we have to hide?"

"Zane, don't start this shit."

"Why?" I repeated. "Why do we have to hide from everyone that we're fucking? Everyone else can fuck, but we can't?"

I was ready for her to yell at me, but instead her shoulders dropped. "I just… I can't bear the risk, okay?" Her voice was small as her gray eyes gazed up at me, all watery and soft. "I've told you this before. I can't bear them finding out."

Fuck me. Her pretty face looked all scared and sad, and it broke me. "Shady's not gonna tell anyone, babe."

"How do you know?"

"Because Shady doesn't give a shit that we're banging."

"But someone else could see me leaving your room," she said. "One of these times, someone will see us. Brody could see us. What if—shit! Were we loud? We were right up against the door. What if someone heard us?"

"No one heard us." But I didn't know if that was true.

And Maggie looked so fucking horrified at the thought. Kinda like the way she looked when she found out the wedding we'd had was real—and not just some elaborate hoax for her dad's benefit.

Best and worst morning of my life.

"That's not gonna happen," I told her. "With Brody. He's not gonna find out. And if he did—"

"Zane—"

"*If* he ever did, I'd put him straight. You can count on me for that, Maggs. No matter what you think, I'm telling you, there's no way I'd ever let him hold this shit against you or let it fuck with your job. Ever. You get that?"

She didn't say anything. Because she didn't get it.

She didn't believe me.

And I knew she had her reasons for not trusting me.

Good reasons.

I knew she was afraid of risking her job over this—risking pretty much everything that mattered to her. Which meant she'd cut me way more slack than I'd ever deserved.

I got that.

I knew I'd disappointed her, hurt her, and in her mind, betrayed her.

But fuck no. Whatever she thought of me in her darkest Zane-hating moments, I'd never fuck with her job. I'd never fucking do that to her. And I'd never let Dirty lose her.

How to convince her of that, though?

The woman was stubborn as shit.

"If Brody or anyone else has a problem with you fucking me," I told her, "I'll deal with them."

"Who cares about the fucking!" she half-yelled. "It's not about the sex, Zane." She took a breath and lowered her voice. "Don't you get that? No one gives a shit who you fuck, because *you are always fucking someone*. If it's me, they might be a little pissed or concerned, for about a minute. But it's not about fucking. It's about *us*. This fucked-up shit between us."

"I know that, Maggs."

"No," she said. "You don't. You just think it's all some stupid game—"

"It's not a game."

"Everything to you is a game. *Life* is a game. You get arrested, you break someone's heart, you end up in the hospital getting stitches, it's all the same to you. The next day you're onto the next thing. You're completely fucking ignorant about the trail of crap you leave in your wake, everywhere you go, because me and Brody and Jude are always cleaning it up for you. You don't have the first fucking clue how this will affect anyone else, because the truth is, you don't actually *care* how it affects anyone else. But it *matters*, Zane."

"I know it matters, Maggie—"

"Do you? Do you know how much it matters? Because I've been managing Dirty for years, and I'm telling you, *this* is gonna totally fuck with the tour and the band. Like some cancer. Like that ugly thing you can't see and can't quite make sense of but it's always there, festering at the corners of your mind, out of your control, until you totally fucking resent it and you just want it *gone*. Want things back the way they were before. But it's not about the sex. It's the secret that's the problem."

"So? If the secret is the problem, then let's just fucking *tell* them."

Maggie sighed, pinching the bridge of her nose.

"Whenever you want," I said, moving closer to her. "However you want."

"Telling them won't make it any better. When are you gonna see that? Whether they know about it or not, this thing between us is *fucked*."

"No, Maggs. It won't be a secret anymore, and we can work out our shit in the open."

"Are you listening to me? There's nothing to work out, Zane."

"That's *bullshit*, Maggie, and you know it. And don't fucking tell me all you want from me is my dick, because if that's all this was about you could've had it years ago. You could've had it every single day since we got married. But you haven't. It's been almost two years since our wedding night and you've let me have you like a dozen times. So you're right. This is about way more than fucking. Let's just call it what it is."

I held her gaze. She said nothing.

I leaned in close, so she couldn't ignore it.

"Maggie, I love y—"

"*NO*. We're not doing that."

I took a deep breath, in through my nose, out again. "Why not?"

"Because we do that, I lose my job, Zane."

"I told you. I'll talk to Brody. He's a brother. We've been friends since I was fourteen. You think he cares more about the business than the band, than me, you're dead wrong."

"That's not how it works, Zane. You think we tell everyone and the next day we just... What? Start dating? Your groupies bounce in and out of your bed, and on the side you buy me flowers and court me, take me to dinner, ask me about my favorite color and my girlhood dreams?" Her gray eyes held mine, cool and unflinching. "Or maybe it's the groupies who're on the side."

I didn't even respond to that. I tried to keep my cool, when I really wanted to slap her upside the head for the first time in my life.

"It's pink," I said calmly. "You pretend your favorite color is lime green, like that suede jacket you always wear, but it's pink."

She frowned at me.

"And your girlhood dream? You wanted to be a genie. Like the girl from that old TV show. Because you wanted to live inside the magic bottle with the wraparound couch, and you had a thing for the astronaut guy."

She frowned deeper and crossed her arms over her chest. "So? He looked hot in his uniform."

"So you said."

"I didn't know you were listening."

I took her by the waist and pulled her to me, but she wouldn't let me get close; her hands went to my chest and held me off.

"You wanna date, we can date," I told her. "You want flowers, I'll get you flowers. Whatever the fuck you want."

"Until what? I catch you in the middle of your latest fuck-bunny orgy?"

"That doesn't have to be the way it is."

She shoved me away, and I let my hands drop.

"You forget who you're talking to," she said flatly. "I've seen it all before."

"Seen what before?"

She shook her head. "It's an old, old story," she said, "and it's fucking boring, and I know how it ends."

Old story?

It hit me then, what she meant.

She wasn't even talking about us.

"I'm not Dizzy," I told her. "I'm not your fucking dad."

"Maybe not."

Jesus. The girl was fucking stubborn. "So why don't you tell me, then. How does it end? Because I'd really like to know, since you're able to see into the fucking future."

"It ends," she said, "when we get a divorce. And after that, if I haven't already, I lose my job. I get dumped, phased out. Whether it's fast or slow, however you want to look at it, you're the rock star, and I'm gone."

Fuck. I could see why she'd think that. I really could.

But that was never gonna fucking happen.

"It won't be like that, Maggie."

"It will."

I clawed my hand through my hair. We were standing a few feet apart. Other than fucking her a few minutes ago, it was the closest I'd been to her in days and it was still way too fucking far. I just wanted to hold her. Grab her and throw her down and squeeze all the fucking bullshit right out of her. Shake it out. Kiss it out and suck it out and fuck it out.

But that had never worked before.

"So that's it? We're doomed to failure? That's all you wanna see?"

"I want you not to tell anyone. So that means you won't tell anyone."

We stared at each other for a long minute.

Then I turned away. I looked at the door, and I thought about just walking straight out. For the first time in my life I actually had the urge to walk out on Maggie.

But I turned back to her.

"And then what? I get you six times a year, when I manage to get you alone?"

"No, Zane." Her gray eyes held mine, tight and cool; I could practically see the wall going up between us. "Even if we fuck six times a year, you don't get me at all."

I just stared at her. Couldn't really believe she'd fucking said that.

But she did.

I did up my jeans. Slowly, so she had time to stop me if she wanted to.

She didn't. Unfortunately for me and my aching dick, didn't seem like there was any chance in hell we were gonna finish that fuck.

So I grabbed my leather jacket and some weed, and I went for the door. "For the record," I said as I opened it, "I am not always fucking someone." Then I paused, half-in and half-out, and looked at her again, totally fucking pissed that it always had to end like this. That one of us was always walking out.

Actually, *she* was always walking out. That was the bullshit pattern.

We fucked. We fought. Maggie got pissed. Maggie walked out.

This time, it was finally my turn. Because I'd never been so pissed off at her in my life.

"And if all I get is six times a year," I told her as I left, "maybe I'd rather have nothing at all."

CHAPTER NINE

Maggie

IT WAS the night of our very last show in L.A.. Though it was a Wet Blanket show, every member of Dirty except Elle had joined the band onstage for at least one song. The whole night was incredible, probably the best Wet Blanket show I'd ever been to.

Not just because of the sheer number of rock stars who took the stage, but because Zane was in such incredible form.

It was arguably his best performance of the tour so far.

The show was at Dylan's nightclub, and though the band had long ago come offstage, the bar had closed and most everyone had been cleared out, the bands were still hanging out, drinking. We were all crowded into the VIP lounge upstairs; Dirty, Steel Trap, and the members of Wet Blanket, along with wives and girlfriends and other friends.

Even Paulie was here; one of Wet Blanket's long-standing guitarists, Paulie had nearly joined Dirty before Seth came back, but had to drop out when his wife was diagnosed with cancer. She was now in a long remission, Paulie had come out for the show, and everyone was in great spirits.

Except me.

Tomorrow, Dirty had a sort-of day off with some light promo, just some phone interviews. The day after that, we headed down to

San Diego for one show there. Then we were done in California. We'd say goodbye to Brody, Ash, Roni and the Wet Blanket guys, as well as my good friend Jessa Mayes, who'd flown down for the L.A. shows to hang with us and see her man, Brody.

Then Dirty and Steel Trap would continue the *Hell & Back* tour, heading onward to Arizona and Nevada.

And I had this weird feeling things were going to change for the worse once we left the west coast. Maybe it was getting farther and farther from home. Or saying goodbye to Brody and Jessa, even though Brody would be back soon.

But I felt a deep unease and sadness about it all.

Like I was about to go into free fall or something.

It was getting late, like almost four in the morning, and things were starting to mellow out. Elle and Seth and Jessa and Brody had already headed back to the hotel a while ago. But Zane was still here, so I was, too.

The Black Keys' "Psychotic Girl" was playing and all the remaining couples were snuggled up together, pawing at each other, the rest of us kinda rolling our eyes in semi-jealousy as we drank.

The usual.

Katie was sitting in Jesse's lap and Amber was sitting in Dylan's, the four of them all cozied up in a booth together. A bunch of our security guys were hanging around, most still on-duty and not drinking. But Jude was up by the bar with Roni, his arms wrapped around her as she played with his hair, a drink in his hand. They were talking, kissing, and pretty much oblivious to anything else going on around them.

It was nice to see Jude be able to relax a little on tour, let down his guard. Have his guys take care of things for a while, while he just enjoyed being with Roni.

It was amazing, really, to see them so in love.

All of them.

My people. My family.

I liked seeing my friends happy, obviously. I especially liked it when the members of Dirty were happy. Made all our lives a hell of a lot more enjoyable, especially on the road.

Plus, it made the fangirls less welcome.

We all loved the fans. We needed and appreciated them. But if I never had to see any of the guys in the band making out with a groupie again, it wouldn't exactly be a hardship.

For his part, our temporary bassist, Matt, had definitely been enjoying his share of groupies on this tour, as had a few of the Steel Trap guys. Though tonight, Matt didn't seem to be looking to hook up.

He was sitting with me.

I wasn't even sure how we'd ended up sitting together, but maybe since we were both pretty much alone, it just happened. We didn't know each other well yet, and he was asking me all kinds of get-to-know-you questions like he was genuinely interested.

I was thinking how nice he was for a hot rock star who could've been a total dick. He wasn't a dick. Matty seemed to be about as sexually-charged as they came; no surprise there. You took a guy with great genes and musical talent, gave him an electric bass and put him onstage, the women were gonna be lining up to fall at his feet.

That was the reality of the world I'd always lived in.

But he definitely wasn't a dick about it.

Actually, I was thinking I could probably like a guy like Matty Brohmer, like... *like* him—you know, if I wasn't already in over my fucking head with Zane Traynor.

I was watching him across the room as I chatted with Matt. He was sitting in a booth with Shady, Alec, and a couple of the Wet Blanket guys. His hair was styled up in a cool, mussy fauxhawk, the way he wore it onstage. He wore ripped jeans and an old Judas Priest *Love Bites* T-shirt with the sleeves and sides cut out, and his elbows were up on the table; I could see his bare waist and the curve of his pectoral muscle. I could see his nipple piercing when he leaned forward.

And Christ... I wanted to lick him all over. Nibble every inch of his amazing body and hear those sounds he made when he was lost in lust.

He wasn't looking back at me. I knew he was still mad at me.

He had every right to be.

But it was *killing* me.

He hadn't spoken to me all night. He hadn't spoken to me in two days, actually. Two. Days. He wouldn't even look my way anymore.

And it was so much harder than when I froze him out. Which was already fucking hard enough.

Was *this* what it felt like for him when I avoided him?

Shit.

I was a terrible, terrible person.

I kind of tuned in and out of the conversation with Matt, managing to keep up my end of it, mostly, while keeping an eye on Zane. I was pretty practiced at this after so many years of wanting him from afar.

But I was distracted as hell.

Did he really mean what he'd said? That he'd rather have nothing, no part of me at all, if he could only have so little?

Did he really want me out of his life?

"Maggie?"

I startled, and refocused my attention on Matt. *Jesus.* How long had I been staring at Zane?

"Yes. Sorry, what was that last part?"

A smile spread slowly across Matt's handsome face. He ruffled his hand through his hair, his forehead crinkling as he raised his eyebrows at me. He had thick brown hair that stuck out in all directions and a crooked smile, and he was definitely too cute to be ignored. "You don't have to sit here," he said, "if there's someone else you'd rather be talking to. I don't want to bore you."

"No. You're totally not—"

"I mean, I'll be wounded. But I won't hold it against you." His keen, kinda soulful hazel eyes danced a little in the candlelight. He was maybe half-serious.

He was maybe flirting, a little.

He was definitely being nice, and I was being a distracted weirdo.

"It's not that. You're far from boring, Matt." True story. The guy had rocked the stage with Wet Blanket tonight, could have any girl sitting here with him, and yet he was sitting with me. The least I could do was put in the effort to carry a decent conversation. "I just have a lot on my mind."

"No doubt. You work too damn hard. Anyone ever tell you that?"

"Kinda."

More like daily.

"Have another one." He slid a fresh beer my way; there were several of them lined up on the table, left behind by Dylan, who'd ordered too many then wandered away. "You've earned it."

"Thank you." I really didn't need another beer, and yet I wanted it tonight.

"I hope they let you know what you're worth to them," he said. "I've been through several managers, Maggie, and what Dirty has with you... it's special. You should know that."

"Thank you. It's really Brody who runs the show, though. I just help him out with whatever needs doing."

Matt laughed. "Sure. Brody's great. He's definitely one of the best managers I've ever had the chance to work with. Believe me, if there was any chance in hell I could join Dirty permanently, I'd be all over it. Not just because of the band and the music, but because of Brody and your team. I'd love to be on board, but I know that's never gonna happen."

"Yeah. Sorry, Matt. It's always so hard for us, too, having guys step in when it's not permanent. Because we know we'll have to let you go at some point."

He just shrugged good-naturedly. "You guys have Elle, so I know there's no room for me. I've got no illusions about that. And like I said, I'd love to keep working with Brody. But it's not just him. If no one's ever told you before, I'll be happy to be the one to tell you, Maggie. What you do for Dirty, day in and day out, the kind of love you have for them, that kind of selfless devotion… the way you put their needs ahead of everything else and genuinely care about *them*, not just making money through them… that's rare and it's fucking invaluable. If you need me to tell Brody you need a raise, just let me know."

I smiled. "Thank you, Matt. They treat me well, and they do tell me that kind of thing. But it's always nice to hear."

Matt raised his beer in toast. "Well, here's to a killer band with a killer management team I'm totally honored to be a part of for a while."

"Cheers. And believe me, we're honored to have you." I sipped my beer. "You know, the guys are very picky about who they'll bring onstage, especially Jesse and Zane. And I know they're all thrilled to have you up there with them. Elle couldn't have dreamed of a better bassist to fill her stylish boots."

He chuckled. "Pretty sure she looked better doing it, but I'll try to make her proud." His gaze scanned my face as we drank our beer. "So. You're in love with him, huh?"

I stared at him, freezing in place as the blood in my veins slowly turned to ice. "I'm not… No." I frowned. "What do you mean?"

Matt grinned. "See. If you weren't, you would've responded to that totally differently. You would've asked *Who?* But you didn't do that. Which means you had someone in mind when I said that."

"Uh, no. I'm just—"

"Who is it?" He leaned in conspiratorially, and I realized he really didn't know who. "You can tell me. I'm not a gossip."

I sipped my beer, straightening my shoulders and sitting up perfectly straight. "I don't even know what you're talking about."

"Right."

I gave him a cool eyeballing. "And for the new guy on the block, you're damn nosy, I'll tell you that."

He raised his hands in surrender. "Hey, I'm just perceptive is all."

"Hmm."

"I mean, when I first came onboard, obviously I noticed you're smoking hot. Noticed you were single. Can't blame a guy for that."

"Is that so?"

"Yep. Gorgeous eyes. Tight little bod..." For the first time since we sat down together—that I'd noticed—his gaze wandered south of my face. Then his eyes met mine again and I raised an eyebrow. I wasn't even sure if he was coming on to me, or working his way toward some sort of point. "No ring on that ring finger..."

"Uh-huh."

"But then I realized, you're not available."

"Meaning what?"

"Meaning, you're not available."

"Except that I am available. Because, as you said, I'm single."

"No, you're not."

"Yes. I am."

"You're totally available?" he challenged.

"Yup."

"Meaning you could hook up tonight with some random dude in this bar."

"Yup."

"Some stranger."

"Yes."

"Like some charming bass player you hardly know..."

"If I wanted to."

"You could just lean in..." He put his elbow on the table between us and leaned in, until he was inches from my face. "And kiss me." His gaze dropped to my lips. "Right now."

"If I wanted to," I repeated.

His eyes met mine. "Here's your chance."

"Lucky me." I made absolutely no move to kiss him, sipping my beer instead.

He grinned. Then he sat back in his seat and drank his beer. He waggled his finger at me. "I'll figure you out, Maggie Omura. I'll find out who it is."

"Just when I thought you were a nice guy, Matt," I said dryly.

He laughed again.

I sipped my beer, and when I glanced in the direction of Zane's booth again, Alec was just walking away. The Wet Blanket guys had disappeared.

Zane and Shady were alone in the booth.

"Excuse me," I said, setting my beer bottle on the table and slipping out of my seat. "I need to go take care of something."

"Mmm." Matt sipped his beer and followed the direction of my gaze. "Wouldn't wanna leave Zane waiting." His eyes locked with mine.

And for just a heartbeat, I gave him the iciest *don't-you-dare-fuck-with-me* look that I could muster.

He winked at me.

I turned and walked away.

Rock stars.

Just when you'd met one you thought might be somewhat of a gentleman, he went and busted your lady balls. While you were drunk and defenseless.

I was, in fact, a wee bit drunker than I'd thought, which I only discovered as I walked across the room and found myself a little less-than-stable on my feet. The heels weren't helping. I was usually pretty damn comfortable in four-inch heels, but the beers I'd just pounded back were making me feel like I had the ankles of Bambi—all four of them.

I managed to weave my way to Zane's table and grab hold of it, steadying myself.

"Hi," I breathed.

"Hey, Maggie," Shady said.

Zane said nothing, just sipped his sparkling water. He didn't even look at me.

It hurt, but it also reinforced what I'd been telling myself all night. My conviction that I needed to be brave here and let down my wall.

Just a wee bit more.

"Mind if I join you guys?"

"Course not." Shady got out of the booth so I could slide in between them.

When we were settled, I chatted with Shady a bit. Just small talk about the tour.

Zane didn't say anything. But he didn't leave.

After a few minutes, Shady seemed to pick up on the tension—or the fact that Zane had said exactly zero words since I sat down—and made an excuse to slip away.

As soon as Zane and I were alone, I told him, "I'm sorry."

Finally, he looked at me. His arctic-blue eyes met mine—and I felt it, way down deep.

Fuck, I'd missed that look.

I'd missed him.

The way he looked at me now, like he loved me... even when he was pissed at me.

I cleared my throat. "This may be hard to believe," I told him, "but I really don't want to fight. I hate fighting with you. And I really can't stand it when you're mad at me."

"Really?" he said. "I don't care if you're mad at me."

My heart squeezed painfully at those words.

"I mean..." His gaze drifted over my face. "You're hot as fuck when you're mad."

Oh.

Relief swept through me. It was a compliment, in a weird Zane way, which meant maybe he wasn't all that pissed anymore.

"I'm not mad," I said.

He said nothing.

"The show was really great tonight," I told him. "You were great. I mean... the last couple of shows, here in L.A., were the best of the tour so far. In my opinion."

"I agree."

"But tonight, with Wet Blanket, you, uh, loosened up a bit. You seemed like you'd really warmed up. The first few shows you seemed kind of tense. I mean, not a lot. Not like the fans would notice or anything. But I did." I squirmed a bit as he just kept staring at me. "You were better tonight. Your voice sounded amazing. It sounded like it should sound. I've... uh... never heard you sing 'Maggie May' quite like that."

He just stared at me.

"So... um... are you okay?" I asked him.

"Okay, how?"

"Like... if there's something bothering you, affecting your performance, we should probably talk about it. Especially if it has anything to do with me. I don't want to make things hard for you, Zane. I don't want this tour to be shit for you because of me."

"It's not shit, Maggie."

"Okay. But... I think you need to tell me if whatever's going on between us is affecting you."

"Affecting me," he repeated, staring at me. "Yeah, it's affecting me."

Well, shit.

Not what I wanted to hear.

My heart had started thudding in my chest, and I knew I just had to get the words out, as difficult as it would be. It was my job to do whatever was in his best interest. And Matt was right; not all managers saw that as their job, but I did.

"If you think you should just stay away from me," I told him, "I can make it so that you don't have to see me any more than absolutely necessary."

"The fuck are you talking about?"

"I'm talking about the tour. I don't have to be in your face all the time. I can stay out of your way so you don't have to see me. If it came down to it... I probably don't have to be here at all. I could work it out with Brody. I'm here because he wants me to be here and Dirty wants me to be here. But I don't have to be. Talia could stay, and I could do my work remotely. I could go back to Vancouver. We could maybe even hire someone else to work with Talia on the road, if it was needed—"

"That's not happening."

"But if it was needed."

"Why the hell would it be needed?"

"I don't know. Tonight's show..."

"Not happening."

"You just seemed like you performed better when you weren't talking to me. When I wasn't on your mind."

Now he did look kinda mad. His jaw ticked and his eyes went dark. "You think for one second you're not on my mind?"

"You seemed to perform better," I repeated.

"It's not happening, Maggie. You're not leaving the tour. Don't say another fucking word about it."

Then he got up and walked away from the booth, leaving me here.

Yeah... so he was still mad.

Definitely.

Which was maybe why he'd performed so well tonight? Nothing like a little rage to fuel a guy onstage.

Or maybe it was just that he didn't have the pressure of it being a Dirty show. Wet Blanket shows were just for fun, the proceeds to charity, the crowd filled with friends and family and generally the pressure was off.

Or maybe it was because I wasn't involved in it at all. Because I wasn't backstage, but out in the club's VIP section?

This one's for a girl I know.

That's what he'd said onstage tonight, without even looking in my direction, right before Wet Blanket ripped into a rocking, punked-up cover of Rod Stewart's "Maggie May." A couple of people had poked me, knowing the song was for me. No biggie. I'd just tried to smile and probably looked embarrassed, which wasn't an act at all.

Zane often dedicated songs at Wet Blanket shows to whomever, and usually with tongue-in-cheek; tonight alone they'd played a song in lament of Elle's hiatus from Dirty ("Since I Don't Have You"), and a song for Jessa, since she was visiting ("Brown Eyed Girl"). And they'd closed the show with a ridiculously awesome AC/DC cover dedicated to Ash and featuring a full stage, with Ash on lead vocals and Zane, Seth, Matty and a couple of the Steel Trap guys singing backup ("Big Balls").

But Zane had never dedicated a song to me onstage. It wasn't like I felt left out or anything; in a weird way, without him saying so, I always just knew that some of the songs he was singing were meant for me.

But this one... this one was something else.

May was my actual middle name, yet only two people in my life had ever called me Maggie May.

My mom and Zane.

Sometime the first year we'd met, Zane had sung "Maggie May" for me by a campfire, just jamming with Jesse on acoustic guitar. He'd done it again a few times over the years, at some Dirty party or casual jam circle; the whole band liked playing it for me, for fun.

But he'd never played "Maggie May" for me onstage.

I glanced across the room, looking for him now. He was standing by the bar, talking to Jude; not looking at me.

The Black Keys were still playing. "Too Afraid to Love You."

I sighed, and my eyes met Matt's. He was sitting at a table with Dylan and Amber, and he was watching me.

I rolled my eyes.

He grinned.

I got up and went over to Jesse and Katie. They were alone in a booth, she was still sitting in his lap, and they were making out.

Too bad.

I knocked on the table and cleared my throat to get their attention, and dropped into the seat across from them.

"So. What are we drinking?"

When a bunch of us eventually found our way back to the hotel, just before the sun came up, it was Zane who walked me to my room.

I wasn't even sure when, exactly, he'd glued himself to my side.

But he was there with me in the elevator and guiding me along the hall, his hand just barely touching my elbow.

Shady was in the elevator too, and he was probably right behind us. But I didn't turn to look.

After some fumbling around, I managed to find my room key card in my purse. I thanked Zane politely for walking me to my door.

But once I had the door open, I caught his hand before he could even think about leaving.

"Please don't go."

I knew this was wrong. I knew I shouldn't be asking him to stay, pulling him into my hotel room with me.

He'd told me the night we were married that he didn't mess around with drunk girls, and though he'd obviously made an exception for me, I knew he had his reasons. Good reasons.

And I was definitely kinda drunk right now.

Plus, I'd pushed him away over and over and over again.

But I still wanted him...

I couldn't help that part. There was nothing I could do to stop it, and when my defenses were all muddled with liquor, and he was right here... it was impossible not to reach for him.

As he stepped into the room with me, even though he held back, watching me with wary eyes, I knew he wanted me, too.

I also knew, this time, he wasn't gonna make the first move.

And not just because I was kinda drunk. Even with all the alcohol in my body, though, I didn't have the courage to make the first move either.

I'd hurt him. I'd really hurt him this time, and I couldn't stand it. I didn't want him to be mad at me; it hurt way too much. But worse, knowing I'd hurt him was pretty much agony. Pain and suffering and guilt of the worst kind, all rolled into one.

And I was afraid of pissing him off, of making him walk out like he did the other night.

So I did the only thing I figured he wouldn't be able to walk out on. I walked deeper into the room and switched on a lamp, then started taking off my dress.

"Don't talk," I said, even though he hadn't tried to say anything. "I'm drunk, and I don't want to talk."

When I turned back to him, he was staring at me.

I definitely had his attention.

I'd dropped the dress and I was standing in my bra and panties and my high-heeled shoes. I stepped out of the dress as Zane walked toward me.

"Don't take off the shoes," he said, his voice rough, quiet. He stood in front of me and looked straight in my eyes.

"Don't talk," I repeated.

So he didn't.

He felt around in the pockets of his leather jacket and his jeans until he pulled out a condom. His eyes were still on mine, and I swallowed.

He slipped off the jacket and dropped it on the floor. He put the condom packet in his teeth, and with his half-lidded eyes locked on mine, he undid his jeans. He peeled his T-shirt over his head. One-by-one I watched him remove every piece of clothing on his body and toss it aside until he stood in front of me, naked and gorgeous in the lamplight.

When I glanced down, a shiver tore through my body. His cock was hard, erect. He took the condom packet from between his teeth, tore it open, and rolled the condom on.

Then he put his hands on my hips and spun me around to face the bed.

He kept a hold of one hip and pushed on my back to bend me over, then slid my panties down around my knees. I braced myself with my hands on the bed. He nudged my legs open a little wider with his knee.

Then he pushed his cock into me and warmth rocked through me.

This. We'd always been best at this...

Communicating without any words at all.

He groaned as I gasped with relief.

He filled me in one thrust, as my body stretched to accommodate him. But I didn't quite take all of him.

He pulled back, then filled me again, deeper.

One hand on my hip, one hand on the small of my back, he filled me slowly, again and again, working his way deeper each time... until I'd taken every inch of him and he was pressed up tight against me.

Then he gripped my hips with both hands and started giving it to me *hard*.

He grunted as he hammered into me, deep and unforgiving. I wanted it hard. I wanted him to punish me. I wanted him to make me feel bad and *oh*-so-good.

I wanted him to forgive me.

I wanted him to tell me, without any words, that he would always, always want me.

In the throes of arousal, it didn't feel so wrong to be selfish.

I'd take whatever Zane would give me.

And he gave it to me *good*.

Then he stopped, suddenly, and pulled out.

I cried out.

He turned me around and laid me out on the bed, on my back, yanking my panties down my legs and off over my shoes. He moved on top of me, wrapping my legs high around his waist as he filled me again. This time, facing me as he fucked me.

As he fucked me *slow*.

With his eyes on mine.

His blond hair fell over me, his breath warmed my face and his lips hovered an inch from mine.

I was in his face, and he *wanted* me in his face.

Zane always wanted me in his face when he fucked me.

And with his face so close to mine, it hit me all at once: how afraid I'd been, when he wasn't talking to me, that he wanted me out of his life.

I didn't even think about my job.

Not once.

The fear that I might get fired because he didn't want me around hadn't even crossed my mind.

I was only worried that Zane didn't want to see me again. When I'd thought he might really be mad enough to turn his back on me, that was all I cared about.

I was afraid of losing him.

Not my job.

Him.

"Maggie..." he whispered, and I kissed him. I didn't always kiss him while we fucked, but I kissed him now. "*Fuck*, you taste like booze..."

"Then don't taste me," I panted.

"You smell like booze."

"Then don't smell me."

But I kissed him again, and he didn't pull away. He kissed me back as I devoured him with desperate, hungry little moans, sucking at his mouth.

For once, my wall had come crashing completely down.

Zane had smashed it down, and I'd let him.

Or maybe the alcohol had.

Either way, I was totally in this with him right now. I was feeling it. I was feeling *him*.

I was feeling everything...

And it was absolutely fucking terrifying.

I was drowning in the bliss of him, in the feeling of being his, of *wanting* to be his. I was suffocating in it as our tongues ravaged each other's mouths and we fused ourselves together.

And all I wanted was for this moment to last. To be here with him. No walls.

To do this, with him, forever.

No fighting. Just *this*.

He reached down between my legs and started rubbing my clit as he fucked me. He groaned as we kissed.

And I came with a scream.

The pleasure ripped through my body like lightning, white-hot, as he pounded into me. I made all kinds of whimpering, desperate, pleading sounds I didn't even know I could make with a man.

"*Yeah*... Fuck, you're so beautiful."

"Ah, *Zane*..." I moaned and gasped and fucked him as hard as I could, until he rammed into me, harder, and pinned me down to the bed. His hips slammed into me a couple of times, and I felt the spasms of his cock deep inside me as he came.

"Fuck, *Maggie*..." He groaned my name. "*Christ*... I love you..."

I rocked my hips, and when Zane responded by slamming into me again, I started to come again. I moaned, rubbing my body against his, every-fucking-where.

I wanted to push him off. I wanted to shove him away when he said those words.

I love you...

But instead, I clung to him.

He kissed me, kissed my face all over with a million soft kisses as the pleasure shook me—body and, yes, soul.

When we'd taken everything we could get from each other, when we'd finally gone still, he smoothed my hair back from my face and stared at me.

"Admit it," he said, kissing me softly on the lips. His weight pressed me to the bed. He was still inside me. Still insisting, with his body, that I was his. "Why can't you just admit that you want this? That you love me..."

And in the moment, all the fight had escaped me—leaving me limp and vulnerable. A soft, broken thing, shattered by his touch.

"Of course I love you," I whispered, as his blue eyes held mine. "But I just can't."

He stared down at me. "Yeah," he said, softly, "you can."

"No. No, I can't. I can't love you, Zane."

"Of course you can."

"No. I *can't*."

He stared at me for a heartbeat. Then he let me go. He pulled out. "*Why*?" He pulled away. "Why the fuck not?"

"Because," I said, drawing the bedspread up over me. My voice was barely a whisper. "You're too much like him."

I knew I sounded like a scared, stupid little girl. But it was nothing but the truth.

The terrible truth.

My truth.

"Like *who*? Like fucking Dizzy?" He moved to sit on the side of the bed and took the condom off. "Is that really what this is all about?" He tossed the condom and scrubbed his hand over his face. "Your fucking daddy issues? *Really*, Maggie?"

Fuck me.

He just didn't get it.

No matter how many times we circled around it, he just didn't get it. I sat up, clutching the blanket around me.

"You know who I love, Zane? *My mom*. She was all I ever had growing up, and we were a joke to him. When he was pissed at us, Mom and me, we were a nuisance, a regret and an inconvenience. We were barely an afterthought. He used my mom and tossed her off when it got old and he never, ever looked back until she was dead."

"I know all that, Maggie," he said, gently.

He did know. Zane was one of the few friends I'd ever really talked to about my dad.

"Yeah? Well, nothing ever got serious for him until it was far too late, and I see you going down that exact same road, Zane. The partying and the easy pussy and your sweet Maggie May, your number one superfan who's always there for you. Until 'always' turns out to be a fucking drag. My mom didn't get her heart broken, because she wasn't in love with my dad. She got a baby at eighteen and a crash course in life as a single parent and a lot of regrets she never thought I knew about, but I knew. If I'm with you, I get all those things, except the baby part, which is the only good thing he ever really gave her anyway, *and* I lose the job that I get out of bed in the morning for, *and* I get a broken heart, because I do love you, Zane. I am in love with you. But I'm smart enough, living the life I live, to know not to give you my heart because a man like you doesn't have the first fucking clue what to do with it."

Zane stared at me.

I stared right back. "You think you love me because you threw down and married me in Vegas to screw with my dad?" I asked him. "You don't know what love is. I have worked my fucking ass off loving you and I know what it is to love someone."

He just stared at me, and for all the things I'd just said to him, he didn't look angry and he didn't look hurt.

"You love me," he said softly, like he was in awe of it or something.

Really?

Out of everything I just said, that was the one thing he really heard?

I got up and started getting dressed.

I just admitted to Zane that I love him.

And I felt raw about it. My heart fucking hurt. It was like the world's worst case of heartburn.

Having him stare at me like that was not helping. That terrible hope on his face. That softness in his blue eyes...

"Maggie..."

"Don't."

"You don't have to run away."

I kept getting dressed.

"You don't have to put up your fucking wall."

"I just have to... I need a minute. I just... Just leave me alone for a minute."

Then I ran out of the room.

But I was gone for much longer than a minute.

CHAPTER TEN

Zane

SHE LOVES ME.

She admitted it to me...

She fucking loves me.

After Maggie left, I lay in bed in her hotel room for a while. It wasn't like lying in bed thinking about her was a new experience for me, but this time I definitely had new food for thought.

She.

Loves.

Me.

When she didn't come back to her room, I called her.

She didn't answer.

I tried to sort through all the shit she just told me. But all I could really think about was the only thing that really sank in; the only thing that really mattered anyway.

She loves me.

Eventually, I dozed off. When I woke up mid-morning, Maggie still hadn't come back. I checked my phone. No missed call from her, no message.

I sent her a text, then got up and went to my own room. I lay in bed, wanting to sleep some more. We'd been up all night and I was still tired, but I couldn't relax.

So I smoked some weed, and I thought about what she said to me again.

She said she loves me.

I thought about all the shit that had gone down between us over the past two years... seeing it in a different light. Reconsidering everything that had gone wrong with the knowledge that Maggie loved me.

That maybe she'd loved me all along.

I thought about how, after we'd gotten married in Vegas, there was that long and difficult nine months of cold war, heated fights, and the occasional angry fuck. Until we screwed the night of Jesse's wedding, almost a year ago now, and something changed. Maggie seemed to soften toward me, a little.

After that night, I'd tried like hell to get her back into bed, to recapture that feeling between us. To make her give in to me again, the way she did that night.

The way she'd looked at me, for just a moment, when I was inside her.

The way she'd said my name.

The way she'd begged for my cock as she came...

And a few times, I'd succeeded.

But things stayed pretty rough between us anyway.

Over the phone, we argued when she wouldn't see me. In person, she'd been careful not to be alone with me, to keep conversation professional. Neutral.

Though sometimes, I'd still managed to get her alone.

And when I did... the result was predictable.

Me and Maggie, in bed.

Or on the floor... or whatever surface was available.

Naked and all over each other.

Then Maggie would flip her bitch switch and freeze me out again.

It was like she was two different people. A woman who wanted me so bad she couldn't resist me... sometimes. And a woman who wanted nothing to do with me, other than our working relationship.

Because anything more than a working relationship was a slippery-ass slope to sex town.

We both knew it.

I loved the fact. Maggie didn't.

And whenever our working relationship forced us together with other people around, like Brody or anyone in the band, she was all charm, overly-fucking-friendly.

Fake-friendly.

That was what really scared me. How fake-friendly she could be in front of everyone else, then totally ice me out.

I'd always thought I was trying to convince Maggie that we could work. That I was trying to charm her or seduce her or just plain persuade her into feeling something more for me than she did. Or, best case, that I was trying to uncover some deeper feelings she might have for me, that I hoped like hell she had, when I didn't really know if she did.

And I thought I was failing.

Epically, and over and over.

For a while, during a particularly long cold spell, I thought it was really over between us.

And I didn't take it so well.

I made some mistakes.

Not Dallas mistakes, but other mistakes.

And as usual, Maggie wasn't so quick to forgive or forget.

But then Dirty reunited with Seth, and things seemed to turn a corner—for everyone. We were all pretty damn happy, and Maggie seemed to cheer the fuck up a bit.

She was happy about the band being whole again, about the album, about the upcoming tour; we all were. Maybe she was just caught up in her work and distracted enough to forget how pissed at me she was.

For whatever reason, my charms seemed to be working on her

again. I knew we were really on an upswing when she started laughing at my jokes. She even came out on the town a few times with me and the boys, after I'd moved up to Vancouver. She wore sexy shit and semi-flirted with me. Or at least she didn't immediately shoot me down when I flirted with her.

Progress.

I'd been texting her, calling her, turning up the heat at every opportunity; Maggie didn't give me many.

But then one night... the night of Jessa's baby shower, I'd somehow managed to convince Maggie to come over and see me. At my place.

Alone.

You know, just to talk.

And we had talked. About the new album.

And about us.

About how she could never seem to trust me, which was fucked up (my words).

About how I didn't deserve her trust (her words).

Then, predictably, I got her undressed.

On my couch.

Underneath me.

I was just about to peel off her panties when my phone started ringing. When we realized the number calling was Jessa's, Maggie freaked out and made me answer it. She was up and getting dressed before I'd even gotten off the phone. By the time I told her Jessa's water had broke, she was out the door.

After that, she avoided me even harder.

She didn't seem as mad. Regretful, maybe. But she clearly didn't want to be alone with me. I let it slide for a while, because I figured she'd come around again, like she always did.

At least she wasn't being as cold to me anymore.

But then Christmas happened.

On the eve of Christmas Eve, I threw a party at my place, and Maggie helped me plan it. Neither of us invited Dallas... but Dallas showed up.

That night, Maggie saw Dallas all over me.

And read the situation totally wrong.

Fact was, women were always coming up to me and feeling me up. A lot of the female population just seemed to think they had a right to. Like my cock was public property or something. In the past, it wasn't like I minded.

These days, I avoided that shit as much as possible.

But chicks could be ruthless.

Wasn't exactly my fault Dallas walked up to me and grabbed my dick before I could stop her. Wasn't really Dallas' fault either; she didn't exactly know I was married. Thanks to Maggie and her *Don't you dare tell anyone* bullshit.

All Maggie saw, though, was Dallas' hand down the front of my pants.

Really, Maggie had seen it all. Most of the time she seemed to just let it roll off. She definitely saw more shit and put up with more shit than any woman should have to.

Half the reason I loved her, probably—she was strong as hell.

But even though she kept refusing to be my wife, when she saw Dallas grope me like that, I knew it cut her.

Even if I never wanted it to happen.

True, I'd fucked Dallas a few times. But that was before I married Maggie. Since we'd been married, I'd only fucked Dallas *once*, and that was in the early days, when Maggie was barely speaking to me and kept demanding a divorce.

I was only human, I was a fucking dude, and besides that, I had a heart and Maggie and her insistence that our marriage was a crock of shit did a number on it for a while.

I'd tried to explain all of that to her, again, after the Christmas party. But she wasn't having it.

Instead, she froze me the fuck out.

And the cold war started all over again.

She pretended like she didn't give a fuck about me or where I put my dick.

But all those times I'd gotten her alone, gotten her naked, and pounded her defenses right down to the ground...

She cared.

I'd seen it in her eyes. Felt it in her anger. Fucking tasted it all over her when she gave in to me.

She cared a fuck of a lot more than she ever admitted.

She fucking loved me.

She just wouldn't admit it to me.

Until now.

There were times when I'd seriously doubted Maggie had any real feelings for me beyond friendship and general annoyance.

Times when I wondered... if maybe she really did regret it. All of it.

Marrying me in Vegas.

Staying married to me.

Ever kissing me or touching me or letting me near her at all.

But now I knew.

She kept pushing me away *because* she loved me.

Which meant that I still had a chance... no matter if she tried to keep pushing me away.

Maggie had real feelings for me she didn't want to admit, but she'd admitted them to me last night. She thought she could avoid those feelings by avoiding me, but that wasn't true. The feelings were still there.

And I was still here.

If she thought she could ignore me and make it all go away, she was wrong. Dead wrong.

All I had to do was keep getting her alone. Keep breaking down her wall, brick by fucking brick, until there was nothing left between us but my feelings for her... and her feelings for me.

Fucking *love*.

I floated around on this dumbass cloud... for not even two days. Not even forty-eight hours, and Maggie Omura sucked the wind right the fuck out of my sails.

It was the night of the San Diego show, and I hadn't seen her since she told me she loved me and ran the fuck away.

I didn't even see her backstage at the show. Apparently, she was refusing to show her face to me, any-fucking-where.

As soon as I came offstage and she was still nowhere to be seen, I went straight outside. We were supposed to drive back to our L.A. hotel tonight, and I didn't even know if Maggie had come with us to San Diego. Her Lady Bus was parked two down from mine, but fuck if I knew if Maggie was on there or not.

I told Shady to stay outside and I disappeared onto my bus, alone. I was still drenched, sweaty, didn't even take a shower along the way. I just tore off my shirt, popped the button on my jeans and grabbed my weed.

I'd barely sat down when someone knocked on the door. It was a soft little knock, and every fibre of my fucking being snapped to attention because I knew it was Maggie.

Then the door opened and Talia poked her head in instead.

"Hey, Zane. Do you have a minute?"

I didn't answer her, but I also didn't tell her to fuck off, so she came right on in. She pulled a couple of papers off her little clipboard thing and laid them out on the table for me as I rolled up a joint. She was already talking, going over a bunch of shit I was supposed to care about, rattling off the dates we were filming concert footage for the "Blackout" video. Then something about album sales? Some interviews I had to do tomorrow on the road, some meet-and-greet in Phoenix.

I barely heard it all. Definitely couldn't make sense of any of it.

Couldn't think of anything but Maggie, disappearing on my ass.

I lit up the joint, took a drag, and finally cut her off. "What're you doing here?"

She looked at me, and I let my eyes wander down. She had a deep tan and her tits were hiked up, kinda bursting out of her tank top, which most guys would probably appreciate. She was a hot little thing, and her tits were bigger than Maggie's.

Fucking annoyed me.

"I'm going over your schedule for tomorrow," she said. "In Phoenix." Like I didn't know where the fuck we were tomorrow.

"I got that. What are *you* doing here?"

"Um..." She looked around the bus, confused. "What do you mean?"

"Who sent you?"

"Maggie. She told me to—"

"Yeah. Well, tell Maggie I'm gonna fire you if I see your face on my bus again."

Her brown eyes went wide, and she just stood there in shock.

When I didn't take it back or say another fucking word, she turned around and got the fuck off my bus.

When she was gone, I threw on some music while I smoked up. Didn't help my mood at all. First song to play on random was Alice in Chains, "Nutshell." Gorgeous, depressing shit.

But instead of getting depressed, I got angry. I felt agitated instead of more mellow.

Then I started pacing like a caged animal.

The last two days, anytime I'd messaged Maggie that I wanted to talk to her, she didn't message back. Ever.

When I texted her about work shit, she replied. Every time.

Or Talia did.

I was starting to actually doubt that things were any better between us now that she'd admitted she loved me. I was realizing, fucking slowly, that maybe they were actually worse.

I was starting to fear another long, fucking painful freeze-out.

And it was pissing me off.

By the time Maggie stormed onto my bus, I was livid. So was she, by the looks of things.

"You said *what* to Talia?"

At least I knew where she was now.

"I said," I growled right back at her, "I'll fire her ass next time I see her on my bus."

"You can't fire Talia."

"Like fuck I can't."

She stared at me, her eyes raking over my bare chest and snagging on my unbuttoned jeans. "Don't make this about her because you're in a bad mood."

"Bad mood?" I laughed. "I'm in a great mood. Why wouldn't I be? Two nights ago, my estranged wife told me she loves me. Good times, right?"

"*Estranged?* I think there has to be some sort of relationship in the first place for one to become 'estranged,' Zane."

"Yeah, maybe. You were always better with the semantics than I was. Had a legal wedding, but we're not married, right? Said your vows, but they weren't real, right? But you did say you love me. I mean, we both heard it. You gonna deny it now? Ignore me? Send Talia to do your work for you so you never have to see me again?"

"It's not my work. It's Talia's work. I've got my own work to do, and plenty of it, and it doesn't include holding your hand and spoon-feeding your damn schedule to you all the time. I'm not your personal bitch, Zane."

"And Talia is?"

"Better her than me," she snapped right back.

Jesus Christ, where did she get off being so mad at me?

And why did it have to get me so fucking hot?

I stared her down, my blood boiling and my dick standing at attention, rock-hard for her, as fucking always. "You want me to fuck her, is that it?"

"What?"

"She supposed to be bait or something? A test? Send her onto my bus alone enough times and see what happens?"

"That's fucking ridiculous."

"See if the same thing happens when I'm alone with her as what happens when I'm alone with you?"

No. Clearly that wasn't her plan.

I could tell by the look of offense, annoyance, and just plain disgust on her face. I could see it... as she started to wonder what exactly *had* happened.

"Did you fuck her?" she asked.

"Would it matter if I did?"

"Well, she's pretty much your employee and she's my assistant, so yes."

"How about the fact that I'm your husband? That rate with you at all?"

She crossed her arms over her chest and said nothing. She was wearing a dress, a short lingerie-looking black dress, under her suede jacket, and it was such fucking bullshit that I wasn't even allowed to touch her.

That if I tried and succeeded, she'd probably just get madder at me.

"Admit it," I said, moving in, "you don't want me to touch Talia. You don't want me to touch anyone else. You want me *with you*."

She didn't admit it. She didn't say a word. But her eyes drifted down my chest again and her nostrils flared.

"You hate it when I'm with other women, and not because it's some bullshit proof to you that I'll never be able to keep my dick in my pants. It's because you're jealous. Because you want me, and you don't want anyone else to have me."

She looked up at me and said, quietly, "No, Zane. I don't let myself want that."

"What? *Why?*"

"Because there's no point wanting something you can never have."

With that, she turned around and walked right off my bus—walked away from me, again.

And all my anger cooled. Instantly.

Because nothing seemed worth it when Maggie walked away from me.

Not being right or winning the fight. I never won anyway.

Neither of us really did.

Fuck.

I sighed, and went after her.

By the time I was off my bus, Maggie was already across the lot and on her bus. Shady pointed me in the right direction.

I went straight over, shirtless, walking right past Katie who was on her phone and sipping a beer outside her bus—and stared at me over the bottle.

Fucking great.

I ignored her. But I had to wonder at what point we were gonna make some dramatic scene in front of a bunch of people and everyone was gonna start realizing what was going on—and Maggie was gonna flip her shit.

Soon, I figured. At this rate... very fucking soon.

And there was a part of me that couldn't fucking wait for it to happen.

The shit-disturber part.

And that other part... the one that wanted all this fighting shit over with. You know, so we could move on forward to other, better shit, like a hell of a lot more fucking.

I yanked the door of Maggie's bus open, ignoring the bullshit NO DUDES sign. There was a chick sitting in the lounge, working on a laptop when I walked in. Freckles and strawberry-blonde hair. Elle's assistant, what's-her-name. Fucking Joanie.

"Anyone else back there?" I asked her.

"You mean, except...?"

"Yeah."

"No."

"Great. Get out."

She blinked at me, then shut her laptop and got to her feet, taking it with her. "Sure. I just need to grab my—"

"Nope."

Her eyes went wide. The girl had been around for a few years now, but this was pretty much the longest conversation we'd ever had. And the rudest.

"Okee dokee..."

She slipped past me and out the door. I locked it behind her, then kicked off my boots and headed straight to the back of the bus.

I found Maggie in her bunk. She'd ditched her jacket and was lying on her back on top of the blanket in her sexy little dress. Before she could react I crowded in with her, lying next to her on my stomach, propped up on my elbows.

"Zane!" she hissed. "What the fuck?"

"We need to talk," I said, calmly, my face inches from hers.

"You're not supposed to be on here."

"I know. The Lady Bus, right?"

"Is Joanie still out there?"

"Nope. We're alone." Alone enough. I knew the door was locked, but there were probably a few people who had a key.

Maggie knew it too; she glared at me. I rolled onto my back and got comfy next to her.

After a moment of silence, she sighed.

There was music playing softly in the lounge. I stared at the underside of the bunk above us, wishing I had a joint on me and wondering if there was a chance in hell Maggie would let me smoke up on her bus.

At least the weed I'd already smoked was kinda helping me mellow out—now that I'd chilled the fuck out a bit.

"What is this Sarah McLachlan-sounding shit?" I asked her.

"It's Feist."

"Sounds like Sarah McLachlan."

"It sounds literally nothing like Sarah McLachlan."

I listened for a bit. "Sounds the same to me."

"Because you've probably never actually listened to Sarah McLachlan." That was true enough. "Let me guess. You don't like it?"

"It's alright. But where's the sex?"

"There's plenty of sex in it," she said, and I could pretty much hear her eyes roll. "You just have to *listen*."

"I guess. Who really listens to this shit, though?"

"Uh, Joanie? Please tell me you weren't rude to her."

I left that alone. "Trust me, I'm not the only dude who's been on this bus, Maggs."

That was met with silence.

Then she turned her head to look at me. "What?"

"Definitely seen other dudes slipping in and out of here." I looked at her; her face was close to mine. We were sharing one of her furry pink pillows. "You telling me you haven't caught them yet?"

"Who?" she demanded.

"Hey, I'm not gonna cockblock a guy for no good reason. I'm just letting you know. I'm not the only one breaking the rules here. And we've already agreed Talia's not getting fired, right?"

"Shit," she muttered, putting the pieces together in her head.

"Go easy on her. And what do you expect Pete and Sophie to do, fuck on a crowded crew bus? Come on, Maggs. You shouldn't make rules no one can follow. Just setting yourself up for disappointment."

"Fuck." She softened beside me, pushing a hand through her hair. "What do you want, Zane? And don't say pussy, because I'm really not in the mood."

"I'm not gonna say that," I told her, honestly, and she tossed me a skeptical look. "Seems to me like we're not getting anywhere, fighting over the same shit again and again. Am I right?"

She didn't say anything. I was right, but she was hardly gonna admit it.

"So, why don't we try getting along? Talk about something else. Like something we can agree on. We used to actually do that sometimes, you know."

"Yeah. I remember."

She didn't go on, but she didn't tell me to leave, so I went on.

"You're beautiful, Maggie," I told her, my voice soft. "You work hard. You deserve to be kissed at the end of the day. Have someone tell you how amazing you are." I was staring at her face, and I meant every word.

"You deserve that, too," she said quietly, but she was staring at the underside of the bunk above us when she said it. Her face looked soft and young, so pretty in the glow of the golden light, and all I wanted to do was kiss her.

So fuck it.

I leaned over and kissed her.

Her lips were soft, and I just savored the feeling. Her warm breath against my face. The smell of her and her familiar taste. I kept my tongue in my mouth and just savored her lips against mine.

Gradually, she started kissing me back.

As we kissed, I shifted my body over hers. And yeah, my dick was up. She was so soft and warm beneath me... Her hands gripped my bare arms, her nails digging in, and my body was overly-aware that I was already half-naked.

And the little gasps she made as my lips moved against hers... *fuck.* I hadn't even touched her with my tongue yet.

I didn't even bring a condom.

I didn't come here to fuck her, but now all I wanted to do was be inside her.

I shifted my hips, moving against her, restless, looking to get comfortable and stay a while... and she spread her legs, wrapping them around my hips.

I nudged my tongue into her mouth and she opened for me, taking me deeper. Tingles prickled down my spine. My balls tightened and my dick throbbed. I moved against her slowly, dragging my rigid dick against her clit.

She moaned, low in her throat, and my dick pulsed. I was already leaking pre-come.

Shit, but I wanted to fuck her. Just bury myself in her and stay there.

I reached down between us and slid my fingers over her pussy. She was warm through her panties, they were damp, and she moaned again, rubbing into my touch.

Definite green light.

I undid my jeans. I got my cock out into my hand, and at the same time, I felt her reach down and hike up her dress. I pushed my dick down between her legs, grabbed her panties and wrenched them aside, and pushed into her.

Her head snapped back and she shuddered with pleasure. Her pussy squeezed my dick as I pumped into her... deeper.... deeper. At the same time, I managed to wriggle out of my jeans, fighting them down until they were finally off, so I could spread my knees and drive into her harder.

Maggie gasped and clutched at my ass, pulling me to her.

She didn't push me back and roll on top or fight me for dominance like she often did.

She just spread her legs for me and took me, deep.

"Condom," she gasped. "We need a condom."

"Don't have one."

"Fuck."

"You have one?"

"Why would I have a condom on the Lady Bus?"

"Why wouldn't you?"

"Because," she said, annoyed. "If I didn't bring any on tour, I couldn't fuck you."

I burst out laughing. I couldn't help it. "That was your plan?"

"Shut up. Don't laugh at me while you're fucking me."

I reached down under her thigh and hiked it up, spreading her legs wider and holding her there, pinned, as I drove into her. "You're right. It's a great plan, Maggs. Really effective."

"You didn't bring one with you...?"

"Really didn't think that far ahead."

She huffed, irritated, but she didn't tell me to stop. Not with words or her body. She just kept taking me as I drove into her, her body gradually relaxing, softening until she was moaning in a steady rhythm to match my thrusts. Her pussy was tight and silky-wet and felt so mindfucking-good against my skin... and I was gonna blow.

Yup. I was gonna blow my load for her in a matter of fucking seconds.

I didn't even want to stop it.

I just wanted to come all over her. Mark her. Make her mine.

"You gonna come, Maggie? Before I blow...?"

"Yeah," she breathed. "Yeah, don't pull out yet..." She was trying to move her hips, so I released my grip on her thigh. I yanked down her silky dress and the bra underneath, popping her tits out. I ran my hand over them and squeezed.

"Gonna come on your tits," I warned her, "about eight seconds..."

"*Fuck...*" She churned her hips as I ground into her, her pussy squeezing me tight, milking me. "Do that thing..."

I fucked her harder, jerking my hips up with each thrust, hitting her clit. "What, this thing...?" Then I pummeled her G-spot, making her breath cut off in desperate little choking sounds as her body arched beneath mine.

"Yeah," she choked out, "*there...*"

I grabbed her hip again, pulled out partway and fucked her in short, hard strokes, working her from the inside-out, forcing her orgasm. I knew it was coming... Her face was flushing. Her nipples were rock-hard as her tits jiggled.

Then her pussy convulsed around my cockhead and she screamed.

I fucked her as long as I could stand, then I ripped my dick out and got up on my knees, fast.

I barely got my hand on myself before I shot off. I aimed for her chest as my cock jerked in my hand. My eyes closed and I braced myself against the wall as the spasms rocked my body. I stroked myself as I came, and suddenly Maggie's hands were stroking me, too.

When I could see again, Maggie was panting beneath me and my come was splattered on her tits, her throat and her chin. She gazed up at me and shuddered out a long sigh.

"Fuck... sweetheart..." I lowered myself down over her. "Hottest fucking thing I've ever seen in my life..." I kissed her soft mouth, touched my fingers to her chin and drifted them down her throat, smearing my come into her skin.

Then I sat back up and looked at her, using both hands to rub my come into her tits, smearing it over her nipples and tweaking the little rosy tips.

She shuddered, sensitive. But she was limp beneath me.

And for a moment, half-undressed and marked with my come, pinned between my knees with my cock still half-hard against her stomach, she looked up at me in total surrender. Soft, vulnerable and spent.

Mine.

Right now, there was no fight in her. She didn't even want to run away. She didn't want me to leave. I could see it in her gray eyes.

I could see how badly she wanted to stay right where she was.

Open to me.

Honest and exposed... stripped and dirty... done for.

That look on her face? It was the kind of shit I'd been dreaming about for eight years.

"It should be like this," I told her, "always. You, fucking covered in my come. Your legs spread. Your pussy wet. Fucking panting and dripping and aching for me to make you come again. Begging me and screaming my name. Fucking *mine*." I slid a hand up around her neck and held her, gently, by the throat, squeezing just lightly as I leaned down in her face. I brushed my lips to hers. "Make you keep coming for me... even when you don't want to."

But she shook her head slowly. "We can't do this," she said. "We can't just keep having sex."

"It's not just sex."

"It is."

I tightened my hand around her throat a bit, holding her there. "For fuck's sake, Maggie. Can you stop saying that? It's not just sex."

She pushed at me, shoved at me to get off, so I let go, shifting over to let her get up.

She sat up and looked over her shoulder at me. "It can't be

more," she said softly, as her eyes filled with tears. "I'm sorry, Zane. I just can't handle more." She slipped out of the bed and stood on shaky legs, fixing her dress. She peeked out toward the front of the bus, and when she looked at me again, she looked scared and fucking sad. "I can't handle this," she told me, and her voice was shaky, too.

And my stomach fucking fell.

She really meant that shit.

And she wasn't even blaming me for it.

It was the first time, ever, she didn't put it all on me, didn't blame me for everything going wrong. She didn't even look mad.

"That's not true."

"It's true," she said. "Please. Get off the bus before someone sees you. I don't want anyone to see you here. Just... *please.*" Her gray eyes fucking pleaded with me.

Then she disappeared into the washroom.

I sat on the side of her bed, scraping myself together. Slowly pulling my jeans back on. But my head felt broken, my brain shattered into a jumble of pieces that didn't seem to want to reconnect. Her words had knocked all the sense out of me.

Fucking shocked me.

I can't handle this.

She wasn't even blaming me.

For once, Maggie wasn't blaming me.

I'd waited for so long for her to stop blaming me. And now that she suddenly did... I didn't know what the fuck to do.

What the fuck was I supposed to do?

If I was the problem, if I'd fucked things up, at least I had a chance of fixing it.

If Maggie was the problem... What the hell was I supposed to do to fix that?

CHAPTER ELEVEN

Maggie

I SHOULD'VE KNOWN everything would *really* fall apart when we rolled into Vegas.

For five days, Zane and I had managed to keep the peace by pretty much staying the fuck away from each other. It was like we both just knew if we got within screaming distance of one another, we'd end up fighting and/or fucking, and hurting ourselves and each other all over again.

So we kept our distance.

I knew he was probably mad at me, again, and hurt, and I couldn't fix it.

But I'd been honest with him. I couldn't handle just having a sexual relationship with him.

And I couldn't handle anything more.

I sure as fuck couldn't handle losing him completely.

Which meant I was smack in the middle of the world's worst Catch-22.

Damned if I do...

Damned if I don't.

Fortunately, the rest of the tour was going strong. I didn't think I could deal with any major catastrophes on that front without dissolving into a puddle of useless mush.

The Phoenix show was incredible, and the rest of Dirty seemed happy.

The day after the Phoenix show, Jesse and Dylan took Katie and Amber on a helicopter tour of the Grand Canyon with a picnic on the canyon floor. Katie invited me along, but I didn't go. Too fucking depressing, being surrounded by all that romance.

I kept myself busy, though. And thank fuck I had Talia in my corner, because I really couldn't face Zane like this.

Because I'd been honest with him about something else, too. I was in love with him, and yay me, I'd finally admitted that to both of us.

Which meant that any way you looked at it, I was incredibly fucked.

It was our first night in Vegas when it really hit me—the fucking sadness. The major fucking downer of being in Las Vegas again, which only brought back all the memories of the last time I was here.

In that penthouse suite of my dad's hotel... with Zane.

We weren't staying there this time, thank God. For whatever reason, my dad had been distracted or disinterested enough that he didn't reach out to invite Dirty to stay there. I was relieved, of course, but I was also a little hurt. Because stupid me. As much as I always dreaded seeing the man, it hurt when he made no effort to see me.

It always had.

Maybe it hurt less now than it did when I was a little girl, but it still hurt. He was still my dad. The only one I had.

When we'd checked into our hotel in the afternoon, Zane had texted me. It was the only time he'd spoken to me in days.

Zane: you talk to Dizzy?

Me: No.

And that was it.

For the rest of that night, as the band went barhopping and I tagged along, and everyone else had a great time, I just felt sad.

Anytime I'd glimpsed Zane, he seemed to catch me looking at him—and he didn't look very happy, either. His jaw was tight, his gaze cold, and he barely seemed to be talking to anyone. I wasn't sure if he was just pissed at me, or also pissed at my dad for not reaching out to me while I was in town.

I wouldn't doubt that.

But I definitely couldn't handle that look on his face.

I couldn't handle fighting with him anymore—about anything.

It was breaking my heart.

And our second day in Vegas only got worse.

People started talking—about Zane. About what a foul fucking mood he was in.

Apparently he'd lost it on some of the crew at a TV interview, which wasn't his style. Zane could be hotheaded, he could be moody and he could definitely be a dick, but he generally didn't go off on random people who were just trying to do their jobs. Especially people whose job was to make him look good.

Glad I wasn't there to see it, and I definitely wasn't gonna watch the footage that had leaked onto the web, showcasing his little tantrum.

Brody called me about it.

I let that call go to voicemail, promising myself I'd deal with it tomorrow.

And for the rest of the day, my spirits just sank.

I didn't see Zane until later, when we all ended up hanging out in Jude's hotel room. The party went late. Hotel management came by a couple of times and politely asked us to shut up.

Normally that might've stressed me out, but I just let Jude deal with it. Jude had a lot of experience greasing palms; something I'd never been able to pull off with much authority. Made me uneasy.

Meanwhile, I'd just kept making drinks. I often played bartender at Dirty parties, and usually it was fun. Kept me busy and feeling like I was looking after everyone—my comfort zone. Though this time it felt weirdly wrong, serving up booze while Zane just sat in a corner with Shady, sipping his water and looking angry.

The party eventually dissolved and we were all now sitting in some diner eating middle-of-the-night breakfast. I couldn't even remember how we'd ended up here. I wasn't drunk. I'd maybe had two drinks over the course of the night. But I was tired and distracted and incredibly disconnected from whatever was going on around me.

All I could think about was Zane, and that night almost two years ago.

Standing at the altar with him.

And the next morning, lying naked in bed with him. *Wanting* to be naked in bed with him. Freaking out when I found out the marriage was real—that I was now legally married to the biggest manwhore I'd ever met, and my career was fucked.

And the ring he'd given me that morning. The gorgeous platinum ring with the giant diamond.

The ring I still sometimes carried around. The ring I was right now wearing, on my middle finger, with the diamond spun around to the inside where no one would see it but I could grip it in my fist.

I didn't even think about it when I'd put it on today. I didn't want to think about why I was putting it on. I was just so sad.

Because I was so totally fucked over the man who'd given it to me.

So. *Fucked.*

When did my life become so fucked?

The moment you decided to work for him.

Yeah. Right about then.

Oh, and when you decided to marry him.

Yeah. Thanks, Mom.

This was my first time back in Vegas since the wedding, and things were even more fucked-up now than they were then. How was that possible? There was a part of me that was just so fucking confused. That couldn't understand why it couldn't just be simpler.

Why we couldn't just work things out and ride off into the sunset together.

Why I couldn't just be with him, trust him, give him a chance.

Or why I couldn't just let him go.

Or why I couldn't just fall in love with a nice, sane rock star instead.

Like Matt.

He was sitting next to me again. He'd been doing that a lot, actually. Our group was all squeezed into a few big booths, and his arm was around my shoulders while I picked at my pancakes. As if I needed a giant stack of pancakes in the middle of the night? Everyone was talking and laughing around me, loudly, but it had all become a buzz of noise. I couldn't make out a single word.

Then someone started yelling.

When I looked up, I noticed that the waitresses in this place were wearing 1950s soda pop girl outfits, and everything was pink and silver and turquoise and happy. Bruno Mars' incredibly upbeat "Runaway Baby" was playing, and Katie, Talia and Sophie were singing along to it in the next booth, putting on a little show for all the rock stars... and I just wanted to cry.

I wanted to be in my hotel room alone, and I wanted to be where Zane was.

I should've removed Matt's arm from my shoulders. But I only realized that about ten seconds after the shit hit the fan.

I was that out of it.

I was staring right at Zane. I realized that belatedly, too... about five seconds after he started tossing cutlery and throwing a world-class rock star tantrum in the middle of the restaurant, and I snapped back to reality.

He was on his feet in the next booth, and he actually took a half-hearted swing at Jesse when Jesse tried to put a hand on his shoulder and reel him back in.

Jesse dodged it.

Then Jude and Seth joined the fray. Jude tried to put a hand on

Zane's arm as he shoved his way out of the booth and Seth said something about not causing a scene, and Zane lost it.

He grabbed a glass coffee pot off the nearby counter and hurled it at the wall. It smashed, coffee and glass flying everywhere. People screamed and ducked. The men at my table got to their feet, except for Matt—who froze and seemed about as shocked as me.

Zane had definitely snarled Matt's name among all the other nasty shit he was spewing. We'd all heard it.

If Matt doesn't stop touching her, I'm gonna fuck up his face.

Now he was screaming something in Jesse's face about *Fuck you* and *You don't fucking know*—and then he turned and lunged for Matt.

Whose arm was still around me.

Zane grabbed Matt by a fistful of shirt; the other fist was already raised to strike by the time I processed what was happening.

"Zane!" I screeched, throwing my hands up—but thank God Jude and Shady were on him. Jude grabbed Zane's raised arm and prevented him from landing that punch. But Zane was strong and he was in a fury.

Had I ever seen him lose it like this?

He was practically frothing at the mouth, and he wouldn't even look at me.

In the end, it took Jude, Shady, Con and Jesse to subdue him while Seth and Flynn got Elle to safety, the other girls got the hell out of the way, Lex and Bane cleared a path and tried to convince the restaurant staff not to call the police, and Matt and I sat in our booth in stunned silence.

At least his arm wasn't around me anymore.

I did an automatic mental headcount of everyone, like I would in the middle of any Dirty disaster. I didn't even know where the hell Dylan was. The washroom?

"What the hell's up your ass?" I heard Jesse ask, as the guys struggled to get Zane to sit down in an empty booth.

"Don't ask," Jude muttered.

"She's my *wife*," Zane spat out. I froze as he turned his ice-cold gaze on Matt, and if looks could kill… I was just glad four large men were holding Zane down.

Jesse looked over at me. "What?"

"*What??*" That was Katie, who was hunkered down in the next booth.

When I dared to look around, everyone else was staring at me, too.

Elle, Seth, Amber, Jude… *everyone.*

Beside me, Matt slowly raised his empty hands. "Hands to myself," he said. "Scout's honor."

Which set Zane off again.

He shot up off his seat, but the guys were on him, and this time they decided to haul him outside. I watched them go, Jude, Shady and Jesse fighting Zane all the way out the door.

Oh, Jesus…

"Take it easy," I kept hearing Shady say. "Take it easy, brother…"

"Alright," Con said loudly, with his trademark charming grin. "Show's over." And gradually people pretended to go back to their food. Then he and Lex herded the rest of our party out the door.

Except for me and Matt, who just sat here in our booth.

Jude walked back in and looked at us, then glanced at the waitress who was cleaning up the broken coffee pot. He sighed and shook his head. "Have Dylan pay the bill," he told me. Then he walked back out, to deal with whatever was going on outside.

Our waitress appeared and laid the bill on our table without looking at our faces, then disappeared.

I was pretty much numb with shock. I couldn't feel anything. I'd finally hit some kind of emotional/sensory overload where I just couldn't take anymore.

I felt Matt looking at me kind of sidelong, like he was afraid to look at me.

"Wife?"

I swallowed. "I, uh, married Zane at the end of the last tour." My voice was small, but I managed to get the words out, quickly. No point lying to Matt's face again, but I'd definitely never felt more like an asshole about the whole thing than I did right now. "Are you alright?"

"Yeah. You?"

"Uh... no."

Someone walked up to our table and I looked up to find Dylan standing over us. Auburn-haired and crazy-tall, Dirty's drummer stood out like a gorgeous sore thumb and didn't even notice half the diner was staring at him. He scanned the three empty booths, then looked at Matt and me. "Where'd everyone go?" he asked lightly.

I put my hand down on the bill and slid it toward him.

"Thank you for the pancakes."

Then I got up and walked out the door, still in shock.

When we got back to the hotel and everyone piled into the lobby, it was freakishly quiet. No one said a thing to me. Which was fine with me; I made eye contact with not one person and went straight for an elevator.

Zane got on with me.

No Shady.

No one else.

They all very purposefully stood back and let the elevator doors close behind us.

Fuck.

They all *knew*.

Because Zane fucking told them.

The shock was gradually wearing off and giving way to an ugly, helpless rage.

Neither of us said a word inside the elevator, but when the door opened again, Zane was quick to close a hand around my arm and escort me up the hall so I couldn't disappear. He pretty much dragged me through the door of my room and tossed me inside.

Then he shut the door and stood his big body in front of it, blocking my only way out. He was already digging around in his vest, and I knew what he was looking for. He was gonna smoke up—and mellow the fuck out.

Which meant if I started yelling, I'd probably be doing it alone.

"*Fuck*, you're an asshole." I bit that out, then turned and walked into the room, throwing my jacket and purse so hard at the bedside table it knocked the lamp off.

"Yup." When I turned to look at him again, he'd produced a joint and was lighting up. "You want help trashing your room? Got some experience in that department."

"No thanks. Bad enough I'm gonna get a bill because you're stinking up my non-smoking room with your weed."

"I'll pay the bill, Maggie," he said, like it was the most inconsequential thing in the world, and took a deep drag. "You just need to calm down." Because now that he had a joint in hand and had rolled right back into king-of-cool mode? *I* was the one who needed to calm down.

"Calm?" I snapped, as calmly as I could. "What, like you? You, who just flipped out in front of everyone and told them I'm your wife?"

"Yeah, I flipped out." He ran his tongue over his bottom lip. "Obviously, if Matty Brohmer thinks he can feel you up, I'm gonna flip out."

"Feel me up? Are you kidding me? He put his arm around my shoulders." Really. Matt was just being friendly.

I'd never seen Zane go off like that, even over a guy touching me.

I hadn't seen Zane in many fights over the years, although there had definitely been a few. And yes, they'd usually been over a woman. Because some dude had rubbed him the wrong way, or he'd said the wrong thing—or put his hand up the wrong girl's skirt—and utter chaos had ensued. Violent chaos.

But if he had some kind of jealous hate-on for Matt, it was news to me.

"You think I don't see how he looks at you?" he said, eyes hard and cold. "How he sits next to you all the fucking time? Touching your hair? Staring at your ass?"

"Well—"

"He's got a hard-on for you, Maggie," he cut me off. "Guy can't keep his mouth shut about you. If he could've wrapped his dick in a pancake and fed it to you right there in that restaurant, he would've."

I tried to ignore that, because I really hadn't noticed Matt playing with my hair. And if he was staring at my ass or talking about my ass in front of the guys, it wasn't my fault.

I scowled at Zane meaningfully. "At least he didn't put his hand down my pants right in front of you."

"Good thing." He stalked over to me and got right in my face. "Because if he did that, I'd have to break his hand and his dick, along with his fucking face, and we'd be out another bass player." He took another drag off his joint, and turned the tip toward me. "You want? Do wonders for your mood."

"What I want," I said, slowly and clearly, "is for you to take your weed and your tantrums and your jealous caveman bullshit and shove it all right up your ass."

Normally, he'd probably have laughed at that or had some clever come-on of a comeback at the ready. But right now? His expression darkened. His eyelids lowered. He flicked his joint in the glass of water I'd left on the table.

Then he pushed me backwards, using his whole body to steer me where he wanted me. His hips crushed me against the wall.

"So, what? You can't handle *this*?" He grabbed the neck of my dress in his fist, yanking me toward him for emphasis. "So now you're just gonna hook up with someone else?"

"Hook up?" I grabbed a fistful of his shirt in return, yanking him toward me. "I was *eating pancakes*. And so what if I hook up with someone else? How is that your business?"

He laughed, but it was more of a snarl. "You kidding me?" He pressed his forehead against mine, hard, so I had to push back. I could already feel his hard-on digging into me—and he was starting to undo his jeans. The rings on his fingers scraped me through my dress as his hand moved between us... and shivers tore through me.

All the blood in my head was rapidly fleeing south. "You so much as think about touching a guy who isn't me," he said, his lips almost bumping mine, "and you better fucking believe I'm gonna make it my business, Maggie."

Breathless. I felt utterly out of breath, my entire body possessed with the need to have him. I was empty, *aching* with emptiness, and the only remedy for that ache was Zane.

Hard and hot and long and deep... filling me completely, over and over again. My clit throbbed with the force of my pulse, and I wanted him in me, *now*.

"I'll hook up with whoever I want to," I informed him, but my voice shook. "I don't belong to you." I knew I was pushing him, just fucking pushing him to screw me and make me his.

He ripped my panties down my thighs, and my pussy clenched.

Oh, *fuck*...

My panties drifted down to my ankles. He shoved his hand between my legs. His fingers were so warm... He smeared them over my swollen flesh, so slippery, and there was no hiding it... I was so wet. He hiked my left leg up around his hip, spreading me open as he pushed against me. I was *quivering*, I was so hot and ready.

Why did his possessive neanderthal bullshit have to get me so fucking wet?

There was something wrong with me. Had to be. Because I already knew who I belonged to and I just kept fighting it. I knew, and there was nothing I could do to change it, no matter how I fought it.

And all it did was turn me on.

And scare the crap out of me.

"*Like. Fuck*," he growled. Then he shoved into me. Every inch of his big dick, straight up inside me. I was that wet, and he was bare. "You'll fuck *me*, Maggie. *Me*."

"Yeah," I panted, as he fucked me against the wall. He hit my limits, fast, stretching me, and I squealed.

"Fuck, yeah... take me, Maggie..."

"Yeah, fuck, give it to me..."

"You want it...?"'

"Yeah, I want it." I clutched at him as he gave it to me, moaning and scrambling to get my legs around him. "Yeah. Yeah, gimme..." I was already way beyond making sense or using my brain to get me out of this.

I didn't want out.

"Gonna show you who your man is," he growled, his fingers digging into my thighs as he hiked me up and pounded into me. "No one else gets this pussy. It's mine. I'm your husband and this shit belongs to me. All of it. Don't even think about giving it to someone else. You're *mine*."

He drove that point home by hiking me up higher and jackhammering into me. He kissed me hard, and I caught his bottom lip in my teeth and sucked, moaning, losing my mind as the sensations flooded my body.

Then he yanked me off the wall and pulled me with him onto the bed so suddenly my head spun. He lay back and held my hips over his and fucked me from beneath.

"Take it, Maggie," he urged me as I rode him.

And I did.

He dug his heels into the bed and pumped up into me, every muscle in his body locked up tight as I braced my hands on his hard chest, gripping his shirt... and I knew why he put me on top. It wasn't to give me control.

It was so I could see him. So I could watch him fuck me.

So he could look me in the eyes while he did it, just like he wanted to.

Then he rolled me over and pulled me right down to the floor. We lost his vest, but the rest of our clothes were still half-on. We kissed and bit and clawed at each other and rolled around in a crazy, dirty, knock-down, drag-out fuck. Me on top of him again and then him on top of me... both of us fucking each other with a vengeance, both of us chasing our own orgasm—and hellbent on making the other one come first.

"You getting the message, Maggs?" he growled as he pounded

into me, almost out of breath. He was on top of me and I was close to orgasm, and he fucking knew it. I was shaking, hyperventilating as I rode him, fast and hard from underneath, meeting every thrust. "You understand who you belong to now? Or do I need to show you some more...?"

"No," I gasped, "I am not yours."

"Yes. You. Are." He held me down by my throat and drilled into my G-spot with this fat cockhead, and *oh my God...*

But I couldn't stop fighting it. I just couldn't stop fighting him.

"This is the last fuck," I choked out as I did my best to strangle him with my inner muscles. "This is the last time I'm fucking you, Zane Traynor."

His face flushed. He was grunting with the effort as he slammed into me, his hips slapping loudly against my thighs. "Fuck you, Maggie," he growled, just as I lost the battle and started to come. I cried out and he stiffened. He shouted something obscene, garbled and barely English, and blew into me with a series of low groans, his hips ramming against me. I could feel him bruising me.

I didn't care.

As my body shook with the tremors of pleasure so extreme I actually felt tears of ecstasy running down my face... I couldn't even fathom it all. I couldn't fathom how I could love someone so much, could want someone so bad, and be so afraid of my feelings for him at the same time. So afraid, I suddenly wanted to gnaw off my own limbs to get out from under him as he collapsed on top of me.

And the condom...

What condom?

There was no condom. Neither of us had stopped to get one or even mentioned it. Zane just came deep inside me and I didn't even care.

Pregnancy, STDs... These vague concepts swirled in my head with the ecstasy and the terror and the strange numbness, as I felt myself detaching from it all... because it was all too much to take.

Just... *fuck.*

Zane was smart enough to use condoms with other women,

right? I was pretty sure about that. I was pretty sure no matter what a manwhore he was, he was probably clean.

And I was pretty sure I was at a point in my cycle when I probably couldn't get pregnant. Or at least... wouldn't likely get pregnant.

Right now, that would have to be enough.

But it wasn't enough.

I swiped the tears from my face before he could see them and shoved his shoulder. "Get off me."

He groaned as he pulled out and pushed himself up on his arms above me. He stared at my face, and he looked about as wrecked as I felt. "You can't have anyone else," he said, his voice all broken like *he* was about to cry.

I shoved at him again and tried to wriggle out from under him. "Why? Why can't I?"

"Because it'll kill me."

I pushed him one more time and he rolled to the side, letting me free.

"What does that mean?" I demanded. "Is that a threat? Are you threatening to start drinking again or something if I end up with someone else?"

"It's not a threat. It's a fact."

"You can't put that on me, Zane," I told him. "You don't get to fuck around and then throw a shit-fit tantrum because another man puts a hand on me."

"Yeah, I fucking will have a problem with it if someone puts a hand on you."

"No. No, you've gotta act like a sane person here, okay? Matt was just being friendly. What are you gonna do when someone actually makes a move on me? Oh wait, I know. Start a food fight." I got up, shakily, covering myself with my dress. "So how about the next time some bitch grabs your junk in front of me, I'll just throw chili at her head, would that work?"

"Go ahead. I wouldn't mind seeing that, actually."

"Of course you wouldn't. Jesus." I raked my fingers through my hair and stared at him. He was just lying there on the floor, half-dressed. "Do you not get this AT ALL? I'm never getting in a catfight over you, Zane. I am never gonna stand between you and other women. I'd be fucking *trampled*, do you get that? I don't want to be the reason you don't fuck other women, and I don't want to be the reason you don't drink, or the reason you don't end up in jail. What I want—no, what I need is for *you* to be the reason you don't do any of those things, FOR YOU."

"Yeah," he said, gazing up at me. "That's pretty much what Rudy said."

Rudy? Rudy Baker?

He'd talked to his AA sponsor about this? About *us*?

"Well then, Rudy's fucking right."

I turned around, searching the floor. Where the hell were my panties and how did he incinerate them so fast? I needed them back on before his come started running down my leg, and the reality of what we just did *without a condom* sank in and I truly lost my shit.

I'd probably just end up fucking him again, since that was what I did, apparently, when I lost my shit in front of Zane.

I started to laugh, this scary-ass, high-pitched giggle that made no sense.

"I need you, Maggie," he said. I heard him getting up off the floor behind me, slowly, and my laughter died. He sounded defeated, and I didn't want to see him like that. But I couldn't even stop myself from turning around.

He looked defeated as he sat on the edge of the bed, his jeans hastily pulled up but still undone, his shirt all askew. He pitched forward with his elbows on his knees and just stared at me.

"I need you, too," I admitted. It was the truth.

I needed Zane, and Jesus Christ I wanted him. Seeing him vulnerable, the way he looked right now, the curve of his shoulders and his blond hair in his face, fucking killed me. I wanted to put my arms around him, so bad.

But I didn't. I couldn't seem to move. I just stood rooted to the spot, wanting him.

"I just can't," I told him, again. "I can't do this with you."

"Fuck, Maggie. Come on."

"I told you. I already told you I can't."

He held my gaze, and he actually looked scared. "Ever?"

"I don't know. Just... not like this." I turned to get away from those blue eyes of his, and I finally glimpsed my panties. I snatched them up and pulled them on. I wanted to run right out the door, but I didn't. It took everything I had to just stand here and not take off, but I didn't.

I turned around and I forced myself to look at Zane again. His eyes were still on me, and he still looked scared. I hated making him look like that. I hated hurting him.

But I seriously didn't know what to do.

I really couldn't handle this.

All I could seem to handle—just barely—was avoiding him, then giving in and fucking the shit out of him... over and again.

Which was no good for anyone.

It just hurt like fuck.

Worse, I was starting to realize that maybe it was *me* who was hurting us both more than anything else... and the guilt of that on top of everything else was gonna fucking destroy me.

"*Fuck,*" I said, because sometimes, there were no other words. I pushed my hands into my hair, wanting to rip it right out at the roots. "You make me fucking crazy. Like no one's ever made me this crazy in my life."

He just stared at me, like he knew exactly what I was talking about. "You love me."

I softened, any remaining fight totally leaving me, because that was the truth, too. I did love him.

I loved him badly.

"Love isn't enough, Zane."

"Maybe not. But it's a fucking start, isn't it?

"Yeah. Yeah, it's a start." I stared at him, sitting there on the bed just two feet from me, and I hugged myself. "Here we are, eight years in... still standing at the starting line."

CHAPTER TWELVE

Zane

I WANTED A DRINK.

I wanted a big, strong, bottomless drink.

It was the middle of the night and this was Vegas. So getting my hands on that bottomless drink would not be a problem.

I should've called Rudy.

Instead, I headed downstairs.

My AA sponsor and friend, Rudy Baker, was a blues musician, a fucking genius musician who'd just about drank his whole life away before he got sober about twenty years ago. He'd been my sponsor ever since we'd connected after my first stint in rehab. He'd been there for me through everything, knew all my dirty shit—or most of it—and was still there for me.

He even knew about Maggie. Knew I was in love with her, but even Rudy didn't know I'd married her in Vegas.

Couldn't quite get myself to confess that one to him.

Rudy lived in L.A., and while it was late, I could've called him anytime of the night.

I didn't.

I didn't even see him while we were in L.A. this time.

I made it as far as the hotel lobby before I stopped myself and sat the fuck down. Right where I was, on a stair. I could see the lights of

The Strip beyond, hear the noise... and I just knew if I walked out there, I wasn't coming back.

Fucking terrifying feeling.

I waved Shady away when he got close. "Just give me a minute. Please."

"Sure, brother."

He faded away, and I sat, looking out across the massive lobby, watching people heading out on the town. I hadn't even thought to throw on a hat or anything. I just sat, unmoving, hoping no one would look my way and try to come talk to me.

There was a loud group of girls in sparkly dresses, obviously half-cut, laughing and arguing over which bar to go to. I could've walked right over to them and joined their little party.

Me plus chicks plus booze...

Instant party.

I remembered how easy that used to be, walking over to a group like that. Wild horses couldn't have kept me away. Wherever I was headed, whatever other shit I was supposed to be doing... a group of chicks like that would've derailed me.

But I also remembered the kind of shit that happened the morning after I'd gone off those rails.

Like waking up to one of my best friends tearing me a new one because I'd ended up in bed with a girl he loved.

Like waking up in the hospital with a broken collarbone and a concussion and stitches in my head because I'd fallen off a fucking balcony.

Like waking up in a jail cell because I'd wrapped my rental car around a pole and by some miracle hadn't killed anyone, including the girl who'd been in the passenger seat, whose name I didn't remember. Was she blonde? Brunette? Tall? Short? I didn't even fucking know.

That kind of shit.

The kind of shit that had finally scared me enough to realize I had a serious problem, and get my ass into rehab.

The kind of shit I never wanted to pull again.

Someone came down the stairs next to me and stopped. I didn't look up, but I saw his snakeskin boots.

Seth.

He sat down next to me and looked at me for a long-ass minute. "You hanging in?"

"Nope."

"You gonna drink?"

"Don't know."

The words just fell out, and it was a fucking relief.

It was the first time anyone had outright asked me, in a long fucking time, if I was gonna drink.

It was also the first time in a long time I'd actually admitted aloud to another human being, besides Rudy or a roomful of random alcoholic strangers at an AA meeting, that I had the urge to drink and I didn't even know if I'd be able to overcome it.

I'd had this urge, many, many times over the past seven years. The entire time I'd been sober.

But not many people really knew that.

Not many people in my life really understood. Most everyone around me thought I was "cured" or something. I was a rehabilitated alcoholic, a nondrinker.

My friends who drank socially, who enjoyed the pleasure of drinking without having it rule and ruin their lives, just assumed I was done with it. That I could sit in a bar full of people drinking around me, or in the middle of some party backstage, or alone in a hotel room, and I didn't need it. I didn't crave it. Because I was over it, it was out of my system, I was strong.

Or some such shit.

But those people were wrong.

The only reason I was able to resist picking up a bottle at all was because I'd gone through the torture of detox, of physically getting the alcohol out of my body—so I could think straight enough to stop myself from taking the next sip, by whatever means necessary. So that I was no longer driven and controlled by the physical need.

I'd been physically off of alcohol for years now. But the whole mental, emotional part was the part that still needed work.

Obviously.

Seth said nothing. He got to his feet, and I didn't blame him. He probably didn't want to watch me destroy myself any more than I wanted him to. He definitely didn't want me dragging him down with me.

"I come back in five minutes," he said slowly, "and you're still here and still dry, we're going for a drive." Then he headed back up the stairs.

Seth was back in five minutes, maybe faster. I was still here, I was still dry, and he had the key for Jude's rental car.

I told Shady to stay behind. He didn't like it, because Jude wouldn't like it, but he stayed.

I got in without asking Seth where we were going, and he didn't tell me. He just drove.

He drove until the lights of Las Vegas were behind us, until every sign of civilization other than the road was behind us... way out into the desert. Until I zoned out to the song that was playing on the radio and completely lost track of where we were.

It was Paul McCartney & Wings, "Maybe I'm Amazed," the live recording from *Wings over America*, 1976. And Jesus Christ, this song...

This was one of those songs that, when I first heard it as a kid—this exact version of this song in particular—playing on some radio station, just like this, I'd been bitten by this sense of hope. A kind of faith that there was something out there so much bigger than myself to believe in, something that could save me if I could just tap into it.

Was this what some people felt when they discovered God?

For me, the only god I'd ever known was music.

I got so lost in the song, I had no idea which direction Seth was driving.

He pulled off the narrow, winding road into an empty stretch of desert and drove some more. Then he parked, turned off the car and got out without a word.

I followed.

Seth walked about a dozen paces into the desert and stopped.

"Where the fuck are we?" I patted my vest, looking for my lighter.

"Wherever," he said.

And that's when it hit me. That Seth had just brought me out into the middle of no-fucking-where—and I didn't have anything on me. I didn't have any weed.

Seth turned slowly, looking around, but there wasn't much to see. Just flat and dark and empty desert in every direction. I searched every pocket in my vest, twice, and fucking sighed.

Fuck me.

"What are we doing here? Peyote?"

He threw me a glance. "No, Morrison. We're here to do whatever the fuck you need to do without getting drunk to do it. Sit. Walk. Sing and dance. Fucking commune with the aliens. Whatever."

"It's fucking cold."

"So jog. Jump up-and-down."

He sat down on the cold, hard Earth and stretched out on his back, like it was the fucking beach and he was gonna grab some rays. He was wearing one of those trucker hats he sometimes wore when he didn't want to be recognized. The one that said *Big J's Drinkin' Hole.* He tugged it down over his eyes, and fucker pretty much looked like he was going to sleep.

He wasn't even wearing a jacket. Just a zip-up sweater thing.

I was already starting to shiver in my vest and thin shirt. Long sleeves or not, it was January. "How are you not cold?"

"Mind over matter," he said.

"The fuck does that mean? Your body temperature is gonna drop. You gonna imagine that away?"

"Eventually, I'll get too cold and I'll have to get up, get back in the car. But for now, you need to be here, I need to be here for you, so I can put off feeling cold."

"Yeah? You gonna mind-over-matter the scorpions away, too?"

"Yup."

I shook my head. This dude and all his Zen shit. Ever since he came back to us clean and sober, he'd been spouting this shit.

"That how you got off heroin, too? Fucking mind over matter?"

"Pretty much."

"Fuck off." I was starting to pace a bit, agitated and cold. "That's a bunch of bullshit. You needed methadone and detox and a medical team, and don't tell me you imagined all that shit in your head."

"Clinic got me off the junk," he said evenly, "but they definitely didn't keep me from using again. That was all me."

"Yeah? That sounds pretty fucking arrogant. What about all that 'higher power' stuff they preach in AA?"

"I never went to AA. NA meetings have worked for me, but I don't really believe in a higher power. At least not one that's gonna take all my fucked-up shit away. I just needed to get my head right. For me, that's what it took."

"That's all, huh?"

"Yup. And that's all it takes, every second of every day, over and over and over again. Definitely not as easy as it sounds."

"Doesn't sound easy at all."

"Never would've worked if I didn't stop mindfucking myself."

Yeah. That I could relate to.

I'd been mindfucking myself all my life. At this point, I was a master of the self-inflicted mindfuck.

I'd mindfucked myself for years over my parents dying when I was so young I couldn't even remember them.

Mindfucked myself before I went onstage, pretty much every time I went onstage.

Definitely mindfucked myself to hell and back over Maggie.

But unlike fucking Buddha here, mind over matter wasn't gonna cut it for me.

I did believe in a higher power: the music we made together as a band.

I believed in the structure of the Big Book, too, the guidance of working through the Twelve Steps, even when I didn't fully buy into them. Even when there were times I totally fucking resented needing them.

I needed AA. Most of all, I needed the meetings. They'd always worked for me, too. When I went to them.

Since this tour had started, I hadn't dragged my ass to one.

"And just to be clear," Seth said, "I'm not preaching anything. Everyone's got their own path to sobriety. You got a road to walk that's yours alone. For a lot of alcoholics, AA works. Belief in a higher power works. I'm not offering solutions and I'm not telling you what to do. I'm telling you what works for me, because you asked. I'm your friend, and I'm a friend who's walking a similar road. So I'm here to listen, to talk, to share, to support, or whatever it is you want me to do short of lying to you, supporting your addiction and getting you booze. And I'm not gonna blow sunshine up your ass, placate you or sugarcoat this shit, either. I brought you to an alcohol-free environment so you could get your shit straight with a clear head, if that's what you want to do."

"What, right now?"

"You got a better time in mind? A better place?"

I looked around at the desert like we were on the surface of the fucking moon. "It's not like I can do this shit in one night."

"It doesn't happen in one night. It happens in one moment."

I looked at Seth, but it was too dark to see his eyes under the brim of his hat or the expression on his face.

"And in every single moment there is, it happens over and over again," he said. "All you really need is one moment."

I ran my hand through my hair. Christ, but I wanted a toke.

Did I really have to listen to this shit?

"Just one, huh?"

"What else have you got? The past is done. The future is uncertain. All you've got is this one moment, right now. You're alive and sober, right now. What are you gonna do with this moment?"

He went silent for a long moment, and I was silent as that sank in. I really didn't have an answer for that question. Which was maybe my problem.

"You gonna have a drink?" he pressed. "Because you take one sip of booze and your life is fucked, I guarantee you that. And by the way, case you haven't figured it out yet, you think your life isn't out of control because you smoke pot daily to mellow out and you're itching for it right now and you're in love with Maggie but you keep fucking it up, you are straight-up deluding yourself."

I stared at him.

I walked over to where he lay and stood over him, staring down, but he didn't move.

"Yeah," he said. "I know you're in love with Maggie, and I know you're probably wondering where the fuck I stashed the car key right now, 'cause you want to get right back in that car and leave me in the dust so you can go get stoned. So. What're you gonna do?"

Fuck.

I rubbed my hands over my face and sighed.

Nothing. I wasn't gonna do anything.

I wasn't even mad at Seth, really. Except that I kinda was. I was itching with the need to smoke up, and I hated myself for it.

I hated people calling me on it. Pointing out my weaknesses to me.

I wasn't fucking stupid. I knew I shouldn't be smoking weed. I knew it was a fucked-up replacement for liquor, in a way. Way less volatile in my life, but no less addictive. No less dangerous to an addict like me.

Fucking insidious shit; it was gonna do me in one way or another.

I'd never wanted to admit that to myself, but I fucking knew.

I knew I was a cranky bastard when I didn't smoke up, when I was craving it, whenever withdrawal started to hit. That I was moody and uneven depending on how much I did or didn't smoke.

It was fucking bullshit, and like the addict I was, I just kept telling myself the solution was more weed.

More weed, and I'd feel better.

Fucking *pathetic*.

I never wanted to end up as fucking pathetic as I'd been at the height of my drinking; when I'd looked back with sober eyes and really seen the shit I'd done.

Or at least, the shit I could remember doing.

But here I was. Heading right down that same hole.

Same fucking shit, different pile.

"So this is the part where I go hit the nearest meeting and start working the Twelve fucking Steps all over again?"

"Told you. I'm not here to tell you what to do. But you want steps? Step one, flush your weed down the nearest toilet, all of it, and stop that shit. And once you stop jonesing and twitching for it and actually have a clear head for once, take a look at Maggie and see what you see. If what you see is the woman you want by your side for the rest of your life, then you find a way to make that shit happen."

Yeah. Fucking brilliant advice.

If only I knew how.

"And here's another guarantee I can give you, brother," he added. "You're never gonna make that happen while you're smoking up and fucking other women."

I turned away and looked out at the fucking desert, like it had any answers.

Empty.

The sky was pretty fucking empty, too. Just a big void of silence, echoing back the truth of Seth's words.

"Maybe if I had her," I said, "I wouldn't be smoking up and fucking other women."

"Uh-huh. Because it's her fault, right?"

I looked at Seth, lying there with his hands folded over his ribs.

Jesus Christ, whose side was this fucker on?

"It's her fault if you fuck other women now," he said, sounding bored, "and she's smart enough to know that down the road, if you're with her and something goes sideways and you end up fucking other women again, you'll make that out to be her fault, too. Just like it's her fault she hasn't thrown caution to the wind to take up with an addict. I haven't known Maggie all that long, and I don't know her all that well, but even I can see she's not the kind of woman who's gonna do that. And if she was, brother, you wouldn't want her anyway."

I'd started pacing again while he spoke, and I paced right back over to him. "So that's it? Everyone else in this band gets the woman of their fucking dreams, huh? Everyone else gets to smoke up, but I can't, right?"

"Yeah, and this is the part where you feel sorry for yourself."

Seth sat up, spinning his hat around backwards so I could see his face. He threw his arms on his knees and looked up at me, meeting my eyes.

"Throw yourself your fucking pity party, Zane, pile on the excuses to go have a drink. But nothing's gonna change the fact that yeah, most of your friends probably can smoke up, and no, you can't. You see me smoking up? It's different for us, and you know this. Other people can have a beer, smoke a joint and have a good time, get up and go on with their lives intact the next day. It's not like that for you and me, and it never was. That shit is poison for us. How many times can you smoke weed before you slip and decide a beer is okay? Once? A thousand times? I don't know the answer to that, and neither do you. But you and I both know, you will slip. And once you take that first sip, you've fucked away your choice about it. That shit gets in your body, and you don't get to choose anymore if you take the next sip or the next. It's over. You want to flush your life down the toilet like that? You want to die?"

"No. Obviously I don't want to fucking die."

"Good to know. You gonna drink?"

I knew what he was doing.

I'd been through this same conversation, more or less, with Rudy, about a thousand times.

"Don't be an asshole. Do you see a fucking roadhouse out here?"

"Yeah," he said. "I'm an asshole. Everyone is an asshole, and you're the king of the assholes, right? You got it all figured out and then some. That's why you're standing in the middle of some desert right now, fucking lost, with no idea what you're gonna do with your next breath."

"Got some idea," I muttered. "Kicking the shit out of you right now sounds like a good one."

"Go ahead, you think it'll make you feel any better," he said, calm as shit. "But it's not gonna change the fact that you're a superstar and you're actually standing here considering shitting your life away. You have everything, and you're just gonna flush it away. Sounds pretty fucking pathetic to me."

"I don't have everything!" I leaned over him and shouted it in his face. Where the fuck did he get off calling me pathetic? Maybe I was, but shit. "I don't have shit," I growled, "because I don't have the one thing I fucking *need*."

"Yeah?" he said, still calm. "Tell me, Zane Traynor. You've got mad talent, fame, friends, pretty much any fucking thing money can buy. What else could you possibly need?"

"Maggie. I need fucking *Maggie*."

"Ah, bullshit."

"What?" I pulled back like he'd bitch-slapped me. "The fuck do you mean *bullshit*?"

"I mean *bullshit*. That. Is. Fucking. Bullshit. It's not Maggie you need so fucking bad that you just keep sabotaging it so you can never have her. It's all that stuff she's got that you want. All that good shit in her that you feel when you're with her. All that stuff you wish you could have. That fucking hole she fills in you with all her beautiful."

I was pacing again, listening to him, wanting him to keep talking because everything he was saying was making some kind of sense—and wanting him to shut the fuck up.

"It's all that shit you probably think you don't have in you and don't deserve," he went on, "which is why you can't get your shit together. But I'm telling you, man, you deal with your shit, you get yourself straight, fill those holes with whatever the fuck you've gotta fill them with... if it's AA or it's music or it's God or it's whatever-the-fuck, as long as it's not booze or drugs or other women, or some other new addiction... if Maggie's really the woman for you, she's gonna come for you like a lightning strike. She won't be able to stay away."

"Yeah?" I pushed back. "That how it was for you and Elle?"

"Yeah. That's how it was for me and Elle. That's how it is for me and Elle, every moment of every day."

Well, fuck.

He was serious about that.

I stared at him for a minute and he stared right back.

Then I turned away. My eyes were starting to burn, because listening to him talk that way about his relationship with Elle... it did something to me. Grabbed my heart in a steel fist and fucking twisted.

I was jealous of that shit. Fuck, was I jealous.

And he was right. I didn't think I really deserved any of that beautiful shit with Maggie.

I never did.

Maybe partly because she'd been pushing me away since the day we met...

But what the fuck was I doing with the weed and the other women? I'd been pushing her away, too.

She wasn't the only one who was hiding from our shit instead of dealing with it head-on.

"It's a choice, brother," Seth said, his tone softening. "Elle and I, we've got some magic shit between us. Can't keep off of her, can't keep her off of me. But it's not an addiction. It's not some unhealthy, fucked-up obsession that we have zero power over, that'll drive us both into an early grave. It's something we're both strong enough to know we could walk away from and we'd both survive on our own, but we don't. We don't, because our lives are better when we're together. It's a choice, every moment, to be together." He blew out a breath. "When you're in a relationship, love isn't a noun, man. It's a fucking verb. Maybe you can't always choose who you fall in love with, but it's a choice to wake up every morning and love the one you're with, to be there for them and do whatever it takes to put their needs right up there front and center with your own."

He went silent, and I really didn't know what to say anymore.

"For addicts like us," he said after a moment, "it's hard. We're selfish fucks. Plus, we're weak."

I glanced at him. He spun his hat back around, tugging it down over his eyes, and lay back down.

"I'm telling you, brother, if Elle left me tomorrow, I'd still love her, but killing myself over it, that would be a choice. Every moment of every day, I choose to live. I choose to stay clean. I choose my relationship. And I choose to love Elle enough to put her ahead of my addiction. If it came down to it, I'd leave her if I had to."

"Bullshit."

"I'm fucking serious. You think I'd let some sketched-out addict around that beautiful woman, and that beautiful kid she's gonna have? I'd leave her before I'd let her live with a junkie, and she knows it. And I don't want to leave her. She doesn't want me to leave. She accepts me for the imperfect person that I am. We've sat up talking until dawn on many, many nights about all the fucked-up shit I've done, and it doesn't scare her away or turn her off. It just makes us closer. That's love."

I stared at him, but that was it. Seth was done. He just lay there in the dark.

I turned and started walking.

"Where you going?" he called after me.

"For a walk."

"You gonna drink?"

"Fuck you."

CHAPTER THIRTEEN

Zane

I WALKED FOR MAYBE AN HOUR, maybe two, mostly pacing. I went as far as I could comfortably go without getting lost. It was black as shit, everything was flat and looked the same, and there was no cell service.

The only light this far from the road was a half-moon and the stars; the car was a tiny little glint in the distance, and I stopped just before I lost sight of it. Some clouds were rolling around the sky and I didn't even think I'd be able to map out any kind of pattern in the stars to find my way back.

I was a city kid. If I was tossed out here by myself, sad truth was I'd probably get eaten by a coyote.

I paced, wearing a fucking path on the desert floor, and I thought about a lot of shit. I thought about my addiction, all the shit I'd tried to convince myself I'd put to rest, and how I'd almost broken right the fuck down tonight. How badly I'd wanted to take a drink—and maybe I would've if Seth didn't intervene.

And how badly I needed to get my ass to an AA meeting.

But mostly, I thought about Maggie.

I thought about how she'd told me she loved me.

And I knew, I fucking knew in my bones that she probably loved me all along. Which meant love was never our problem.

Because I'd definitely loved her all along, too.

I'd loved Maggie Omura with everything I had in my broke-ass heart of holes, for a long, long time. Seth was right; there were a shit-ton of holes in me. Holes left by my parents a long time ago. Holes with deep black roots, that I'd never known how to fill. It was like Swiss fucking cheese in there.

I used to think I could fill those holes with booze and pussy and the adulation of a few million fans.

But that was all bullshit.

All that shit just went through me like a fucking sieve.

What I needed was the love of this one woman. And I really didn't need Seth to tell me I was never gonna get it until I started filling those fucking holes myself.

The signs were there all along.

I just didn't want to see them.

So I kept fucking things up instead.

I loved Maggie, and yet the common thread through all our shit was me fucking it up.

According to her, I'd fucked up pretty much everything—right down to our wedding song.

She'd told me as much a couple of months after our wedding, when things were at their fucking worst between us. I'd stopped by her place one night to talk to her, but instead, we'd ended up in a massive fight. I knew any second she was gonna throw my ass out.

But then she paused to take a breath from reaming me out. And she sighed and said to me, *I love this song.*

I'd barely even noticed she had music playing. It was some acoustic song with a dude singing; I'd later found out it was Stereophonics, "You're My Star." But at the time, I didn't know what song it was. Only that Maggie apparently loved it, and I'd ruined it for her.

I really hope something can save this song for me one day, she'd told me, *because you've just ruined it for me. You know, I heard it for the first time a few months ago and I thought, now there's a song I'd love to have play at my wedding someday. But I guess you ruined that, too. Lucky me... I got married in Vegas in some tacky theme chapel, to my dad's bullshit "Schoolgirl" song playing on repeat.*

Objectively, I knew that part was her dad's fault as much as it was mine, but at that moment, I wasn't gonna argue the finer points with her.

Married to a man who can't keep it in his pants to save his life, she'd added. *Or at least, to save his marriage.*

And she was right. I didn't keep it in my pants.

As a husband, I was a fucking failure.

Out in the world, I was a rock star. Like Seth said; I was a superstar.

I didn't set out to be a superstar.

I set out to be a musician, and the rest was golden icing on the cake. I was never gonna say I didn't want it. Far from it; I got a taste of the sweet life at twenty-two, when Dirty's debut album hit, and all I wanted was more.

There was a time I'd fucking glutted myself on it.

And in that life, in the eyes of the world, I was a kind of demigod.

But in Maggie's eyes... a failure.

A man who'd pretty much tricked her into marrying him, then failed to be any kind of decent husband.

Fact was, I didn't know how to make her happy, and it fucking killed me. When it came to my relationship with Maggie, I *felt* like a fucking failure. Every time I looked at her and she looked back at me with those all-seeing gray eyes of hers, I felt like a fucking fraud.

And every time I disappointed her, all the ugly shit it stirred up in me... It was the kind of ugly shit that, when I was drinking, would've flipped me right into self-destruct mode.

I didn't drink, but there was always weed and a lot of it.

And there were always women.

A lot of them.

I hadn't been with all that many women since I'd married Maggie... but since when was even one okay?

According to Maggie, it wasn't, no matter how bad things were between us.

According to my conscience, it wasn't either. Which just made me want to drink.

Which made me want to smoke up.

Vicious fucking cycle.

It wasn't like I wanted to be a failure or a fraud. Wasn't like I'd accepted those fucking roles in Maggie's life.

I fought them like hell, and I still failed.

I kept trying to please her, trying to give her what I thought she wanted so I could win her over, and all I did was fuck it up. I'd tried to win her over with sex about a million times, but just because she'd fucked me a handful of times didn't mean it was any kind of victory. I knew that now.

She wanted me, and just like her love for me, that want probably went way back, too.

So she'd let me have her body.

She'd never let me near her heart.

She was protecting herself from me, and for good reason.

As I went over all this shit in my head, I knew she'd already told me all this stuff at some point or another. A lot of it, she'd told me repeatedly.

That she didn't trust me. That she couldn't give me her heart. That she couldn't love me because I made it impossible for her to do that.

I'd just never heard her.

I didn't want to believe her, because I'd convinced myself that all I had to do was get her between the sheets again and she'd come around to the inescapable truth that we were meant to be together.

But if we were meant to be together, I should've been able to get my shit together and treat her right, right?

I didn't treat her right.

I treated her like every other woman I'd tried to get into bed. Like sex with her was some kind of currency. Something I could use to persuade her to open up to me.

Or something I could use to hurt her, by having sex with other women when she'd hurt me.

Sex was the most powerful tool I'd ever had when it came to women, and with Maggie, all my other shit was pretty much useless anyway. My talent, my fame; she took those in stride. Because of her job, and long before that, her fucking dad, she was surrounded by rock stars and all the bullshit that came with them. Unlike so many other women I met, none of that shit was gonna faze her or impress her.

I'd tried the money thing, maybe just a little, with the engagement ring and the watch. But I knew that really wasn't gonna do it either.

Sex. Sex was the only thing that ever let me through Maggie's wall.

If that really wasn't gonna do it anymore... what the fuck did I have?

I was powerless.

Powerless, just like I was with my fucking addiction. And the only thing that ever worked to get me off the booze was to completely surrender to the fact that I was powerless. That I had a weakness. A destructive obsession that was wreaking utter fucking havoc on my life, that would destroy my life. That I needed help.

That I couldn't overcome it alone.

And that no one else could fix it for me, either.

I had to do it myself—with help and support. Because I didn't have all the answers. My sponsor didn't have all the answers. As wise as his ass sounded, Seth didn't have all the answers.

And as much as I would've loved to find them deep in Maggie's pussy, she didn't have all the answers, either.

The truth was I'd been living like I'd overcome all this shit, like I was done with it. I'd hoped I was done with it... but I'd never be done.

The path of recovery was a long and winding road, and one I'd just have to keep walking. Some people, for a time, would walk it with me. When I asked for help, and even when I didn't.

I might fall down, and I might fuck up.

I had no idea what tomorrow would bring.

I only knew there was no cure for what I had.

It was part of me.

But in this moment, right now, the only moment I had, I wasn't drinking. I wanted to drink, but I wasn't gonna drink.

And I was always gonna walk this road.

Like Seth said in the song he wrote, it was the road to hell and back.

We'd both been to hell. We'd both hit bottom, young and fast. And we'd both be walking back from that place for the rest of our lives.

Seth, that fortunate bastard, had fallen in love with a woman who loved him enough to walk that road with him.

I just didn't know if Maggie was ever gonna walk mine with me.

And if she wouldn't... Was I ever gonna find a reason to do it, besides keeping air in my lungs, that would feel worthwhile?

Because at the end of the day, the music and the money, the fame and the fans and all the pussy in the universe didn't make it worthwhile.

Nothing made it feel worthwhile, without her.

Because I loved her.

I wasn't addicted to Maggie. She wasn't some obsession, and I wasn't gonna let her kill me. She could try, but it wasn't happening.

I just wanted to love her.

As I made my way back to the car, the sky was lightening to a pale violet-gray in the east. Some clouds were bunched around the mountains on the horizon, the sun about to break through, a new day about to start.

Fucking Buddha of the desert had fallen asleep.

I kicked his snakeskin boot and he jolted awake. He straightened his hat and sat up with a shiver. "Fuck. It's cold."

"No shit."

"I've got a bottle of Jack in my hotel room."

Seth said nothing in response to my confession as he drove.

I raked my hand through my hair, clawing it back from my face. Not even a couple of hours of pacing in the desert had mellowed me out. If anything, I was more agitated than before.

And I was fucking jonesing.

"What," I fired at him, "you just spewed more words at me in that desert than I've probably ever heard out of your mouth, and now you've got nothing to say?"

He said nothing.

I sighed, but it came out an aggravated growl.

"Okay. *Fuck*, you're an asshole. The truth is, I do this sometimes. Most of the time. *No.* All the time. I have a full, sealed bottle on me. On the road. At home. Everywhere." I glanced at him. He just kept his eyes on the road ahead.

Nothing.

Seth said not one thing.

I sighed again.

"You ever hear that thing about Gandhi," I asked him, "how he slept surrounded by naked women to prove he could resist temptation?"

Fucking finally, he spoke. "Sounds like bullshit."

"Maybe."

"So you got a bottle with you, what, to prove you can resist the temptation?"

"I tell myself it's this monument to my sobriety, that I can resist it, that it doesn't have control of me anymore. But in reality, it's there to assure me that I can have it if I break the fuck apart and need it."

Seth didn't say anything.

"I've never told anyone that."

"Even your sponsor?"

"Even Rudy."

"Then here's what we do. We get back to the hotel, we get rid of that bottle. Then you call Rudy and you tell him."

I wasn't gonna argue with that. And I knew what I was in for. Rudy was pretty much Seth, still sober and twenty years into the future.

"There's this thing Rudy always says. Something about fame and fortune... how it gives you the means to have a fantastic life, or to fantastically kill yourself."

Seth gave a dry laugh. "True enough."

"I don't know what the fuck I'd do without him. If it wasn't for Rudy, I think I might be dead." There was a weird lump in my throat as the truth of that sat, heavy in my chest. "If it wasn't for Maggie..." I didn't even finish that sentence. "You know, I got sober a few months after I met her. She was a big part of that. I mean, she probably doesn't know it. But she was."

"There were plenty of times I would've killed myself," Seth said, "if it wasn't for someone saving my ass. Elle, finding me on the floor after I'd OD'd on that tour bus. Jude, getting me into rehab, over and again. My foster father, giving me a home and a name and some pride. You," he said, glancing over at me, "picking me up off the street and bringing me home, bringing me into the band. Jessa and Jesse and Dylan... there were a lot of people over the years who cared about me."

"Yeah."

"You need people in your corner, Zane, but you can't get clean for them."

I didn't say anything.

"No one wants to be your reason," he said. "Maggie doesn't want to be the reason you drink, and she doesn't want to be the reason you stay sober. Don't put that on her. This is all *you*."

I sighed and rubbed my hands over my face.

I don't want to be the reason you don't fuck other women, and I don't want to be the reason you don't drink, or the reason you don't end up in jail.

That's what she'd said to me.

We can't just keep having sex.

I can't handle more.

She'd said that, too. Admitted she couldn't handle what was between us.

And I couldn't handle *anything*. Not like this.

I definitely couldn't handle losing her.

Jesus and fuck. Were we seriously doomed? Because we were both too fucked-up to keep a relationship together?

"What do I do if I can't fuck her?" I gave Seth a sharp look when I felt his response to that. "Don't laugh. I'm serious."

"Okay."

"What the fuck do I do if I can't touch her?"

He looked at me, a few times, before answering. "What were you gonna do, just fuck all your problems away?"

Silence. I didn't fucking answer that.

And maybe it slowly dawned on him that that was exactly what I was gonna do. I'd been fucking away my problems with women for years. Thing was, that approach had always been sufficient before, since I never wanted any of those other women to stick around *after* we fucked.

"Have you talked to her?" he asked me. "You know you can actually talk to her, right?"

"Uh-huh," I said, but mostly just to get him to stop talking. Was already sorry I asked. "Stop fucking laughing."

"I'm not.

"I can hear it in your head."

Silence.

Then he burst the fuck out laughing, until I punched him on the shoulder and he reeled it in.

"Okay," he said, biting back his shit. "So try this. Next time you feel like fucking Maggie, keep your pants on, sit on your fucking hands, and talk to her instead."

"About what?"

"About the weather and the state of the economy. What do you think?"

"I've already told her how I feel about her. She doesn't even want to hear it. And by the way, for a nice guy, the level of sheer dickheadedness that comes out of you is stunning at times. Has Elle seen this side of you?"

"Never claimed to be a nice guy. And unfortunately, Elle's seen every side of me." He said that in a way that made my stomach turn.

Reminded me exactly what she'd seen.

I'd seen the aftermath of it, the medics hauling Seth's lifeless-looking body out to the ambulance on a stretcher, and that was bad enough. Elle was the one who'd found him unconscious, covered in puke and blood.

"And by the way," he said, "the amount of women you've been with, the lack of shit you know about the female gender is stunning."

"Yeah?"

"Yeah. I thought I had a hard time understanding women..."

I stared at him. Then I took off his hat and pulled it down on my head. "I'm keeping this hat."

A grin flickered over Seth's face, dimple and all. "Look, if I can tell you're in love with Maggie, I'm pretty sure Maggie can tell you're in love with Maggie. She probably doesn't need to hear how you feel about her as much as she needs to hear all the other shit."

"What other shit?"

"You know what shit. If you're trying to be a rock star for her, trying to be that guy who only exists on the album cover and on the stage, that's never gonna last."

I slid down deeper into my seat and crossed my arms, tucking my hands in my armpits. The sun was up now; we'd been up all night. But I was still listening to every word Seth said.

"She needs the shit you don't wanna say, brother. The shit you don't talk about with anyone else. Your addiction, your demons, whatever it is. You can't talk to her about that shit..." He shook his head. "Might as well burn that marriage certificate they gave you two in Vegas."

When we got back to the hotel, Seth cracked open my bottle of Jack Daniels and flushed it down the toilet, along with all my weed. He rinsed the bottle and took it with him when he left, so I wouldn't even have to smell the fumes. He also took my rolling papers and my lighters.

As soon as I was alone, I sat down on the bed and called my sponsor. It was early, but Rudy was already up, having his morning coffee with his wife.

I told him everything.

I told him about the bottle of Jack. I told him about the wedding and everything I'd fucked up with Maggie. And he listened, because that was what Rudy did best.

At the end of the call, I told him I'd check in again later. And he actually said to me, "Proud of you, son."

Rudy never told me he loved me, but truth was, over the years he'd become much more than my sponsor. I looked to him like something of a father figure and we'd crossed a line there that probably wasn't ideal, but I didn't care.

Fuck it. I loved the guy.

"Give Laney my love." Laney was Rudy's wife, and while I never told him I loved him, either, I'd tell his wife, which was pretty much the same thing.

When we got off the phone, I texted Shady to let him know I was back. I was planning to call Brody to ask him if we could talk—but according to the texts he'd sent me, he was up.

And he was here in Vegas.

I scrolled through the many, many text messages on my phone. Apparently, right after the giant scene I'd caused in the diner—on the heels of that other scene I'd caused with the TV crew the day before—Jude had been on the phone to Brody in Vancouver, and Brody had flown straight out.

Which meant they were worried about me.

Fuck me.

As it turned out, they'd been up all night. Brody, Jude and Maggie, who were all in Brody's hotel room.

I had missed calls and voicemails from all of them.

Jude: *Hey, brother. Shady says you just took off with Seth in my rental car. No idea where you're going, but check in, alright?*

Brody: *Hey, Zane. I wanted to talk to you and Maggie, but no one can seem to find you, so... Call me or send me a text, yeah? Let me know where you are.*

Maggie: *Hey. Where are you? Everyone's flipping out. It's almost dawn and they all think you've gone off on some bender and maybe Seth has, too. Elle's being the voice of reason here. She's trying to convince Brody that there's no way Seth would do that, and they're, uh, calming down. But... can you please call someone and just let us know you're okay?*

Maggie: *Zane. Everyone's worried about you, okay? Please call.*

Her voice sounded so small and faraway. She was fucking worried about me, and who knew what the guys had put in her head if they were flipping out about me going off the deep end in Vegas.

I would've liked to believe that she'd know I wouldn't, but *shit.* Wasn't even gonna kid myself that I'd ever given her that kind of faith in me.

There were more messages, but I stopped listening and got my ass over to Brody's hotel room.

Brody opened the door, but I barely saw him.

Maggie was slumped in a chair clutching a takeout coffee cup, and she didn't even look at me. But I saw her give a kind of sobbing sigh as Jude pulled me into his arms. Her eyes were pink, but not like she'd been crying. She looked miserable.

I'd never seen her look like that.

"We were worried about you, brother." Jude slapped me on the back and I hugged him back.

"Yeah. Sorry. Didn't even think about that. Just had some shit to deal with."

When he released me, Brody's hands were at his hips. He shook his head. He was pissed, obviously, probably because of that look I'd put on Maggie's face.

"Fuck, you're an asshole." He sighed and swept me up in a hug, then released me. "Sit your ass down. Please."

I sat in a chair across the coffee table from Maggie. Brody sat down on the couch and Jude stood.

"You gonna tell us why you took off?" Brody nodded at Maggie. "You had Maggie worried."

I looked at her. She still wouldn't look at me.

"I... uh..." I cleared my throat; kinda felt like I'd tried to swallow a whole, live frog. "I wanted a drink."

No one said anything.

"So Seth took me for a drive."

"Where?" Brody asked.

"Out of town. Into the desert." I knew what they were all probably picturing. Me going hog-wild at some strip joint. "We talked for a bit."

"You alright?" Jude asked.

"I will be."

"Did you drink?" When I looked at Brody again, he was staring at me, hard and direct. "You know I've gotta ask, brother."

"I didn't drink."

When I looked at Maggie again, her eyes finally lifted to mine. Gray and soft, raw and pink. She blinked like she was holding back tears. But I saw the relief in her shoulders as they softened a bit.

Then she kept staring at me, and I had to look away.

"I had some time to think," I told them all, staring at the coffee table, "and I talked some shit through with Rudy just now. The way I see it, I've gotta cut myself some slack, but not too much. So I've given myself two choices. I can leave the tour right now and check myself into rehab before I actually drink, or I can get my shit together right here, on tour, before I drink. Because drinking is not an option. I've decided, after talking to Rudy, that I'm giving myself one chance. Just one. And if I break, if I fuck up and take a drink, I'm asking Jude to take me to rehab."

"Yeah, brother," Jude said. "Whatever you need. You've got my support to stay on the tour. You know that. I've got your back and Shady's got your back, and the second you need anything to change, you say the word. You need me to take you to rehab, I take you, no questions asked."

I glanced up at Jude. He was standing there with his big arms crossed and his dark eyes leveled at me. I nodded, swallowing around the lump in my throat.

"Same goes with the weed," I said. "I'm done with it."

The expression on Jude's face didn't falter. Whether he believed I could hold up my end of that or not, he didn't show any sign of doubt. "Okay."

I glanced at Brody, and he nodded too. "We're all onboard," he said. "Whatever you need."

"Good. Because I'm gonna need you guys to work out a new schedule for me, keep me busy during the day. But no interviews for a while. And no meeting fans backstage. We can tell them I'm saving my voice for the shows. I need the shows. But I can't handle the people in my face right now."

"You've got it," Brody said.

"And I need no booze or drugs backstage."

"Not a problem," Jude said.

"It's not forever, just for a while. Seth's gonna be around when I want to talk. I'm gonna need support." I felt Maggie's eyes on me, and I couldn't even look at her. "I know it's not her job, but since Talia won't be as tied up with my promo shit, I thought maybe she could find me AA meetings to go to, each town we hit. You know I don't want all that Betty Ford shit. I like going to regular meetings with regular people in whatever church basement. I don't care."

"Yeah, Zane," Brody said, his voice soft. "We know."

I lowered my head. I was getting fucking teary-eyed, but I didn't want to cry. I just couldn't believe I was having a moment like this, when I'd convinced myself all these moments were behind me now. That I had all my shit under control.

Seth was right, though. I was out of control.

And I was falling apart in front of the people who loved me most.

"I'm sorry," I said, and my voice fucking broke. "I'm sorry I'm putting this on you all right now, when I should've dealt with it before the tour. I can see that now."

Someone moved in, and I saw Jude's boots in front of me. He pulled me up into another hug. "You know we'd do anything for you, brother," he said, quietly, right in my ear. "Anything you need."

When he released me, Maggie was right there. She reached for me and I scooped her into my arms, hugging her so tight I almost couldn't breathe. I wasn't expecting her to come anywhere near me, but she was hugging me right back, tight.

She didn't say anything, and when she started to let go, I let her go.

Brody was looking from me to her, as we stood side-by-side but not touching. "And what about this... uh... marriage?" He looked uncomfortable, if anything, so I figured they didn't talk about it without me here.

But someone had definitely told him what I'd said at the diner.

Got the feeling it wasn't Maggie.

I didn't even have to look at her now to know what she'd want me to say.

"Me and Maggie," I said, forcing the words out, "we're not together."

When Brody's gaze flicked to her, out of the corner of my eye, I saw Maggie give a little nod of agreement.

"Who else knows about this?" he asked.

"My dad and his girlfriend," Maggie said softly. "They were at the wedding, but they won't tell anyone."

"Flynn was there, too," Jude said.

"Shady knows, and so does Seth," I said. "I told them. And Rudy."

I felt Maggie looking at me, and I met her eyes. I shrugged a little and she rolled her eyes.

"Fuck," she said, sighing, and she looked at Brody. "I told Jessa. I'm sorry, Brody."

Pretty sure we both read the look on Brody's face at that one... as he realized his woman knew about our secret bullshit and never told him.

Jesus. I did not want to be there for that conversation.

"I asked her not to tell anyone," Maggie added gently.

"Anyone else?" he asked. And I knew Brody; he was trying not to be pissed off, but he was pissed off.

"Not that I know of," she said.

I shook my head. I didn't think anyone else knew. Suspected something was up, maybe.

"We all need some sleep," Brody concluded with a heavy sigh. "I'm gonna be in touch with Alec, let him know we'll roll out to the arena a little later than usual today. And let's call a band meeting for tomorrow night, when we get into Salt Lake. Lay a few things out for everyone." He looked at me. "The whole band needs to know what's going on so we can all be on the same page about your sobriety." Then he told Maggie, "Let's circle tomorrow before that and go over some things."

"Sure."

"I'm assuming we want to keep the whole marriage thing under wraps?"

"Yes," Maggie said.

"And I'm assuming Rudy is tight?" he asked me.

"He'd never tell anyone my shit," I said.

"You want to talk to Flynn and Shady?" Brody asked Jude. "Make sure they know to keep their mouths shut?"

"They know," Jude said. "But yeah, I'll talk to them." He glanced at Maggie, then nodded at me, patting my shoulder as he left.

"I can clear Zane's promotional schedule and have Talia help," Maggie told Brody. "I'll get her on top of mapping out some open AA meetings in advance of each city, and coordinate with Zane whatever he needs. We'll have the other band members cover his interviews. Everyone's wanting to talk to Matt and Elle and Seth right now anyway, about the baby and her being off the tour, and what it's like for Matt filling in for her, all that stuff. We can definitely make it work."

"Good," Brody said.

"Can I go now? I have some calls to make."

"Yeah. But make sure you get some sleep, Maggie."

Maggie nodded, then glanced at me. I really couldn't read that look, but it was somewhere between sympathy and uncertainty.

I wanted to reach out and pull her into my arms again.

But then she left.

Brody looked me in the eye as soon as the door had shut behind her. "Anything you need. Whatever it is. I don't care what time it is. I don't care what it is or where you are or how bad it is, or what you think I'm gonna think. You call me, and I'll get you what you need. No judgment. I'll make sure you have whatever you need. As long as it's not booze or drugs. Or anything that's gonna make Maggie kick me in the balls."

I would've laughed at that, but I wasn't in the laughing mood. "Thank you," I forced out.

"I mean it. The tour doesn't go on without you. That's not pressure, Zane, that's fucking reality. We went on without Seth for years. We all felt the loss, but we went on. And it sucks, but we're doing a whole tour without Elle. We could go on without Jesse or Dylan, have someone fill in for them for a while. Wouldn't be the same, but we'd make it work. But we can't do it without you. We're never gonna do it without you. You're our frontman, and it doesn't work without you, without your voice. Everyone in the band knows that. We've already discussed it."

What? *When?*

He held up his hand to silence me, like he knew what I was gonna ask. "We already talked about it, years ago, when you went into rehab. The show doesn't go on without you. Dirty isn't Dirty without Zane Traynor, and we all know it. You need this tour to stop, you need everything to stop, then it stops."

I just nodded. I couldn't get any more words out. I moved toward him and he pulled me in for another hug. He hugged me for a while, and when he let me go he said, "Proud of you, brother."

I headed for the door before I started crying like a baby. I was fucking exhausted. Emotionally tapped out.

"And this Maggie thing," he said behind me, all the softness leaving his voice. I paused and glanced back at him. "We'll talk about that later, yeah?"

"Yeah," I said.

Then I went to my room to try to get some sleep, because I had a show to do tonight. My band was counting on me, and fuck if I was gonna let Dirty suffer because of me.

CHAPTER FOURTEEN

Maggie

THE NEXT DAY, I woke up late. I hadn't even fallen asleep until well after dawn, again. I'd been up all night after the Vegas show, unable to sleep, but I still hadn't fully processed everything that had happened.

Everything I'd done wrong.

All I knew was I'd hurt Zane in a profound way.

I'd spoken briefly with Alec and Brody before the show yesterday, but mercifully no one brought up my marriage to Zane or the whole ugly incident the other night. Brody wasn't going to let it go; I knew he wasn't. But for the time being, he looked like he felt too sorry for me to say anything.

It was early afternoon when I climbed onto the Lady Bus. Most of the buses had already hit the road to Salt Lake City, but some of us took our time rallying out of Vegas. Luckily there was no big hurry, and no one was complaining.

As I quickly discovered, the news about the little drama the other night had spread—especially after last night's show, when Jude's crew cleared out all the booze backstage and security was extra tight—and everyone was concerned.

The girls on the Lady Bus all seemed relieved that Zane had

resurfaced from the desert sober and unscathed, but they knew this was serious; they were all waiting for me in the lounge.

Talia gave me a hug. "Is he okay?" she asked me. Joanie and Sophie were waiting for the answer to that question, too.

We'd all witnessed his performance at last night's show. He was great; his voice sounded great. But he was definitely tense. There was a ton of tension at the show, and no one was exactly smiling backstage.

The whole crew felt it.

Zane's alcohol addiction was no secret to anyone on Dirty's crew, and obviously everyone cared about his continued sobriety. They either cared because they truly cared about Zane, and/or because they were scared they'd be out a job if the tour fell apart.

"Yeah," I said. "He's okay. But there are gonna be some changes. We're having a band meeting tonight, and I'll have some things to go over with you."

"Of course," Talia said. "Anything I can do to help..."

"Let me know if I can help, too," Joanie offered. "I honestly don't know how Zane does it, being around booze all the time, and the rest of the band drinking. Seth, too. If there's anything we can do to make it a more supportive environment for both of them, I'd be happy to help any way I can. I know Elle will, too."

"Thank you."

"Yeah," Sophie agreed. "Zane is so sweet. I feel so bad for him."

That made me pause and smile. I didn't often hear a woman describe Zane Traynor as *sweet*. But Sophie was pretty sweet herself.

"I didn't get much sleep the last couple nights, so I'm just gonna rest for a bit," I informed them. "We'll talk later," I told Talia, before disappearing into my bunk.

I put on some music in my earbuds and lay down. I'd barely been up for two hours, but the day felt long.

Maybe because I kinda felt like I'd been run over by a very large truck the other night, and I still hadn't recovered.

I'd been so fucking worried about Zane.

I'd never been more relieved than when he walked into Brody's hotel room... just to see him in one piece. I was mad, too, but so relieved to find out he'd been with Seth in the desert. That he didn't drink or do something else stupid.

Like fall into the arms of some random woman.

It kinda stunned me, actually, because when he'd walked out of my hotel room after I told him *I can't do this with you* and *Love isn't enough*, the look on his face... It was kinda like he was in shock. Like he definitely didn't want to hear what he'd just heard. Like he needed to find somewhere to sit down—somewhere far away from me—and lean on something for a while.

Like maybe a case of booze.

If I'd ever truly and deeply feared that Zane might pick up a bottle, that moment was it.

I'd asked him to sit back down, because honest to God I thought he might pass out or something. He was in a weird kind of daze... kinda like what happened before he went onstage sometimes. Like this private, mini panic attack, where he disappeared inside himself and went blank.

It scared the shit out of me.

When he didn't stop, when he left the room despite my protests, I decided it would be better to let him go, give him space.

But then Jude called me looking for him. He told me Brody was flying out to talk to me and Zane, and I quickly discovered that no one could find him... and I panicked.

For the next few hours, I ran through every horrendous possibility in my head.

He was fucking someone else.

He was drinking.

He'd been arrested.

He was injured.

Each scenario just got worse and worse, until I actually feared, when he didn't answer his phone the umpteenth time I called, that he might be dead.

That all our bullshit had pushed him to drink, and now he was gone.

Forever.

When he came back, and I hugged him in Brody's hotel room and I felt his warmth, smelled his familiar smell and felt his heart beating against my chest, so strong... I didn't want to let go. I never wanted to let him go again.

But I knew—that wasn't up to me anymore.

I wanted a drink.

Hearing Zane say those words... it crushed me.

Because of me, because I'd hurt him, he could've gone on a bender that ended in some horrendous tragedy... A tragedy that might've been avoided if I'd stopped fighting him. If I'd just let myself love him.

But he didn't drink. Instead he came back and told us what happened.

Which meant that whatever Zane and I were going through, together or apart, I knew it wasn't up to me anymore to decide if and when it was okay for me to get close to him again.

It was up to Zane.

That night in Salt Lake City, we had our band meeting in the hotel, in Brody's room. No one was in the room except the members of Dirty and me, Brody, Jude and Shady.

Brody filled everyone in on the situation, and he pulled no punches. The fact that Zane had almost drank in Vegas. That he was giving himself one chance to continue with the tour and stay sober while he did it.

That he wasn't smoking weed anymore.

That it was the responsibility of every person in this room to support him.

He informed them all that Talia would be handling Zane's

personal schedule. That Zane would be spending his time at the gym and AA meetings in favor of parties and bars, and that until further notice there would be no booze and no drugs of any kind backstage.

He also informed them that yes, Zane and I were married, legally, but that we currently weren't together, and beyond that, it was the business of absolutely no one but Zane and I.

Brody did all the talking, so Zane and I wouldn't have to. When he was done, he asked, "Any questions?"

There were no questions at all. We'd all been through this before—at least, the addiction part—and we all knew how serious it was. And one thing I knew for sure: every person in this room cared more about Zane than about the tour.

"I have something to say," Zane said, turning to Matt. "I owe you an apology for flipping my shit on you. Maggie said you weren't doing anything out of line. Just hard for me to see it that way. I get kinda bent out of shape about it, you know, since she's my wife."

Everyone was silent. It probably wasn't lost on anyone that Zane had just described me as his wife. Again.

And there was definitely a little bite in his tone. Kinda like an apology-slash-laying-of-claim.

I felt Elle's eyes on me.

"I didn't know, man," Matt said.

"No one knew," I offered, trying to let Matt off the hook. Maybe *some* people knew, but it wasn't Matt's fault he didn't.

Matt glanced at me, then looked at Zane again. "I'm not gonna lie," he added, cautiously, "and pretend my intentions were entirely honorable. But it won't happen again."

Zane's eyes narrowed as he considered that. Then he said, "Then we don't have a problem."

There was nothing else to discuss, at least not in a group setting, so the meeting broke. I was relieved to see Matt walk up to Zane and the two of them have a hug. By the looks of things, everyone else was headed in Zane's direction to do the same.

I headed for the door, but Elle caught up to me. For a pregnant woman, she moved pretty quick.

"Are you alright, Maggie?" she asked me, her steel-gray eyes full of concern. She smoothed a hand over her belly and studied me.

"Yeah," I said. "I'm alright."

"If you want to talk..."

"I don't want to talk right now. Is that okay?"

"Of course," she said. "Of course it's okay. If you change your mind, you know where to find me."

"I do," I said. Then I thanked her and slipped out.

I was standing backstage at the Salt Lake City show two nights later. It was only the second concert Zane would play without smoking up in God-knew-how-long.

And I was nervous for him.

I was with him and the rest of the band in a dressing room, and he didn't look particularly nervous. He was talking with Jesse and Seth, joking around and semi-arguing about the changes they'd made to the set list, and I just watched him.

At every show on this tour, for a few minutes before the band went onstage, they'd had this alone time. Only the band, Jude and me were welcome in the room, and of course Brody, if he was in town.

Everyone else had to wait outside while Dirty got ready to take the stage together.

I didn't always join into these informal little meetings, but when I did, I didn't say much. I just stood back and kept out of the way in case I was needed.

Which was exactly what I did tonight.

Usually, Jesse busted out the bourbon and everyone except Zane and Seth did a shot right before showtime. I was pretty sure Jesse still did his pre-show shot with Katie, but he kept it on the downlow; there was definitely no booze in this room.

When it was time to hit the stage, we all headed out, Jude in the lead and me in back. But just before he went onstage, Zane reached back and caught my hand.

We were standing at the bottom of the stairs leading up to the stage, and while the rest of the band headed up, he gave me a hug. But he didn't say anything.

Then he ran up there and did his thing.

I watched him perform from backstage with Katie. He looked gorgeous, as usual, with his hair all white-blond under the lights and sweat running down his face, a little smudge of black eyeliner that made his blue eyes pop. His arms looked chiseled in his sleeveless Danzig T-shirt, his shoulders broad. He was wearing charcoal-black leather pants; Zane didn't often wear leather pants, but when he did... as he ran around the stage, they clung to him in a way that made me bite my tongue.

He was *incredible* tonight, and listening to him sing had my heart racing. Especially when he sang, "I'll Go," which they'd just added to the set list.

My heart always raced when Zane sang. But this time, my respect for him was exploding, too.

He hadn't broken when I feared he would.

And I realized, as I watched him out there, rocking the place down—clean and sober—that I'd never actually believed he'd be able to give up pot. I'd doubted his ability to do that in every way.

To be fair, I'd never seen him totally give up pot before.

But I'd definitely never believed that he could or that he *would*.

The truth was, I never believed he actually wanted to.

Now, I was seeing him in a whole new light...

It had only been a few days. But Zane had stopped smoking pot, on his own, because he wanted to.

Just like that.

I was afraid it wouldn't stick.

I was afraid he'd change his mind or fall apart or just plain fail.

But I was hopeful, too.

For the first time in... *ever*, I actually had hope that Zane might stay clean.

And what that could mean for *us*...? I wasn't even sure I could go there yet.

But yes. It gave me hope.

It gave me even more hope, in a weird way, when at the same time he'd stopped smoking pot, he'd also stopped trying to get in my pants.

It wasn't like he'd lost his mojo or anything.

That much was clear.

As I watched him out on that stage, he was still just as sexy as he'd ever been. And all the women out there, screaming for him? They clearly agreed with me.

Zane Traynor was as hot as ever.

Hotter.

Was that possible...?

Was it possible that I was even more attracted to him when he wasn't coming on to me all the time?

I'd been through something like this with Zane once before, seven years ago. After I'd first come to work with Dirty and he first got sober. But even then, when he came back from rehab and was working through his recovery, he never stopped trying to get in my pants.

Never.

And he never really stopped smoking up.

This time, he hadn't even tried to touch me or flirt with me. Not since the shit hit the fan in Vegas.

But he didn't seem angry, either. He wasn't acting distant or cold or mean.

He was definitely a little moody. He seemed anxious, twitchy and restless offstage. And he seemed anxious around me, for sure.

I knew it was to be expected. I'd talked to Seth a bit about marijuana withdrawal, what he knew about it, and I'd read up on it a bit.

Offstage, Zane was showing most of the signs that could be expected of someone who'd just stopped smoking, cold-turkey.

But he also seemed happy. I'd never thought of Zane as an

unhappy person, until I saw him so happy right now, onstage... Though maybe happy wasn't even the right word?

Awake, maybe.

Focused.

Present.

He seemed fully present, and it was amazing to be around.

He was vibrant up on that stage. And when he came off, he was glowing. He seemed calm, and not because a fat joint was waiting to help him get there.

His blue eyes met mine, and he walked over to me. He pulled me in for a steaming hug; he was literally dripping with sweat. His clothes were soaked. He smelled like himself times a hundred, pheromones and sex god mixed with the musk of sweat.

I hugged him back.

And before I could tell him *You were amazing out there tonight*, he said in my ear, "You look so pretty, Maggie." Then he released me and he was gone, headed off to his dressing room with Shady... without even trying to grope me.

It was so entirely new and different.

And I liked it.

After the show in Salt Lake, the *Hell & Back* tour continued to roll smoothly along.

Night after night, Zane was incredible onstage. The whole band was incredible, and the way everyone pulled together to support Zane... it almost brought me to tears. I got choked up sometimes, just watching Dirty perform.

But I kept the tears to myself.

"Somewhere" had been released as the second single off the *To Hell & Back* album, and had quickly joined the "To Hell & Back" single at the top of the charts. The video for "Somewhere" was gorgeous, moving, and deceptively simple—like the song itself—featuring the members of Dirty playing the song out in the desert.

Concert footage would be filmed at our two upcoming shows in Chicago for the "Blackout" video, which would be the next single.

Things were going so well with this album and tour so far, actually, that it was exceeding all our wildest dreams. Brody and I were hopeful that this album, overall, would be Dirty's second most successful album of all time in terms of sales and the charts; second only to *Love Struck*, Dirty's debut.

And we were on track to pull it off. The tenth-anniversary angle and the strength of the songwriting that Seth and Jessa Mayes had brought back to the band were proving a major win with the fans and the industry at large.

I felt hopeful about the future, in a way I hadn't allowed myself to feel in a long time.

Hopeful for Dirty.

Hopeful for myself and for Zane.

We still weren't together. But my feelings for him hadn't changed. By now, I knew how I felt about Zane.

I wasn't even gonna try to kid myself about it anymore.

I wasn't with anyone else, had never even wanted to be with anyone else since I married him, so I had no intention of being with anyone else now.

And I knew he wasn't with anyone else, either.

The girls were still all over him; they always would be. And who could blame them? Everywhere Zane went, Shady was constantly having to peel them off.

But he wasn't messing around—with me or anyone else.

I knew this because Talia had pretty tight tabs on him, considering she was managing his schedule. She was doing an incredible job, researching every city we were playing in advance to find AA meetings and convenient gyms for his workouts, and even picking up healthy snacks for him. She'd consult with me and I'd help organize his day, making it easy for him and Shady to navigate where they needed to be and have proper meal breaks and down time.

Zane spent a lot of time with Shady, actually, and not just because he had to. The two of them had grown really close.

It was nice to see.

Shady was in his forties and seemed to be playing the role of a laid-back older brother in Zane's life. A brother who made him laugh, watched his back, and genuinely cared about him.

I loved Shady for that.

And I loved Jude for hiring him.

Zane spent a lot of time with Jude, too, and Seth. He also spent more time with Jesse, and one of the incredible side effects of Zane giving up pot? Jesse Mayes found him far more tolerable a companion than he did when he was getting stoned all the time. Who knew?

Jesse and Zane were now hanging out together like I hadn't seen them do in years… maybe since before Jesse hooked up with Elle and tensions in the band started running high.

Dylan had become Zane's workout buddy, and instead of lazing in bed with Amber all morning, our drummer was getting up and hitting the gym with Zane. Dylan usually worked out in the afternoon; he liked to work out before he went onstage, because he was an animal like that. But he'd changed that up to fit Zane's schedule.

As for Elle, she was coming around a lot, checking on Zane, just sitting with him and talking.

That actually did make me cry, once. Seeing him like that—spending time with a female friend he wasn't trying to fuck, just talking about her pregnancy and whatever else she wanted to talk about.

Katie did her part, too. She baked Zane cookies.

When Dirty played Minneapolis, Katie and Jesse stayed with a friend of Jesse's, and Katie used their kitchen to make Zane a bunch of healthy cookies with seeds and nuts and dried fruit in them. *Rock god power cookies*, she called them. Apparently she made them for Jesse at home, because he wouldn't eat all the sweet stuff she baked.

They were delicious.

Really, it was incredible to me how the whole Dirty family was pitching in to support Zane, in ways I never would've expected.

The sense of love and care was overwhelming.

Sophie, who was younger than Zane, had seemed to take him under her wing like some doting aunt. She drank virgin Caesars with him in the mornings before he hit the gym, and soon became his unofficial hair stylist. The girl could sell merch like nobody's business, but she definitely had some serious talent with hair; hers was always in some fabulous 1940s-era updo. She'd even managed to convince Zane to let her style his fauxhawk into a victory roll for a photo shoot.

Actually looked really cool.

Then she shaved a little heart into the short hair behind his ear, and Jesse informed him that Sophie was turning him into a pussy. I disagreed. The heart was cute. And of all the guys in the band, Zane was the only one who'd ever even tried to pull off eyeliner or nail polish, and he'd succeeded. When you were as badass as Zane Traynor was, even makeup didn't change that. Heart or no, Zane was still badass.

Losing weed definitely hadn't made him lose his cool.

Far from it.

I saw him before and after every show, and I watched him sticking with the program, adhering to the schedule and the regimen Brody and Talia and I had laid out for him. Staying away from the bars and the parties and the fans.

Staying away from weed.

And I knew it couldn't be easy. I knew he'd had some physical side effects, too; stomach pains and insomnia. Cravings, obviously.

Brody had a couple of doctors check in with Zane on the road, so his withdrawal was being properly monitored. The doctors had actually recommended a more gradual detox, but Zane had insisted on sticking with the cold-turkey thing.

And he was succeeding.

I would've known if he'd gotten high; Talia and I usually had an eye on him, and I would've seen it in his eyes. I would've smelled it. I would've felt it, and I would've known by the change in his moods.

He definitely wasn't getting high, and it was stunning how quickly I could see the changes in him.

Without smoking up pretty much daily, like he'd been doing for so many years, he was more clearheaded. He was sharper and, as the peak of his withdrawal symptoms faded, he was way more even-keeled.

He was definitely more reasonable.

And he wasn't as moody.

But instead of dulling his edge, it made him shine.

He smiled easily, and it wasn't a sly, calculating smile. He wasn't laying on the charm. He wasn't trying to charm anyone. He was just smiling.

He laughed more, too.

But when he was close to me… he remained kind of reserved, if not anxious. His smiles were more tentative. He put his hands in his pockets and used few words, and usually moved on pretty quick. He didn't seem to be avoiding me, exactly. But he definitely wasn't lingering in my vicinity.

That was new.

I didn't love it, but I wasn't about to complain. I wasn't going to put any kind of pressure on Zane right now, about anything.

So I let him set the tone and the direction and the duration of each conversation, each interaction.

And at the end of each night, when he gave me a quick hug and took off, I accepted it.

For fifteen nights in a row.

Yes, I counted.

On the sixteenth night, when he tried to let me go, I tightened my arms around him.

We were standing in a restaurant near our hotel after dinner, while Jesse and Dylan took care of the bill. "Wait," I whispered. And after a moment, he softened and continued the hug. He was wearing a leather jacket, and he smelled of leather and winter and Zane.

Eventually, I let him go. He stood about a foot away from me with his hands buried in his pockets. "Good night, Maggie."

"You're going back to your room?" I asked him.

"Yeah."

It was late. We'd had a late dinner, and I knew a lot of our group was heading out for drinks after this. I wasn't sure what Madison, Wisconsin had to offer in terms of night life, especially on a frigid February night, mid-week. But whatever there was to find out there, Dirty would find it.

I could've gone with them, but all I wanted to do was hang with Zane.

Talk to him.

Touch him.

Shit, but I wanted to touch him.

"Do you, uh, want me to come with you?" I offered. It was the most awkward come-on in the history of women trying to get some. At least, that's how it felt to me. I didn't exactly have a lot of experience with trying to seduce Zane Traynor.

Usually he handled the seducing.

He just stared at me for a long moment, his jaw going kinda slack, like I'd stunned him or something.

"Maggie, uh... I don't think—" He was cut off right there by Jesse, who chose that exact moment to toss his arm around Zane and start telling him how proud he was of him for staying the sober course and all that.

Obviously he was drunk, because Jesse only got verbal about his love for Zane after a few.

I'd never hated Jesse Mayes more.

Actually, I'd never hated Jesse at all. But right now?

I gave him an incredibly dirty look, which he didn't even notice.

As I turned to walk away, Zane caught my hand. "See you tomorrow," he said, his eyes on mine. Jesse's arm was still slung around his shoulders as Zane leaned in to give me a kiss on the cheek.

Jesse went right on talking to Zane as I walked away.

"Your husband's a pussyblock," I grumbled at Katie as I made my way past her out of the restaurant.

"Oh, shit," she said, her eyes going wide.

What else could she say?

She knew about Zane and I being married; by now, everyone in the Dirty family did. But we hadn't talked about it. She'd tried; I'd shut it down. Told her I wasn't ready to talk yet.

I wasn't sure if she was more stunned by the fact that I was trying to get in Zane's pants or by the fact that her husband had pussyblocked me.

"Have fun tonight," I told her. Then I left her to get drunk and laid with her hot husband.

I disappeared back to the hotel alone, before anyone could guilt-trip me for not coming out with them.

About ten minutes later, Zane texted me.

Zane: sorry, Maggie

Zane: you surprised me

Zane: but we shouldn't be having sex

I didn't even know what to say to that, so I didn't reply.

I'd told myself to let him call the shots. I just had to be patient.

Eventually, when he was ready, he'd want to be with me again... right?

CHAPTER FIFTEEN

Maggie

WE PULLED off the road for breakfast about an hour from Chicago and I got off my bus. I didn't see Zane outside. I had some paperwork in my hand, some scheduling notes from Talia for him, as an excuse to talk to him.

Lame, obviously. But I was going with it.

After the whole *we shouldn't be having sex* thing the other night, I was thrown for a bit of a loop.

I'd already promised myself that I'd let Zane steer the direction of things and I'd respect his needs, give him time and give him space. He had more important things to deal with right now than his fucked-up marriage to me. Which meant I had to accept the quick hugs and the general non-sexuality of our relationship.

But I'd never been outright denied access to Zane's dick before. And I had to admit to myself that it made me feel weirdly off-kilter.

And a little nervous.

I'd never had a chance to relate to Zane like this before, and as much as I'd thought I wanted it, at times... I really didn't.

I mean, it was nice and all, having a little break from him chasing me all the time... for a while. But yeah. I was over that now.

I could really use an ass-squeeze or a kiss or *something*.

Anything to assure me that yes, he still felt the same about me, and yes, I was going to be able to touch him again, someday.

When I didn't see him anywhere, I went over to his bus. I'd already seen his driver disappear into the restaurant, and I found Shady smoking a cigarette outside.

"Zane's inside?" I asked, and Shady gave me a nod.

I knocked on the door, then popped my head in. "Zane?" I called.

"Yeah."

The sound of his voice, a little rough, a little soft, gave me goosebumps.

That definitely hadn't changed.

I climbed up into the bus and shut the door. Zane was standing in the lounge, alone. He'd just finished whatever he was doing on his phone and set it on the table as he turned to me.

I gripped the papers in my hand, ready to serve up my excuse for needing to talk to him... but I didn't even get that far.

He was wearing soft, plaid pajama pants—and nothing else.

They clung way-low on his hips, like not-suitable-for-children-low, and my eyes followed his chiseled abs down to the amazing sculpted V of his groin... the deep indentations inside his hipbones, and his neatly shaven, golden treasure trail... and I fucking salivated.

I must've been ovulating or something, because no matter how much I'd gotten myself off last night, I was still horny as fucking hell.

I'd been up half the night, unable to sleep, I was *that* horny.

For him.

He pulled up the pants a bit, adjusting them on his hips. It didn't do much to cover him any better, but *he pulled up his pants*.

Zane had never in his life attempted to cover more of his body in my presence.

"Uh, Maggs? Got a face up here."

My eyes jumped up to his face. His beautiful face. And *shit*, he was wearing his glasses. The little frameless glasses he wore sometimes to read and stuff.

I fucking loved his little glasses.

His light-blue eyes danced with amusement. Or maybe it was affection. But he definitely didn't smirk or gloat.

And I was reminded of that Seinfeld episode... Men get smarter when they don't have sex, and women get stupider?

I smiled a little sheepishly. "Hi."

"What's up?" he asked, gently, taking the glasses off... all laid-back and sexy.

For the last almost-three weeks, despite whatever personal hell he may have been going through with his withdrawal, he'd been all laid-back and non-cocky and fucking sensible with me—and it was definitely turning me on.

Granted, Zane Traynor had been turning me on since the day we met. Since before that, actually, if you counted all the times I'd gotten myself off fantasizing about him when I didn't even know him yet. I couldn't possibly remember all the orgasms I'd had either as a result of him touching me, or me touching myself thinking about him touching me.

But I didn't think I'd *ever* been as turned on by him as I was these past few weeks.

And *now* he didn't want to have sex with me?

I swallowed, my eyes dropping from his face, because eye contact with Zane when I wasn't supposed to be having sex with Zane was a bad idea. I tried really hard not to stare at his pierced nipple. It had a small steel barbell through it, and that tiny, sensitive dark-pink nub looked like it was just begging to be flicked by my tongue.

I remembered the way he'd groaned when I'd licked it in the past, and my clit throbbed.

"I, uh, brought you a couple of things." I laid the papers Talia had given me on the table and tried to find anywhere to stare that wasn't Zane's naked flesh.

"Thanks."

"You're welcome."

Silence.

Awkward silence.

I looked up into his eyes again… and there was that feeling.

When I'd first met Zane, every time our eyes met, there was an explosion of butterflies in my stomach. Considering I was around him all the time and soon had to witness firsthand what a manwhore he was, I managed to convince the butterflies to cool their jets.

Ever since his pilgrimage into the desert with Seth, the night he'd laid out his plan to give himself one more chance to stay sober and stay on this tour? Butterflies. A whole mad chaotic swarm of them, every time his eyes met mine.

Maybe it was how much clearer his eyes looked now that he wasn't smoking pot.

Maybe it was that calmer, steadier vibe he was starting to put off.

Maybe it was something to do with the respect I'd gained for him when he didn't fall apart but instead stood strong.

Whatever it was… it was like Zane was new to me again. In a very good way. Or at least, the butterflies hibernating in my stomach seemed to think so.

"Is that all?" he asked, when I just kept staring at him.

"No," I admitted. "I was just thinking… I miss you."

"Maggie," he said, slowly. "I really think—"

"Not like that. Not sex." *Well… not just sex.* "I just meant… I miss talking to you. I haven't really had anyone to talk to about what's been going on, you know? There's Jessa, but she's so far away."

Concern etched his features, and it felt good that he cared. I didn't want him to worry about me, but I definitely didn't want him to stop caring. "What about Katie? You two are tight."

"Yeah. But I think I feel guilty for not being honest with her all along. I feel weird talking to her about everything now, like I betrayed her or something."

"I'm sure she doesn't think that. Why don't you just talk to her?"

"Yeah. I will."

That seemed like as good a place as any to make a graceful exit.

But I made no move toward the door.

Zane's eyes scanned my face, slowly. "And, hey, if you really need someone to talk to, I could be your girlfriend. I could just tuck it."

"Tuck...?"

I glanced down, at the bulge of his dick in his thin pajama pants... then looked back up to meet his small grin.

Then I burst out laughing. I laughed until tears shimmered in my eyes.

Zane's eyes shone, too, with something like happiness.

I cleared my throat and got my shit together.

"Thank you for the offer, I guess. But... I don't want you to tuck it."

Zane's slight grin faded, but he still looked happy.

I felt my own smile vanish. "I like you the way you are," I told him, my voice kinda lusty and scratchy as I squeezed out the words.

I moved closer to him, a lot closer, and slipped my hand around the back of his neck. Then I leaned into him, stretching up on my tiptoes so I could kiss him, just a bit.

"Maggie..." he started to say, but I cut him off by pressing my lips to his. I ran my other hand down his body and grabbed his cock through his soft pants. He wasn't hard yet, but he was getting there. His cock was swollen and starting to firm. I loved the weight of it in my hand. I squeezed his cock and balls and he groaned... A few quick strokes, and he was rock-hard. Then I wrapped my hand around his fat cockhead and squeezed.

"Maggie... stop, okay?"

I heard the words he whispered against my mouth, but they didn't compute. The taste of him on my lips, the feel of him hard and ready in my hand, the smell of him... all these sensations triggered the overwhelming auto-responses in my body.

Sent all the signals to my lady parts that they knew so well...

I needed him inside me.

I knew, distantly, that he'd asked me to stop. But he didn't really mean it, right? He was so hard...

I dropped down to my knees on the floor at the same time I

yanked his pants down and got a hold of his bare cock. He swore and groaned as I fed him into my mouth, even as his hands landed on my shoulders and he started to push me back. I held on, closing my mouth around his cockhead, my hand around his shaft, and squeezed hard. Sucking and licking...

"Maggie... ah, *fuck*... babe... we can't."

His hands slid down my arms and he lifted me away, yanking me off his dick and depositing me on the couch.

I just blinked at him.

"Did you just pull me off your dick?"

He laughed shortly and kind of grimaced as he shoved his cock back in his pants, which tented ridiculously. "Yeah. I did."

"Why?" I asked, dazed, his text from last night suddenly coming back to me.

In the moment, I'd almost forgotten about it.

we shouldn't be having sex

He stared at me for a moment, his chest heaving a little with his breaths as he swiped a hand through his hair.

I'd definitely gotten him worked up, but he didn't look happy about it.

He looked uncomfortable.

Since when did sex make Zane Traynor uncomfortable?

"When I started in AA," he said slowly, "Rudy advised me not to start up any new relationships with women for at least a year. I didn't exactly listen to that. But this time, it's different. I'm not new to the program and I'm not newly sober, but dropping pot has been a big change and it's not easy for me. I don't want to fuck this up."

By *this*, I wasn't even sure if he meant the drinking thing or the pot thing or the *us* thing—or all of the above. I was still stuck on two specific words he'd said.

"*A year?* You want me to wait for you... for a year?" I swallowed thickly as my pussy throbbed in agony at the thought.

Zane's eyebrows went up. He looked genuinely surprised that I was mildly freaking out. Then the corner of his mouth turned up in the slightest hint of a smile.

"Well... maybe not a *whole* year..."

I tried to collect my thoughts. It was all a little hazy, what with the lust clouding my judgment and his dick still pointing at me. I knew, rationally, that this was what he needed. If he was setting a limit with me on this, it was important.

Zane had never set a limit with me when it came to sex.

And Brody was right; it was my responsibility to support Zane. To give him what he needed in his fight to stay sober.

His sobriety was the most important thing here.

It was definitely more important than my frustrated libido.

But that didn't change the fact that seeing him like this was such a turn-on. Everything he did and said lately was a turn-on. He just seemed so in-control, and it was so damn sexy it was killing me slowly.

I glanced down at his massive hard-on and asked him, "Are you sure?" Because as much as I knew, rationally, that I should be listening to him right now, my body was still screaming at me to jump on that dick and fuck it into next Tuesday.

When my eyes jumped back to his face, my thoughts must've been written all over me—because his eyes went almost comically-wide with panic.

"You need to go," he said, suddenly bolting for the door.

"Go?" I stared at him, my brain blanking out. I couldn't make sense of the word.

Zane had never asked me to go anywhere. Other than to bed with him, or to some party where he planned to put the moves on me.

And once, to a wedding chapel.

"I need you to go," he said, standing by the door and not even looking at me.

I blinked at him.

I got up, slowly, and went to the door. I stood in front of him and looked at his face, but he wouldn't meet my eyes.

I drifted my hand up his bare chest, just lightly, grazing his nipple piercing, and he flinched at my touch. I could feel the barely-restrained tension. I could sense every muscle hardening as his whole body went rigid.

He wanted me. I was sure of that.

I ran my hand up his neck and cupped his face. Finally, his ice-blue eyes met mine. I stood up on my tiptoes and gave him a super-quick kiss on the cheek.

"I'm sorry," I said.

"Me too." Then he reached past me and opened the door, and gently nudged me through it.

I stood in the lot outside, my back to Zane's bus as he shut the door behind me. I was partly in shock, incredibly aroused... and deeply confused.

He asked me to leave.

I just stood here for a long moment trying to process it. When it finally sank in, more or less, I started to move. I crossed the lot to my bus and climbed on, headed straight to the back, to my locker... and I started to pack.

By nine o'clock that night, I'd arrived at Jessa and Brody's home in North Vancouver. I'd called Jessa to let her know I was coming, and she'd put on a pot of tea. However, I was in the mood for something stronger and arrived with a bottle of wine in hand.

When my tour bus had arrived in Chicago, I'd gotten off the bus, gotten into a taxi and headed for the airport, and caught the next available flight to Vancouver. The first thing I did when I landed was pick up the wine. And the first thing I asked Jessa as we settled into a couple of cushy seats by the fireplace on her rooftop patio was, "Is Brody mad at me?"

"That's what you're worried about right now?" My good friend looked over at me. She'd been tinkering with her baby monitor; Nicky was sleeping inside.

Brody was in Chicago; he'd flown out for the Chicago shows and the filming of the "Blackout" video. His mom lived in Chicago, too, so maybe he'd see her while he was there.

"Yeah," I admitted, taking a generous gulp of wine. "That's one of the many things I'm worried about right now." I'd had a couple of drinks on the plane, too. Now that I wasn't around Zane, having a drink—or a few—had become top priority.

"I don't think he's mad at you. I think he's worried about you." Jessa set the baby monitor on the table and sat back in her chair. "He was mad at me, though. You know, for not telling him about you and Zane."

"Really?"

"Yeah. Really." She picked up her mug of tea and sipped.

"Shit, Jessa. I'm sorry. I should never have put that on you. I should never have asked you to keep a secret from Brody like that. He's your man. I honestly didn't think about that part when I told you."

"It's okay."

"It's not. I should never, ever have asked you to lie to Brody for me."

"You didn't. You asked me to keep your secret. And I never really lied to him. It's not like he ever asked me, 'So, do you think Maggie and Zane are secretly married?'"

I cracked a smile. "Thank God for that."

"If he'd ever asked me something like that, I don't know what I would've done. I wouldn't have been able to lie to him, even if I wanted to. But I never would've voluntarily told him, Maggie. You told me in confidence, and even Brody respected that once he got over being offended that I didn't tell him. I never said a word about it to anyone."

"I know you didn't. And thank you."

"You're welcome." She picked up her iPhone. "Music?"

"Yes, please." I sat up to refresh my wine glass; my first few gulps had already put a dent into it. "Put on your girlie mix or something."

"Uh-uh. Not what you need right now." Instead, she put on Soundgarden, "Fell On Black Days."

"Oh shit, yes." I melted back into my seat, glass of wine in hand. "This is better. Turn it up."

She did, and we both sat back and just listened, let Chris Cornell and the boys take care of things for a few minutes.

About halfway through the song, Jessa turned it down a bit. "Okay, I can't stand it. I've gotta ask. What are you going to do about Zane and the marriage thing?"

"I don't know."

"Why did you leave the tour?"

"I don't know."

"Are you going back soon?"

"I don't know."

Jessa was clearly dissatisfied with those responses. "Well... how are things between you and Zane?"

"I don't know."

"Maggie."

"I seriously don't know," I told her. "I tried to get in his pants this morning. I mean, I did get in his pants, for about two seconds. I got his cock in my mouth. And then he took it back."

"Excuse me?"

"He pulled his dick out of my mouth and told me to stop. And kicked me off his tour bus."

Jessa smushed her mouth shut, biting back her first response to that. Then she sipped her tea. "That's... um... gotta be a first."

"Yup."

Together we stared into the fire, listening to the music and the soft crackle of the flames.

"You know, everyone says he's doing well, but in reality he's probably in a pretty rough place right now," she offered. "And in the middle of a tour... You probably need to be patient with him."

"Yeah."

"You once asked me what I would do about it if I were you," she said. "About the marriage. And I told you that would depend on how much I loved him. So... how much do you love him?"

"Enough to stay married to him for almost two years, in secret, and pretty much put myself through hell."

"So," she concluded, "a lot. Enough to make a marriage work."

I looked over at her, and she was looking back at me, steady.

Jessa Mayes had changed in the last year. She'd grown up. Matured and softened and gotten stronger all at once. She looked good, too. Obviously, she always looked good. She was a lingerie model, for one. Long brown hair with golden highlights and this undeniably gorgeous face; similar brown eyes and dazzling smile as her rock star brother.

But these days, she looked like she was *feeling* good, too. Coming home, coming back to Dirty and writing with the band again, being with Brody and having baby Nick, becoming a mom and someone we could all count on... she'd become part of us again. Part of our family. It was good for her, and it was good for us.

It was good for me, because she'd become someone I could count on again.

"I've never talked to anyone else about him," I told her. "Just you."

"You can talk to me about anything, Maggie."

"Yeah."

She fiddled with her phone, and a new song started. It was "Maggie May" by Rod Stewart.

I groaned. "You're a bitch. I hate this song."

"And you forget I was there," she said, big brown eyes blinking at me innocently. "I was at the Wet Blanket show in L.A. when Zane sang this song, and you definitely didn't hate it that night. You looked pretty starry-eyed, if I recall."

"I hate you a little right now."

Jessa grinned, but she left the song playing quietly. And I wondered what I'd come here to talk to her about, exactly. Or if I'd even wanted to talk.

Maybe I just wanted to be with someone who understood.

I knew Jessa understood both Zane and substance abuse in ways maybe I didn't, and maybe never would.

"You know," I confessed, "sometimes I think he must think I'm crazy. Or other people will, when I try to explain our fucked-up relationship to them. Like maybe no one will understand why Zane smoking pot is such a big deal to me. What's wrong with someone smoking pot? It's not like he's shooting up in some skeezy alley or binging on hookers and blow. And he's not like your typical stoner cliche, you know? He's not a burnout. He's Zane Fucking Traynor. The man gets shit done. He's still a rock god, no matter how much pot he smokes."

Jessa shook her head. "It's not about that," she said gently. "It's not about the type of drug someone uses or how much they use or how fucked-up they get on it. It's the fact that he can't stop doing it. I mean, if he can't. If he chooses getting stoned over any other important thing in his life, even once... that's the addiction part. And even if it seemed under control, it won't stay that way."

"Right. I know that. I've seen it all, with my dad, you know? I know where it all leads. And Zane wasn't in control. From my point of view, things have been amazing since he stopped smoking up. But I guess we'll just have to see how it goes? I'm afraid to get my hopes up too high, Jessa."

"I don't blame you."

"Like I think when I went after his dick this morning, part of me just wanted to see what would happen. See if us fucking would trigger him to flip right back into his old ways, or if he's really done with all that shit. I don't want to be a trigger for him, and I don't want sex to be, either. I guess I don't know what might set him off, and it puts me in a scary place. It's fucked-up. I've just never known how to trust him. That's on him, because he's definitely done a lot of shit to make me lose faith in him, but it's also on me. I've got trust issues through the roof."

Jessa took that in, and she didn't seem too quick to want to blame me, but I knew I had ownership in this mess. It wasn't all Zane.

"You know, I've known Zane since we were kids," she mused. "He's always been like a brother to me. And I never messed around with him, was never infatuated with him or anything, so I probably understand him better than most women would, in a way. I never had rose-colored glasses on when it came to Zane, you know? I could see his issues pretty clearly, even when I was neck-deep in my own. I know what he's made of, and I probably know things about him that most people don't."

"Yeah. Most definitely. You see that boy you grew up with and the man he became, right? The real, multi-dimensional Zane. A lot of people can't see past the rock star thing."

"Yeah." Jessa fixed me with her brown eyes. "Which means I know he has a huge, beautiful heart, Maggie."

My chest tightened at her words and tears sparked in my eyes. Because she was right about that.

"And I know he can be loyal, and I know he's complicated."

"Yeah," I agreed.

"And I know he can be a royal fucking asshole when he wants to be."

"Amen to that."

"I know he has demons and he struggles with addiction and he's slutted his way through many a world tour," she said, "but I also know he lost his parents young, younger than I did, and I know what that does to a person. How it shapes you in a way that's so unfair, that's beyond your control because you're too young to even know it's happening. And there's this hole that stays with you, this missing piece, because you never get to find out how different you might've been if your parents had been there to parent you. I know he's far from perfect, Maggie, despite what a lot of his fans might think. And I can see why he would fall for you. If I had to choose a woman for Zane Traynor, I don't think I could find a woman better for him than you. But if you asked me if he's the right man for you... I don't think I could answer that."

"Would you think I was crazy if I said I think the answer to that is yes? And I think the only thing really standing in the way of us is that I'm too scared?"

"You're not crazy, Maggie," she told me. "But what are you scared of?"

I took a breath and braced myself to admit to her what, so far, I'd only admitted aloud to Zane. "I'm scared that he's too much like my dad."

"Ah."

"I've known too many men like him, Jessa," I said, feeling the need to elaborate, even though she hadn't balked at my confession or judged. "I've seen the broken marriages and the addictions and the womanizing and the damage and the pain and the bullshit. I've seen it up close, and I don't know that I'm strong enough to deal with it. I don't know if I can handle having my heart broken like that. I feel like I've already lived through it all, my whole life, with my dad, and I just don't want to do it anymore. Even just thinking about it is painful. All the conversations I've had with my dad when he's wasted, and visiting him when he's been in the hospital, and all the forgotten birthdays, having him disappear for months at a time, showing up with a different girl on his arm every other time I see him... He keeps getting older, but the girls stay the same age." I shook my head at the thought, so disturbing to me. "I've seen Zane with so many women over the years, and I don't think I could bear to see him live like that for the rest of my life if we really did attempt to be together and it didn't work out. I've always been afraid that if that happened, I'd be fired from Dirty, but to be honest, I think I'd have to leave anyway. If Zane and I were together and then we weren't, even if he and Brody and the rest of the band wanted me to stay, I'd have to go."

"I wouldn't blame you," Jessa said, without the slightest hesitation. "And I know Brody and Elle wouldn't blame you either. Seth would probably understand, too, given what he's lived through with his own addiction and recovery. And the rest of them can go fuck themselves if they don't understand. Because who would want to live like that? That's not a life for you, Maggie. I love you, and I'm telling you, I don't want you to be miserable. You deserve so much better than that. What woman would be strong enough to deal with that anyway? I don't even think it has to do with strength, because honestly, you're one of the strongest people I've ever known. I don't think there's any question that you're strong enough to make a marriage work, even with a lunatic like Zane Traynor, as long as he mans up on his side of things. But I understand what you're saying. If you two didn't stay together, I don't see how you could keep working with Dirty."

"I couldn't. I know I couldn't."

Jessa sighed sympathetically and sipped her tea. "Then maybe you just need to ask yourself if you're willing to take that kind of risk, Maggie. Is Zane worth that risk to you?"

She was right. At the end of the day, that really was the most important question I needed to ask myself. And when I did, the answer came to me very clearly.

"He is worth the risk," I told her, quietly. "If he's clean and sober."

"Well, then, that is one hell of a risk," she said, holding my gaze. "Because I don't think any addict can guarantee you they'll be clean every day for the rest of their life."

"They can't," I agreed, thinking of my dad and all his useless, empty promises over the years. "There are few guarantees in life, right? And you and I both know that one would never be iron-clad."

"Which means..."

"Which means," I finished for her, "I either trust him or I don't. I take a chance or I don't. Because there is no guarantee of anything here, and the risk is real."

"Yeah," Jessa agreed. "But if you love someone with your whole heart, Maggie, the risk is always real."

CHAPTER SIXTEEN

Zane

I WAS on a plane to Vancouver around midnight, eight hours after Maggie's flight took off—after I'd finished my work and as fast as Talia could arrange a flight for me. I had some shit to do in Chicago, including a creative meeting for the "Blackout" video that Brody strongly advised me not to bail on.

Then I hit the air.

It was a private jet, straight from O'Hare to Vancouver, and since we were flying back two time zones and Talia had a car waiting for me at the Vancouver airport, I got to Maggie's place just after midnight, Vancouver time.

I would've brought flowers and candy and teddy bears and fucking balloons if I thought it would help, but since it probably wouldn't, I came alone and empty-handed. I left Shady in the car and rang the bell.

I didn't message Maggie on the way or let her know I was coming. I never told anyone exactly why I was suddenly jetting to Vancouver. Likely, they knew. Maybe they gave her a heads-up.

I had no idea.

But it took her a long-ass time to open the door.

A light went on inside, then there was a definite pause as she checked me out through the peephole. The lock clunked open and the door cracked, and Maggie looked at me, uncertain, through the gap. She looked tired, but not like I'd woken her up. More like she'd been trying to sleep and failing miserably.

"What are you doing here?" she asked softly.

"What are *you* doing here?"

She didn't answer that, but she opened the door wider. "You want to come in?"

"Yeah, I want to come in."

She stepped aside and I went in, kicking off my boots. I walked into her living room as she turned on another light. One of her travel bags was still sitting in the hall, but nothing else was out of place.

I fucking loved Maggie's place. It was so *her*.

Neat. Orderly. Pretty.

It was a modern condo, about eight years old, everything white and steel and minimalist. But everything Maggie touched turned to soft and pretty. The billowy curtains, the furry pillows and blankets draped everywhere, the twinkly lights strung around the fireplace and windows.

It even smelled like her.

A guy could sit down on that girly pink couch and just never want to get back up.

Which was pretty much what I did.

She sat down next to me, and I noticed she was wearing sweatpants. Maggie never wore sweats. At least, not in front of me. They were pink. And she was wearing a soft white T-shirt that was falling off one shoulder, with a lime green bra underneath. And fluffy slippers. She'd probably only gotten dressed when I rang the bell.

Was she sleeping naked? Or wearing those silk jammies she wore when we shared that hotel suite in Vegas?

She had no makeup on, and her hair was straight but a bit bed-messy. She had slight circles under her eyes, and she was kinda chewing on her full bottom lip as she stared at me with something like trepidation mixed with want.

Fuck, but I was in love with her.

I just wanted into her bed and into her heart and I wanted to be all wrapped up in her and hang out with her in her pink sweatpants and watch movies with her in her fluffy slippers.

I wanted it bad... and I still didn't know how I was ever gonna get it.

I still didn't know if I'd earned her trust, and being not even three weeks clean didn't exactly make me feel like I had a right to ask just yet.

We still had a long way to go.

I knew that.

I leaned my elbows on my knees and stared at the floor and took a breath, blowing it out again in a deep sigh as I tried to gather my thoughts and not say the wrong fucking thing like I usually did.

I didn't want to say the wrong thing, but I didn't want to pussyfoot around, either.

"Just please tell me you're not leaving the tour."

"I'm not leaving the tour."

"Why did you fly home? You didn't tell me you were going. I had to find out from Talia." I looked at her, and her gray eyes widened.

"I'm sorry. I didn't do it to hurt you," she said, like she was realizing for the first time that it did hurt me.

"When I asked you to go," I said carefully, "I meant I needed you off my bus. You know, so I could cool off. I didn't mean for you to leave the country."

"You said you needed some time, Zane, and I wanted to respect that. You needed me out of your space."

I stared at her, processing that. "Look. I know it's been part of your job for the last—what? Almost eight years now? But maybe you need to stop telling me what I need," I told her.

She blinked at me. She started to speak a couple of times, her mouth popping open and closing again before the words finally came out. "Okay. *I* needed to think. And to not feel like I'm there putting pressure on you when you're fighting to stay sober."

"You're not."

"Zane. I know you. I know things about you..." She trailed off and ran a hand through her hair. "I'm sure you think I've been incredibly, overly hard on you, and I have, but—"

"I don't think that. You've been more than fair. *And* you've been hard on me. And you have reasons for that."

Her pretty eyes softened as she looked at me, and I fucking melted.

Fuck, but I wanted to kiss her.

"It's just that... it used to be the booze," she said softly. "But then it became other things. You use pot, and you use women and sex instead of dealing with your shit."

"That's true."

She looked genuinely surprised that I wasn't trying to deny it. That I actually got it.

"Yeah," she said softly. "It is. And maybe I'm the only one who really calls you on it."

"That's not true, believe me. Brody treads lightly. But Jude calls me on it. Jesse calls me on it. Rudy calls me on it, and Seth sure as fuck calls me on it. But I've never listened to any of them like I listen to you."

Maggie stared at me for a moment, seeming to process that. Then she looked away. She stared at the floor for what felt like a fucking eternity.

Then she shifted, turning her body toward me a little. She looked up into my eyes like whatever she had to say was going to be hard.

I braced myself for whatever it was gonna be.

Whatever shit she had to say to me, I knew I had to hear it.

"I don't want to have this conversation with you in some heated moment when we fall into bed," she said slowly. "So I'm telling you now. I know you said you want to wait a while before you get involved with someone, that Rudy advised you long ago to do that. And I respect that. But we're already involved, Zane. You can't deny that. We've been involved since the day we met."

I nodded. "I know, Maggie."

Her gray eyes held mine. "So maybe we could work through this together. I mean, you told me we'd get through this together. On the first day of the tour, you came on my bus and that's what you told me. So now I'm telling you the same thing right back."

Well, shit. She was serious.

She really meant that.

And hearing her say shit like that? Felt like I'd been waiting my entire life to hear Maggie say shit like that to me.

Did she even have any idea how much I loved her right now?

"I mean, if you want," she went on. "If that works for you. No pressure. I guess what I'm trying to say is... um, I'm here for you. *Damn.*" She took a breath and started again. "This is hard for me, Zane. I'm not used to stepping back and letting someone else call the shots."

"I know, Maggs."

"Not when it comes to my personal life, anyway," she said. "But... you're a huge part of my personal life, and I know I can't call the shots right now. Not with you. I can't guide this and I can't control it. I can set my personal limits and boundaries, but I can't take control of the reigns of our relationship like I can your day-to-day band business. We both know there are some things that you need to deal with, and I can help you in some ways, but I can't make it happen. I'll tell you, honestly, this is a really uncomfortable place for me to be. But I know I have to step back. What you're doing is even harder, way harder, and I respect the hell out of you for doing it. So I'm here for you. In whatever way you need me to be. As your friend. Or as more... when you're ready for that."

I absorbed every word she said. I knew she meant every word of it. But... "I know you mean that," I told her, "as long as I stay sober. But I won't hold you to it if I don't."

She shook her head. "I would never say that to you. I don't want to put an ultimatum on you or that kind of pressure."

"It's okay. You don't have to say it. I know it."

She stared at me, and she looked really fucking sad. Like she wanted to argue that. But we both knew she couldn't.

"I'm sorry," she said. "I love you, Zane. I'll love you no matter what you do. I've always loved you." Her voice dropped to a whisper on that last part, like it was hard for her to say.

"I love you too, Maggs," I said, the words heavy with emotion.

And *fuck*... Right about now, I would've been reaching for a joint, if I could. Actually *feeling* shit like this... I wasn't used to it.

At least, not clean and sober.

Everything I felt for Maggie, since I'd gotten clean, had only intensified. The feelings were always this intense, but the pot just kinda dulled them down, or distracted me from them. Intense feelings, in general, without anything to *do* about them—like get stoned —were a lot to deal with right now.

Definitely didn't make it any easier to stay off the weed.

But I had to admit, actually experiencing the intensity of my feelings for Maggie, while pretty overwhelming, was pretty fucking incredible, too.

Like when we'd had sex without a condom... There was nothing to buffer the connection between us. It was raw, powerful; naked.

"*But*," she said, "I just can't be in a relationship with you if you're using, Zane. You're really... different... when you're drinking."

"No doubt."

"And when you smoke pot..." She shook her head and sighed a little, like she was really trying to find the right words. "I like who you are, Zane. I really do. I wish you could understand how much that's true, despite how much I've pushed you away. But I feel like the pot is just a slippery slope to all the other stuff."

"I know you do. And you'd be right."

She stared at me, surprised.

"You wouldn't be the first person to say that to me, Maggie."

"Oh." She went silent for a moment, thinking. "Okay. So here's the thing. I feel like when you need to smoke weed it means you're out of control, even just a bit, and it scares me." She shrugged with discomfort, her shirt slipping a little farther off her shoulder. "I guess... it's my hard limit. Does that make sense?"

"Hard limit..." I repeated, considering that. "So you're saying... spanking and tying you up is okay, then?"

Her eyes narrowed at me a little. Then her full lips twitched in the hint of a smile. "Good to know giving up weed hasn't dulled your sex drive."

"Actually," I admitted, "it's kinda made me hornier."

At that, her eyes went wide. "I'm... uh... not really surprised. It's definitely made you... clearer. It's subtle, but your eyes are clearer. You've been brighter, in general, since you stopped smoking up."

I had to hold back a smile. "Brighter?"

"Yeah. Like all your dazzling-golden-sun-god shit just got more blinding. It's annoying, really."

Now I full-on grinned. "Sun god?"

"You know that's what they call you. *Rock's golden god.* Like, girls get a sun tan just gazing at you."

I laughed.

She frowned. "I think we're getting beside the point..." Then she wrapped her arms around herself.

And this was it. The moment Maggie started raising her defenses and I turned up the charm, cranked up the flirt, pressed into her space and got my hands on her, daring her to resist.

But I didn't. Not this time.

My pulse was beating in my dick, my growing hard-on getting uncomfortable in my jeans, and yes, I wanted to fuck her. I wanted to pull her to me, peel off her clothes, jam my tongue in her mouth and my cock in her pussy and never let her go. I wanted to fuck her on the floor and on every piece of furniture she had. Never mind that we'd fucked right here on this couch about six months ago.

But I knew I had to keep it platonic, as hard as that might be. For now. Because I wasn't ready to touch her.

Because if I fucked her again and she put up her wall, I could spiral.

I had no fallback now. No parachute. No bag of weed in my pocket to take the edge off.

And no way was I touching another woman.

It was Maggie for me, but it wasn't even about proving that to her anymore. I definitely didn't need to prove it to myself. I didn't need to convince anyone that Maggie was the woman for me.

I didn't care about any of that anymore.

All I cared about was staying clean and doing right by her.

"Here's the point," I informed her. "You're gonna grab your bags, get dressed if you want to. You can wear sweatpants, I don't care. You're getting in the car with me and we're going to the airport, and we're flying back to Chicago. You're not leaving the tour, and you're not taking a break from the tour either."

I studied her response to that. Maggie wasn't used to me telling her what to do; I knew that. I mean, not like I hadn't fucking tried. But she never really listened.

On this, she had to listen, because I was right. No way was she leaving the tour. I wouldn't let her leave the tour.

Brody wouldn't either.

I'd already talked to him. And while he was clearly a little pissed at me over the whole secret marriage thing—and probably worried I'd fuck things up with Maggie—he'd assured me fucking up-and-down that Maggie's job was safe, that he was never gonna let *anyone* fuck with it. Even me.

"You need some time off," I added, taking a gentler tone, "you can take time off, but you're doing it on the road."

Maggie shook her head slowly. "I don't need time off, Zane."

"Great. Go get your shit."

"I'll need to book us a flight," she said.

"No worries," I told her. "Got a jet on standby."

When we were seated in the plane, I said, "Surprised you didn't say anything about the private jet."

Maggie looked at me. She'd sat right next to me, even though the cabin was huge and she could've sat anywhere. She'd gotten dressed and she'd even put on a little makeup. Her gray eyes looked tired and pretty. "Like what?"

"Usually you tell me not to waste my money."

"Usually I don't mind flying first class with you." Her eyes moved slowly over my face. "But I don't really want to deal with the bombardment of attention. You know... fans. Horny flight attendants." She looked away. "I really don't need people or their camera phones in my face right now."

That was fine with me; I didn't want that either. I just wanted to be with her.

"I don't want to share you, either," I told her.

She looked at me again, but she didn't say anything.

Once we were in the air, she started reading on her iPad. I put in my earbuds and listened to some music.

After a while, she put the iPad aside, dropped her head on the headrest and went to sleep. Or at least I thought she went to sleep. But then she reached her hand onto my armrest, palm-up, without opening her eyes.

I put my hand in hers, and we curled our fingers together. And we held hands like that for the rest of the flight... even when we both fell asleep.

CHAPTER SEVENTEEN

Maggie

Five weeks later…

"MAGGIE. You're really cramping my style here."

I looked up into the ice-blue eyes of the man I'd married almost two years ago to find him gazing down at me with a twisted, amused smirk on his face. Which was when I realized how tightly I was holding his hand.

"Oh. Uh… sorry." I released my death grip. I also realized I'd been leaning heavily on his arm, flinching in sympathy pain, the little stool I was sitting on pressed tight up against the chair where he was sitting while he got tattooed.

"Shit, you're strong," he muttered, flexing his newly-freed hand and wiggling his fingers. "Not sure the blood's coming back anytime soon."

"Oops."

I'd sworn to him this morning that if he let me come along with him to the tattoo parlor today while he got his tattoo, I wasn't gonna freak out. Just because I'd almost fainted when I saw Jude getting a tattoo once didn't mean I was gonna be a freak about this.

Or so I'd hoped.

It wasn't like I'd ever seen *Zane* get a tattoo before, though. How did I know for sure how I'd react to watching him get tortured?

Until today, Zane didn't have any tattoos. Jude had a ton of them, Brody had several, and Jesse had one big one on his forearm, but for a bunch of rock stars, the members of Dirty weren't all that into tattoos. Zane himself had claimed aloud, more than once, that he didn't want to "desecrate" the work of art God had made—i.e., his body—by putting ink on it.

I was pretty sure that comment was aimed at Jesse, since Jesse's tattoo was pretty damn sexy and girls were always wanting to touch it.

When I asked Zane this morning, seriously, why he'd never gotten a tattoo before and why he suddenly felt the need to get this one, he told me, *Just feels right.*

He was getting a Viking ship, one of those cool dragon boat things, on his right shoulder. Except that the dragon part of the boat turned into this giant serpent that wrapped around the boat. He had it all sketched out by a tattoo artist; he'd been conversing with this guy Jude had connected him with for a couple of weeks already, and had made an appointment to see him while we were here in Nashville.

When I'd asked Zane the meaning behind the tattoo, he'd asked me in return, *What are Vikings famous for?*

When I'd answered, *Uh, raping and pillaging?* he'd given me a mildly dirty look and said, *Boats, Maggie. They were seafarers, explorers. Feel like I'm conquering new ground here, that's all.*

Later, I'd heard him tell the guys, *It's to commemorate some big shit in my life. I'm fucking serious about staying clean, and marring the beauty of this God-given body of mine? Serious as it gets.*

Then he'd winked at me, and I knew that last part was kind of a joke. Except that it also really wasn't.

He was serious as hell about staying clean.

Then he'd explained to me privately that the serpent symbolized his addiction, that it would always be with him, but he wasn't going to let it take him down.

I'd almost cried when he told me that, I was so proud of him... But I'd managed to keep my cool.

Right now, I was totally losing it.

"Maggs," he said, "why don't you go get some air, stretch your legs? You know, take a walk around the block and chill out."

"Oh..." I glanced nervously at that buzzing needle scraping at his flesh and shivered. "I can stay with you though, you know, for moral support."

"Sweetheart," the tattoo artist drawled, "that's his polite way of asking you to get gone."

I looked at Zane and he just smiled.

"You want me to go?"

"Why don't you go find somewhere for us to eat? And I'll take you for lunch after this."

"Oh. Okay." I got up and retrieved my purse, taking a final glance at the ink that was permanently marking him. The tattoo artist glanced up at me and smirked. I gave him a narrow eye, then told Zane, "Text me when you're done."

Then I went to find someplace yummy for us to eat... even though the thought of eating right now was making me feel a little queasy.

I pushed through the door of the tattoo parlor to be greeted by sunshine and crisp spring air, and Shady, who was leaning against a lamp post. I waved at him and took a deep breath, trying to relax my nerves.

Apparently, I had a major aversion to seeing Zane in physical pain, and watching him get inked made me want to stab that tattoo guy in the eye with his tattoo gun.

But other than that... it was a pretty good day.

For the last five weeks, I'd been enjoying my life as assistant manager to Dirty again—a hell of a lot—and working literally side-by-side with Zane.

Actually, I'd been spending every possible moment with him.

I'd even started accompanying him to his interviews and appearances. He'd started doing them again, at a much gentler pace than usual, and so far, so good.

I hadn't gone to a single interview on this tour before Zane got clean. I could have. I worked closely with our publicity teams and was the main point of contact for all of them—we had a main publicist in Vancouver, a company we worked with out of L.A., and another one in Europe—and I probably would've gone along with the band members more often for their day-to-day promo stuff on this tour, if it didn't mean I'd have to see Zane so much.

Now, it was like my priorities had totally flipped upside-down.

Instead of me spending my days holed away in my hotel room or the Lady Bus or some random cafe, where I hoped I wouldn't run into Zane, I found myself materializing outside his hotel room or his bus, or in the hotel lobby, waiting to spend the day with him.

He didn't complain.

The first time it happened was a couple days after we'd flown back from Vancouver together, while we were in Chicago. Bright and early, I was waiting in front of the hotel with a Rolls-Royce Phantom stretch limo, laptop and coffee in hand, ready to start the day—with Zane—when the band members started rolling out of the hotel.

To everyone's surprise, the car, which was a step up from your standard luxury sedan, was for Zane and Zane only. Well, and me and Shady. Zane had been clean for just over three weeks, and by three weeks, the doctors had expected the worst of his withdrawal symptoms to subside.

Subside, they had.

It was a major accomplishment, and I thought we could celebrate. I was proud of him and I wanted him to know it.

That day, I'd accompanied the band to a photo shoot, and all of us had lunch together.

From that day on, I went pretty much everywhere with Zane.

I'd hang out behind the scenes or at a nearby café, working on my laptop and phone while he did his thing, or I'd run errands, and when he was done we'd meet up. We'd eat meals together or with the rest of the band or with Shady.

We even hit the gym together sometimes. I'd do a yoga class while he lifted weights with Dylan or Jesse and Jude, and Shady smoked outside; big and burly as he was, Shady wasn't much for working out.

Or we'd sit in the back of the car or in his tour bus together and work, side-by-side. He'd write lyrics in his notebook. I'd make phone calls.

Sometimes we'd enjoy long silences.

Sometimes we'd talk.

And when we did... we talked about a lot of shit.

He told me, at length, about a ton of shit he'd done over the years that he wasn't proud of. A whole laundry list of his self-proclaimed faults and fuck-ups, that he wanted me to know.

I listened, but honestly, it didn't make me think any less of him. Partly because I pretty much knew all that shit about him already, and partly because I thought it was incredibly brave of him to tell me. That instead of chasing me down and trying to win me over, he was just being real. He was opening up to me in a way he never really had before.

I already knew most of his dark shit, but not because he'd actually talked to me about it.

More because I'd been a reluctant witness.

I figured he was scared that it all might scare me away. But actually, it just made me feel closer to him—that he chose to trust me with all these things he felt so bad about.

He also told me how hard it had been giving up pot, that it wasn't as easy as he'd probably made it look. That he still craved it, that he still had some difficult nights and moments he wanted to break right down and smoke up.

Just like he sometimes still wanted to take a drink.

It was pretty brave of him to tell me this, too, because I was pretty sure it scared the shit out of him to admit it to me.

Zane had never wanted me to see his weaknesses; I knew that

about him by now. He didn't want me to decide that he was a failure; that he was going to fail at this, that he couldn't do it—and give up on him.

So we talked about that, too.

We talked about pretty much everything.

Everything except our relationship.

It wasn't a point of contention between us. It was a nonissue, actually; something we'd finally been able to call a bit of a truce on and put aside, for now.

We didn't need to fight about it or even discuss it. We knew it was there, waiting to be dealt with, when we were both ready.

For now, we were getting along. Things were good between us. We weren't together, but we were copacetic.

For fucking once in our lives.

And he still wasn't trying to get in my pants. He never tried to touch me for anything more intimate than a hug.

But all the while... he looked at me like a man who loved me.

He spoke to me like a man who loved me.

By my side, he felt like a man who loved me.

The man.

He never once put pressure on me to discuss our relationship or to further our relationship. I never asked him to further our relationship, because I'd realized it was pretty damn sweet as it was, and maybe it should just stay this way for a while; respectful, peaceful, mutually comfortable.

Platonic; at least on the surface.

When I walked back into the tattoo parlor this afternoon, though, that all changed.

"What do you think?" Zane asked me. He'd gotten up out of the chair and stood before me, his T-shirt sleeve rolled up over his newly-tattooed right shoulder, which was turned to me.

The tattoo wasn't massive or crazy-elaborate, but it covered most of his shoulder. The skin looked tender, which still made me cringe, but the tattoo was gorgeous. Both the boat and the serpent were pretty detailed, outlined beautifully in crisp black.

He'd already told me the tattoo artist had a friend in New York that he was going to see in a few weeks, to have the colors inked in.

"It's beautiful, Zane," I told him honestly. "Are you happy with it?"

"Yeah," he said. "It's exactly what I wanted. But... I think this one is my favorite."

Then he showed me his left hand. I had to blink at it several times before it really sank in.

Those ring tattoos some people got around their ring finger when they got married? Like in lieu of or in addition to an actual wedding ring...

Zane now had one.

In very delicate, tiny, gorgeous script, the name *Maggie* was now inked on his ring finger, right where a wedding ring would go.

Permanently inked.

My jaw dropped.

When he turned his hand over to show me the other side, it said *May*.

"Oh my God... Zane." I looked up at him. My vision was blurring. "You didn't." I blinked furiously, looking at his hand again... but there it was. I grabbed his hand and pulled it toward me.

"Easy," he said, eying me. "It's tender, babe."

"Sorry." I gentled my touch, lifting his ring finger and turning his hand, back and forth, reading the little script-ring.

Maggie May

"You hate it."

I looked up into his blue eyes, startled. The look he gave me back was guarded, his eyelids lowered.

"No. No, I don't hate it, Zane. I'm just a little... stunned. I mean... it's so..." I swallowed. "Permanent."

"Yeah?" Now there was a spark of challenge in his eyes that I knew all too well. "Well, so were my vows to you. Even if you divorce me, right the fuck now, what I said at that altar stands. The fact that I married you stands. Even if we aren't together, all that shit is real and it's forever. At least, it is for me."

I couldn't even speak. I was stunned and speechless.

I glanced back down at the ring tattoo. My name on his finger, *forever*.

"Don't worry, I'm gonna cover it with a ring," he told me. "I'll just throw one of my regular rings over it. You know, I wear a lot of them. No one's gonna think anything of it if I wear a skull ring or whatever on that finger. No one has to see it except—"

"I want one," I blurted.

The words came out fast and certain, surprising us both. His eyes widened, and I knew I was staring at him like a crazy person, but I meant it.

I turned to the tattoo artist before he could say anything. "Can I have one? Just like his. A tiny little script ring—it shouldn't take long, right?"

The guy eyed me up and down. "You sure, sweetheart?"

"Yes." I scowled a little. "I'm *sure*. I want it on my finger. Right now. Please."

"I just meant it's gonna hurt," he informed me. "Tattoos on the fingers... painful."

"Yeah, well. If he can do it, I can do it." I dropped my purse and plopped my ass down in the chair. "Hell, if my dad can do it, I can do it." I shot Zane a look, and while he raised his eyebrows at that, he wasn't gonna argue. My dad had a ton of tattoos, and no way was he braver than me.

The tattoo artist just shrugged and started prepping to do my tattoo. At which point it really sank into me that this *was* gonna hurt, and I sank my fingernails into the leather arms of the chair.

Zane dropped onto the rolling stool and rolled over next to me.

"You sure about this, Maggie...? It's forever, right?"

"We already went over that," I said, giving him a quick glance. I tried not to focus on the tattoo gun, but I really wanted to watch what the guy was doing. "I want Zane on the outside," I informed him. "And Adrian on the inside. And I'm going to spell it out so you can write it down first. I've seen photos on the internet of people with misspelled tattoos, and I'm telling you right now, I'm gonna throw a shit fit if his name is spelled wrong. Just thought I should tell you that upfront, to be fair."

"Fair enough," the dude said, with an amused glance at Zane. Then he turned to get a pen and paper.

I looked at Zane. He looked back at me. He didn't say anything, but he definitely looked worried that maybe I'd lost my mind and would hate him for this tomorrow.

It was impulsive, yes, but so what? I'd done impulsive shit before.

Like marrying him in Vegas.

Because let's just be honest. There was a part of me—a big, huge part—that just kept wanting me to attach myself to Zane Traynor in every way I could.

You know... the part of me that just wanted to love him and forget about everything else.

"I'll cover it," I told him, "with the wedding band you gave me at the chapel."

"And when people notice you're wearing a wedding ring?"

"I'll tell them to mind their own damn business."

He continued to stare at me as I spelled out his name for the tattoo artist. *Zane Adrian.* "I want something really fancy for the Z," I told him, thinking on the fly. "Like, can you embellish it a bit?"

"Sure," he said. "I can do it the same style as his and add some little curls on the ends of the Z, but still keep it the same height as the other letters. Sound good?"

"Uh, can I see what the Z looks like in that font? Like, can you show me an example? So we can make it perfect...? I want it to be perfect."

"Sure, sweetheart." He reached for his notebook again, with another glance at Zane that seemed to say, *And you married this chick, because...?*

"You're amazing, you know that?" Zane said, just staring at me.

"Yeah, well." I nodded at the tattoo guy. "Opinions on that may vary."

Zane smiled, slowly.

I smiled back.

We were barely in the door of the hotel room when Zane reached to take my hand in his. He tugged me close to him as the door shut behind us and slipped my purse off my shoulder, placing it gently aside.

It was his hotel room, and it smelled faintly of him; the smell of his bodywash from his morning shower.

We were alone, completely alone, for the first time in a long time.

Even when we'd worked in the lounge of his tour bus, we'd left the door unlocked and Shady had drifted in and out.

The door was definitely locked now.

When he'd asked me to come back to the hotel with him after we had our lunch, I'd said yes without hesitation. I didn't ask why, but I didn't need to. We both wanted to be alone together and we both knew what it meant.

We hadn't been alone like this in his hotel room or mine since the night of his disappearance into the desert.

I'd told him when he'd followed me home to Vancouver that we could get through this together; that I'd be here for him as his friend, or more—when he was ready. Since that night five weeks ago, I'd been telling myself I could be Zane's friend, indefinitely, without more between us, because that's what was best for both of us.

It was what was best for him as he struggled to stay clean.

It was what was best for our relationship.

But it wasn't easy.

As Zane slipped his fingers into my hair and cupped my face, tingles skittered through my body. Fire ignited as he skimmed his thumb across my cheek. Warmth swelled through me; the anticipation of more of his touch. My nipples tightened and butterflies stirred in my stomach. My clit pulsed. The restless need for him was already building between my legs. My heart was pounding and that back-of-knee-sweat thing? Yup.

As I slipped my hands under his leather jacket, onto his waist, they were kinda shaking.

Because Zane Traynor would always be so much more to me than a friend.

Right now, I wanted him more than I'd *ever* wanted him... and I hoped to God he was ready.

I'd had a lot of restless nights lately, and as much as I told myself it was all for the best and the greater good... I'd missed Zane like this. The intimacy of his face this close to mine, the feel of his breath on my skin and the warmth of his hands on my body. The look in his ice-blue eyes, his pupils dilating as he looked at me.

This lust-charged space between us. The bone-deep—no; *soul*-deep magnetic pull.

We'd been sucked into each other's orbits the day we met, and we were still going around and around.

Would we ever stop?

No. I couldn't imagine that ever happening.

I'd only been able to stuff my desire for him down—just barely—and focus on work because, frankly, I knew how to do that. And because I knew it would be incredibly unfair to jump on him and shove sex in his face when I'd given him so much flack over the years about staying sober, giving up pot and retiring his manslut ways.

When he'd finally done all I'd ever asked of him, and told me he needed some time without being involved with anyone, including me... how could I disrespect his efforts to stay clean by trying to lure him right back into bed?

It wouldn't be fair, it wouldn't be respectful, and it definitely wouldn't be love. And the fact was I loved this man. I'd just gotten his name tattooed on my body, for fuck's sake.

Love.

I loved him more right now, in this moment, than I probably ever had, and I'd do *anything* to support him staying clean and living a long, healthy and happy life... Even if it meant I couldn't be with him.

I'd sworn that to myself.

That if Zane decided he didn't want to be with me once he got clean and stayed that way, I wasn't going to fuck up his life by chasing after him and complicating things for him.

One thing I knew: Zane Traynor was a man who knew what he wanted.

If he wanted me, he'd make it known.

If he didn't... there was nothing I could do to change his mind.

I was just going to let him go, so to speak, and wait for him to come back to me.

However... I was still human, I was horny as hell, and he hadn't touched me in a long, long time. And I wanted him so fucking bad it hurt.

I'd never been a dude, so I really had no way to compare, but I was pretty sure blue balls had nothing on this.

"Do you still want me?" I blurted out as his thumb traced over my cheek for what felt like the dozenth time. It was like he was in some kind of trance, staring at my mouth. But my words seemed to stir him out of it.

"Want you?" His eyes met mine and he blinked, like he was struggling to make sense of the question.

"Yeah. We haven't... You haven't tried to touch me in a long time, and I just wondered—"

"Wondered?"

"If it was the same between us. If maybe... you feel differently."

"Differently..." he repeated. "Jesus, Maggie, are you serious? I just got a ring tattoo with your name on it."

"I know. I know, but... I just meant, you know, is other stuff still the same?"

"Stuff?" His gaze drifted down to my mouth again, and he swiped his tongue over his lip. "You mean, stuff like this?" He moved my hand to his crotch, pressing it down against the erection in his jeans.

I swallowed, heat thrilling through my core as the relief hit me.

"I just wondered..." I said breathlessly.

"The only reason I've managed not to touch you," he pretty much growled out, "is because I've been rubbing myself raw thinking about you every fucking day."

"You did that for me?" I swallowed again. "Alone?"

Maybe it shouldn't have surprised me so much, but yeah, it kinda did. Like, I knew a man with a sex drive like Zane's had probably jerked off thinking about me a few times. But... *this* man was a rock star.

A drop-dead gorgeous rock star with a very public reputation for having a huge dick and the skills to go along with it; he could've had a woman take care of his needs anytime, anywhere.

For some reason it was still hard for me to think of him hanging out alone in his hotel room, keeping his legendary dick to himself, when he could've been picking up chicks.

God, but my dad had jaded me.

Zane laughed shortly, but the sound was cut off and strangled as it ended in a low groan. He was still holding my hand, grinding my palm against his hard shaft.

"What am I, a fucking animal?" he said, his voice low. "I can be faithful, Maggie. Jerking off is nothing compared to the satisfaction I get with you, but neither is being with another woman. And besides... I never want to hurt you like that again."

He rolled my palm over the plump head of his cock, pressing down on it in a way that I would've thought would be painful... but he didn't look like he was in pain.

"You fucking feel me on that, Maggie?" he murmured, his eyes darkening with desire.

"Yeah. I feel you..."

"Plus... my dick has a distinct preference." His gaze wandered down my body. "I start bringing around second-rate pussy, it's not gonna be happy."

I rolled my eyes but kinda had to smile. "I really don't think you should do that," I offered, starting to rub him up-and-down myself. "Your dick deserves better..." I bit my lip and he bit back a growl as he backed me up against the wall.

"My dick agrees with you." His face was so close to mine, we could easily have kissed. "That feels good," he muttered, but he made no move to kiss me.

"Yeah..."

"I want you. I never stopped wanting you, Maggie. You stop wanting me?"

"No."

"You're in my room."

"I am."

"You just got my name tattooed on your finger..."

"Yeah," I said, my voice dropping to a whisper. "So did you."

"Then I guess we are in this together."

"I guess so."

His gaze dropped to my mouth. "You gonna let me kiss you?"

"I'm not gonna stop you, Zane."

I didn't. His lips met mine and it was like all the air was instantly sucked from the room. My breath caught; I didn't even need to breathe.

I just needed *him*.

My hands went to his neck and gripped him, holding him close as I kissed him over and over, my tongue lapping against his. Then we were moving; he was drawing me with him into the bedroom and then he was peeling off my clothes, and all I wanted was to be naked with him. I *needed* him against my skin.

I started undressing him, too, and by the time we were both naked, all I could do was press myself up against him, wanting all his warmth, wanting every part of his body touching every part of mine as we kissed, deeper and deeper. It was like we were trying to climb into each other... Like we could make the rest of the world just go away.

Like all we needed was one another.

Not air, not food... not anything or anyone else.

By the time we ended up in a horizontal position, entwined with each other, I hardly knew where we were...

The floor. We were on the floor, laid out on top of one of the hotel robes, which he'd somehow spread out beneath me, because my man was considerate like that.

"Condom?" he asked, and I shook my head.

"No. We can just... I *just* had my period. We won't get pregnant."

He stared at me. "And if we do?"

I didn't answer that.

He didn't ask again.

My legs were spread around his waist and I was gripping him tight, my thighs squeezing him, my fingernails digging into his back... and he pushed into me. He did it slow, and warmth radiated through me. My core clenched, my pussy squeezing him as he pushed deeper.

And *oh God*, I'd missed this.

I savored the sounds of his labored breathing, the low groans in his throat as he kissed me, his chest expanding against mine.

He filled me and withdrew and filled me again... and there was no way I could ever get enough of this.

Some sex was just sex.

This sex was... life-altering.

Every time Zane fucked me, something between us changed.

Deepened.

We grew more complicated and more entwined, and I became more unable to imagine any kind of life without him.

The feel of Zane inside me? Pure ecstasy... far beyond any mere sexual pleasure I'd ever experienced.

I felt him everywhere.

I wanted him everywhere.

And I wanted him to feel everything I was feeling.

"Harder," I breathed. "Fuck me harder, Zane. Hard... hard..."

I urged him deeper with my hips, urged him to fuck me harder with my ragged pleas. I yanked him against me, taking his full weight as he grasped my hands, lacing his fingers through mine. He pinned my hands on either side of my head as he fucked me and I begged him as I kissed him, "I need you... I need you to fuck me for hours... We can't leave. We can never leave this room. I need you to fuck me like this forever."

"We can't," he breathed. "I'm useless with you. Can't last for two fucking seconds, Maggs..."

"Fuck that..." I gripped his hands tight and bucked up against him, meeting every thrust as I rolled my hips, my focus shifting completely at his words. "Just come. I want to feel you come."

"You first..."

"Fuck. No... I want you to come. Right now. Just come, baby..."

"Maggie..."

"*Yeah...*"

He panted heavily as he picked up speed. His hips slammed roughly against mine and I fucking loved it. I crossed my feet behind his back, locking them at the ankles, squeezing him in a vise grip. I gripped his hands as tightly as I had at the tattoo parlor, probably cutting off blood.

And I felt it, everywhere, when he started to come... The familiar feelings as his body started to lock up, muscles flexing. The hitch in his rough breaths. The way his cock seemed to swell and stiffen, right before the orgasm peaked.

And when it did... I felt him pulse inside me several times.

And *fuck*, that feeling...

He groaned into my neck, lost in pleasure as my body gripped his, savoring his release... and I felt my own climax building. I was on the edge, my body raw with desire, every nerve humming and striving for that peak...

I rubbed myself against him, trembling, and the slight movement was enough to set me off. I cried out, biting his shoulder as the pleasure soared through my body and my head spun.

When we'd both panted through our release and started kissing again, making out even as we fought to catch our breath... wrapped in one another's arms, our bodies still locked together... I felt it. I felt how different this was.

I didn't want to avoid this.

I wanted to stay right here in Zane's arms and feel this.

I wanted to feel his love for me.

I wanted to love him, and I didn't even feel scared. In this moment... there was so much love and I was so full of it... there was no room for fear.

I knew we'd end up here, naked together, eventually. Sooner or later... we'd be here again.

But this time... the sex was different. Instead of some desperate, anger-fueled frenzy or some brutal tug-of-war, it was like jumping off a cliff—together.

Like plummeting into a space where nothing existed except *us*.

It was like falling... deep. Deep into something I'd never be able to understand until I was in it.

It wasn't just what I felt for Zane or what he felt for me.

It wasn't just being in love.

It was what we *became* together.

It was what we were to each other and what we became in one another's arms. Something we could never be without each other and something that didn't exist outside this space. Something that just had to be, that maybe was meant to be; something that was so right, I couldn't have launched any kind of battle against it if I'd tried.

It was me and Zane together, and there was nothing like it in the world.

There was a part of me that always knew this would happen... That if I ever really let Zane in, I'd fall for him so fucking hard and so deep I'd never get out.

It was like he said at the tattoo parlor...

This was forever.

No matter what we let happen between us or didn't, how long we stayed together, how much we fought it or fucked it up... this thing between us, it was a forever thing.

Eventually, Zane rolled over, taking me with him and arranging us on our sides more comfortably, wedging me in under his arm with his bicep as my pillow. It was his left arm, and as it wrapped around me, his hand resting on my arm, I could see his ring finger.

"Please tell me," I whispered, "that you'll never regret it. That you're never gonna look at that tattoo on your finger and regret it."

"It's just ink on my skin, Maggie," he said, without even opening his eyes. "You're already in here." He laid his other hand over his heart.

And if I'd never been sure that I loved Zane Traynor before this moment, I would've fallen in love with him right now.

Thing was, I'd loved Zane forever.

"You gonna regret it?" he asked me.

"No," I said. "You were right. This thing between us... it's forever, Zane."

He opened his blue eyes and looked deep into mine. "For real," he asked, "what happens when people see it? You gonna flip out...? Run away?"

"No. I meant what I said. I'll wear the wedding band over it. I have it with me anyway."

"You do?" He seemed genuinely surprised about that.

"Yeah. I carry it and the engagement ring you gave me everywhere. I might not wear them, but they mean a lot to me, Zane."

"Maggie..." He put his hand on the side of my face, lightly, and drifted his thumb over my bottom lip. "Jesus... you still surprise me."

I smiled. He surprised me too, in incredible ways.

We'd just gotten tattooed together. I'd never seen that one coming.

"I'll wear the wedding band," I promised him, "and a lot of people probably won't notice it. I'll wear the ruby ring my mom gave me, too. I wear that a lot. And if anyone has the balls to ask... Our friends have already been told we're married but not together. If they notice the ring, I'm sure it'll imply that there's more going on than they've been told. But we're all adults here. I think my friends can respect that I don't want to talk about it just yet. Hell, if they can't respect that, what kind of friends are they anyway?"

I wasn't sure what he thought of that; he didn't say anything.

"And people who don't know me..." I went on. "They have no reason to think there's any connection between you and me."

"Other than the fact you're with me all the time."

"As Dirty's assistant manager."

"Maggie. You start wearing a wedding band and showing up everywhere with me, the media is gonna sniff it out sooner or later."

"Let them sniff. They've got no proof of anything."

"You know we could just make this easier on ourselves and tell them, right? Tell everyone."

"Yeah. I know. And one day we will. But let's just give this some time to be real. Just the two of us." I gazed up at him, wanting that more than anything. To just be with him without any external pressure and enjoy it for a while. Without worrying what other people would think, or dealing with women hating on me or the media swarming. "Okay?"

"Okay," he said, with surprisingly little resistance. His eyes searched my face. "Just tell me you're happy, okay?"

He'd never asked me that before. I only realized that now, because it stood out. Honestly, from the day Zane had married me, he'd never asked me that.

He'd asked me to be his wife, yes. He'd asked me to love him and to try to make our marriage work.

But he'd never asked me if any of it would make me happy. He'd never asked me if I thought he could make me happy, or if I *was* happy.

I looked at my tattoo. It was wild and impulsive. It was so like Zane, but it really didn't seem like me.

The thing was, it *felt* like me in a way I wasn't sure how to explain to him or to anyone.

It felt right, just like lying here with him did.

"That's hard for me to answer," I told him, honestly. "I'm definitely not unhappy. But this is all so new. I don't mean our relationship, even though it's definitely changed some in the last several weeks. It's grown, and it feels good. But I mean, I'm kind of new."

I looked at him, wondering if he understood what I meant by that. If he'd noticed the subtle changes in me, even while he was going through more dramatic changes of his own.

"I'm different with you, Zane Traynor. I think when I'm with you, I'm more of the person I would've wanted to be if my whole relationship with my father hadn't left me so starving for security and control." I shook my head. "You know, I never thought I was a fearful person. But the fact is I've let fear pretty much rule my whole relationship with you. I always thought I was strong because I was in control of my life. The truth was, I was desperate to be in control because I was so scared. Being around you always scared me because the things I feel for you make me question everything about the way I've been living my life."

His fingers stroked lightly up-and-down my arm as he took that in. "The thought of being my wife still scares you?"

"Actually," I confessed, "it doesn't. It's curious and thrilling and... I don't know... delicious? I don't know any other word to describe this feeling. The feeling of lying here in your arms and knowing this thing between us isn't going anywhere." I looked up into his eyes. "It's delicious, and I want more of it."

"You know you're just making me fall more in love with you, right?"

I smiled. "Am I?"

"Yeah. But it's not your fault. I pretty much fall in love with you more every day, no matter what you do. It's pretty fucking ridiculous."

"I think I know what you mean..."

He kissed me, softly. Then he told me, "I love you, Maggie."

And for the first time hearing those words from his lips, I truly believed him.

"I've never loved before like I love you," I told him, and I think he believed me, too. "This kind of love... it's a once-in-a-lifetime love, Zane."

CHAPTER EIGHTEEN

Zane

SHE REALLY SHOULD'VE KNOWN I wasn't gonna let this shit lie.

I mean, my wife knew me by now, right?

Maggie had to know sooner or later I'd be pressing her to tell the universe we were married.

Or someone else would tell... and I'd just go along with it. Maybe I wouldn't blab just yet, but I wasn't gonna deny it if it came out. I wasn't gonna lie about it, and I wasn't gonna be ashamed.

Fuck shame. I had none.

As I watched Maggie eating her mushroom risotto, one of her favorite meals, way too quietly, I figured she already suspected I was buttering her up because I was itching to spill. Brag to the media. Shout it from the rooftops. Piss her name in the snow.

She already had my name tattooed on her finger. Might as well brand her with hickies and start wearing matching shit.

I wasn't exactly a quiet, private or subtle dude. I definitely lacked manners, tact, and that impulse control thing she was always going on about.

I would've happily leaked a sex tape, if the thought of random assholes jacking off to my wife didn't make my trigger finger itch.

But I had no problem with the entire fucking universe knowing I owned that sweet ass.

Fortunately for me, it now kinda did.

Unfortunately for me, Maggie was gonna be pissed about it.

I was pretty sure about that.

She hadn't said a word since she started eating, but she did keep glancing my way through narrowed eyes, like she was reading my fucked-up thoughts. "Aren't you going to finish your lunch?"

"I'm good."

Truth was I was too worked up to eat. Too antsy going over all the shit in my head I wanted to say but didn't quite know how to.

How to tell her about the Maxxi shit?

How not to make her pissed at me when I did?

How not to freak her the fuck out by staring at her too long without saying anything at all?

I decided to stop staring at her and looked out the window of the jet instead, into the sea of clouds below. I relaxed back into my seat. It was a five-and-a-half-hour drive up to Detroit from Louisville, so I figured we'd fly in style instead. Maggie didn't seem to find anything suspicious about that, at first.

But I knew the way I was acting was tweaking her Zane's-up-to-shit radar.

Maggie had sharp radar.

And I was definitely up to shit.

I'd never actually cared about upsetting people with whatever came out of my mouth before. I definitely lacked a filter, but fuck it. I didn't like being filtered. Wasn't used to anyone telling me what I could and couldn't say.

Brody and our publicity team gave me "suggestions."

I usually ignored them.

I was used to saying whatever the fuck I wanted and maybe apologizing for it later.

Maybe.

Having to consider what my wife would think and how she'd

feel about everything that came out of my mouth, before it came out of my mouth, was like a whole new fucking world.

Seth was right.

No idea if it was just because I was an addict, and/or because I was an only child or my parents died when I was so young, or because I'd become so successful I was used to getting my way with most things... but I was selfish. And getting used to putting someone else's needs right up front with my own? Took some getting used to.

But practice makes perfect, right?

And maybe Seth was right about something else. Motivation was key. I had to have a reason for doing the right thing, and that reason had to be internal.

And it was.

I wanted to ace this husband thing.

I figured I'd been doing pretty good with it—so far.

Maggie and I hadn't gotten into any serious arguments since Vegas—nine weeks and counting. I was keeping up with going to AA meetings, hitting the gym, eating well and sleeping well, and generally keeping my shit together.

I was making this shit look good, too. I knew I was. People kept telling me so. Even people who had no idea I'd kicked pot and had no reason to comment that I looked or sounded better or whatever.

I was getting positive feedback left and right; that was a fact.

And not just from chicks.

The crew seemed to think I was a nicer dude now, too. Guys who used to steer clear of me backstage were starting to look me in the eye and wish me a good show.

Felt good.

Who knew not being such a self-obsessed prick would make life so much more enjoyable?

I'd even apologized to Talia for threatening to fire her, and apologized to a few other people for various shit I'd pulled.

I'd gradually gotten back into a routine of promo work; no solo interviews, but interviews with the other members of my band, no more than two a day. And I hadn't even slipped or put my foot in my mouth at any of those interviews.

But no one was exactly asking about my sobriety or my marriage, because neither of these topics had hit the media.

Until this morning.

It was pretty much my personal version of hell to have to sit through interview after interview fucking dodging every question about my personal life and being all fucking evasive and secretive, but I'd been doing it. For Maggie.

No; for my relationship with Maggie.

All the while, I just wanted to shout the truth in everyone's faces.

I'm in love with Maggie Omura, oh, and by the way, we're married. Send gifts.

Except...

Maggie would've been pissed. And not the kind of pissed that could be channeled into sexual frustration and end in a nice angry fuck. Like seriously pissed—the kind where she stopped fucking me *and* talking to me.

Wasn't going down that road, ever again, if I could help it.

So, I'd bit my fucking tongue and slogged through the torture.

And I kept doing my best to make my wife happy. Not something I had a great track record with, but I was figuring it out. I was finally learning all the ways *besides* sex I could put a smile on Maggie Omura's face, and I was committing this shit to memory.

Coffee with honey in the morning, mocha if she could get it.

Chocolate.

Yoga.

A few hours of quiet each day to get work done and some time alone every few days, usually involving a bubble bath or the spa, for "Maggie time."

Time to chat with her girls.

High-heeled shoes.

Pretty pink shit.

These were the things that made Maggie Omura happy, day-to-day.

She also liked it when I washed her hair in the shower, and when I had deep conversations with her that didn't lead to sex. Go figure. Took me a while to figure that one out, but it definitely went a long way to making Maggie happy when we spent quality time together without me putting the moves on.

Bonus: it usually made her so happy she ended up putting the moves on me anyway.

Win-win.

Oh, and girl-on-top. Because sexual satisfaction was now a guaranteed way to give Maggie that happy glow. And no matter who was calling the shots, Maggie loved being on top when we had sex.

And let's be honest; she was usually calling the shots. Even if I pretended it was otherwise.

Since I loved her being on top, that was another win-win anyway. And even if she was calling the shots... I could still make her lose her shit.

So no one was complaining.

Which got me thinking...

I glanced over at her. She'd finished her risotto and the flight attendant was clearing away our plates. Maggie met my eyes and gave me a hesitant smile.

I knew I wasn't supposed to be trying to solve problems with sex anymore... but fuck it. My head was already deep in the gutter. And in my books, it was always the right time for sex.

I'd once fucked a girl at a funeral, so there was that.

Shame; I had none.

If Maggie was pissed at me, I knew it was gonna be harder to make her lose her shit. So instead, I figured I'd make her happy first, before she got pissed at me.

This was my entire plan.

One, make her happy.

Two, make her lose her shit.

And three, when she was in the happy afterglow phase, break the Maxxi thing to her gently.

Shouldn't be too hard... We were alone, on a private jet; just me and Maggie. I'd had the two rooms of the cabin filled with pink flowers for her, and the one in the back had a bed. I'd made sure of that.

When the flight attendant set the piece of nine-layer chocolate cake in front of her, though, she was definitely on to me.

"You're up to something," she said as she eyed the thick slice of cake. "You know I know that, right?"

"Can't a guy treat his girl to a private jet?"

She narrowed her gray eyes at me.

"Aren't you gonna eat your cake?"

She ate her cake.

After she ate, I showed her the room in back. There was a flimsy door between the two rooms that I shut, then I tugged her straight toward the bed.

Maggie's eyes widened when she saw it... but she couldn't exactly be shocked that what I was "up to" was angling to get laid.

"What if the flight attendant comes back here?" she asked, eying the flimsy door.

"He's not gonna bother us. You're hot as fuck and there's a bed. You think he doesn't know why I brought you back here?" I was already taking off her clothes, peeling off her little ruffled top and her skirt. I left on her sexy boots, picked her up by the waist and tossed her on the bed.

Then I stripped down myself. Slowly. While she watched me, her eyes glazing over with lust as I skimmed my shirt over my head, then started undoing my jeans.

"And none of this five-minutes-til-I-make-Zane-blow bullshit," I told her, getting a little distracted as I watched her strip off her bra.

"We've got another half-hour in the air, I'm fucking you every second of it."

"Okay." She tugged her panties down and off, a wicked gleam flashing in her eyes as I shoved my jeans down. "But you know you can't last that long..."

Challenge accepted.

"What am I, thirteen?" I kicked off my jeans and socks.

She narrowed her eyes at me. "Even you weren't having sex at thirteen, so don't start."

I prowled over to her, naked. "You know, I *can* last longer than ten seconds." I stood over her and let my eyes roam over her body as I rolled on the condom. She was laid out before me on her back, naked, her knees pulled up and slightly spread so I could see every part of her. "It's not my fault you're so hot and so damn greedy, you want it fast and five-hundred times a night."

She did.

Maggie loved it when I finished fast. Go-fucking-figure. With other women, swear to Christ, I could fuck for hours. "Sex god" and all that shit; I'd earned my reputation with women for good reason. You could ask those other women.

But with Maggie, I lost my shit almost every fucking time. Something about *this* woman just fucked with me in a major way.

"*Five* times," she said, as I laid my hands on her knees and spread them. "I believe that's our record..."

I settled onto the bed, kneeling over her. Her gray eyes were wide and dark as she watched me. So fucking beautiful. "I remember. I was sore the next day." I lowered myself over her, forcing her legs wide. "Totally worth it."

It was. This past week, we'd fucked so many times I'd lost count. She could've broken every bone in my body and I'd still want to fuck her.

"What can I say?" she teased, wrapping her arms and legs around me as I started rubbing my cock against her soft pussy. "I'm a quantity over quality type of girl..."

"That's bullshit."

"Why?"

"Because. You chose this dick... you chose the best, baby."

Maggie laughed her husky-soft laugh. Then she shoved at me a little, tried to push me over so she could roll on top.

"Uh-uh," I said, pinning her down. "I'm on top, and you're doing what I say." I had her thighs open wide with my spread knees, one hand in the middle of her chest, holding her down, and I started grinding my dick against her. I was hellbent on keeping control. Much as I loved giving it up to her, she wasn't taking it this time.

She wriggled beneath me, increasing the friction, and she started making those husky little gasping noises I knew so well as she tried to rub herself off on my dick.

"And slow the fuck down," I ordered, even as my voice got low and rough with lust. "You're not going off until I say."

"What? You don't want to rush it, fine. But I'm gonna get me some."

"No, you're not."

I peeled her arms off me and pinned her wrists above her head. I leaned low on my elbows and got in her face, fusing my body to hers as I slowly but forcefully pushed the head of my cock into her.

She gasped and moaned. "Zane... *yeah.*"

And the fact that she loved it? Went straight to my balls and took all the blood in my head with it.

I shoved my way in slowly, deeper... until I bottomed out and the heat swept through my body. The feeling of being squeezed by her, so hot and tight, the pressure gripping me... Pure fucking heaven.

Maggie squirmed, wanting more, but I just stayed like this, deep inside her, for a long moment. I kissed her, catching her full bottom lip and nibbling as she squirmed. But I was holding onto control.

Just barely.

"You gonna calm down?"

She blinked at me, dazed. "What?"

"Stop wiggling around and calm down, I'll feed you some more cock." I kissed her softly. "You like that?"

Her eyelids lowered and maybe she tried to glare at me a bit; didn't really work. She relaxed a little beneath me. "Okay."

I lifted my hips, drawing my dick back out to the very tip, and slamming back in. Maggie's eyes rolled closed and she breathed this soft, raspy sound... "*Baby...*" she sighed.

And that was about it.

My self-control went out the window without a fucking parachute.

I buried my tongue in her mouth, squeezed her wrists tight and started fucking her hard and deep, kind of mid-tempo and hungry. I wasn't chasing the finish, but I wasn't holding back either. I wasn't even thinking about coming. I just wanted to make Maggie come. Feel her shiver and shake and run out of breath in my arms and fall the fuck apart.

Make her feel the way she always made me feel...

I wasn't gonna eat her out or play with her clit or tease her to get her there. I was just gonna smother her until all she could feel with every part of her hot little body was *me*. I was gonna crush her, devour her, fuck the hell out of that tight, swollen little pussy of hers until she screamed so loud they heard it in the cockpit.

So that's what I did, with single-minded focus.

I fucked her until I was lost, too. Until all I could feel was her body pinned beneath mine. All I could taste was her taste; chocolate cake and Maggie. All I could hear were her soft, panting cries in my mouth, against my skin. All I could breathe was her soft smell.

Until her pussy convulsed around my dick and she screamed... that soft, ragged Maggie scream that totally did me in.

I felt the rush, the high of making her come gripping me... and the pleasure tearing right through me.

My balls seized and my cock blew up. I drove into her hard, shooting deep, as she murmured, "*Yes...*" against my skin. I felt her nails digging into me, her teeth in my neck, her grip on me heightening the pleasure.

Fucking Christ. No way I could hold that one back.

Maggie panted softly beneath me, kissing my neck and kinda

humming happily. As my body gradually relaxed against hers, she twitched and squirmed a little. I was still inside her and every time she moved, it sent a twinge of raw pleasure up my spine.

"Fuck..." I sighed. "Sorry, babe. I couldn't even help it..."

"I loved it," she said, her voice soft. She gazed up at me. "Why do you apologize? I love it when you come."

"Yeah. Can't even hold it back with you. You just make me lose my shit..."

Her gray eyes searched mine. "Why does it bother you?"

"That I can't last for shit with you?" I rolled off her, carefully pulling out. "Because I'd love to be able to fuck you for hours, obviously."

"You do fuck me for hours. Just because you come multiple times, and so do I, it's not a fail, Zane. I love that you can't hold back. Don't you know that?" She drifted her hand over my chest and down my abs, making my muscles tighten. Everything was so fucking sensitive.

Maggie knew it. She leaned in and flicked my pierced nipple with her tongue, sending pleasure sparking through my body. Then she sucked it into her mouth, and Jesus Christ, I wanted to fuck her again.

Then she kissed her way up my chest. "I love it that you lose control with me," she told me. "I love making you lose control." She smoothed my hair back from my face and smirked. "I guess this is the one area of your life that I don't mind you being so out of control. So unpredictable."

"It's predictable as fuck, Maggie." I relaxed beneath her with a satisfied sigh as she lay half on top of me. "Get you anywhere near my dick, and I can tell you exactly what's gonna happen."

She grinned at me. "Well, your dick's not complaining, and neither am I. So just enjoy it."

My gaze wandered down her face to her tits, which were pressed against me. "Never said I didn't enjoy it."

"Good."

She started to sit up, and my dick twitched at the sight of her perfect naked breasts, her perky, rosy nipples. "Fuck it. Let's do it again."

She laughed.

"I know what this is about, Zane."

I looked over at Maggie as we got dressed; she was tucking her top into her skirt as I did up my jeans. We didn't end up doing it again. I would've loved to have this conversation while we were horizontal, but the jet was about to descend and the flight attendant had already knocked on the door.

"You want us to tell everyone we're together," she said gently. "I know you do. You bring it up every day."

"I do? Thought I was being subtle."

"This is your idea of subtle? A private jet and a florist's entire stock of pink flowers?"

"Two florists, actually."

She just shook her head at me.

"You don't like it?"

She sighed. "What girl wouldn't like it?"

"What was your favorite part?" I asked her, seriously. I was pretty bent on adding more shit to that growing list of things that made her happy.

She glanced down my body as I pulled on my shirt. "I'd have to say the bed was a nice touch."

"Yeah?" Fully dressed, I walked over to her.

"Yeah," she said as I took her in my arms. "I've never mile-highed it before."

I grinned and kissed her. "Fuck, I love deflowering you..."

"But... I'm still not ready to go public," she said firmly. "It's not that I don't want everyone to know, Zane—in theory."

I cocked an eyebrow at her. The hell did that mean?

"I don't like hiding it any more than you do," she said. "Honestly. I just don't want to rush this."

"This?" I kissed her again.

"Yeah." She softened against me. "This thing between us. It's real and it's good, and even though I've loved you for so long, *this* is new. You and me. And when we share it with the world, it's gonna change. It could be a big change or it could be a small change, but it will change. It'll be different when everyone knows. And for just a little while, I want this to just be ours."

"Okay, Maggie." I kissed her on the forehead, then let her go. "But I really don't think our relationship is gonna change just because people know."

"I wish that were the case. But I don't think that's realistic." She seemed to consider the look on my face, then sighed. "I know. I'm a buzzkill. I swear, I keep hoping it won't be a big deal. But literally the day I started wearing the ring, people started asking." She waved her left hand at me, where she wore the wedding band. "I mean, the girls started asking. Katie. Amber. Even Jessa messaged me from Vancouver to tell me she'd heard, probably from Katie. And Brody keeps doing this thing... Whenever we finish a conversation, he goes silent for a moment, like he's waiting for me to say something. I don't, because I'm still figuring out how to explain to him what this is and how it's not going to affect my job. I just haven't found the words yet."

"I know, Maggs."

She gazed up at me, chewing on her lip a bit. "I told the girls that you and I are working on things, privately, and I asked them to give me some space. They were totally supportive, of course. But I keep trying to figure out how to face up to all the little lies I've had to tell and answer all their burning questions, and it all just seems so daunting. I don't even know how I can begin to deal with it and deal with us at the same time, you know?"

"I think you're making it a lot harder than it has to be," I told her, gently.

"Yeah. You know, I used to think that was your domain. You were always making everything too difficult. But now I can see what you mean... I don't exactly make life easy, do I?"

"You make my life better. That's all that matters to me."

Total truth.

She smiled at me softly. "Thank you."

I wanted to smile back, but it felt wrong. I really, really didn't want to fuck up all these good vibes we had going between us—for one thing, we were now able to calmly discuss our personal shortcomings without going off on each other, and that was fucking refreshing—but we were heading back to Earth and soon enough, she was gonna turn her phone back on.

So I took her hands in mine. "Maggie... I've gotta tell you something."

She stared at me, and as those words and the seriousness of my tone sank in, I could see the trepidation in her eyes. I could feel it as she started to brace herself for the worst.

And what would the worst be, in her mind?

I'd fallen off the wagon?

I'd fucked someone else?

"There was a story this morning online," I told her. "Brody sent it to me. I'm sure he sent it to you, too... but you know how I confiscated your phone?"

She blinked at me, and I could see her pulling the pieces together in her head. How I'd bounced out of bed this morning and grabbed her phone, shoved it down my pants and told her she wasn't working today because we were gonna spend the day together.

Then she pulled her hands from mine. "Yes...?" she said, warily.

"Our wedding in Vegas was mentioned in the article."

She stared at me. "What about our wedding?"

"It was an eyewitness account. From someone who was there."

"I know what an eyewitness account is," she said, her tone cooling. "Are you telling me my dad talked to the media about us?"

"It wasn't your dad. It was that girl he brought to the wedding."

"Maxxi?" She gaped at me, stunned. "That little... My dad's girlfriend talked to the media about us?"

"She, uh, said a whole shitload of stuff about your dad, too. We weren't exactly the focus of the story. But yeah, she threw our wedding in there. I'm thinking they must've had a falling out or something? And she felt the need to expose all his private shit to try to hurt him?"

"Oh." Maggie sat down on the edge of the bed. "*Shit*," she muttered. And that was it.

She was taking this pretty fucking well, considering I'd been mentally preparing for a screaming fit.

There was a knock on the door. "The pilot requests that you take your seats and buckle in..." the flight attendant called in, for the second time.

"We've gotta go sit down," I told Maggie gently, reaching for her.

She looked up at me, but she didn't take my hand. And that's when I really saw the look in her eyes.

Nope. She wasn't taking this well.

Not at all.

"You stole my phone and hijacked me so I couldn't see it? So I couldn't react?"

"So it wouldn't totally ruin your day," I corrected her, "and we could talk about it before either of us reacted."

She stared at me. She wasn't yelling, but somehow, as she glanced at my hand and refused to take it, this felt worse. She looked resigned and fucking disappointed, like she couldn't even be bothered to fight. "You don't even care, do you?"

"Of course I care."

"You care how I'm going to react. But you don't care that it's out there."

"I'm not gonna lie to you, Maggie. I don't give a shit that it's out there."

She got to her feet and looked into my eyes, ignoring the hand I'd offered her. She shook her head at me with that disappointment in her eyes. She didn't touch me, but somehow it felt worse than a slap in the face.

Then she whispered, "I need to talk to my dad," and left the room.

CHAPTER NINETEEN

Maggie

I ARRIVED at my dad's place in Las Vegas late that afternoon. I'd considered simply calling him, but then it would've been too easy for him to just hang up on me. Instead I'd texted him to confirm that he'd be home, and got my ass on a plane.

While I was on the plane, I'd reread the offending article repeatedly—it was rapidly circulating the less-reputable entertainment gossip sites—and I knew I was making the right move.

This was really more of a go-ream-him-out-in-person situation.

By the time my taxi pulled up to my dad's house, though, I'd lost most of my gusto. I knew the odds I'd actually ream him out over this or anything else were pretty slim.

I'd never given the man a tenth of the flack he'd deserved.

Standing in his tacky home, surrounded by all his flashy, gaudy bullshit, and giving him hell? Unlikely. Looking my father and his ridiculous life in the face always disarmed me. Made me realize how futile anything I could say to him really was.

It had been a long time since I'd been inside my father's home. Maybe... six years? Seven? He'd lived in this one for over a decade, in this gated community in Summerlin, and I'd never enjoyed coming here. I'd never really enjoyed being in any of my dad's homes over the years, but this one was easily my least-favorite.

Maybe because when I walked into it, it seemed so grossly unlikely that a man who'd fathered me could actually live here.

It looked like a Goodfella lived in it. All marble and glossy and too much gold. And my dad himself, in his paisley silk pajama pants and robe, was the picture of *Look at me, I'm rich and sleazy*.

There was even a new young thing on his arm.

Well, she wasn't exactly on his arm. She was lounging on his couch, half-naked, when I followed him into the expansive, shiny living room. She was topless, to be precise, and had a tiny, fluffy white dog in her lap.

When she saw me, she looked me over slowly and speculatively, making no move whatsoever to cover her breasts. And my dad, the epitome of grace and manners, didn't even introduce us properly.

"This is Margery," he told her. And that was it.

"Maggie," I said. My dad only ever called me Margery to be an ass, because he knew I preferred Maggie.

"Charmaine," the girl said, still looking me over. And not in a friendly way.

"I'm his daughter," I informed her, before she could say anything I could never unhear, like asking him if I'd dropped by for a threesome. "Could you please give us a little time to talk, alone?"

She didn't say anything, but she got up and made a point of walking over to my dad, boobs still out, and gave him a gratuitous kiss before handing him the dog. Then she threw me another look. Like Maxxi, she was young and slightly plump, but where Maxxi had brown hair with fuchsia at the tips, this one was a peroxide-blonde.

She also had a definite skank vibe about her.

Sadly, I kinda missed Maxxi.

When she'd wandered out of the room, I asked my dad, "What happened to Maxxi?"

"Gone," he said, with a lack of feeling that was pretty disturbing, though I really couldn't be surprised. I watched him stroke the dog's fur and deposit the tiny thing gently on the couch. Then I looked around.

Why would I even hope to find Maxxi here?

Just because he'd kept her around longer than a lot of the other ones didn't mean she'd be staying forever.

I sighed and set my purse on a table. Unfortunately, I wasn't going to get the kinds of answers I was hoping for. This became abundantly clear when I took a good, long read of my dad.

It was barely four-thirty on a Wednesday and he was definitely not sober. And he was mixing himself a fresh drink on his gaudy drink cart, this mirror-and-rhinestone thing that looked like it belonged on the set of a 1970s porno.

Looked a hell of a lot like the one he'd sent me and Zane as a wedding gift, actually.

Needless to say, we didn't keep it.

On the wall behind him, there was a giant painting of—I shit you not—*himself*, with the dog. He also had a new tattoo on his wrist of a naked chick. Which brought the total count of naked chick tattoos on my dad's body to three, as far as I knew.

"Maxxi was nice," I offered. It was true enough; the one time I'd met Maxxi, the night I married Zane, she was nice. She was pretty wasted, but she was nice. Probably nicer than my dad deserved, honestly. "You were with her for a while. A couple of years, right?"

My dad made a disgusted sound. "Maxxi's a useless cunt."

Okaaay.

I watched him take his drink and settle onto the couch, drawing the dog into his lap, completely unaffected by my presence. Well... he looked mildly annoyed, maybe.

Holy shit, this was gonna be hard.

Harder than I'd anticipated, even.

My father was the very opposite of a nice, loving father or a nice, loving man. All he had to do was open his mouth to remind me of it.

Calling his ex-girlfriend a useless cunt?

How would I ever get through to a man who would do that?

No matter how pissed off I was about the girl spilling my private shit to the media, she didn't deserve my dad talking about her like that. Maybe she was a little... air-headed? But from what I knew, she was barely twenty-one when I met her.

My dad was turning sixty this year.

It would've been swell if this age disparity was an anomaly in my dad's dating history, but not so. Fact was, Dizzy Bowman, fading rock star, was drawn to girls with major daddy issues.

Admittedly, I had daddy issues of my own, so it wasn't exactly difficult to recognize. I'd never been into dating vastly older men, but I couldn't exactly judge.

"You want one?" he asked me as he looked me over. He gestured belatedly toward the bar cart, where he hadn't bothered to pour me a drink.

"No, thank you," I said, and my dad actually rolled his eyes. Because, you know, good fathers always rolled their eyes when their daughters wouldn't drink alcohol with them. "I came to talk." I chose a chair across from the couch that didn't look like anyone had had sex on it recently, and perched carefully on the edge. "Look, Dizzy. I wanted to ask you—"

"*Dizzy*." He cut me off with a bitter chuckle. "Are we back to this shit?"

Uh... we never got off this shit. But okay...

"Dad," I amended, though it pained me. I was pretty sure he only preferred me calling him Dad because of the power trip. *I'm your father, you owe me your life.* That kind of thing. "I need to talk to you about something important."

"So?" He sipped his drink. "What's up?"

What's up?

Seriously?

We hadn't seen each other since my wedding almost two years ago, and we'd spoken less than a handful of times this year.

Any number of things could've been up.

I'm dying of cancer, Dad.

I've got three months to live.

I won the lottery and I'm leaving it all to you.

Jesus, I wanted to say something terrible to get some kind of reaction from him.

Five minutes in the man's company, and I already felt like an angry teenager all over again.

"What's up," I said slowly, "is that Maxxi said a bunch of stuff to the media about us."

"She's not here," was his response.

"Yes, I see that. Did you see what she said, online?"

"Yeah. I saw."

Okay. So at least he knew what I was talking about. Though he didn't seem the least bit concerned.

"They quoted her, Dad. She gave them her name. She didn't even try to hide who she was. Which means she was probably trying to hurt you. And to do that... she was probably pretty upset with you."

"So?"

"So... what happened between you two?"

He grunted. "What happened? I treated her like a queen, and this is how she returns my generosity. Dragging my name through the mud."

Right... Because his name was so pristine up until that point.

"She said she was at my wedding to Zane," I went on. "Which was supposed to be a private event. She wasn't supposed to tell anyone."

My dad stared at me blankly. "That was a long time ago, Maggie."

Like that mattered?

I tried another tack. "She spilled a lot of unflattering stuff about you, too. I think this was just one of many things she thought might hurt you."

"Why would it hurt me?"

"Uh... because I'm your daughter? And it was supposed to be a secret."

That didn't seem to compute at all. I could already see him

checking out of the conversation, though it wasn't like he'd really checked in in the first place.

"I was supposed to be able to trust you," I added.

Now my father gave me a cold look. And when Dizzy Bowman gave you a cold look, it put frost on your spine. "It wasn't me who blabbed about your wedding."

"Right. But you're the one who brought her to the wedding. We trusted you, and you vouched for her, and we trusted that. This is a breach of that trust. Do you get that?"

I looked deep into his gray eyes, and no, he definitely didn't get that.

"It's not my fault if some bitch can't keep her mouth shut," he said. "This what you came here for? To hassle me in my living room?" He took a slurp of his drink.

"I'm not hassling you, Di—Dad. But you should know, it really upset me when I read what she said to the press—"

"Don't be a bitch, Maggie."

And there it was.

Had I ever gotten through a conversation with my dad without him calling me a bitch or a slut or a waste of air?

Not that I could recall.

Which was maybe why I had such a hard time standing up to him. Because I knew that when I did, the insults would start flying.

And it would hurt.

I sat back and looked at him. He was still handsome, in a way. My father was never the best-looking guy, but there was something about him. This kind of haphazard charm he tossed around. Made people want to buy into his bullshit, at least for a while. There was a reason the young girls kept coming around, and it wasn't just the money.

With his scraggly, bleach-blond hair and tattoos, his dark tan and jewelry, there was something attractive about him, I supposed, to a certain type of girl. It was his confidence, maybe. His unshakable sense of self-importance.

"I'm not being a bitch, Dad," I told him calmly. "I'm just trying to be honest with you. I want you to know how I feel."

He made a disgusted sound and sipped his drink. It was almost empty. "Well, what do you want me to do about it?"

As if I wanted anything.

I watched him stroke his dog. She wore a gold bow, and if memory served, her name was Cookie. I'd never met her before, but he'd definitely sent me pictures of her. She was pretty damn cute, so it was impossible to hate her. But it was painfully clear to me that Cookie got a shit-ton more love from my dad than I ever had.

I was pretty damn sure, based on this exchange and so many others over the years, that all I'd ever been to my dad was a pain in his ass. Even though I'd never actually asked him for much.

Although... maybe I did want something.

For as long as I could remember, I'd wanted to work in the music industry and manage bands—and not because I loved music. I did, but the real reason I'd always been so driven to succeed in my career was because deep down I'd been seeking my father's recognition and approval all along.

I knew this.

My musical talent was pretty much nil, but the business side of things had proven a solid fit for me, and I knew that was the only way I'd have a chance of making a name for myself in the industry.

The only thing my dad had ever seemed to care about besides himself was the music industry.

Well, and his dog.

And yes, I wanted his approval.

That was never more clear to me than when I sat here in his tacky house and felt his supreme *lack* of approval.

It wasn't that my father disapproved of me, exactly.

He just didn't approve.

And seeing him like this, fawning over Cookie? He was now feeding her treats from a silvered-glass bowl... and Jesus Christ.

I was jealous of a dog.

"I don't expect anything from you, Dad," I told him, which was true enough. Maybe I did want, but I'd learned long ago not to expect.

"How's your husband?" he asked, switching topics like I hadn't even spoken. Was he *trying* to be an asshole? Because he definitely hadn't asked me how *I* was since I'd stepped in the door. "You know, I asked him to meet up with me when Dirty played Vegas. What was that, two months ago? He never called me back."

Perfect. I should've known.

I'd never heard from my dad while we were in Vegas on this tour... yet he'd reached out to Zane.

Zane never told me about that, but I didn't blame him. He would've known it would only hurt me.

"He's okay," I said flatly.

I could've said, *He's mad at me right now because I freaked out that our wedding is now in the press, thanks to you, and we spent an hour arguing about it this afternoon while he tried to talk me out of coming to see you, you know, on account of you being such an irretrievable asshole*, but I didn't.

"Okay?" He grunted. "You're not making him happy?"

"I try," I said; no idea if he'd pick up on the sarcasm. "My mission in life is to make my husband happy, of course."

"Should be. You play your cards right, he'll take care of you for the rest of your life. I would've taken care of your mother, if she'd stepped up."

Cards?

Play?

Like my marriage to Zane was some kind of strategic game?

And my mother...?

My mom did step up—and raised me by herself. With pretty much zero help from him. While he'd fucked groupies and snorted coke in his gold-plated mansion, we'd scraped by.

I watched him suck back the last dregs of his drink, his eyes unfocused. He was barely following our conversation, and it wasn't just that he was drunk and/or high.

He also truly didn't give a shit.

Not one shit.

"What are you on?" I asked him. It wasn't something I normally asked. Because really, why bother? But I was morbidly curious.

"Grow up, Margery," he snarled. "You know I've got the pills for my back."

Right. The mysterious phantom back pain that had afflicted him for the last thirty years.

"I didn't know that was still bothering you."

"Why're you here?" he asked me, and I could tell that he seriously had no clue. I had no idea if he'd already forgotten about the whole Maxxi-leaking-shit-to-the-media thing or if he'd entirely missed how significant it was to me. But he definitely had no clue why I was still sitting here.

Frankly, neither did I.

I stood up and got my purse.

"I do want Zane to be happy," I told him. "Maybe someday you'll meet someone who'll want that for you, too."

He glanced up at me as Cookie ate a treat from his hand. "Did you meet Charmaine?"

I stared at him, searching his face. *Jesus*, he was drunk.

"Oh, yeah. She seems like a real keeper."

As I headed out to the front foyer, he called after me, "Tell Zane to give me a call, Maggie."

"Sure, Dad."

I'll get right on that.

If only he knew... that if Zane had come with me to have this conversation—which he'd wanted to do, but I'd talked him out of—he'd probably have cut off my dad's balls already and fed them to him.

I'd probably have let him.

I wasn't a little girl anymore, and I definitely saw Derek "Dizzy" Bowman for what he was—a womanizing, alcoholic narcissist who was much more in love with himself than he'd ever been with my mom, and who really didn't give a crap about me. All I was was a footnote in his life, the mere fact of my existence a credit to his excellence as a human being.

Yup, I'm a dad. Got a beautiful daughter...

I was pretty sure a line like that had gotten him laid more times than I cared to know.

As I walked out his front door, I knew I needed to let go of the hope that I was ever going to win his approval, much less his love. And I knew I shouldn't have felt so hurt about it, or about the fact that his latest girlfriend had betrayed my trust.

My need to be loved by a man who could probably never love me, who probably had no real capacity to love anyone but himself, was the most fucked-up ongoing disappointment in my life—and it was the hardest to reckon with.

I really shouldn't have needed my dad's love anymore. I shouldn't have wanted it. But I still did. I knew that painful truth, deep inside.

I wanted it, but I was never going to get it.

Because you couldn't have something that didn't exist.

I arrived back in Detroit late that night, exhausted, my emotions rubbed raw and wanting nothing more than to fall into Zane's arms. I found him easily enough, in the lounge of the bar, which was closed for a private Dirty party. Brody and Jessa were with us again, Roni had also flown out, some other friends of the band had come down from Toronto and the place was packed.

I'd said hello to Brody and a few other people before I spotted Zane. He was standing at the back of the room, talking with Dylan and some other guys I didn't know.

I made my way through the crowd toward them, and when Zane saw me his face lit right up. His eyes locked on mine and I felt that look all the way down deep. The butterflies swarmed, my heart swelled, and my shoulders softened with relief.

About two seconds later, I saw *her*.

Dallas.

She was standing over at the bar with a few other girls, including Katie, and Jesse was standing nearby. And granted, Katie and Jesse had no reason to know about my bullshit drama with Dallas, or what an evil wench she was, but it really rubbed me the wrong way. Katie and Jesse were my friends.

Zane was my husband, and this was my family.

Dallas was the enemy.

What the hell was she doing here? In her shiny red mini-dress and *I'm-a-slut* heels, with her thick blonde hair and fake game-show-co-host smile...

By the time I reached Zane and he pulled me to him, I was far more angry and distraught than I was happy to see him.

"What's she doing here?" I demanded, before he could get a word out.

"Who?" The light in his face died a bit, so maybe he already knew who.

"Dallas," I bit out.

Zane glanced over toward the bar, where Dallas stood. So yeah, he knew she was there.

"Hey, Maggie. Welcome back." Dylan laid a warm hand on my back and I let him draw me into a hug.

"Thanks, Dylan," I forced out. "Nice to be back."

Then Zane yanked me away from Dylan and pulled me aside—into the very back corner of the bar.

"You alright?" he asked, looking me over. "What happened with Dizzy?"

"Fuck Dizzy. Did you invite her?"

"No," he said. "I didn't invite her. I haven't even talked to her yet."

"*Yet?*" My hands curled into fists at my sides, and I wondered what the odds were that I'd punch him—or Dallas—before the night was through. With the fury that was running through my veins right now, it was feeling pretty damn likely. I was shaking, I was so wrung out from the awkward-painful conversation with my dad, and now *this...*

"It's a party, Maggie," he said, eying me cautiously. Maybe wondering if I was gonna use the fists. "She showed up. That's what people do."

"Yeah. She showed up. Just like she showed up at your Christmas party, and you let her stay there, too. There she is, and you know how I feel about her. I told you how I feel about her after that party. So unless *you* have some kind of feelings for her, I can't see any reason why she's still here."

"I'm not involved with her anymore," he said, eyes narrowing. So now he was getting mad at me? Where did he get off getting mad at me over this? "I've told you that. You never believe me."

"Okay," I practically seethed. "I believe you. But you still put up with her. You still entertain her bullshit."

"What bullshit?" he challenged. "When she shoved her hand down my pants at the Christmas party? I told you, nothing happened after that."

"I know. You didn't even kick her ass out."

"I didn't fuck her either, Maggie. I spent most of the night with *you*."

That was true.

"Even though you were barely speaking to me," he added, with a little growl in his voice.

That was true, too.

I glared at him anyway.

He glared right back at me. He towered over me, with his head bent close to mine. We were maybe an inch apart, and even more than I wanted to kiss him... I wanted to throttle him.

Fuck. Were we ever gonna get along for any length of time?

And would I ever stop seeing my fucking dad when I looked at him?

Maybe not. Because I couldn't seem to stop seeing women like Dallas when I looked at him.

Women I *knew* were beneath me—which meant I wasn't gonna

make some scene by kicking her out myself. I shouldn't have to kick her out myself.

I shouldn't have to ask Jude to kick her out, either.

She wasn't here for me or Jude.

"She's not a good person, Zane," I informed him, because to be fair, maybe he'd never seen that side of her. With him, she was probably sweet as pie. "I don't want to see her. Is it too much to ask that she doesn't show up at every party?"

"She's not at every party," he said. "And I get that you don't like her, but—"

"But what? There's no *but*. I have reasons for not liking her, Zane."

"Why, because she grabbed my dick? She didn't know I was with you when she did that, because *you don't let me tell anyone I'm with you.*"

"Right. So it's my fault. And that makes it okay for her to grab your dick."

"Well, it doesn't make it not okay," he said.

"You did not just say that."

"Maggie. I'm not fucking Dallas and I'm not looking to have my dick grabbed by anyone. When are you gonna believe me when I say that?"

Silence. It was loud in the party, but we just stared at each other for a long moment in our silent, heated corner.

"I understand that you don't like Dallas," he said again, slowly. "I just don't understand why she needs to be punished. If you need to punish someone, punish me. I'm the one who slept with her when I shouldn't have. That's not her fault."

I shook my head at him, still angry. I was mad at myself, too, for flipping out on him about this, about that stupid girl, when I couldn't even stand up to the one person who really deserved my anger—my dad.

"I can't believe you don't see it," I told him quietly.

"See what?"

"You think she's a nice girl? Ask her what she thinks of me."

I turned to walk away, because stupid tears were actually forming in my eyes—but Zane grabbed my arm, stopping me. He spun me around to face him and held me by my shoulders. "What does that mean?"

I blinked back my tears, trying to cover the pain with anger. But I couldn't deal. I was so done. I had nothing left.

Dealing with my dad had taken it all.

"I overheard her talking about me at the Christmas party." My lips actually quivered as I said the words.

"Talking about you? What do you mean, talking about you?" Zane's hands tightened on my shoulders, his fingers digging into me.

A part of me couldn't believe I was really telling him this... But I told him anyway.

"It was late, after a lot of people had left. I found her in the kitchen with her girlfriend. They were drunk, and I guess they were looking in your fridge for booze. They didn't see me. But I heard her say, 'Where's that little brown girl who makes the drinks?'"

Zane stared at me.

I didn't want to say it, but there it was. I'd never wanted to repeat those ugly words to him.

Zane knew who I was and what I was worth, and everything I did for Dirty. But to some people, all I'd ever be was the little brown girl who made the drinks at a Dirty party.

"She said *what*?"

I swallowed a sob that threatened to escape. "She said, 'Where's that little brown girl who—'"

"Don't. Don't fucking say it again."

I went silent.

"Give me a minute," he growled. Then he practically tossed me aside as he walked away, leaving me standing here, alone.

I turned right around and left the party. I headed up to my room, just barely holding back the tears. As soon as I'd shut myself into my hotel room, though, the tears won.

I tossed myself on the bed and cried for five solid minutes or so, until I was too exhausted to do it anymore and felt like a useless idiot. What had crying ever done for anyone?

It hadn't done anything for me when I was a kid. It definitely never solved any of my problems or magically turned my dad into a nice guy.

Then I rolled over onto my back and stared blankly at the ceiling, kinda wishing I'd never gotten up this morning.

Well... the sex on the private jet with Zane... I'd get out of bed for that. And the chocolate cake.

But the rest of it?

To hell with the rest of it.

Maybe fifteen minutes later, there was a soft knock on my hotel room door.

I opened it to find Dallas, her eyes red-rimmed from crying. Her gaze barely met mine, and I hoped I didn't look half the mess that she did.

I'd never had a conversation with this woman before. I really didn't know her, and she didn't know me.

I only knew her name because my husband had fucked her.

What the hell did we have to say to each other?

"I'm sorry," she whispered, but there wasn't much remorse in it.

Clearly, she was sorry about whatever just happened between her and Zane, though.

Shady was standing behind her. When I looked at him, he took her by the elbow, gently, and ushered her away.

CHAPTER TWENTY

Zane

WHEN MAGGIE OPENED the door of her hotel room for me, she looked like she'd been crying—and it gutted me. How many times had I ever seen Maggie actually cry? Like tears running down her face and everything?

When her mom died. When her stepdad died, too.

And when Dylan's dad died, she'd been pretty weepy at the funeral.

That was about it.

"What happened at Dizzy's place?" I demanded as I walked in. "What did he say to you?"

"What did you say to Dallas?" She stood there with her arms wrapped around herself, looking small and off-balance, like she didn't know if she should hug me or start crying again or what.

And I softened, instantly.

"She's not coming back," I told her, taking a gentler tone. "You don't have to worry about seeing her again."

"Just like that?"

"Just like that." I looked her over carefully. She was still wearing the sexy little gray dress I'd seen her in downstairs. "You want me to take you back to the party?"

"No."

"You want me to leave?"

"No."

"Good. Because I'm not going to."

She stared at me for a moment. "What did you say to Dallas, Zane?"

"Doesn't matter."

"Zane."

I swiped my hand through my hair, smoothing it back from my face. "What do you think I said to her? I told her she's a fake-ass bitch and she's never gonna see me again."

True enough, but actually what I told her was worse than that. A little more colorful. With the shit Maggie told me replaying in my head, wasn't too hard to completely lose my shit on Dallas.

Didn't even care that I made her cry. Really couldn't remember why I'd ever put my dick in her in the first place.

Okay... so maybe I'd been frustrated with Maggie refusing to trust me. I kept thinking she was using her hatred of Dallas as an excuse to treat me like some class-A asshole she could never forgive—and maybe I'd let that blind me to the fact that I should've kicked Dallas' ass to the curb long ago.

Didn't even rate with me that Dallas was still hanging around trying to get her claws in me, because I didn't care. That was my bad, though. I should've seen it, but I didn't. I didn't realize how Maggie would take it. That she'd think I thought a lot more of Dallas than I did.

True, I didn't have any particularly negative feelings toward Dallas until tonight, but that didn't mean I had *feelings* for her. Just because I'd fucked her more than once didn't mean I cared about her any more than I'd cared about any other chick I'd screwed over the years.

Besides Maggie.

The fact was, Maggie was precious to me. She was my *wife*.

Even angry and PMSing and tearing me a new one, Maggie Omura was worth more to me than a lineup of Dallases, naked and willing. And a chick like that making fucking degrading comments about her?

Fuck. That.

"And by the way," I said, starting to pace a little, "you ever hear anyone talking about you like that again, you tell me." The whole thing was fucking agitating me. That she didn't give me a chance to make it right before this. Or at least tell Jude or someone. "Or you tell Jude. Or Jesse or Brody or Shady, or whoever's nearby. That shit does not stand, Maggie."

"Okay," she said, but I really didn't feel it.

"You feel me on that? I'm fucking serious about this."

She eyed me carefully as I paced back and forth in front of her. "You may be serious," she said, slowly, "but I really don't think you want to hear all the shit people say about me behind your back, Zane."

That stopped me cold. "What are you talking about?"

She sighed a little, in that way she did when I was being an idiot. "I'm female, I'm young, I'm mixed-race, and I'm pretty, and I work in a business that's driven by money, men, and sexuality. You think I haven't heard every sexist, racist, ignorant and cruel comment there is? Not to mention that if we go public with our marriage, every other girl from here to Tokyo is going to hate on me. Publicly."

Well, shit.

I never really thought of it like that before.

Personally, I thought the fucking world of Maggie. Always had. Pretty much everyone around me in the Dirty world treated the woman like solid gold, and that's what I was accustomed to. Comfortably accustomed to.

It never occurred to me that anyone would look down on her or be mean to her because she was young or pretty or had darker skin than mine.

Definitely hadn't occurred to me that anyone would hate her because I loved her.

Jesus Christ.

I sat down on the couch. And I tried to really feel the weight of it; how hard this was gonna be for her.

Maggie never asked to be famous. She never set out to fall in love with a rock star... or someone so like her dad. Someone who'd bring so much drama into her life.

"They're not gonna hate you," I said, slowly, thinking it through. "The fans love Katie."

"Sure. A lot of them do. But I'm not Katie and you're not Jesse, and you really don't know how they're going to react."

"You're right. I don't know. And I'm sure Katie's had her share of hate mail, so to speak. I don't exactly see that keeping her and Jesse apart, though. I'd dare any chick to say an unkind word about Katie, see how he reacts."

"I know you'd stand up for me, Zane, if you could. But that's not the entire picture." Maggie came over and sat down beside me on the couch. "You know, my mom used to get letters, over the years, from fans of my dad. Total strangers who admired her for mothering his child, or who condemned her for mothering his child. People who'd made up all these grand fantasies about her in their heads that weren't even true. She wrote back to almost all of them. I could never do that. I don't want a bunch of strangers weighing in on my life. I know you welcome it, that you like being the center of attention. And there's nothing wrong with that. You thrive on it. I definitely don't. It's just one of the things about us that's at odds, that we like about each other anyway, right? But you're not always going to be there to make the Dallases of the world apologize to me."

"Yeah," I told her. "I will. That's what a marriage is."

Maggie's eyes softened as she stared at me. "Zane..."

"You keep telling me I don't know what marriage is or I don't know what love is, Maggie. But I *know* I love you. And the thought of anyone hurting you makes me want to grab the nearest gun and start shooting."

She just stared at me.

"Your dad never even tried to protect you or your mom, Maggs. Your mom should never have had to read those letters alone. She wouldn't have had to face that shit alone if Dizzy had ever cared for either of you the way he should have."

She nodded.

"You feel that?"

"Yeah," she whispered. "I feel that."

"Good. I feel it too, Maggie. It kills me that you've gone through what he's put you through. I'm not gonna stand by and let anyone hurt you. I don't care who knows I love you. I don't care who knows I'm married to you. If anyone's got a problem with it, I don't give a fuck. I haven't talked to anyone about the wedding or that gossip article since you took off to see Dizzy. I haven't even talked to Brody. Because you asked me not to, and you trusted me not to. But I'm not gonna keep my mouth shut forever. People have been asking me about it all day, and I'm not gonna deny that we had a wedding when they keep asking me. It's fucking true."

Her expression darkened. It was still a sticky point with her, and the girl wasn't giving up on it easily. "But it's not up to you to decide that, Zane."

"I'm not gonna lie about it, Maggie. Let people say what they're gonna say about us. They're gonna do it anyway. I'm not gonna let that control our lives."

"It's not a lie. We just need to decide *what* we want to say publicly, and when."

"It is a lie if I say anything other than the truth. They've already printed the truth. It's already out there."

"But we need to discuss it first," she said, getting frustrated.

"What's to discuss? It's *true*. We got married."

"We did," she said, her gray eyes on mine, steady. "And if you really want us to have a marriage, you can't make decisions about this kind of thing without me. We're in this *together*, right?"

I swiped my hand over my face. "You know what? You're right."

She stared at me and blinked, like a little gray-eyed owl. "Excuse me?"

"You heard me. *You're right*. You're usually right."

Maggie actually looked stunned at those words out of my mouth. But fuck it; I thought she was right most of the time.

"I am?"

"You're right about most things, Maggie. But honestly, if you want my opinion, I really don't think you should've run off to talk to your dad today. What did that get you?"

"Nothing," she admitted.

"Right. It got you sweet fuck-all, because that's all the man has to give. If you ask me, you should've stayed right here, with me, so we could deal with this shit together."

"Yeah," she said softly. "You're right about that. I see that now." She sighed. "Does it make me the world's worst idiot because I actually hoped he'd care that I was upset?"

"No. It doesn't make you an idiot, Maggie." I sighed myself; it fucking ate me up when she talked to that prick, because it always ended the same way—with Maggie hurt and upset.

And *shit*, but I wanted to be a better man than her father.

I was pretty fucking sure I was. I was pretty sure Maggie didn't think I was the dirtbag her dad was, either... but I wasn't sure her heart really *felt* the difference between the two of us yet.

"Don't be too hard on yourself, Maggs, okay? I'm telling you. When it comes to our relationship, you always knew better than I did where we were at. If it was up to me, we would've been fucking from day one, and that would've been a travesty because I was a fucking drunk, and I know I would've fucked everything up even worse than I have now, and we never would've made it this far."

"You haven't fucked everything up, Zane," she said, her voice soft.

"Right."

She slipped her hand over my knee. "I told you the night we got married that you were a damn good husband. In a lot of ways, you really have been."

I cocked an eyebrow at her. "I have?"

"Yeah," she said. "You love me. I don't doubt that you love me with every part of you."

I slid my hand over hers and squeezed gently. "What can I say? You're under my skin, Maggie May."

She sighed unhappily at that and shook her head. "God. You must think I'm a real bitch."

A smile twitched at my lips. "Sometimes."

She frowned and bit her lip.

"You think I'm just like your dad," I reminded her.

"Actually," she said, her eyes searching my face, "I think I'm finally seeing that you're not like him at all. You care, Zane. You care about me, a lot."

"No shit."

"I mean, you really care. You care how I feel about things. You care if they forget to bring the honey for my coffee at breakfast, and you care if you're going onstage and I haven't come by to see you yet, and you care if my dad is an asshole to me."

"Yeah, well. You hate it when you have to use those little sweetener packets instead."

"You care," she said, her eyes soft as she gazed up at me, "about all the stupid little things, and the big things, too."

"Yeah."

She smiled at me a little, and I got lost in her gray eyes for a long moment. I wanted to kiss her, but it didn't feel right.

Not until I knew she was happy, and she wasn't hung up on this Dizzy shit anymore.

"Hey," I said, clearing my throat, "you remember that time the airline lost your luggage? It was like the first flight we ever took together, the first year you were with Dirty? I was pretty fresh back from rehab, so I was the only one not out at the bar. I saw you talking to the airline on your phone in the lobby of our hotel and trying not to lose your shit. You were so frazzled. It was late, and you were wearing a little dress and high heels that you'd flown in. I figured you'd want something comfortable to change into, so I swung by your room a little later with one of my T-shirts and a pair of sweats. You invited me in, and then you went into the bathroom to change, and when you came back out you looked so fucking adorable in my big T-shirt. You had my sweats all rolled up at the waist. You were swimming in my clothes. I had no idea what I was gonna wear to the gym in the morning. All I knew was I needed you in my clothes that night. You looked so fucking sexy—and so grateful, by the way—and I didn't even try to get in your pants. That's how much I care, Maggie."

"Wow," she whispered. "Such a gentleman." I wasn't even totally sure if she was being sarcastic or not.

"I know."

Then she leaned in and kissed me, her lips just barely brushing mine. It was a sweet, soft kiss that made my toes fucking curl. My dick snapped to attention and my nipples hardened, too, the piercing in the left one pulling at my shirt a bit.

She'd been gone for most of the day today. It was a matter of hours, but *fuck*, I'd missed her. And when she was here... we'd pretty much been fighting.

This was a hell of a lot better.

She smelled good, too. So good...

"Think I fell in love with you that night," I whispered against her lips.

She pulled back a bit and looked up into my eyes, like she wanted to know for sure if that was true.

It was.

"I mean... that was the first time."

Full truth was, I'd fallen in love with Maggie Omura many, many times. By now, it was pretty much a daily occurrence.

"You tried to get in my pants long before that," she pointed out.

"Yeah. I thought about you from the first moment we met. But that night... we watched TV in your hotel room together, remember?"

"*I Dream of Jeannie*," she said. "I remember. It was on some random channel..."

"You told me you wanted to marry the astronaut guy, and I actually felt jealous. That's when I knew. I was jealous of a fictional character who had your heart. I kept looking at you all snuggled up in my clothes at the other end of the couch, and I knew... I was so totally fucked."

"Shit, Zane. Why did you have to go and tell me all that? I actually feel bad for you now."

"It gets worse. When the show ended, you kicked me out."

"I had to." She gave me a slightly embarrassed look that made my dick throb. "You looked like a giant slab of sex lounging on my couch, and I hadn't been laid in a while."

"I would've stayed and helped you out with that."

"I know. That's why you had to go."

Her lips were so close I could practically taste them. Our noses were touching. I slipped my hands up around her neck, cupping her jaw with my palms and smoothing my thumbs over her cheeks. I drew her toward me gently...

"You want me to go now...?" I asked as our lips brushed.

"Please don't go," she breathed, and she threw a leg over me and climbed into my lap. She pushed me back against the couch. Then she kissed me, slow and deep, sliding her tongue into my mouth.

And this feeling...

Maggie, giving herself to me...

Taking what she wanted from me...

I'd do anything for this. To feel this, every day.

But I stopped the kiss, holding her face so I could look at her.

"Maggie... I just want to love you," I told her. "I want to be able to love you and not have to hide it."

"Okay."

But I wasn't even sure she really heard me. If she really understood. Her eyes were kind of hazy with desire and she'd started rocking her hips, slowly, grinding her pussy against me. Her dress was short, and the only thing keeping her from being naked against me was the crotch of her thin panties, and my jeans.

I could feel the warmth between her legs as she rubbed herself against my cock through the denim. I was harder than fuck by now, and it was a fucking feat to think straight—but I did my best. Because the woman in my lap was worth it.

"I want you to love me, unconditionally," I told her. I'd been thinking about it a lot, and all this shit needed to be said. "I told you it was okay... that I understood you couldn't love me if I was drinking. But it's not okay. I need you to love me without putting any limits on it. That means we're together, and if I fuck up, you still love me. If I fall off the wagon, you still love me. I have plenty of imperfections, Maggie, and I always will, but I still need you to love me."

"I already told you," she said, looking into my eyes. "I'll love you no matter what you do."

I absorbed that, but it still didn't feel like enough.

Even though she was still rubbing her pussy slowly up-and-down against my dick, it wasn't enough.

I needed her to know...

"Seth said he would leave Elle, if he was gonna use again."

At that, she went still. She was sitting on me, pressed tight against me, but she'd stopped dry-humping me.

"But I don't think I could, Maggie," I confessed. I felt fucking weak about it, but I had to be honest with her. "I don't think I could leave you. You'd have to be the one to leave. And if I start drinking, I don't expect you to stay with me. If you have to leave me because I can't get my shit together, that's your right. And we both know that means you might have to leave Dirty, and that's the last thing either of us wants. But if you say you love me and I love you, then to me that means we are in this together. And you keep loving me through whatever comes. For you that might mean losing Dirty, for a while or even permanently. For me that might mean leaving the band for rehab, or worse. But you know what? I'm not gonna let anything stop me from loving you. I don't want anything to stop you from loving me. So I need you to be fully in this, right now, with me. No conditions. No limits." I gazed up at her, at her fucking gorgeous face in my hands. "Can you do that?"

"Yeah," she said, her full bottom lip quivering just a bit as she took a breath. "Yeah, Zane. I can do that."

"Even going public and telling the world you're mine."

She squirmed just a bit in my lap, like she was still uncomfortable with the idea. "Yeah," she said, nibbling on her lip. But her gray eyes held mine. "I can do that."

"Then come here." I pulled her to me and kissed her, hard. She moaned and our tongues entwined, and my hands sank into her hair.

Then she got to work on my jeans. She had my bare cock in her hands in no time, and I felt her yanking the crotch of her panties aside. My dick flexed in her hand, so fucking hard, I couldn't even think anymore.

Good thing I'd gotten out whatever I wanted to say, because right now, I could barely remember what it was.

Had I ever wanted inside her so badly...?

Well, yeah. All the fucking time.

But, *fuck*...

"Take me, Maggie," I groaned, as she worked her small hands all over my cock, driving me fucking crazy.

"Going to..." she breathed, just before burying her tongue in my mouth again.

I was hoping she'd take me bare. But I wasn't gonna press the issue. We'd both been tested by now but she still wasn't on the pill, wasn't going on the pill. We'd use condoms when she thought we should. She said she tracked her cycle and all that.

I trusted her to make that call.

I knew neither of us had any infectious shit we were gonna pass to each other, but as for getting her pregnant? I wasn't ready for that. I knew I wasn't.

She'd told me she wasn't either.

But if it happened... I wasn't gonna be disappointed.

Scared as shit, maybe.

But I wasn't going anywhere.

Maggie wasn't going anywhere, either.

We'd deal with it together.

Because me and Maggie? We *belonged* together.

As I slid into her, her weight pressing down on me as she took me, bare... it was the first time I ever felt like I truly belonged to her. Like I was *hers*.

I'd always been Maggie's, in a way. But she just didn't accept it, fully, until this moment.

I knew it. I felt it...

And I wanted this.

I'd never wanted to belong to a woman before her.

Only her. I'd wanted to belong to Maggie Omura for a long time... and now, I knew I did.

Even her worst fears and my worst fuck-ups couldn't destroy this.

"You're mine, Maggie," I whispered against her lips as she rode me slowly. She kissed my face and her hair drifted over me. She moaned as my heart pounded, hard and fast in my chest.

"Zane," she gasped, clutching at my shoulders. "Yeah..."

"And I'm yours."

Her eyes met mine.

"Yeah," she said softly. "That, too."

"From now on," I told her, gripping her chin to force her to hold my gaze and hear this, "you're in my bed every night, naked. And when you're not naked, you're in those pink sweats of yours."

"Yeah?" She smiled. And when Maggie smiled... it fucking undid me. Especially when she was slowly riding my cock, bareback, while she did it. "You like my pink sweats...?"

"Yeah, babe." I slid my hand under her dress and squeezed her ass cheek. "Easy access. I want it."

She laughed, that throaty, sexy laugh of hers. "Okay, Zane," she whispered. "Whatever you want..."

And for about the millionth time in my life, I fell in love with her... just a little bit more.

CHAPTER TWENTY-ONE

Maggie

THE NEXT MORNING, Zane bounced out of bed early—before my eyes were open—and I actually heard him singing in the shower. He didn't even try to get laid first.

I'd never heard him sing in the shower before, but then again I wasn't nearby for many of his showers, historically. Maybe he did this all the time? He *was* a singer, and he sounded pretty damn happy doing it.

And it was *loud*.

As I lay in bed, half-awake, he belted out "We Are The Champions" and hotel guests could probably hear it three rooms over.

I smiled to myself and cuddled into the pillow that smelled of him, my eyes still closed.

A little while later, I woke up again as Zane came out of the bathroom all refreshed and sparkling, smelling like freshly-showered rock god and delicious spiced bodywash. His damp blond hair was slicked back, a smile was on his face, and he was singing Paul McCartney's "Maybe I'm Amazed" under his breath. I didn't think he'd even noticed I was awake as I looked him over.

His faded jeans hung low on his hips but, unfortunately, he was wearing a shirt. It was a T-shirt with the sleeves and sides cut out though, so I could see his ribcage and waist, his sleek muscles shifting as he moved.

Yum. Would I ever get tired of gazing at him?

Nope. Not possible.

He strolled over to the couch, which I could see through the open doorway from the bedroom, and sprawled on it, picking up the room service menu. His eyes met mine and he stopped singing, that killer Viking smile of his splitting his face.

I smiled back.

"What do you want for breakfast, babe?"

I stretched lazily. "Whatever you're having. With some fruit on it." I dragged my ass out of bed and his gaze darkened, sliding down my naked body. I flung on a robe half-heartedly and wandered to the bathroom, yawning. "And whatever they have that's chocolate. Lots of it."

He cocked an eyebrow at me, but the grin never left his face.

I half-expected him to follow me into the shower. Okay, three-quarters-expected. But not so.

When I reemerged about forty-five minutes later, my hair washed, dried and smoothed straight and makeup on, he had our breakfast all set up on the coffee table, the fake fire glowing in the fireplace and real candles lit. And fresh flowers.

I stopped to admire the pretty, all-pink arrangement, a mix of tulips, frilly carnations, miniature roses, alstroemeria and other stuff I didn't even recognize.

Zane was sitting on the floor in front of the fire, his back against an armchair, legs stretched out in front of him and crossed at the ankles. His bare toes twitched with excited energy and there was a definite sparkle in his eyes. He had a pen in his hand and one of his writing notebooks in his lap, open to a page where he appeared to be jotting notes or writing song lyrics or something.

How many times had I seen him writing in one of his notebooks like that?

It always made me happy.

"You're in a great mood," I remarked, somewhat warily.

He just grinned.

"Please tell me you're not on something."

I was teasing; I didn't really think he was. But I was feeling pretty anxious myself.

He gave me a look that was somehow reproachful while still smiling. "Can't a guy be happy?"

"And you're happy because...?"

"Because we're finally gonna tell everyone about us."

"Oh, yeah..." I whispered, my voice fading. "That."

Last night, before and after all the hot sex, we'd definitely come to an agreement that we were both in this for keeps—and we were telling everyone exactly that. I'd told him I was finally ready. And I was. Kinda. Mentally.

But I still didn't totally *feel* ready.

I definitely didn't feel as twinkly about it as he clearly did.

His eyes narrowed at me a fraction. "Yeah, *that*. Which means I can officially start groping you in public now. And telling dudes who get in your face to fuck the hell off, instead of having Jude do it for me."

"Oh. Well... congratulations?"

"Thank you. There's champagne if you want it." He gestured at the table, where there was indeed a bottle of champagne in a bucket of ice, as well as a large bottle of sparkling mineral water and two champagne flutes. Then he returned his attention to his notebook, jotting something down. "Been waiting a long time for this day, Maggs..." he muttered.

Well, that was incredibly sweet.

I melted all over just watching him there by the fire. His hair had dried and pieces of it were drifting over his face. And I wanted to touch him.

But somehow I felt all stiff and strange and couldn't seem to move my feet, either to go over to him and cuddle into his lap, or to go get dressed.

"Yeah," I said quietly, just standing in the middle of the room. "Me, too."

I had been waiting for this day. Maybe not in the same way that he had, but in my own way. It still hadn't quite sunk in, though, that this day had actually come. It still felt surreal.

And scary.

"I mean, I'm glad this is happening," I told him, my voice barely above a whisper as he glanced up at me. "With you. I mean... you and me." I cleared my throat, which suddenly felt tight.

The grin spread across Zane's beautiful face, and I almost had to look away. In the past, I would have. I would've avoided his joy because it made me uncomfortable, for so many reasons.

Now, I just looked at him.

My husband.

My dear friend.

The love of my life.

I swallowed, and before he could say anything to make me do something stupid like cry, I said, "Just let me tell my dad first, okay? I made a big deal about it being a secret and telling him he broke my trust. It's only fair I tell him what's going on. I'll call him this morning."

At that, Zane's face changed. For the first time this morning, a dark cloud passed over his features. Unfortunately, this was the way he usually looked when I mentioned my dad. His smile vanished. His jaw spasmed as whatever dark thought rolled through his head... though he managed to keep it to himself.

Instead, he said, "You still love him."

"You know me." I gave him a shaky smile. "I'm stubborn that way."

He considered that, then put his notebook and pen aside as he got to his feet. He came over and drew me into his arms, gently. He tucked my head under his chin and held me, and I leaned into him, just relishing his strength and his warmth and his stillness as his heart beat against me.

"You're always gonna love him," he muttered, almost to himself. "I'll just have to get used to it, I guess, and suppress my murderous urges."

"Would you, please? For me?"

"Yeah, babe. I can do that. Only for you, though." He kissed the top of my head, and it felt so good, the warmth of that gentle touch radiating through me.

I hugged him tight and whispered, "I'm always gonna love you, too."

He squeezed me back. "I fucking hope so."

"Put it this way." I peeked up into his blue eyes. "You're never gonna fuck up as bad as he has, right?"

A small smirk tugged at the corner of his mouth. "I don't think that's possible, Maggie."

"You're right," I agreed. "It's not."

As soon as I'd gotten dressed and we'd sat down to breakfast, Zane wanted to know the plan.

"The plan?" I asked him blankly.

"Yeah." His eyes bore into mine. "You said you're gonna call Dizzy this morning. But what about everyone else? The band, friends, the public... How do you want to roll this out, and when?"

I blinked at him. "Uh..."

"And just so we're clear, *today* is the right answer to that question."

"Oh. Well, thank you for letting me know." I tried to give him a dirty look but failed. I was pretty sure it was the first time in history that Zane wanted to know "the plan" about something before I'd even begun to figure it out. It was pretty damn cute. "You know, you're cute when you're getting organized."

"Don't try to change the subject. Won't work."

I sighed. "Yeah. I suppose we can discuss it..."

"When?"

"Well... I'm assuming from the look on your face that the right answer to that question is... Now?"

"You assume correctly. So who're we telling first? After Dizzy."

I took a breath and considered that. "I think... I really owe Brody the respect of telling him first. Like maybe I could meet with him alone, and let him know what's happening? We'll need to bring the publicists up to speed, but we should really schedule a phone meeting for that. I'll see what Brody has to say about it. And you should really give Dolly a call so she doesn't have to find out through the media."

"Dolly knows," he said.

"What?"

"I told her." He blinked his blue eyes at me. It was a rather innocent look, given that the man didn't do innocent looks. "Last year. I've been talking to her about it all along. What?" He shrugged at the look on my face. "You can't expect me not to tell Dolly. It's *Dolly*."

I took that in... and once I got over the initial shock of it, I sighed and gave in, because he was right. Dolly was not only Zane's grandma but the woman who'd raised him and the only family he had. And he definitely had a way different relationship with her than I had with my father. Much closer. I was pretty sure, from what I'd witnessed over the years, that Zane told Dolly everything. Right down to the dirtiest details of his nastiest sexploits.

The woman probably knew far more than she'd ever wanted to know about her beloved wild-child of a grandson.

God knew *I* knew more about Zane's sex life, pre-me, than I'd ever wanted to know.

"Okay. So you can *update* Dolly. And then we can tell the rest of the band and close friends together. Maybe get everyone together for dinner tonight?"

"Sounds great."

He eyed me closely as I nibbled at my breakfast. He'd ordered me the same as his; egg white omelette loaded with vegetables, lean ham on the side, and mine had an added bowl of fruit.

And two chocolate brownies that I was pretty sure I would've eaten first if he wasn't here to see it. Because right now, I was so nervous I could've eaten a giant chocolate cake—myself. I was under no illusions that one of the brownies was for Zane, anyway; he didn't care much for sweets, and he'd definitely ordered them for me.

Which was why I was married to the man, right? If this didn't make him husband material, I didn't know what did.

Almost made up for the whole manslut thing.

I smiled at him anxiously.

"Why are you so nervous, Maggs?" he asked, reading my mind.

"Because," I said carefully. "I'm scared." I sipped my sparkling water. I didn't want to waste the champagne he'd paid for, but I really didn't feel good about drinking in front of him these days. I'd have to give it to Katie later.

"Scared? Why?" he demanded. "*Still?*"

"Yes. Still. I mean, my fears weren't gonna just magically evaporate overnight."

As he stared at me, I realized that was exactly what he'd thought would happen. Or hoped would happen.

"You know," I added, trying to soften that in case it made him feel bad, "it's like I've told you before. I don't really think of myself as a fearful person. Heights, spiders, horror movies... whatever. I just don't have any weird phobias about scary stuff—"

"How about clown dolls?" he asked, raising an eyebrow at me.

"Uh, no."

"No? So... that time we were in the toy store picking out gifts for baby Nick, and that clown doll with the acid-trip eyes made you scream... you weren't scared?"

"That doesn't count. It *jumped* on me from the shelf."

"Pretty sure it fell."

"And I didn't *scream*."

"Oh yes, you did. Like Ned Flanders."

"*Anyway*," I said. "Like I was saying. I don't scare easily. But when it comes to *this*... I don't know, Zane... My bones feel kinda mushy and I see spots. Honestly... I've never been so scared of anything in my life."

"Spots?"

"Yeah. Like these dark spots kinda float around and I feel like I might pass out." Zane stared at me, searching my face, like he might be able to see these dark spots if he tried hard enough. "But hey, at least I don't pass out, right?"

"If you do," he said, still eying me, "I'll try to catch you before you crack your head open on something."

"Thanks. That's sweet." I swallowed, picking at my food. I'd definitely been picking at it more than eating it.

"Babe." He reached to take my hand in his. He ran his thumb over my knuckles, exactly the way he'd smoothed it over my wedding ring when we'd stood together at the altar. "Tell me why you're so scared."

"Well..." I cleared my throat again and looked into his eyes. "Maybe because I've never cared this much about anything in my life?"

His eyes scanned my face again, like he was trying to assess the truth in that. "Never?" And I knew what he was thinking. He was thinking about my job, how obsessive and serious I was about it.

But the fact was, a good chunk of the reason for that was... well... *him*.

Besides—stupidly—wanting to impress my dad, I'd also always wanted to please Zane.

"Never," I told him. "I don't want to lose you, Zane." I looked down at his hand and gave it a squeeze. "I can't lose you."

"You won't." He touched my chin and tipped my face toward his so our eyes met again. "If I know one thing that's true beyond all other things, Maggie Omura, it's that you're never gonna lose me."

I absorbed that, nodding. "We should eat," I said, too nervous to really enjoy the romance in what he'd said. "I should, uh, get to that phone call. As soon as I'm done with my dad, I'll meet up with Brody, okay? And I'll organize a dinner for tonight. Somewhere nice where we can get a big table in a private room or something."

"Sounds perfect."

I looked at my plate, but the beautifully prepared breakfast didn't look so appetizing anymore.

"You gonna be okay?"

"Actually, I feel like I might be a little sick. Like... is it okay if I throw up a bit?"

"Sure, babe. Whatever you've gotta do."

"Is this how you feel before you go onstage?"

"No."

"Stop smiling."

I could hear it in his voice, even though I wasn't looking at his face.

"I can do all the talking, Maggie," he offered, gently. "You don't even have to say anything. All you have to do is sit there and look gorgeous."

I looked at him. His eyes were twinkling a little again—this time, amused and sympathetic. I couldn't even help smiling back. But my stomach churned with nerves.

And I realized there was another reason I was so nervous.

I didn't want to let Zane down. I'd promised him we were doing this, and I really didn't want to fuck it up or somehow hurt him... ever again.

"No," I said. "It should come from me. I feel like it has to come from me. I'm the one who made you wait this long. I'm the one who made us both lie to everyone for so long and keep this secret."

"You had your reasons. It's not all on you, Maggie."

"Yeah. But I need to be the one to break the silence."

He held my gaze, and I tried to convey my conviction and dedication to this, even as my stomach rolled. "If that's how you want it to be."

"That's how I need it to be."

"Okay." He squeezed my hand. But he didn't even try to kiss me —like he understood that it would distract me from eating, and in order to get through this day, I really needed to eat.

Then he put on some music. It was Guns N' Roses, "Think About You."

We ate the rest of our breakfast without a word. And I managed to keep mine down... even when Zane kept smiling at me.

The next time I saw my husband, I was walking into the private dining room I'd booked in a restaurant near our hotel.

We'd both had a busy day. Him with promotional work, and me with trying not to hyperventilate every time I thought about the two of us being together, for real, out in the open... and calculated the odds of either of us somehow screwing it up.

Zane was already seated at the table. It was a long, wide table, and there were two place settings at the head of the table where he sat. One setting for him... and one, the only one at the table that wasn't yet taken, obviously for me.

I sat down next to him without a word. I would've been on time or early, as usual, if it wasn't for the fact that I'd had what I figured was my first legit anxiety attack in the ladies' room on the way in. Heart pounding, cold sweats, and the overwhelming desire to climb out the window.

But I'd gotten past it.

Zane kissed me on the cheek, though I didn't think anyone particularly noticed. No one seemed to notice anything was out of the ordinary, even though he was being all glittery about me sitting next to him. He was flashing his panty-wetting smiles all over the place, and everyone else seemed to be in a great mood too.

It was already loud in the room. The table was set for sixteen people, and it was now full. Every member of Dirty was here along with their partners. Brody, whom I'd met with privately this afternoon, just like I'd told Zane I would, was here with Jessa. Jude, Roni, Alec and Talia were here, and I'd also invited Shady.

As far as everyone in the room knew, this was just a regular Dirty dinner party on a Thursday evening. A *dry* dinner party; in honor of Zane, there wasn't a drop of booze in the room. In order to make sure everyone showed up, I'd told them we were going to have a little nonalcoholic toast to acknowledge that Zane had been clean for two months.

For a little while, I chatted with Katie about... what? I had no idea. I was just kinda running on autopilot and hoping no one would notice how unusually sweaty I was.

Then, as soon as the food had been ordered, Zane put his hand on my thigh under the table and squeezed. But it definitely wasn't a trying-to-slip-his-hand-under-my-short-dress squeeze. More of a *Can-we-do-this-now?* squeeze.

He was excited. Every time I looked at him, I could see it. The twinkle in his blue eyes... The little grin that never left his face. I could feel it emanating off of him like invisible rock star glitter.

He glanced at me now and I rolled my eyes.

He just grinned bigger.

Then he picked up his water glass and started clinking his rings on the side of it, until everyone somewhat quieted down. When that didn't totally work, he got to his feet and shouted out, "EVERY-ONE! SHUT IT. Jesse Mayes, that means you."

Everyone stopped talking and finally gave Zane their full attention. Even Jesse.

Zane offered me his hand and helped me to my feet, which was good, because I was feeling a little unsteady in my heels.

"Maggie and I have something to say," he announced.

He let go of my hand and waited for me to speak.

"Right," I said, my voice about as wobbly as my knees. "First of all, thank you all for being here on time and everything. I mean, I know you all have other stuff to do and it's nice we can all, uh, get together. And as you know, I wanted to acknowledge Zane and how amazing he's been doing... I mean, he's been clean for over two months now. Sixty-six days, to be exact. Totally clean, and... I'm really proud of him. So, I thought we could have a little dry toast. To Zane Traynor."

It wasn't the word's greatest toast. I fumbled my way through it, definitely feeling less-eloquent than usual, but oh well. The backs of my knees were all clammy and my heart was hammering pretty hard, too.

I had no problem giving orders and telling people what to do on a daily basis. But having to stand up and speak in front of a bunch of people I cared about, about personal stuff?

I felt mildly petrified, like the world's creepiest clown doll had just attacked my face.

I lifted my glass and so did everyone else, and a bunch of people called out supportive comments like, "We love you, Zane!"

I glanced at him; he was staring at me, and he looked pretty astonished, actually. He had no idea I was going to do this.

"To Zane," Brody said from the other end of the table, where he was sitting with Jessa. I caught Jessa's eye, and she smiled at me.

"To Zane," everyone said, and they clinked glasses.

I clinked my glass to the two people closest to me—Katie, who was seated beside me, and Shady, who was on the other side of Zane. Then I raised my glass to Zane himself, and he touched his glass to mine. "Proud of you," I whispered to him.

The sparkle in his eyes shifted in the candlelight… from surprised and joyful to proud and touched. Then we all took a sip of our nonalcoholic drinks.

Zane's blue eyes stayed on me, and I knew he was waiting for me to say that other thing….

"Oh… and, uh, before you all get talking again…" I said, holding everyone's attention, "there's something else."

I set my glass down and took a deep breath. Everyone was staring at me. I felt Zane next to me, solid and still. I could feel the warmth coming off his arm. We weren't even touching, but it felt like they all knew anyway. We were standing so damn *close*.

Even though Brody and I had discussed it today, it was somehow still totally nerve-wracking, standing up here, preparing to tell them all about *us*. I'd been candid with Brody about my fears, about the risk I knew I was taking; that I knew I'd probably have to leave Dirty if things between Zane and I didn't work out. He'd said he understood, but assured me absolutely nothing regarding my job was going to change, and if I ever left, it would be my choice—not because anyone was ever going to ask me to leave.

But it still felt awkward.

I feared their judgment, their doubt, and their response to this. And I *really* didn't want to cause drama or be the center of attention.

I just had to do this anyway. For Zane, and for me.

For us.

"Zane and I just... uh... wanted to let you all know that... *well...*" My voice kinda faded out on a little squeak.

Fuck.

How was I supposed to do this?

Just rip the bandage off, Maggie. You can do it.

Well, shit. *Why can't you be here for this, Mom?*

I looked down the table at all the familiar faces, everyone waiting for me to speak, but I couldn't quite see their eyes.

Tell them already. Give them a chance to be happy for you.

But what if they're not, Mom?

They will be.

But how do you know that?

Because they love you like I do.

My vision was getting a little wobbly. Dark spots... And all I could see clearly was Brody's face at the end of the table. He gave me a nod, and I blinked.

"We're together," I blurted out, my voice filling the silence. "We've been together, sort of, for a while now, and we've had some ups and downs, but we just want it to be clear that we're together now."

Silence.

"I mean, we're a couple." Wasn't sure why I felt the need to clarify that, but there it was.

No one said anything. A few of the guys looked at Zane, like they were waiting for him to say something.

Then Jesse raised his hand, slowly, like he wanted to speak, until Katie noticed and snatched it back, shoved it in her lap—and sealed her hand over his mouth.

"We're married," I went on, my voice cracking a little, kinda like it did at the altar when I said *I do*. Jesus, there were so many eyes on me... "Husband and wife. And that's how it's going to be."

Oh my God, I'm dying.

I could feel the heat creeping up into my face as I turned that special shade of red that a girl with my skin tone should never turn. They all just kept staring at me, and even though the dark spots were dancing over my vision and I couldn't seem to focus on anyone in particular, I could feel the raised eyebrows and the smirks.

I cleared my throat.

"That's all. Thank you."

I smoothed my dress to sit down, feeling so stiff I wasn't sure I could hinge enough at the waist to get my ass into my seat. I threw a desperate glance at Zane, who kinda snorted with suppressed laughter, then grabbed me before I could sit down.

He laid a kiss on me so hard it almost knocked me over—would have, if he wasn't already cradling me in his arms, dipping me way-low while he mauled my mouth.

In front of everyone.

People started applauding and making rude noises. I heard some girly cheering and someone shouted "Get a room!" but it was kinda fuzzy and far away, like I was underwater or something... as I kissed Zane right back. And everyone else in the room just kinda disappeared.

The spots cleared, replaced with a different kind of blurred vision as the heat cranked up between us, and Zane held me tight against his hard body. Then he pulled his mouth away from mine with a grin and I gasped for air, as discreetly as I could.

He stood me back up, holding me tight against him.

He grinned down the table at our friends, who were clapping and whistling. It was pretty damn loud, and everyone seemed to be getting to their feet as the blood thumped in my head.

"That's all *I* have to say," Zane shouted over the ruckus, and then he sat down in his seat like a king, taking me with him. He pulled me into his lap and I buried my face in his neck, hiding my tomato-red face. "It's alright, babe," he murmured in my ear. "You did good."

Then I felt a hand on my back that wasn't Zane's. I peeked up to find Katie standing over me, smiling and bouncing up-and-down, waving me into her arms. There were tears in her eyes.

Zane let me go as I got up and hugged her. I clung to her, actually, as she whispered, "Are you happy?"

"Yes," I practically sobbed back. All my emotions were twisted up and amplified, like everything Zane and I had been through was coming together in this one beautiful, embarrassing moment.

"*Oh my god*, Maggie," Katie gushed in my ear, "I'm so happy for you!"

I groaned in pain. "Is this what it's like for you? Everyone staring all the time...?" I saw people lining up behind her to hug me; Jessa and Amber and Talia... as the guys piled in on the other side to congratulate Zane.

"Pretty much." Katie laughed and gave me a final squeeze of reassurance. "Or staring at my husband. But you know what? You get used to it."

Sweet Jesus, I hoped so.

CHAPTER TWENTY-TWO

Zane

JESUS, my wife was feisty.

First she told me she was so scared she was gonna puke, then she blindsided me with an emotional toast that got me all choked up, then she screwed the hell out of me in the ladies' room of the restaurant... Then I woke up in my hotel bed in the morning to find her binding my wrists over my head with my own belt and climbing on top of me.

I was hard as fuck, because she'd woken me up from a really good dream... Although, on second thought, maybe she'd caused the dream. She was running her hands all over my naked body and who knew how long she'd been doing that?

She was kissing her way down my stomach, too, nibbling and full-on biting as she went, and goosebumps broke out all over me.

"Shit, woman... what're you doing...?" I asked sleepily, not really caring what the answer was as long as she kept doing *that*.

Maggie bit my hip, then swirled her tongue over the spot where she'd probably left little teeth marks.

"I just really, really need to taste you," she whispered in her husky-sweet morning voice, her warm breath tickling my skin. Her soft fingertips drifted over my rigid dick and I tensed all over. Every nerve was waking up and sparking to life, and I groaned as she licked her way down to my dick. "I need to fuck you, right now..."

But she didn't fuck me.

She took a deep breath instead, her nose against my skin, smelling me. Making little *mmmmm* noises as she brushed her lips over my skin, licking and teasing, but never putting her mouth anywhere close enough to my cock.

"Oh God," she gushed, like she was almost in pain. "You smell so good. Like, I smell you and I have to have you, immediately. It's an automatic response..."

"Welcome to my life..."

She grunted a bit of a laugh as she sat up and finally threw her leg over me. She was straddling my hips on her knees, and I felt the warmth and the softness of her bare pussy just brushing against my dick, and it was pure torture.

"I'm gonna fuck you," she informed me, almost in a daze. As I looked up at her in the hazy morning light, her lips were swollen from kissing me and her eyelids were low. "Without a condom. But you have to make sure you don't come inside me." She reached down between her legs to grasp my cock and stroke me, twisting slowly as she spoke. "You have to warn me and I'll get off."

"Get off...?"

She smirked as she angled my dick where she wanted it. "Get off your dick, I mean."

"Okay, but—"

She started pushing down onto me, and the words failed in my open mouth. I groaned as I filled her. She was wet and so fucking tight, and it felt like pure, sweet heaven being squeezed by her. If there was an actual heaven, I couldn't imagine it being any better than this.

Maggie, horny, and taking control of me...

Sure, I could've bucked her off and seized control, even with my hands belted above my head.

But where was the fun in that?

Fuck that.

I just lay here, spread out on the bed, my bound arms limp above my head, as Maggie fucked me in an eager but semi-slow rhythm, her mouth open and sexy little sounds coming out, her hands planted on my chest, fingers curling into my skin, her nails digging deep into my pecs.

"Just don't come too fast okay?" she said, gazing down at me.

"Uh-huh... *fuck*, you're sexy."

"Just wait... just wait a while, while I fuck you..."

"Yeah, babe."

I did as she told me to, as the tension and the pressure built between us. Tingles moved up and down my spine. My balls tightened. My nipples fucking throbbed.

I could've easily come fast if that's what she wanted, but my cock was in its happy place, so why rush? Normally, I might've been happy to fuck her fast and furious, so we could just do it again right afterwards.

I was greedy like that.

Usually, Maggie was, too.

But she was in no hurry right now.

My dick was definitely loving it, but the rest of me was getting restless, impatient to take over and fuck those husky little screams out of her. And the more I thought about that, the harder it was not to come.

"Can I come yet?" I asked her as she rode me faster, losing her rhythm as her own pleasure built.

"No, you can't come yet."

"Holy shit, Maggie." I groaned, fucking suffering. "Don't be cruel..."

"I'm not cruel. I'm incredibly kind. You feel what's happening to your dick right now...?"

I laughed, fucking delirious with arousal and pleasure. More than that... I was happy. Like really fucking happy.

If this was my life?

For the rest of my life...?

I was gonna die one day a very happy man.

"I love you," I told her, sincerely. "But please come on my dick before I die."

A slow smile spread across Maggie's face. Then she switched up her moves. Instead of the up-and-down thing she'd been doing pretty steadily, she started grinding back and forth a little with each thrust, working her body against mine exactly how she needed it. The smile faded and her breaths got raspier. Her nails clawed deeper into my chest.

"Don't come," she gasped. And then she came with a soft scream and a couple of jerks of her hips. She dropped her head as she moaned and her silky hair brushed my skin.

"Maggie... let me see your face."

She lifted her head and her gray eyes met mine as she kept riding me, slowly and jerkily. She was still coming, still in ecstasy.

And fuck, I wanted my hands back. I wanted them on her face, on her tits and all up inside her.

"Babe. Babe, you gotta move..."

But I didn't wait for her to move. I just rolled, taking her with me. I managed to loop my belted arms around her as she tumbled onto her side on the bed. I snapped my hips up, hammering into her a few times, my dick switching into autopilot mode.

Then I pulled out, and she caught my dick in her hands just as I came. She smoothed her hands up and down my shaft as I shot on her stomach with a groan. She rolled her palm over the head of my cock and pressed her body tight against mine. My come was smeared all over both of us.

We kissed and just lay like this for a long time. Kissing, breathing... hearts pounding. I closed my eyes and I could feel her pulse, beating against me.

Eventually, I found my voice. "I'm all sticky."

"Me too." I didn't even have to open my eyes to know she was smiling.

"I'm lying in the wet spot. Is that love or what?"

"Hate to tell you. We're both in the wet spot."

I tugged halfheartedly at the belt that still bound my wrists behind her back. "I can't get up. Nothing works."

"Same here."

"I've lost the feeling in my hands."

She laughed. "Poor baby."

Yup; feisty as fuck.

After the killer morning sex, we had breakfast in the hotel room, then showered together. Predictably, we ended up having more sex in the shower... steamy, slow sex.

Maybe it was because she'd unbelted my hands and they were now free to roam all over her hot, slippery-wet body, but I literally could not keep my hands off her.

I hiked her legs up around my hips and screwed her up against the wall... Then I washed her and dried her, too.

Then we stood at the his-and-her sinks and got ready for our day together, and you know what?

It was the best morning I'd ever had.

Ever.

Had plenty of mornings waking up in a pile of naked chicks with a hangover, and those were alright, too. For different reasons. Glad I'd experienced them, in a way.

But this?

I wouldn't trade this for anything. Just hanging out with Maggie, listening to her talk about what she had to do today (I'd asked her), and how she felt about the big announcement at dinner last night (I'd also asked), and watching her get dressed. Just being close to her and doing stupid regular shit. Enjoying each other.

No drama or fighting.

Feeling all cozy with her in the hotel suite, with the fireplace on and the lights dimmed low as we gradually started our day. Soaking up the husky-soft sound of her voice and the feminine scents of her lotion and the girly stuff she put in her hair.

And all her little idiosyncrasies.

The way she laid her toothbrush and toothpaste perfectly parallel to one another and perpendicular to the edge of the counter.

The way she jiggled her tits into her bra cups and hiked them up —no idea how I'd missed that maneuver before.

The way she flattened her naturally-straight hair with a straightener and fussed over it until it was glossy-smooth.

The way she answered her phone, "Hey, sweet stuff," when Katie called. I'd never heard that one before, but it was cute as shit. We were out in the living room and she was organizing shit in her purse when her phone rang; she even did this girly laugh, then gave me a dirty look, taking the phone into the bathroom when she realized I was listening.

Cute.

So cute, I was probably gonna have to fuck her again—asap.

Shitty fact: I was definitely gonna mess up her hair while I did it, and she was gonna be annoyed about it.

Too bad.

Shittier fact: I really didn't have time to do it right now. Had to get to the venue.

Where the fuck was everybody, anyway?

I dropped onto the couch and checked my phone. It was a little earlier than I'd planned to head out, but fuck it. I was anxious to get going. So I sent a chat to the band.

Me: ready to go?

I texted Shady to let him know I was ready to leave.

Then Jesse responded to the chat.

Jesse: What time you going down?

Me: NOW

Jesse: What's the rush??

Me: you need to learn the song, asshat

Jesse: Already know it.

Me: we need to rehearse

Jesse: Maybe YOU need to rehearse...

I considered calling him to tell him what an asshat he was more personally, but it felt good to see shit written out in black-and-white. Had a certain impact.

Me: just stop fingering your wife and move your ass

Jesse: OH SHIT. You didn't.

Jesse: I'm giving you one free pass on that one.

Jesse: But you've got a wife now and she is NOT off-limits for that shit.

Fuck me. Didn't think about that.

No way was I listening to Jesse Fucking Mayes' asshat comments about me fingering my wife, for the rest of my life.

This shit could not go both ways.

Which meant I was gonna have to be a little more of a gentleman towards Katie and his relationship with her in general.

Okay... a *lot* more of a gentleman.

Me: noted

Me: please stop making love to your wife and let's go

Me: better?

Jesse: Marginally. Hard not to be an uberdouche all the time, huh?

Me: thank you for the constructive criticism

Jesse: I'm here to help.

I sent him an emoji of two dudes holding hands.

He sent me back a heart.

And a photo of my wife.

I stared at it, lifting the phone toward my face. Obviously taken at some party, it was a closeup of her face—and her perky tits, in a sparkly top that dipped low. Maggie's tits weren't large, but she definitely knew how to work what she had. She was looking at someone off-camera and had a saucy look on her face, and the whole thing was just begging for a caption like: *sexy bitch I need to fuck*.

I actually dug out my glasses and put them on. Where the shit did he get that photo?

I downloaded it, obviously. Definite keeper.

Then I noticed the slender arm slung around Maggie's shoulders—and realized Jesse had cropped his wife out of the photo, just to fuck with me.

Asshat.

"Babe?" I called out. "You off the phone?"

"Yeah?"

"I've gotta run soon," I told her while I answered Dylan. He'd popped into the chat; had to get him to stop fingering his woman next. "We need to do a little rehearsal at sound check."

"Rehearsal?"

"Yeah. I'm adding a song into tonight's set list."

Maggie came out of the bathroom, putting in her earrings. "You're changing the set list?"

"Yup."

"Please tell me you're keeping the encore the way it is, though. I love the progression of 'Blackout,' 'Road Back Home' and 'To Hell & Back' at the end of the show. It's perfection."

I grinned at the compliment. Call me a vain asshole, but I fucking loved it when Maggie complimented me, even indirectly. "Okay, babe. No changes there."

"What are you changing?" She turned my notebook, which was sitting on a table, toward her, taking a peek.

"Uh, none of your business, Miss Nosy Manager Type." I gave her a sharp look and went back to my phone.

She rolled her eyes. "So sorry, Mr. Rock Star."

"And it's not in there. Just come to the show and you'll find out with everyone else."

"Oh, yeah?" She slinked over to me and dropped into my lap, wrapping her arms around my shoulders, pressing her hot little bod up against me and playing with my hair. "No special privileges for the wife of the frontman, huh?"

"Nope." I slid my hand down around her hip and cupped her ass cheek, giving it a squeeze. "None at all."

"Huh. Maybe I'll have to rethink this whole marriage thing, then..." She started to get up, but I yanked her tight against me, tossing my phone aside and using both hands to lock her ass in place.

"How about you stick around, I throw in some perks?"

"I'm listening..."

"Front row seats?"

"I prefer backstage."

"Backstage pass?"

"Already have one."

"Party with the band?"

"Pretty sure Brody can get me in." She smiled prettily. "Or Jesse."

"Fuck Jesse." I kissed her, hard. "Personal tour of my bus after the show...?"

She rolled her eyes, but her lips were flushed from my kiss and her eyes were darkening. "How is that a perk?"

"I'll let you touch my favorite pen."

"Is that some bad euphemism?"

"It's the one I write songs with."

"Hmm." She considered that for a while, smoothing her thumb over the short hair behind my ear. That slow touch, back and forth, sent shivers right down my spine and straight to my balls. I was getting hard, which was inconvenient, since I had no time to do anything about it. "Okay."

"Really? That's all it took? A pen?"

"Well... I'm pretty sure it's still a euphemism."

"It is. I don't actually have a favorite pen." As if to drive home that point, my rock-hard dick was now jabbing into her ass.

"See?" She wriggled her hips a bit, rubbing herself into me. "Because I'm your wife, I already knew that."

I gazed at her in honest-to-God wonder. "We're so made for each other."

She smiled, eying my glasses. "You know, you're definitely a bigger dork than the world takes you for."

"Shh. Don't tell anyone." Then I kissed her for real, forcing her mouth open with mine and deep-throating her with my tongue.

"Jesus," she said, when I let her up for air. "You've got the devil's tongue, Zane Traynor..." I took that as another compliment, since she looked pretty damn flustered about it. Like horny-flustered. Her cheeks were even a little pink. "Can you fuck me with your little glasses on next time? You've never done that."

I laughed. "Really?"

"Yeah. Maybe you can sit by the fire with a book like some hot coed, and I can be the naughty headmistress who slips out of her office, you know, to visit her sexy student in the library after hours..."

"Wow."

"Or... maybe I'm just on my way back from cheerleading practice? And I notice my hot professor's light is on, and I think, 'Maybe he'd like some company...'"

"That's elaborate, babe."

"Not really."

"Is this the shit you think about when we bang?"

She scrunched her eyebrows. "What do you think about when we have sex?"

"You," I said, kissing her and nibbling at her full bottom lip. "Your pussy. It's not complicated."

She laughed her husky laugh, pulling back. "Well, I've never had either of those fantasies while we're doing it, either." She gazed at me pretty damn adoringly. "But what am I supposed to fantasize about when I'm already having sex with the sexiest man in the world?"

That was pure flattery, but somehow, I knew she meant it, too.

Still, I cocked an eyebrow at her. "You're having sex with Blake Shelton?"

"What?"

"People magazine, babe. Sexiest Man Alive? I do actually read with these glasses, you know. They're not just for your slutty coed fantasies."

She laughed again. "Zane. Baby. Blake Shelton's got nothing on you. Well... except the official title of Sexiest Man Alive. And Gwen Stefani."

"I did once have this Gwen Stefani fantasy..."

She silenced me with a finger to my lips. "Don't even."

"You have an outfit for this cheerleader thing?"

"We can get one."

"Hmm. I think I like the horny headmistress thing better. Come to think of it, I was a really, really bad student..."

"Okay, now you're just getting me hot. Which means," she said, sliding out of my lap and leaning over me, "I'm going to have to teach you what happens when you act up in my class." Then she kissed me suggestively, biting my lip for emphasis.

Then she shoved me right down on my back and climbed on top.

"Holy shit," I muttered, "you got into character fast..."

The grin had faded from her face and the horniness had taken over, and she dove right in. We made out like we hadn't fucked in weeks, forget that we'd done it twice this morning.

Then some asshole knocked on the door.

"Shiiiit," I groaned. "That'll be Shady. I've gotta go."

"Okay." She smiled down at me.

I groaned again and made a grab for her ass.

Then she slid off me and we both got up. "I'll see you later," she said sweetly.

But I didn't budge. As I stood looking down into Maggie's gray eyes, I actually found myself wishing I didn't have a show to do tonight so I could hang out with a woman instead.

Huh. That was new.

I sighed and kissed her, squeezing her round little ass one last time. "You're gonna be there early, right? Kiss me before I go onstage?"

"Of course."

"Good." I let her go and pulled on my leather vest. "See you tonight, Maggie May." We kissed one last time, getting totally wrapped up in each other's arms for way too long, then finally peeled ourselves apart again.

She gave me another smile. "Glasses."

"Oh. Thanks." I took them off, then waggled my tongue at her as I headed for the door.

"And you better let me touch that pen of yours," she called after me. "Or I'm gonna spank you with my ruler!"

The door closed behind me and Shady didn't even pretend not to hear that shit.

"Let's go," I said, deadpan.

"Sure, brother."

But when he'd turned his back, I definitely grinned like some lovesick schoolboy.

After sound check, the band grabbed some food at a restaurant where we were eventually pretty swarmed by fans. Always happened when too many of us showed up in one place in broad daylight.

We signed some shit, then had to leave out the back door.

As we all piled into the waiting cars, Jesse got in with me and shooed everyone else into the other ones. He even asked Shady to follow in a cab.

"What's up?" I asked him, as he settled in next to me.

"Just wanted to talk to you."

"Cool."

"You know," he said, "I've gotta bust your balls and all that. Because... I don't know. It's like, the law of nature between us or something?"

"Yeah," I agreed. "Or something."

He eyed me sidelong. "But you've been doing really good. You know, giving up pot."

"Thanks."

"And if Maggie's gonna put up with you, hey, you're one lucky son-of-a, right?"

"Yup." We'd already talked about that, actually. About a week after I'd kicked weed, when maybe he felt certain enough that he wasn't gonna send me spiraling off a cliff by coming down on me, Jesse had told me exactly what he thought of me marrying Maggie in Vegas and keeping it a secret from him all this time.

And putting Maggie through what I did the night I took off into the desert with Seth.

And all the times he'd seen me at some party with some chick who wasn't Maggie in the time since I'd married her.

If memory served, he'd dropped the word *asshole* a few hundred times.

Not sure what else there was to say about it.

"So, uh... what I'm saying is..." he went on, looking anywhere but at my face, "I know you've been working hard. Taking care of yourself. Going to meetings and keeping clean and taking shit seriously. We can all feel it, and it definitely shows onstage. To be honest, I never would've thought you could get any better than you already were at what you do, but you actually have."

I stared at him, taking that in, and he finally looked me in the eye. "Thanks, man."

"You miss it?" he asked me.

"What, the devil's lettuce?"

He smirked at the term.

"Yeah. Sometimes. The ritual of it. The habit, more than the high, maybe."

He nodded like he understood, but I was pretty sure he didn't. Jesse had never had any issues with drugs or booze.

"Clean and sober is good on you, Zane," he said after a moment. "And when I think about it, I can't really remember the last time you showed up somewhere with some random chick on your arm. It's been a long while. And from what I gather from Katie, Maggie wants this. She wants you. So you must be doing something right there. I guess I'm trying to tell you I'm proud of you... and all that stuff."

Wow. Watching Jesse Mayes squirm his way through a heart-to-heart? Awesome and painful at the same time.

"Thanks, brother. You really don't have to say all this."

"Sure I do."

I put him out of his misery and gave him a damn hug. Which felt pretty awkward in the back of a car. Plus, he was wearing his sexy-ass leather pants, and we were both in short sleeves so there was some definite skin-on-skin. Only saving grace was I knew it was more awkward for him, so I made sure it lasted a little too long.

"You're shit at this," I told him. "You know that, right?"

He pushed me away. "Just want you to know I love you and all that shit. Always have."

"Yeah. Same here."

"I know I rarely say it. But it doesn't mean I don't feel it. You know, half the time I'm pissed at you because I envy you."

"I know that, brother." I punched him lightly on the shoulder. Sure, I'd taunted the dude relentlessly over the many years of our friendship, goading him to admit just that. But hearing him say it out loud? I could let him off the hook. Truth was, I'd always envied him, too. "Guess we can both be douchecanoes."

"Huh?"

"That's what you called me this morning, right?"

"Uh, that was uberdouche. Can't really take credit for that one, though. Katie called me that, few days ago, when I looked at her sketchbook without asking." He rubbed the back of his neck the way he only did when he was anxious. "She hates when I do that shit."

"So stop doing it."

"Yeah. She was, uh, pretty mad."

I stared at him. He actually looked pretty bent out of shape about it. "I didn't think you guys fought like that."

"We don't. I still feel bad about it."

"So, go tell her you love her and you'll do anything to fix it."

He blinked at me, looking halfway stunned. As if I had no clue how to talk to a woman or something.

"What? It's not hard. You just look in those big blue eyes of hers and admit you made a mistake."

"Christ. Are you giving me relationship advice now?"

"Yeah. Think I just did."

Jesse groaned, maybe realizing his love life was in serious danger. He looked out the window as we moved through traffic. After a moment, he said, "They're blue-green."

"What?"

"Katie's eyes. They're blue-green. They're kind of like a turquoise color."

"Uh-huh."

He looked at me. "You never noticed that?"

"Would you want me to notice that?"

He just shrugged and looked lost.

"What's up with you?"

"Nothing."

Right.

"She's, uh, been kinda moody lately," he said.

And I actually got a bit worried. Something was definitely off.

"What's going on between you two?"

"Nothing. She's gonna kill me for telling you, but... she's pregnant."

I stared at him. Maybe I was waiting for the punchline for a moment or two... until it kicked in that he was serious.

And the fucking relief hit me.

"*Holy shit.* Jesse, man." I gave him another hug. "Thought you were gonna tell me your marriage was falling apart or some shit. But... *shit.*"

"Yeah. You can stop hugging me, though."

"Is this a good thing?" I let him go with a little shove, and a smile crept slowly across his face.

"Yeah. It's a very good thing. She just doesn't want to talk about it yet. We just found out yesterday, and she says she wants to get through the first trimester before we tell anyone. She's only six weeks along and she's pretty paranoid something's gonna go wrong because it took us over a year to get her pregnant. I keep telling her that's not gonna work on tour, that everyone's gonna find out somehow. You know, close quarters and all that. She already cracked and told Maggie yesterday."

"Maggie knows?"

"Yeah. She gave Katie a bottle of champagne, and since Katie couldn't drink it, she totally broke. Girl can't lie to anyone. She's gonna keep cracking for sure." He sighed and rubbed a hand over his face. "Anyway, I'm a shit husband. I already broke and told Jude last night, and I'm pretty sure when we get out of this car I'm gonna go blab to Brody."

I laughed and gave his shoulder another shove. "Shit, brother. Everyone's gonna know by the end of the night. You know that, right?"

"Yeah. Probably. Just don't tell anyone, okay? I'm hoping Katie will just keep caving so it's not all my fault. She's been emotional lately and I don't want it raining down on me. I'm still hoping to get laid sometime before this baby comes..."

I shook my head. Normally, I might've loved to hear about Jesse

Mayes' problems getting laid, but I was pretty fucking sure he was kidding about that. "Jesus. It's raining babies..." First Brody and Jessa, then Seth and Elle... and now Jesse and Katie? "Some crazy shit in the water around here, huh?"

"Yeah," he said, kinda smirking at me. "Think it's called love."

That night at the Detroit show, I was beyond stoked. By the time we were about to play our final pre-encore song of the night, the crowd was all hyped up and my spirits were through the fucking roof. As soon as we finished "Come Lately," I told the audience, "We're gonna wrap up here with a special song tonight, for a special woman."

Then I gave Jude the cue; he was standing at the back corner of the stage where I could just see him.

"We're gonna play a song right now by this little band called The Beatles, who influenced me in a big way when I was young and pretty sure I'd never end up in a place like this, singing for all you beautiful people."

The crowd roared their approval, and I looked out over the audience, where what looked like a million cell phones were lit up in the dark.

"Some of you may have read some shit online or wherever that I got married two years ago in Vegas." The crowd answered with a mixture of screams and cheers and boos. "And it's true. I married this incredible woman." More screams. "This is gonna embarrass the shit out of her. But too bad, right?" I turned toward the back of the stage. "Come on out here, Maggie."

She was standing in the shadows at the edge of the stage, Jude standing behind her so she couldn't bolt. He'd managed to get her out here, even though she was shaking her head at me.

At least she looked too embarrassed and petrified to be mad at me right now.

Katie and Amber were right there with her, flanking her, which wasn't my idea, but it was a good one. Katie took Maggie's hand and pretty much dragged her out onstage, Amber following, clinging to Maggie's other hand and looking about as uncomfortable as Maggie did.

I waved them over to me, center-stage, as a couple of crew guys ran out with folding chairs, setting them up in a row for the girls. The three of them held hands while the crowd roared. Katie was grinning, Amber was wearing the hint of a nervous smile, and Maggie had her fist to her mouth.

"You ready for this, babe?" I asked into the mic, and Maggie just shook her head once... *No.*

Katie giggled and put an arm around her. There was a sparkle of tears in Amber's eyes, but she gave me a little nod of approval as she gripped Maggie's hand.

"Take a seat," I told them. The crew had disappeared and the girls sat down, Maggie in the middle.

I walked around behind them so they couldn't hide behind me, and I stood behind Maggie. I lifted my hand high over her head and pointed down at her. "This is my lovely wife, Maggie."

My wife was definitely covering part of her face with her fist, and Katie laughed as the crowd screamed and applauded.

I pointed down at Katie next. "If you don't know who this is, you've been living under a rock or something. This is Katie Mayes."

Katie gave a little wave and Jesse played a hot little riff on his guitar that made Katie laugh again.

"And this," I said, pointing at Amber, "is Dirty's tour photographer, and girlfriend of this guy named Dylan Cope." Dylan did a little drum roll and a couple of cymbal crashes.

The crowd thundered their excitement, people clapping and whistling for the girls as anticipation of the final song built.

I walked around beside the girls, so Maggie could see me, and said, "This one's for you, Maggie May."

I glanced over at Jesse, who grinned at me. Seth and Matt and Dylan were all in position, waiting.

Then I belted out, "*OOOH! DARLING...!*" and the band launched into our cover of The Beatles' "Oh! Darling."

Katie and Amber applauded as I serenaded Maggie, smiling all the way. Maggie just sat there with her fist pressed to her mouth for pretty much the whole song, her gray eyes glistening.

Seth and Jesse came over and stood on either side of the girls as they played. Through the whole song, I sang my ass off for Maggie with heart, soul, and tongue-in-cheek, and I put everything I felt for her into it.

We were in a stadium with over forty thousand people... but for a few moments there... it was just us.

Maggie.

Me.

I sang until Katie was crying through her smile and a tear streaked down Amber's cheek. They both had an arm around Maggie, who just sat there looking stunned.

At the end of it, the roar of the crowd was pretty much deafening. Katie flung herself into Jesse's arms and Amber bolted in the direction of Dylan's drum kit.

Maggie got up a little slower, looking unsteady. I scooped her up into my arms as the stage lights went down.

"You mad at me?" I said into her ear. I knew it was a risk, that she might be. We didn't talk about this. We never agreed this was the way we were going public.

But fuck it. This was a huge part of who I was, and she was just gonna have to get used to it.

Maggie made plans, and I loved her for that.

But sometimes... I just had to go rogue.

Not like she didn't know it when she married me.

She snuggled into me, holding me tight. "No, Zane," she said in my ear. "I'm not mad."

Well thank fuck...

We headed offstage and I pulled her into a dark corner backstage, ignoring everyone else. She was still clinging to me. I slid my mouth over hers, and we just stood like this for a long time. We kissed and kissed, murmuring *I love you* back and forth, until I had to go back out onstage.

"I gotta go kick ass on 'Blackout,'" I told her. "But I'll see you here after the encore."

"Yeah," she said. "See you here."

Then we kissed again, and I let her go, heading back out to the stage. When I glanced back, Maggie was still there. She gave me a little wave and a look of raw wonder with tears in her eyes.

Pretty sure it was the first time my "rock star" status had ever actually dazzled her.

I just grinned to myself.

It was also the first time I could remember ever walking out onstage feeling so damn happy... I didn't even have any room left to feel self-doubt or any of that other mindfuckery.

Just happy.

CHAPTER TWENTY-THREE

Maggie

Six weeks later...

"KATIE, seriously. Let's get this show on the road."

I glanced back at her but she was playing on her phone, yet again.

Fuck me.

I sat down on the stairs this time.

We were at the Crystal, on the fabulous sweeping staircase in the hotel lobby that led up to the second floor and the ballroom, and Katie had stopped again. It was taking us like ten minutes to get up half a flight of stairs.

"Just a sec..."

"Who the hell is it?"

"Um. It's Jessa."

"Please don't tell me she's running late."

"Nope."

"Good." I sighed and checked my phone. Seven-thirteen.

I was supposed to have Katie here at seven o'clock, and for some reason she was really dragging her heels.

As the guest of honor at this thing, she was acting really weird.

Now that Dirty had reached the end of the North American leg of the tour and we were all home for a few days following the Vancouver show, we were having a little party for Jesse and Katie, to celebrate their big news—that Katie was pregnant. She was three months along now and everyone had known for a while, but it just seemed like a good time to celebrate it.

Jessa, being Katie's sister-in-law, had the honor of handling most of the planning, including booking out the beautiful ballroom at the Crystal for the party. Probably a bigger room than was necessary, but I was sure the party would be top-notch.

I mean, I could only guess.

I was still trying not to be disgruntled about the fact that I wasn't asked to help plan the party.

At all.

Because, you know, it wasn't like planning was my thing or anything. Seemed like everyone had forgotten about that particular talent of mine, because no one seemed to want my input. On anything.

I wasn't hurt about it, but I was kinda hurt.

At least I'd been able to keep myself busy.

Officially, we all had a few days off before we left for Europe, but the women's shelter I volunteered at whenever I was home didn't exactly take days off. I was always welcome there, and I'd put in some long hours the last few days—which had helped keep my mind off the whole party thing.

Still killed me just a little that all that planning was going on and I wasn't a part of it.

"Okay," Katie said, finally. "We're good to go."

"Alrighty." I got to my feet and up we went the last several steps to the big hallway outside the ballroom. Giant set of ornate double doors, closed, and total silence from inside, but maybe the doors were soundproofed? Definitely didn't sound like there were a few dozen people in there waiting for us.

And no sign whatsoever of Jesse. Wasn't he supposed to meet us at the door?

It was more than a little weird, actually, that we hadn't run into anyone on our way in. Not one party guest in the lobby.

And I was starting to get this horrible feeling on Katie's behalf...

What if everyone was running late? Or something had gone wrong?

They *really* should've had me involved in planning this thing. Maybe they'd know better now, for next time. Good thing; if I was shut out of planning Jessa's bridal shower this summer, it was gonna get ugly.

I paused just outside the doors, feeling weird about this. Where was Jesse? Zane was supposed to bring him.

"Just a sec, okay?"

"Sure." Katie stood dutifully by while I typed furiously on my phone, sending a text to Zane: *Where the fuck are you?*

He replied almost instantaneously, at least.

Zane: we'll be there

I showed the message to Katie and she smiled a little awkwardly.

Fuck. This party was all fucked-up. I could feel it. Something was way off, and it wasn't my fault, but now I was gonna have to help fix it. I just hoped Katie's feelings weren't hurt when it all fell apart...

I sighed to myself and opened the door.

And stared.

Okay...

So maybe it wasn't falling apart?

The room was full of people. Like, many dozens of people. Way more than I thought were coming to this thing.

I'd stopped short, and Katie nudged me into the room. I stood aside to let her in, but she hooked her arm through mine and we walked in together.

And... *wow.*

Apparently they didn't need my help planning.

Everyone was on their feet, staring at us. I could see catering staff standing by at the edges of the room in crisp uniforms, and some of Dirty's security team in the shadows. Antique furniture, tables laid out with food, and twinkly lights all over the place...

And the room was awfully... pink.

Pink flowers everywhere. Shiny pink balloons in giant bunches in the corners of the ceiling. There was even a huge pink disco ball over the dance floor.

Was Katie having a girl or something? Could they find out the gender this soon...?

It was weirdly quiet, as everyone just stood staring at us with the lights twinkling in their eyes. Then Jessa materialized next to us with a weird, hopeful look and a gorgeous grin on her face. Though she wasn't looking at Katie.

She was smiling that smile at me.

Come to think of it, where the fuck was her brother? Like, the guy who'd knocked Katie up?

I turned to look at Katie, who gave me the same hopeful-expectant-giddy smile.

"Surprise?" she kinda whispered at me. Then she hugged me, and Jessa hugged us both with her long supermodel arms.

"Oh." I heard the word slip out of my mouth, but then I went kinda blank. Then other people were piling in, hugging me.

And then there was Zane, patiently waiting to get his arms around me.

"You're here," I said stupidly when the crowd parted to let him through.

In a suit.

I blinked at him. My rock star husband was wearing a suit. Or at least, part of a suit. Black dress pants, black dress shirt with the sleeves rolled up and a black suede vest, all perfectly tailored to his gorgeous body.

"You look gorgeous," I gushed, as he enveloped me in his arms. "Shit, am I dressed right for this? What's happening?" I clung to him, thinking over my outfit. Cute blue cocktail dress, but nothing as special as what he was wearing. "It's not my birthday..."

"No," he whispered into my ear. "But it's as close to our wedding anniversary as I could get everyone together. Sorry it's a month late." I peered up into his blue eyes. "Welcome to our wedding reception, Maggie."

"What?" I peeked out over his shoulder at the beautiful room and all our beautiful friends, smiling at me.

"We never had one," he said simply. "Thought you might like one, here at home."

Pretty sure that was when I started to cry.

I definitely had tears streaming down my face by the time he handed me off to Jessa and Katie again and Jessa told me, "Let's go get you changed. We've got a dress for you." Zane just kept kissing my head, until I finally let go of his arm.

I couldn't even see anything around me.

Total shock.

We ended up in a beautiful powder room in a little alcove off the ballroom, where dresses and lingerie were hung up for me.

"Oh my God, you didn't," I gushed, blinking up at the dresses on the rack as Jessa and Katie shut the door behind us.

"We did," Jessa said.

"We're sneaky that way," Katie added brightly.

"Now get undressed," Jessa ordered, as Katie started pouring us pink drinks from a glass pitcher on the antique vanity.

I was still in shock.

Jessa started pulling lingerie from the hangers and I drifted behind the pretty folding screen. I slipped off my shoes and started taking off my dress in a daze, as she draped panties and bras over the top of the screen for me.

"We got a few different sizes and cuts for the panties and bras," she informed me, "just in case."

I heard her, but all I could think was, *They did all this... for me?*

Zane did this for me?

"And don't worry about your face," Jessa went on. "We've got a makeup artist all set up in the next room to take care of you. But

Maggie, you need to stop crying right now. That's an order. There's a photographer out there, too."

"Amber?" I asked, just trying to wrap my brain around everything.

"She's here, but she's not taking photos tonight. We've hired someone else so she can just party with the rest of us."

"I like that," I said, as Katie reached around the screen to hand me a drink.

"And it's a dry party," Katie informed me, "in honor of your husband."

"Thank you," I practically sobbed, almost breaking down in tears again. I gave her a quick hug, even though I was already in my underwear.

I took a sip of the drink and it was delicious; some kind of sparkling pomegranate thing.

Then I finished stripping down and pulled on one of the panty-and-bra sets. It was blush pink and fit perfectly. I chose the skimpier panties over the boy-cut ones, the see-through lace with the keyhole and bow, rather than the silk, because I thought Zane would like them.

Then I stepped out.

Jessa and Katie made happy noises of approval.

"Now," Jessa said, "all the bras are strapless so you can wear whichever you like best with the dress. We wanted you to have options, since this is all being kind of sprung on you..."

"Kind of...?" I said, still half in shock.

Katie made a sweeping *Ta-da!* gesture at the dresses. There were three of them, and I'd barely had to glance at them to know what they were.

Five days ago, the three of us and Roni had gone dress shopping, to get fitted for dresses for Jessa's wedding to Brody later this summer. I'd been extensively measured, and Jessa had made me try on about a hundred dresses.

Now I knew why.

The one we'd all liked best on me was hanging right here in

front of me now, in three different colors. None of them were the coral color Jessa had chosen for her bridesmaids to wear. Two of them were in soft pink shades that they had to know I would love.

The other one was white.

"We got one in white, just in case," Jessa said.

"No pressure," Katie added, grinning. "Just choose the one you like best."

"The white one," I said automatically, and my girlfriends both beamed.

"Yay!" Katie said.

"I didn't wear a white dress at the wedding," I told them. "So this is... perfect."

Jessa got the dress down and handed it to me. It was short, with a flared skirt and a deep V neckline, the whole thing overlaid with a subtle white lace, the same lace used for the long, flared sleeves. It wasn't a traditional bridal dress or bridesmaid dress. It was utterly cool, a little rock 'n' roll, and I was pretty sure Zane was gonna love it on me.

I put it on, and Jessa turned me toward the giant wall mirror as Katie did up the little buttons on the back. It was perfectly tailored for my body.

Was this really happening?

I took a long look at myself. And I felt like I was in a dream.

"Maggie Omura, you look like a fucking dream," Jessa said, as if reading my mind. And since it was coming from a lingerie model, I took it as a huge compliment.

"Thank you."

Then she got right down to business again. "Bare legs, or do you want the stockings and garters?"

"Bare," I said, knowing Zane would like that, too.

Jessa nodded and whipped out some leg cream, a tinted moisturizer with a little shimmer in it, and started rubbing down my legs. "Damn," she muttered, "you have the most beautiful skin tone. You don't even need this shit..."

At the same time, Katie played with my hair. "Up or down?" she asked. "The makeup girl does hair too, so she can put it up for you if you want."

"No. That's okay," I said. "Zane likes it down."

Katie grinned at me in the mirror.

"Now... shoes." Jessa turned me around. "We've got these little booties that will go with the dress, but I'm thinking—"

"The glittery ones," I said. My eyes had already fixated on them. They were pink gold, with a few thin straps that zig-zagged across the foot.

Jessa and Katie helped me get them on. The heels were four inches and gave me a nice boost of height, made my short legs look long in my dress, and added the perfect hit of dazzle to complement the somewhat simple but edgy dress.

"Is this happening?" I asked, as they both stood back to admire me.

"Yes," Katie said firmly.

"And it couldn't happen to a better person," Jessa added.

"But what about your baby party?" I asked Katie, feeling a little guilty.

"Ah," she said with a shrug and a smile, patting her still-flat belly. "We'll deal with that later."

Then they steered me out the door to get my makeup touched up.

By the time the three of us made our grand reentry into the ballroom, the party was underway. People were mingling and chatting, laughing and drinking their non-alcoholic mocktails, and music was playing.

It was a remix of Sarah Vaughan's "Fever," and I was pretty sure I didn't even need to look to know who the DJ was at this event. Then the music went low, and I heard a familiar voice over the sound system. "Here comes the bride!"

I smiled and looked across the room to find DJ Summer, a

good friend of Dirty's, all set up at the far end of the dance floor. Long, dark hair, scarlet-red jumpsuit, big smile. She blew me a kiss as she turned the music back up, and everyone applauded for me.

I clung to Katie's hand until she passed me off to Zane, who was waiting for me.

He took in my dress... and my bare legs... and the hint of cleavage bared by the deep V of my neckline, and he nodded in approval. "Holy fuck, Maggie. You clean up nice."

I rolled my eyes. "Yeah. I really came in here in rags."

He smirked. "You look fucking gorgeous. You always look gorgeous. I'd be happy to do this thing with you in those pink sweatpants of yours, if you want."

"No, thanks. I'll keep the dress." I did a little spin so the flared skirt did its thing and he got an eyeful of thigh. Plus the sparkly, sexy shoes.

His pierced eyebrow went up in a look of appreciation and pure sex. "Think you can dance in those things...?"

"Yes. I'm a professional. I can fuck in them, too."

He pulled me up against his hard body and growled. "Careful what you wish for. We've got a lot of guests here, waiting on us."

Then my eyes went wide. "Don't tell me you're actually planning to dance with me tonight."

"I might. Have a few things planned. Maybe a special song for you, later... First dance for the bride and groom. You know, after the vows."

I stared at him. "What vows? I thought this was just a wedding reception."

"It is a wedding reception. We're already married. Doesn't mean we can't renew our vows."

I swallowed. "Uh... we're renewing our vows tonight?"

"Yeah. I thought we could," he said, kinda nonchalantly. But I knew this wasn't nonchalant. I knew he'd planned the hell out of this. "If you want to." His gaze moved over my face. "I don't know about you, but the first time I was pretty nervous and emotional.

Have a hard time remembering it all. Might be nice to do it again, with our loved ones here."

"Yeah." I blinked at him. Just... *wow*. Was he for real? Who was this man? "Me too. I mean, I was nervous, too."

He leaned in and kissed me softly, his lips just brushing mine. So soft... It was very possibly the sweetest kiss he'd ever given me, and I felt it all the way to my toes. *Tingles.* I was tingling all over...

"You're not gonna be nervous and emotional this time?" I asked him, swallowing, feeling kinda nervous myself.

"Emotional, probably. Nervous, no. This time, I'm not so afraid of losing you right afterward."

"Because you won't." I kissed him again, wrapping my arms around his neck. "I can't believe you did all this for me."

"For us," he said. "Definitely wasn't easy, planning a surprise for the girl who plans everything."

"You did an amazing job."

"Yeah?"

"Yeah. I like your spontaneity, too... but it makes me horny when you plan stuff."

He kissed me again, his lips lingering this time like he wanted more.

Much, much more...

"You think we could slip away and fuck without anyone noticing...? I'll be quick."

I groaned a little. *I wish.* "Maybe later. After I've had a chance to at least talk to everyone and thank them for coming."

And "everyone" was pretty accurate.

Everyone who was important to me was in this room. Zane had managed to pull them all together, somehow, and I was incredibly moved.

It took me a long while to make the rounds. And it was definitely a family affair.

Brody was one of the first to give me a hug. He told me baby Nick sent his love, but he was home with a sitter.

All of Dirty was here, of course, with their partners. Including

Elle and her enormous baby belly. She'd flown home from the tour a couple of weeks ago, just in case, and she was literally ready to pop at any second; she was actually three days past her due date now.

Matt was here, solo.

Jude and Roni were here, and so was Jude's brother, Piper, who'd always been pretty tight with Zane.

My two cousins on my mom's side, the only living relatives I had besides my dad, were here with their families.

Some of Dylan's family was here, too, and Elle's sister and her parents. Katie's parents, and her sister and her husband. Katie's best friend, Devi, and her date, some cute model guy. Amber's sister Liv, one of our favorite video directors, and her girlfriend, Laura. And Seth's foster father, Ray, a lovely man I was meeting for the first time tonight.

All the members of Steel Trap were here, with dates.

Ashley Player was here, though I wasn't even sure if he'd brought a date. He didn't seem to be drunk, either, which was a nice change from the last several times I'd seen him.

Alec and Talia and some of our key crew from this tour had come, along with Jude's entire security crew. And Woo, Dirty's record producer, our Vancouver publicists and several other people both Zane and I had worked closely with over the years.

Rudy, Zane's AA sponsor, had come up from L.A. with his wife, Laney. I spent quite a while talking to them.

Definitely felt like they were family now, too.

I gave Rudy a long hug that ended with me in tears, again. I felt like I owed a huge debt of gratitude to this man for playing a role in saving my husband's life, probably on many occasions, and helping him in ways I'd never even understand.

"Thank you," I said to him, not even sure how to put all of that into words.

"You've got a good man, there, Maggie," was all he said.

And then I sat down with Dolly.

I found her, sitting alone, on one of the many beautiful antique couches, close to where Jesse and Katie stood. She was sipping a mocktail and she offered me a cheers. I clinked my glass to hers.

"Let me see..." she said, in her kindly way, looking me over. "Sore feet?"

"They're actually quite comfortable," I said, kicking up my foot as we admired my new shoes.

"They're beautiful."

"Jessa picked them out."

"You're beautiful, dear," Dolly said.

"Thank you." I put my foot down and looked in her pale blue eyes, so like her grandson's. "Uh... I feel a little silly. I never actually talked to you about the fact that I married your grandson, or that I was in love with him or anything. Right now, sitting here with you, that feels like such a fail."

"It's alright, Maggie."

"I should have. I should have talked to you. It feels... disrespectful."

She laughed. "Why? You should've asked me for his hand in marriage?"

"Maybe." I shrugged. "Something like that. Between him and me... you're the most important parental figure we have left."

I could see that she took that to heart, and her eyes got a little misty. "Maggie, dear. I love you dearly."

"I love you, too." I gave her a hug, and in her arms, I got very emotional. It was hard to get the words out of my mouth when I said, "Thank you for taking such good care of him."

When we drew apart, she looked across the room, and I followed her gaze. We could both see Zane sitting on the other side of the dance floor, talking to Elle, Seth, and Matt. He was smiling at whatever Elle was saying and as we watched, he laid his hand gently on her belly.

"You know, when I look at him," Dolly said softly, "I still see that little boy in my kitchen, getting all under my feet and asking me to play with him while I was trying to make dinner. His parents were gone from his life too soon, Maggie. And he just wanted me to play with him. 'Will you come play with me, Grandma?' How many times did he ask me that? Must've been thousands over the years. I can still hear his little voice, and see that bright look in his eyes. He thought if he turned on the charm, if he was just cute enough, I'd drop what I was doing and come play with him. It usually worked." She laughed a little and I sniffled, trying not to cry.

Jesus, this party was gonna kill me.

I looked at Zane's grandma as she fixed her blue eyes on me again. She placed her soft hand on my knee.

"All that boy wanted was to be loved, Maggie."

And I understood her. I knew what she meant.

Zane had pursued me, for my love, from the moment we met, and I was pretty sure he would've pursued me to the ends of the Earth and the end of his days trying to get it.

I took her hand and squeezed gently. She felt so frail, but there was strength in her yet. "I love him, Dolly," I told her, and it felt like a promise.

She nodded. "All I ever wanted for him was to be happy and to be truly loved." Then she cupped my face with her free hand. "What more could I wish for him than you?"

After my talk with Dolly, I beelined across the room for Zane, feeling a little lightheaded. I scooped him away from Elle, pulling him aside. He wrapped me gently in his arms like he could sense I needed the support.

"You okay?" His eyes were soft as he searched my face.

"I'm great. Just had a little talk with Dolly."

A smile tugged at his lips. "Good?" he asked, still trying to read my face as I blinked back the tears that hadn't quite fallen.

"Yeah. I can't believe all the people you brought together here for me. For us." I gazed up into his eyes. "I noticed my dad's not here, though..."

"Yeah." His expression hardened a bit. "I didn't invite Dizzy.

Didn't want you to think I did and he didn't show, but I also didn't want to give him the chance to disappoint you. Kinda wrestled with that decision. Hope I made the right one?"

"Yes," I told him. It was sad, but it was the right decision. "I just want to be surrounded by people who really love me right now."

He gathered me tighter in his arms and lowered his face down to mine. "Like this?"

"Yeah," I said, and kissed him softly on the lips. "Just like this."

"Besides," he said, "Dizzy was the only one who got to witness our first wedding. Figured it was only fair we give our other friends and family a chance this time."

"Fair enough."

"So where do you want to do it?"

I peered up into his eyes, where I glimpsed the evil gleam I knew all too well. "Uh, do it...?"

"Our vow renewal. I'm ready if you are."

"Oh. Right. That..."

He grinned at me, and I grinned back.

In the end, we decided to renew our vows out on the balcony, under the moon and stars.

There was a long, beautiful balcony loaded with flowers that opened right off the ballroom, overlooking the city and the mountains and the dark of the waters beyond. It was a May evening, the flowers were fragrant and it was a little cool but not cold in my dress.

I was pretty sure no one could even hear us from the ballroom, but it didn't matter. These vows were for us, a private moment between Zane and I.

And our impromptu wedding party. It was small, just two people, because making it any bigger just got us into a silly argument.

Jessa and Jesse; my oldest friend, and his oldest friend.

After that he wanted Brody and Jude, I wanted Katie and Talia, but then he wanted Seth, too, which meant he wanted Dylan, and then he wanted Ash... and I wanted Elle, but then I didn't want to leave Amber and Roni out, or my female cousin... and the whole thing snowballed into a ridiculous negotiation over who would get left out, until we would've had the entire guest list crammed out here on the balcony to make each other happy.

So instead... just Jessa and Jesse.

And our vows?

We made them up on the fly.

Well, Zane had maybe a little more time than me to prepare his, but we improvised a lot.

"I love you, Maggie, and I'm always gonna love you, so you're just gonna have to deal with it," was how he started.

"Absolutely the same right back at you," I said.

"And I'm never gonna promise you I won't fuck up. We both know I'm gonna fuck up, but I'm never gonna give up on trying to do right by you."

"Same here."

"This marriage means more to me than any other thing in my life, and I'm gonna make sure you know that, every day."

"Me, too."

"You can't just ditto your way through these vows, Maggs," he said, a happy sparkle in his eyes.

"I know." I squeezed his hands. "You just pretty much said it all. I love you. That's where this all started, but that's not where it ends. You know... Seth said something to me the other day, about love being a verb—"

He kinda rolled his eyes. "Fucking Seth."

"Don't roll your eyes at me. You hate it when I do that to you, Mr. Omura."

He cocked an eyebrow. "Mr. Omura?"

"Well, I'm not taking your last name."

"I'm not taking yours, either. Mine's pretty famous, Maggs."

"Which is why I'm not taking it."

The cocked eyebrow went higher. "Are you turning our vows into an argument?"

"As I was saying. Seth said love is a verb, and he's right. I'm telling you right here and now at our wedding reception and vow renewal party that I love you, Zane Traynor. And to me that means I'm going to love you, actively love you, every day for the rest of my life. My love for you will be... you know, the wind beneath my wings and all that."

"Holy shit. You are not gonna start serenading me with Sarah McLachlan...?"

"Holy Christ. It's Bette Midler. What rock have you been living under?"

"Are you still talking? These are the worst vows ever."

"Agreed. I didn't have much time to prepare."

"Maybe we'll just have to redo them." He grinned at me. "You know, again. In two more years."

"Yeah." I grinned back. "But they're the best vows ever, okay? Because they're ours." I squeezed his hands again, pulling him closer to me. "Seriously. You're the love of my life and my best friend, and you're kinda my *life* in a way that, as a strong, independent woman of the now, I don't like to admit. But you know what? I couldn't be who or what I am without you, and I swear to you I will fight for that. I'll fight for you and for us to my dying breath, because you are it for me, Zane." Suddenly the humor had faded and this shit had gotten real. My breath hitched and his blue eyes softened.

"Maggie..."

"I love you in ways I never knew I could love until I met you. And to quote your vows from our first wedding, 'I'm never letting you go.'"

"You remember," he murmured.

"I remember." I blinked back the tears that were glittering in my vision. "Yes, I remember."

"I love you, Maggie May Omura."

"I love you, Mr. Omura."

He cracked a smile. "Don't start."

Then he kissed me.

When he pulled away, he said, "I love you so much it fucking hurts, Maggie. In the best way possible. The only thing I can really promise you is the most important thing there is, as far as I'm concerned. I'll never leave you fighting alone."

I smiled and the tears sparkled in my eyes. He knew how those words would hit me, because he knew it was a promise no man had ever made me before; not even my dad.

"I'll be here for you whenever you need me," he said, "and even when you don't... I'll be hanging around just in case. I'm fucking crazy about you, and I'm pretty damn sure, if the past is any indication, I'm gonna spend every day of the rest of my life loving you more than the last one."

Then we kissed.

And we *kissed*... Until my pussy started throbbing so incessantly it sucked all my attention downward with its gravitational force, and I started calculating the quickest way to get his dick inside me...

"Uh... Maggie," he whispered. He'd stopped my hand, which was on his dick, squeezing him through his pants. "I'm all for that, but maybe we get rid of Jesse first?"

"Nice vows," Jesse said, and I glanced up to find our tiny little wedding party standing patiently by, watching us. Both of them with a little sparkle of happy tears in their eyes.

Shit. I snatched my hand back. They heard all that?

Totally forgot they were here.

"Thanks," I mumbled, as Jessa swiped a tear from her eye. She was holding her brother's hand.

Both of them moved in to hug each of us, then Zane took my hand in his and we all headed back into the ballroom. Jesse announced loudly, "PRESENTING MR. AND MRS. MAGGIE OMURA!"

To which Zane punched him in the kidney.

"*Ooph.* I mean, MR. AND MRS... ZANE TRAYNOR...?" He threw me a look, covering his vital organs with his arms like he was expecting another punch.

I just shook my head.

"Uh, ZANE AND MAGGIE! Let's eat."

So we ate. And we mingled.

And then we sat down and just enjoyed the feeling of being in this room together.

Our wedding reception.

There was no formal dinner, but the small army of catering staff circulated the room nonstop with loaded trays of food, and there was a massive buffet table of desserts. There was also a chocolate fountain, because my husband loved me like that.

And there was a full bar of exotic non-alcoholic drinks.

Fortunately, our friends were fucking cool and they knew how to party without alcohol. Although I was pretty sure more than a few people snuck out onto that gorgeous balcony for a toke throughout the night...

Zane didn't seem to mind.

He took it all in stride, happy that his friends were happy. That I was happy.

"You're really good with all this?" he asked me, leaning over to speak close in my ear as we snuggled on one of the antique velvet loungers. "I know you love planning and being in control. I was hoping you'd still have fun tonight."

"It's amazing. You did a great job, and I love it," I assured him.

"You're happy?"

"Yeah. Hells yes, I'm happy." I kissed him softly, and then we toasted with our cranberry mocktails. "Here's to many happy years together, okay?"

"Okay." His eyes twinkled at me over his glass as we sipped. "You know, you'll be able to drink again. If you want, you can take off with the girls later to the bar and celebrate. I won't be mad. A little jealous, maybe..."

"Fuck that. I'm screwing you later until we both pass out from exhaustion."

The grin spread across his face. "That sounds like a way fucking better plan. I knew I married you for a reason."

"And what reason would that be?" I asked, as he set our drinks aside.

"Because you're fucking smart, Maggie," he said, lounging back and taking me with him. "You always know where it's at."

"Of course I do," I said. "It's in your pants."

He laughed, pulling me into his side as he wrapped his arm around me. He held my hand, drawing it into his lap and brushing my knuckles very purposefully against his dick. Teasing me. Reminding me exactly where it was gonna be at later.

His ice-blue eyes said it all.

I just licked my lip and stared.

Zane's eyes darkened... Then he smirked and looked away. I watched him looking at our friends, laughing and carrying on around us. It was loud. The music had gone up, the lights had gone down and people were dancing.

But all I wanted to do was stare at Zane.

My man wasn't perfect. But he was definitely... *epic*. He was sexy and smart and devoted, and he still made the backs of my knees sweat.

Our relationship wasn't perfect, either. But yeah... it was pretty fucking epic, too.

I stared at his gorgeous blond hair, styled in an edgy fauxhawk... His strong, defined, slightly crooked nose... His broad shoulders in his black shirt and vest. His strong hands with all the rings... and his bare ring finger, which bore the tattoo of my name.

My tattoo was visible, too. I'd stopped covering it up once we went public with our relationship.

And as it turned out, things did change once our marriage was totally out in the open. For the better.

We'd had all kinds of reactions from all kinds of people, both good and bad. Though mostly good. Anyone who really mattered to us, whose opinion really mattered, had been supportive, in the end.

And Zane was right. When our relationship went public and everyone weighed in on it, the fans had their say and the media swarmed all over it... it really didn't change *us*.

Instead of heaping the pressure on, it had taken the pressure off.

No more secrets. No more little lies.

No more sneaking around.

I ran the tip of my finger over his ring tattoo and he looked at me. Our heads were close together as I leaned into him, our cheeks practically touching.

"I'm sorry your mom's not here to see this," he said, sincerely. I knew he meant it, deeply, because he loved me that much.

He loved me enough to know what I needed and where my heart was at. To pay attention to all the little things, and the big things, too.

And God, I loved him.

I squeezed his hand and shrugged, knowing exactly what my mom would say to that. "Maybe she is."

Zane didn't say anything, but he kept staring at me.

I kept staring right back.

"What?" he asked, softly.

"Is it weird," I asked him, "that this is the first time I've truly felt like we were a married couple?"

He smoothed his thumb slowly over my ring finger, back and forth. "I know what you mean. I feel it, too."

"I think something happened out on that balcony under the stars, Zane."

"Yeah, Maggie," he said, gazing into my eyes. "We got married."

EPILOGUE

Ash

WE WERE all set up in front of Summer's DJ platform at the far end of the dance floor, ready to go. Jesse, Seth and me.

The crew was pretty slick getting us all hooked up, like a bunch of rock 'n' roll ninjas. Jesse and Seth had guitars and I had a mic stand, and the three of us were all seated in a row like gentlemen; not my usual way to perform.

The last time I'd performed a song sitting down was at Jesse's wedding.

Summer was playing The Miracles' "Shop Around," not a remix, just the regular old Motown classic, and she had all the old people dancing. Brody was dancing with grandma Dolly—carefully; that woman was getting old. Elle's parents were dancing. Matt was dancing with Dylan's mom, Katie was dancing with Seth's foster father, and Piper, of all people, was dancing with Katie's mom while Katie's dad danced with Jessa.

It was kinda nice seeing everyone cut loose... and all the people Dylan cared about so much under one roof.

Jesse poked me and pointed out Amber, who was dancing with Shady—or at least, trying to dance with Shady. The man couldn't dance for shit, but she was doing her best to keep him shuffling his feet around while not breaking her toes.

She looked pretty in her pale yellow dress with a flower in her hair, her pointy little eyeteeth flashing as she laughed.

I smiled a little.

Was good to see her happy. It didn't make me unhappy like I thought it might. And I wasn't all that nervous about seeing her anymore.

I wasn't nervous about the song, either. It was a pretty vocally-intense and emotional song, sure. But for some fucked-up reason, I was actually a little nervous about singing in front of Dylan.

I just had to breathe and maybe forget he was in the room.

As soon as "Shop Around" was done, Summer would introduce us—but it felt like the longest song in history right now. She might as well have put on "In-A-Gadda-Da-Vida" and called it a night. I was sweating a little, and it had nothing to do with the heat in the room.

It wasn't hot.

The doors along the balcony were wide open, and I could feel the fresh air.

Just had to breathe...

And remind myself that this thing was gonna be beautiful.

Was definitely gonna get Zane laid tonight.

Luckily, Maggie hadn't noticed us sitting here. The full dance floor helped. Plus, Zane was doing a good job keeping her distracted at the other end of the ballroom. As soon as "Shop Around" started playing, that was his cue to redirect her.

I'd seen them circling the dessert table; pretty sure he had her dipping into the chocolate fountain right about now.

Then "Shop Around" finally came to an end. I didn't even have to look at Jesse or Seth. They sat on either side of me, and I could feel them shifting in their seats, getting ready.

We'd rehearsed to perfection. I didn't need a cheat sheet for the lyrics or anything. The lyrics were pretty simple. Zane had chosen the song; it wasn't a new song, but it was new to me, and I'd made sure to commit it to heart this week.

"Zane? Oh, Zaaaaane," Summer purred over her mic. "Where's

that beautiful wife of yours? Bring her on out to the dance floor, would ya?"

Everyone started looking around for Zane and Maggie, and the crowd parted as they made their way onto the dance floor. Zane in the lead, drawing Maggie along by her hand.

"And the rest of you lovely people," Summer called out. "Can you clear the dance floor for this gorgeous couple?"

Everyone did as instructed, and the crowd got pretty thick all around the dance floor, everyone gathering to watch as Zane steered Maggie right into the middle of the floor, under the mirrored ball.

She'd seen us by now.

A smile lit up her face, and when she looked at her man, he pulled her close.

"I'd like to welcome some dear friends of Zane and Maggie to the floor," Summer said. "This is Ashley, Jesse and Seth, and they're going to play a song for Maggie right now that Zane chose for her."

There was some applause and some happy shouting and whistling, and when everyone finally died down, Jesse started the song, leading on guitar. Seth joined in... and then I started to sing.

The song was "You're My Star," the acoustic version, by Stereophonics, and if you asked me we did a pretty killer cover of it. Judging from the tears I could see running down Maggie's cheeks by the time I got the first line out of my mouth, I'd put money on it.

According to Zane, the song was important to Maggie somehow.

Seemed that was true.

Eventually, the two of them started dancing slowly in the middle of the floor, wrapped tight around each other. I got kinda lost in the song myself, but somewhere well before the end I noticed they'd stopped dancing to just stand there again and listen, watching us play.

When the song ended, Maggie pulled Zane right on over to us, and before I was even on my feet she'd launched herself into my arms.

"Ash! That was so beautiful," she sobbed, and yeah, she was definitely crying like a baby. "Thank you so much."

"You're welcome. Congrats, Maggie."

"Thank you."

She finally let me go to hug the other guys, and Zane pulled me in for a hug. I already knew he was grateful; I knew he would've liked to serenade Maggie himself, but this night wasn't about him taking the stage. I was honored he'd asked me to step in, and he'd already thanked me about a thousand times. Now, he patted me on the back and told me, "You have no idea, man."

"Anytime."

When we drew apart and he moved on to thank the other guys, Amber was standing there. Teary-eyed, she gave me a hug. "That was amazing." She kissed my cheek, her soft, caramel hair brushing my face. Then she looked me in the eye and told me, sincerely, "I miss you."

"Thanks, Amber," I said. It was all I could really say.

Dylan was next, pulling me in for a tight hug. "That was great, man."

"Thanks."

After that, there was a bit of a lineup of people wanting to shake my hand. Eventually, I managed to work my way off the dance floor and visit with a few more people who pulled me aside.

Elle was one of them.

"You look great," I told her. It was the first time I'd spoken to her all night. I'd been busy enough; the party was pretty full of people to talk to, and besides that, I still wasn't all that comfortable hanging with her. Wasn't sure why, but it still felt weird to me that she had Seth's baby in her belly so damn fast after we fell apart.

Not that we were ever really together, according to her.

"Thank you," she said, smoothing her hand over her giant belly. "The song was just beautiful. Thank you for doing that with the guys. I know it means a lot to Zane and Maggie."

"No worries."

"So... My feet hurt and my hips ache all the time, but other than that, I feel pretty good," she volunteered, when I didn't ask how she was doing. "We're hoping the baby decides to make an appearance soon."

"Cool," I said. I wasn't sure what else to say.

I'd already heard, from Dylan, that no matter when the baby came, Paulie was joining Dirty for the first few weeks of the European tour, filling in for Seth so he could spend some time at home with Elle and the baby. After that... maybe he'd rejoin the tour and leave Elle and the baby here for a while, or maybe she'd bring the baby on the road. I didn't know. Didn't really care to know.

I kissed her forehead. "Take care, okay? Let me know when the baby comes. I'll swing by."

"Of course," she said.

After that, I circled back to Summer, bringing her a non-alcoholic blender drink from the bar. I hopped up onto her platform and let her congratulate me on my performance. She'd already heard me practicing the song earlier in the week, and I knew she approved.

"You sounded great," she told me, kissing my cheek. "Not a dry eye in the house, I'm telling you."

"Yeah. Thanks. Fuck, that felt good."

"It should. You killed it."

It really did feel good. Was the first time I'd played in front of any kind of audience in way too long.

Fucking missed it.

Plus, Jesse Mayes and Seth Brothers were pretty kick-ass backup.

Unfortunately, my band, the Penny Pushers, were officially done. But no one really knew that yet. Our management company knew. Summer knew and Dylan knew. We'd announced on all our social media shit that we were on hiatus. And that was about it. Rumors were flying around left and right, but we hadn't officially cut ties.

We'd be doing it soon.

No use kicking a dead horse.

It was all for the best, anyway. In a way, it would be freeing, right?

Painful, but freeing.

Like a breakup from someone who was a great person, someone you'd come to love and you'd gotten really fucking used to having around... but was just wrong for you.

I gave Summer a kiss on the temple and a squeeze and left her at her deck to continue on my rounds. I could see Dylan and Amber together across the room, and Elle with Seth.

And when I saw them all like that, from enough of a distance... looking exactly how they were supposed to be... I knew it was finally time for me to let go.

It was time to move on.

Fact was, I really wasn't sure where the fuck I belonged anymore, but it wasn't with any of them.

Later, I headed out to the balcony. It was well after midnight and the party was dwindling. Most of the older guests and the ones with babysitters at home had already taken off.

Without booze to keep the party going, the remaining guests were discussing afterparty options as they gathered by the doors.

But I wasn't feeling much like partying tonight.

Dylan and Amber already had their coats on when I'd said goodnight to them. Most of Dirty seemed ready to head out, but I was waiting for Summer; told her I'd hang with her after. She was playing Three Dog Night, "Mama Told Me (Not to Come)," her final song of the night, and the lights were up in the ballroom as everyone said their goodbyes.

But it was dark out on the balcony, and empty except for me. I was smoking down at the far end when someone came up behind me.

Half of me hoped it was Dylan... and half of me didn't.

"Hey, brother."

I looked up to find Zane watching me. He was alone.

I mashed my joint out on the stone wall and flicked what was left in a pot of flowers. "Sorry. Dry wedding party, and I'm the asshole smoking up."

"No worries." He came over and stood next to me, looking me over. He had a pink drink with berries floating in it in his hand. "You good?"

I considered how to answer that. How many people had asked me that in the last six months? How many times had I said yes?

And how tired was I of saying yes to make them feel better?

Fucking *tired*.

"I'm not," I answered honestly. "But I will be."

"Soon?"

"Not sure."

He leaned on the low stone wall next to me as we both looked out over the city below. "Few people coming back to our place. You coming?"

Our place. That would be his house in West Vancouver, the one he bought last year, which Maggie had just moved into. I'd definitely enjoyed my share of parties in that house already.

But Dylan and Amber would probably be there, and I wasn't in the mood for that.

"Think I'll pass this time."

He nodded. "Yeah. Okay."

We both fell silent. I fished out my cigarettes; I doubted people were supposed to smoke out here at all, but fuck it.

I thought Zane might leave as I lit up, but he didn't. I offered him one but he passed, sipping his non-alcoholic drink instead.

"So," he said, breaking the silence. "You fuck Dylan or what?"

I laughed, a little, because it was typical shit for Zane to say. The dude seriously lacked a filter.

I could relate.

But he was probably also trying to crack the palpable tension.

"Does it matter?"

"Nope," he said. "I'm just perversely curious like that."

"I never fucked Dylan. Wasn't like that."

"He fuck you?"

I shook my head. "Not his type. His type's in there, with the flower in her hair."

"You guys still cool?"

"Kind of." We really were.

Thing was, we were a little *too* cool.

Dylan was happy. He wanted me to be happy. I wasn't happy. We were still best friends, and I hoped that would never change. But something was different. It was the pity he felt for me, maybe. Or the pity I imagined he felt.

Or maybe it was just the broken heart I kept dragging around that made things so unclear.

Hard to see things clearly, maybe, when you were wasted more than you were sober and too busy bouncing in and out of beds to ponder shit like feelings.

"You think Amber's worth it?" Zane asked after a moment. "Cute girl. She seems good for Dylan. But is she worth this?" He looked me over again, assessing me with his cool blue eyes.

I shrugged. "Amber's not the problem."

"So what is?"

"Nothing," I said, which was pretty much bullshit. But whatever. If I knew what my problem was, I'd fix it, right? "Actually… I've been thinking. I think it's time for my breakup party."

"Yeah?"

"Yeah. I kinda had my heart smashed in a major way. And I know what you're thinking. What else is new? But this was a big one. You know, double whammy."

Zane just nodded. He didn't ask for clarification on that, and I had no idea if he knew I was talking about Dylan and Amber both breaking my heart or what.

Though if we wanted to get technical about it, it was kind of a triple whammy. Because Elle hadn't left my heart so intact, and I'd never had a breakup party to put that one to bed either.

"So," I asked him, "you ready for that shit?"

Because no doubt, Zane would have to host this thing. It was pretty much tradition.

Ever since my breakup party after my relationship with Summer ended... the best breakup party *ever*... the one that started at Zane's place in L.A. and ended with me at a ski resort in Alaska, partying with a bunch of members of a traveling freak show, crashing a bachelorette party, snowboarding naked and getting tattooed... he definitely had to host it.

"Bitch, please," he said with a smirk. "I'm always ready for that shit."

"Yeah? Think you can handle it? You know, now that you're all married...?"

He threw me a dry-as-fuck look. "Pretty sure I can come up with something."

"I don't even care if it's dry or whatever," I said, seriously. "You know, it's not about getting laid or getting wasted. I can do that any day of the week. It's about hitting the reset button."

"I get it. Not sure how I'll top jetting you off to Alaska..." He cocked an eyebrow at me. "You still got that tattoo?"

"Actually, it fell off while I was asleep one night. The fuck do you think?"

"Dunno. Laser removal or some shit?"

I shrugged. "It's not that bad."

"Dude. I saw it."

I sighed. Yeah; a lot of people saw it. For a while there, I'd gotten into the habit of showing it off when I was good and drunk. The girly pink flower tattoo with the words *Danny 4Ever*, right up under my balls. And since it was right up there, a lot of people had seen other stuff, too. Like my ball sac.

"You ever gonna tell me who Danny is?" he inquired, not for the first time.

"Don't know."

He sipped his drink, considering. "And why the pink flower?"

"I seriously don't know."

"Do I get to pick the tattoo this time? I'll get you something real nice." He flashed me a diabolical smile, and I laughed.

"No more tattoos unless I'm stone cold sober. You can take that to the bank."

"Alright, brother." Zane punched me lightly on the shoulder. "Give me a few days to throw something together. I fly out to Europe next week. We'll do it before then."

A grin spread across my face, and it felt like a long time since I'd smiled this big. Or looked so forward to... well, anything. "Looking forward to it."

"Cool. Do I need a guest list?"

"Huh?"

"I mean, am I supposed to invite Summer to this thing? Dylan?"

Right. Good questions...

"Summer, yes," I told him. "Dylan and Amber... no."

"Got it."

"And, uh... no Elle. But I'm pretty sure she's gonna be busy anyway."

"Right."

I pushed off the wall and we did a man-hug, back-slap, high-five thing.

"You know," he said, just as we were about to walk back into the ballroom together, "you've got big balls, Ashley Player."

I paused. "How the fuck do you figure that?"

Zane stopped and gave me an affectionate little shove. "Come on. Not many people could pull off what you just did in there, in front of all those people, with shit the way it is... You know, your double whammy?"

"Right."

"You should've heard yourself, man. You made my grandma cry. Chicks were creaming... I got a little hard myself."

I grinned. "It's a talent."

"Seriously. You got a new Pushers album coming or what?"

I took a breath. "No," I said, shaking my head. "No Pushers album."

And *fuck*.

I felt the weight of those words. The loss of my band brothers...

and all the years, all the blood, sweat and fucking tears we'd put into something that in the end really hadn't taken us very far. Alone, we were probably all more talented than we'd been as a band, and that was the hard truth I'd had to swallow this last year as we fell the fuck apart.

Zane gave me a thoughtful look. And I knew, when he didn't exactly start crying over the news, he was thinking something along the same lines.

"But I'm pretty fucking sure you haven't heard the last of me yet," I assured him.

"Thank fuck." He clapped me on the shoulder and looked me in the eye. "Telling you. I can live without the Penny Pushers. What the world needs is more Ashley Player."

And I hoped to hell he was right.

THANK YOU FOR READING!

Turn to the end of this book to read an excerpt from
Ash and Danica's story, the first book in the spinoff Players series...

Hot Mess

A mistaken identity. A regrettable tattoo.
A love that was meant to be.

ACKNOWLEDGMENTS

Thank you to my incredible ARC Team. And all the bloggers who've supported me along the way, posting, reviewing and sharing.

Thank you to my dad for introducing me to a world of music when I was young. I was definitely the only nine-year-old girl I knew who was listening to Pink Floyd, Led Zeppelin and Queen. Many songs on the Dirty playlists entered my consciousness because I first heard them on your vinyl records so many years ago, and that music shaped who I am. I wouldn't have it any other way.

Thank you to Lauren for sending me a dress pic that ended up becoming inspiration for Maggie's wedding reception dress.

Thank you to all my friends and family who've supported and championed me along the way, and just been there for me. Mom, Brittany, Gladys, Marjorie, Guin, Chris... to name a few.

Mr. Diamond... here we are at the "end" of our first big series, and we're already so excited about all the books to come. I could not have made it here so fast and so damn well without you. I'm THRILLED that you're now joining me in this journey full-time, and look forward to all the incredible projects we'll work on together. Thank you for literally everything; you're a part of this beautiful thing in every way. You might even say you're my star.

To my readers: An enormous, loving THANK YOU for reading this book. Your ongoing excitement, support and passion makes what I do incredibly rewarding. I now hear from readers all over the world who read and love my books (Israel, Holland, Germany, Australia, etc...!) and all I can really say about that is that it's quite literally a dream come true. I'm so honored that you chose to read this love story; my intent as a romance author is to spread love. If you've enjoyed Zane and Maggie's story, please consider posting a review and telling your friends about this book; your support means the world to me.

With love and gratitude,
Jaine

PLAYLIST

Find links to the full playlist on Spotify and Apple Music here:
http://jainediamond.com/dirty-like-zane/

Since I Don't Have You — Guns N' Roses
Can't Stand Losing You — The Police
Shake That (feat. Nate Dogg) — Eminem
California Love — 2Pac
Wild Horses (Acoustic) — Bishop Briggs
My Girl — The Temptations
I Get a Kick out of You (Cinematic Orchestra Mix) — Ella Fitzgerald
Sail — Awolnation
In for the Kill (Skream's Let's Get Ravey Remix) — La Roux
(I Can't Get No) Satisfaction — The Rolling Stones
Don't Let Me Be Misunderstood — The Animals
Stop Draggin' My Heart Around — Stevie Nicks & Tom Petty
I'm Not Calling You A Liar — Florence + The Machine
Better With You — Michl
Little One — Highly Suspect
Psychotic Girl — The Black Keys
Too Afraid to Love You — The Black Keys
Big God — Florence + The Machine

Cupid — Jack Johnson
Comfortably Numb — Pink Floyd
Nutshell — Alice in Chains
Inside And Out — Feist
Sour Girl — Stone Temple Pilots
Runaway Baby — Bruno Mars
Gold Guns Girls — Metric
I Ain't Gonna Be The First To Cry — Bob Moses
Maybe I'm Amazed (Live) — Paul McCartney & Wings
Burden in My Hand — Soundgarden
Fall To Pieces — Velvet Revolver
Caught Me Thinking — Bahamas
Warning Sign — Coldplay
Like A Stone — Audioslave
Sit Next to Me — Foster the People
Gloria — Them/Van Morrison
Fell On Black Days — Soundgarden
Maggie May — Rod Stewart
The Girl — City And Colour
Magic — Coldplay
Hey! Ya, You — The Elwins
Way Down We Go — Kaleo
No. 1 Party Anthem — Arctic Monkeys
A Message — Coldplay
We Are The Champions — Queen
Think About You — Guns N' Roses
Don't Panic — Coldplay
Woman Woman — Awolnation
Oh! Darling — The Beatles
I Would Do Anything for You — Foster the People
Fever (*Adam Freeland Remix*) — Sarah Vaughan
Hymn for the Weekend — Coldplay
Shop Around — The Miracles
You're My Star (*Acoustic 2015*) — Stereophonics
Mama Told Me (*Not to Come*) — Three Dog Night

EXCERPT: HOT MESS

Hot Mess

*A steamy, swoony second chance romance—with a twist—
featuring a mistaken identity, an embarrassing tattoo,
a broken, irresistible bad boy,
and the woman who's destined to be his.*

PROLOGUE

Ash

I'd never believed there was any kind of grand purpose to my life, or to the relationships that came and went from it.

I'd never believed in fate, or karma, or any of that shit.

With all the bullshit I'd been through, why would I?

I definitely wasn't feeling any kind of manifest destiny that day.

I couldn't feel much at all.

Then I got off the chairlift at the top of the mountain, the edge of my snowboard caught in the ice and I went down, hard, twisting the shit out of my knee.

It had been three days since I'd broken up with my girlfriend, Summer. Three days since I'd had my heart smashed.

Three days since I'd started partying.

It was a gorgeous, clear morning. Bluebird day; fresh powder, perfect conditions. I'd planned to spend all fucking day on my board, sweating out the alcohol.

Then, you know, start drinking again.

But then I fell getting off the fucking chairlift.

I was barely able to crawl out of the way in time before the guys getting off the chair behind me ended up on top of me. It was two of my bandmates, Pepper and Janner, who pretty much pissed themselves laughing at me. Zero sympathy.

I could've boarded circles around either of these guys, hungover or not, but in that moment, they weren't the ones on their asses in the snow.

At least Johnny, who'd been on my chair with me, gave me a hand up.

It was our first run of the day. The four of us had just dragged our asses out of the hotel, and my day of boarding was already done. Couldn't put much weight on my knee, couldn't even coast my ass down the hill. Had to sit down in the snow and wait for help, while Janner sat with me—and laughed at me.

Guess that's what you get after staying up most of the night, drinking way too much tequila with a bunch of rock stars.

And circus freaks.

And a bachelorette party.

Long story.

The medics had to collect me and give me a ride down the hill on a snowmobile. They took a look at my knee and wrapped it up, told me to go easy on it for a few days. I passed when they asked for photos; I wasn't in the mood to play rock star. But I signed their skis before I limped on my way.

By the time I got back to the hotel, it was a ghost town. Everyone was on the slopes. So I got changed and did the only thing there was to do: start drinking. I hit up the empty lounge, sat at the bar, ordered a beer and chatted a bit with the bartender.

Johnny came back to the hotel not long after I did.

I was alone at the bar when he found me. Said he was too hungover to board and ordered himself a drink.

"Shot of bourbon," he told the bartender. "And one for my wounded friend here."

I looked at Johnny then. Really looked.

I didn't know Johnny O'Reilly well. I didn't know we were friends.

I'd only met him a few times before. We were both rock stars on the rise, both from Vancouver, spent a lot of time in L.A.. Ran in the same circles, hit the same parties.

Two days before, he'd come to my breakup party in L.A., and here we were.

In Alaska.

Alone in some bar.

And he'd sat down pretty damn close to me.

Johnny had that striking combo of a deep tan, bleach-blond hair and blue-green eyes. The tattoo over his shoulder climbed out of his thermal shirt and up one side of his neck—the shirt that clung to his sculpted chest and arms. He had a guitarist's callused fingers and clean, square fingernails. Nice hands, white teeth, slow to smile.

And dark, serious eyebrows that made it look like he was always thinking, like he cared about something, about you, even when he didn't.

... And that air of fucking calculated recklessness. The one that told you he was always in control.

Thing was, I kinda had a weakness for guys like Johnny O.

Bad boys.

Not exactly my type, but... tempting.

The shots came and he slid one over to me.

And that was it.

I clinked my shot glass to Johnny's, and when I looked into his eyes, my fate was sealed.

Granted, I sealed it myself.

Maybe I was still kinda drunk from the night before and just getting drunker, but I knew what I was doing. No one forced that shot down my throat.

If I hadn't done that first shot with Johnny that day, no fucking doubt, things would've gone down differently than they did that night.

But then maybe, just maybe, I never would've met *her*.

ABOUT THE AUTHOR

Jaine Diamond is a Top 5 international bestselling author. She writes contemporary romance featuring badass, swoon-worthy heroes endowed with massive hearts, strong heroines armed with sweetness and sass, and explosive, page-turning chemistry.

She lives on the beautiful west coast of Canada with her real-life romantic hero and daughter, where she reads, writes and makes extensive playlists for her books while binge drinking tea.

For the most up-to-date list of Jaine's published books and reading order please go to: jainediamond.com/books

Get the Diamond Club Newsletter at jainediamond.com for new release info, insider updates, giveaways and bonus content.

Join the private readers' group to connect with Jaine and other readers: facebook.com/groups/jainediamondsVIPs

goodreads.com/jainediamond
bookbub.com/authors/jaine-diamond
instagram.com/jainediamond
tiktok.com/@jainediamond
facebook.com/JaineDiamond

Printed in Dunstable, United Kingdom